Loud Unspoken Memories

SAMANTHA CHRISTY

Athena
Books Publishing Group

Saint Johns, FL 32259

Cover designed by Maria @ Steamy Designs.

Loud Unspoken Memories

Samantha Christy

Chapter One

Dallas

I roll over in bed and smile. My beautiful wife is sleeping peacefully. It may be cold outside, but just lying next to her has warmth flowing through me like a freshly brewed cup of coffee.

I brush a chunk of blonde hair off her forehead and a wave of nausea washes over me when the hair sticks to my hand and pulls away from her head to reveal the gray, ashy pallor of her face.

She turns to me and her sunken eyes spring open. "I'll always love you, Dallas."

Bolting awake, I run to the bathroom and hover over the toilet like I've done so many times before, certain I'm going to hurl. Sinking down onto the cold plank floor, my forehead meets the wall, pounding against it until the dream starts to fade.

"Fuck!" I yell to no one, the word echoing off the walls of my small cabin.

When the nausea passes, I go back into the other room and check the time. It's three-thirty in the afternoon. I suppose the good news is I did get six hours of sleep—after the totally sleepless night I endured upon returning from my brother's wedding.

I wolf down a protein bar, top it off with Gatorade, and layer up in my running clothes.

It doesn't matter how hot or cold it is, or if it's raining, snowing, or storming, or even if it's two in the morning, I always work out or run after I dream of her. Or him. Or them.

On my way out the door, I look up at the sky. It's as gray as Phoebe's skin was in my dream. Weather is coming. There's already a thin layer of frost coating the ground. It's lying completely undisturbed. No footprints. No tire tracks. It's exactly why I picked this cabin. It's so far away from… everything, that I even had to pay to get a cell tower installed so I could have decent enough internet to work up here.

They erected the small tower halfway between my cabin and the only other one up here within thirty miles. Not that Abe Miller needs the internet. That old guy couldn't work a computer any better than a primitive caveman. But I did talk him into getting a cell phone at the very least. And he has his trusty dog to keep him company.

Abe lived here long before I moved in. I often wonder why he chose to live a life like this. Though we're friendly, it's not like we have Tuesday poker nights. We barely even cross paths unless we happen to be making a supply run at the same time. And only then because there's exactly one road in, and one road out.

Luckily, if bad weather is coming, I'm completely stocked, having been to town right before I left to go to Blake's wedding in Calloway Creek.

I eye the five-hundred-gallon propane tank that sits eighty feet from the rear of my cabin, wondering when it's scheduled to be filled next. A quick check on my phone confirms it's tomorrow. Good thing.

Picking up the pace as I head toward the road, Blake's wedding once again takes over my thoughts. It was the first wedding I'd been to since losing Phoebe and DJ. Well, the first wedding that actually resulted in a marriage, that is. My other brother, Lucas, infamously known as the runaway groom of Cal Creek, recently bolted yet again, leaving his fourth fiancée at or near the altar. Maybe that's why I went to that one. I knew there wouldn't be a ceremony.

But a few months ago, when Blake told me he was getting married after a whirlwind romance, I knew it would be different. I knew it would happen and I'd have to watch him and Ellie smile and laugh and cry and declare their love for each other. And as expected, every second of it ripped my fucking heart out.

I stupidly had a few too many drinks at the reception, only staying as long as I needed to become sober. Thankfully, my younger brother knows me well enough not to have asked me to make a speech. That would have only driven the stake further inside me. Lucas's speech wouldn't have been any better, so our father did it. The whole time, my eyes traced the movements of a spider making its way up a nearby trellis, my mind making up a story about where he's going to weave his web and how big it might become.

Being only the second guest to leave, following closely behind a woman with an infant, I made the four-hour drive back home.

Home. This is my home now. Has been for the last two and a half years. The middle of nowhere in the Tug Hill Region of New York. It's the polar opposite of the small town of Calloway Creek where I was born and lived for twenty-six years. A town where all you need to do is look outside your window to see your neighbors' kids playing in the yard. Where couples stroll the sidewalk hand-in-hand. Where families meet at the ice-cream shop, the parents having coffee as their kids inhale their cones then run around the playground laughing.

No—that was never going to be home for me again. Not after losing everything.

The drive seemed uncharacteristically long. It had rained earlier, and the frigid temperature allowed ice to form on some of the sparsely traveled roads. I drive the biggest, baddest truck around, but still nearly skidded into a gully. I stopped, pounded the steering wheel, and shouted to God—if he even exists—because what kind of God would take my family like that? I screamed at the top of my lungs for him to make something happen. Take me. Slam me into a fucking tree so I can join them if that's what it takes. Anything to get me out of this pitiful existence.

Eventually, I made it home in one piece, tried to sleep, but just kept seeing Phoebe walking down the aisle toward me just like Ellie walked toward Blake. Closing my eyes almost always results in seeing her. Seeing DJ. It's why I live half my life as a sleep-deprived zombie.

Finally, at eight in the morning, when my body was shaking from stress and lack of sleep, I resorted to taking a sleeping pill—something I only do when things get critical. At least it allowed my body to recharge enough to think. To eat. To run.

So that's what I'm doing now. Running. From them. My dreams. My demons. Next to my job, it's what I do best. Between that and chopping wood, I'm in the best shape of my life. Not that it matters. There's nobody in my life to appreciate it. I don't date. I'm not in competition with, or for, anyone. I barely leave the cabin. I crunch numbers. Alone. Because as CFO, that's what I do. Numbers don't have faces or feelings. Numbers are safe. They don't talk back. And they don't die.

I'm not sure how long I've been running, but when I trip over a snow-covered root, it brings me back to the here and now and I realize I should probably turn around and head home. I know the forest like the back of my hand by now, which means I know how dangerous it can be in a storm. I might have turned reckless in the past few years, but I'm not stupid. Breaking my leg and starving or freezing to death out here is definitely not at the top of the list of ways I'd like to leave this life.

And yes, there is a list. But not one I'd ever act upon. Because if I failed and lived, Mom would fucking kill me, not to mention what my little sister Allie would do. Blake, Lucas, and Dad would be okay. They'd get over it. But not Mom and Al. They'd become like me. And that's not something I'd wish for anyone.

A sound in the distance has me stopping and listening. A gust of wind pushes it away. Maybe I was imagining it. Like I often imagine the sharp piercing sound of the CO detector alarm that could have saved my family. The alarm that was never there because *I* failed to install one.

I hear it again. I'm definitely not dreaming. It's not an alarm either. It's a horn.

Making a detour on my way back—because if anyone is in trouble, I may be the only person around to know about it—I follow the sound as it becomes louder and louder.

Ah, shit. My feet slip out from under me, and I fall hard onto my ass. There must be a thin layer of ice under the inch or two of snow. Before I get up, I see the rear of a car sticking out of a ditch. A Honda or Kia or… definitely something without snow tires. Who the hell comes to the middle of nowhere New York in late November without snow tires? Stupid fucker.

Standing up and getting my footing, I make my way over. The blaring horn is starting to get on my nerves. *Must* the driver keep pressing it? I mean, Jesus.

I freeze when the whole car comes into view. Because I know the driver isn't pressing the horn. The front end of the small red car is crumpled against the large trunk of a tree. I race over to the driver's side and try the door. It won't budge.

I'm almost afraid to look at what lies within. But movement inside the car has me doing it.

It's a woman. Blood trickles down her forehead and she's holding her left arm in her right hand.

"Are you okay?" I shout over the horn.

She looks over at me, relieved to see another person, but terrified all the same. "I—I don't know."

The hood is mangled and twisted. I've become pretty good at knowing car engines. With that knowledge, I reach inside, feel around and finally pull the plug on the horn. Ahh, sweet silence.

Then my stomach hollows with dread when I see the hole in the front windshield. But it's not the hole that has bile rising in my throat. It's the empty child's car seat I see in the middle rear seat.

Terror licks at my heart as I turn and vomit into the fresh snow.

Chapter Two

Martina

What is this guy doing?

I could swear he just tossed his cookies. And now he's frantically looking around my car like a maniac. Why isn't he helping me get out? Or at the very least calling 911.

I can't find my phone that is Lord-knows-where, along with the rest of the contents of my purse that went flying after my car skidded and ran into the tree.

Holding my sore wrist, I wonder what other horrible things are in store for me after the hellish few days I've already had.

"Excuse me!" I shout.

It's like he doesn't even hear me. He's searching the ground behind the tree I hit. He's looking all around the car. What the hell? It'd be just my luck to have wrecked my car in the middle of nowhere and have the only guy around be some unmedicated schizophrenic. Or worse, a serial killer living out in the boonies just waiting for helpless women to drive down his road.

I let my head fall back and rest against the seat. Why did I go off route? I curse my old GPS. Or rather, I curse myself for not paying the few hundred dollars to update it at my last service appointment.

"Hey!" I yell.

The guy *has* to hear me; the front windshield is broken.

I look around. Deflated airbags. Broken glass. The hood a crumpled mess. I fear there will be no salvaging this old trusty car. All I can hope is that I can find my phone, call a tow truck, and get to the nearest car rental place.

Taking stock of my injuries, I breathe a deep sigh of relief that I can wiggle my toes, feel all my extremities, and don't seem to have any kind of whiplash—though I'm no medical professional. For all I know, I have a brain injury that will kill me in five minutes time.

For now though, I focus on the good. With the exception of my wrist, all in all, I dodged a major bullet here.

I think.

Unless the crazy man outside is the bullet.

"Mister!" I yell at the top of my lungs. "Are you going to help me out of here or what?"

Finally, he stops looking at the ground and runs over. "How old is your child?"

"Uh, three," I say, confused as to why he's asking.

His face goes completely pale, and he turns to scan the ground.

"Mister! Get me the fuck out of here!"

"Not until I find your child."

Everything begins to make sense as I put myself in his position. The empty car seat in the back. The hole in the windshield. I look at the heavy branch that settled into the passenger seat, happy no one was there to be impaled by it.

"He's not with me."

The man stills, takes the biggest breath I've ever seen anyone inhale, and walks back over to me. "Jesus Christ, why didn't you say so?"

"Me?" I furrow my brows, taking offense. "You're the one out there going all batshit crazy while I'm trapped inside my car. Now… do you mind? And maybe call 911 or a tow truck or something in the meantime. I can't find my phone."

In the ten minutes I've been stuck here, snow has started piling up on what's left of the windshield, some of it coming in through the broken glass and coating the dash.

The guy seems to totally ignore my request. Either that, or he doesn't have a phone on him. *Who doesn't carry a phone?*

"Can you open your door from the inside?" he asks.

"Do you think I'd still be sitting here if I could?"

I think he rolls his eyes. I can't be sure, however, as chunks of his longish hair have come out from under his hat, concealing the upper part of his face.

He goes around to the passenger side and that door opens easily. "Are your legs injured?" he asks. "Can you crawl over?"

Without calling the man stupid, I look between him and the large branch now occupying the passenger seat.

He doesn't call me out on my sarcastic eye movements. Instead, he says, "Let me see if I can get this out of here."

He tugs and pulls and twists, but the branch doesn't budge. He steps back and removes his outerwear—a light rain jacket and hoodie—leaving him in a skin-tight, long-sleeved T-shirt.

My eyes trace the outline of his muscles when he reaches back inside and manipulates the branch until he can lift and push it back through the windshield.

Damn. This guy is strong. Lumberjack strong.

And now, instead of being worried he's a serial killer, I'm having thoughts of him being an eccentric recluse who lives in the woods, cuts logs, and, I don't know, reads and sips wine every night just waiting for his soulmate to show up at his door.

Stop it, I tell myself. How can I think of such things after Charles just died?

Because it's been years since you've been with a man, my subconscious reminds me.

And this man—wow—I can't think of a finer specimen.

Sweat dotting his brow, he removes his wool beanie, and I swear to God I forget all about the pain in my wrist and my mouth actually waters. His dark-blond hair falls down to meet his shoulders. It has body most women would kill for. Not curly, not straight, but the perfect combination of both. His chocolate brown eyes are striking, but they aren't even his best facial feature. That would be his chiseled jawline. Or his full lips. Or his five o'clock shadow that looks like it's been through a dozen five o'clocks.

If only I wasn't in a hurry to get to my son, I could stay here and live out a full-on romance novel. I can see it now: woman gets into accident, is rescued by gorgeous hermit who whisks her off to his secluded cabin where they laugh and cook all day and make love all night. Throw in an accidental pregnancy and I'm thinking it could be a NYT best seller.

"Lady?"

I shake my head, realizing I've been staring—maybe even a bit obsessively.

Ouch! The sharp head movement triggers a pounding near my left temple. I reach up and feel something sticky. I look from my blood-covered fingers to the stranger, fear in my eyes.

"I don't think it's bad," he says, reading my expression. "From the looks of it, you might have banged your head on the window. Can you crawl over now?"

"My wrist hurts, but I can try." I go to unhook the seat belt, but it doesn't release. I keep pushing the button. "It isn't coming off."

He reaches around his back and swivels around something that looks like a cross between a fanny pack and what a handyman carries on his belt. Fishing through it, he comes out with a knife sheathed in a leather casing. My eyes widen and I gulp down my breath. *Holy shit!* Is this hot, reclusive, lumberjack actually some psycho murderer dude who's going to stab me right here? Or maybe he's just salivating at the chance to lure me back to his lair.

My heart beats a million times a minute, all kinds of horrible scenarios playing out in my head.

I pull away, moving my body as close to my door as possible while still tethered by the seat belt.

"Relax," the guy says. "I'm just going to cut you out, not cut you to pieces."

An exasperated burst of air escapes me. "Are you *trying* to make me have a panic attack?"

He backs off and moves the knife away. "Okay, maybe we got off on the wrong foot." He holds out his hand. "I'm Dallas Montana. I live around here. I was out for a run and heard your car horn. Good thing as nobody travels these roads. What the heck are you doing this far away from the highway? You don't know Abe, do you?"

"Abe? No. I'm um… going to pick up my son in Cicero. I'm from Florida. Drove straight through the night. I was supposed to get off on I-90 and go west to Syracuse then pick up I-81 north, but around the Utica area my GPS messed up. Or I did. I ended up on NY-12 north and then my GPS went blank, along with my cell service. I figured I just needed to keep going west so…"

His brows knit together, and he looks down at his still outstretched hand. "Was there a name in there somewhere, or should I just keep calling you *lady?"*

I roll my eyes and shake his hand. "Martina Carver. My friends call me Marti."

"Okay, Martina—"

"Marti," I interrupt.

He flashes me a look of amusement. "So now we're friends?"

"Are you going to get me out of here or what?"

"Are you going to keep freaking out about my knife?"

"About that," I say. "Exactly why do you carry an eight-inch knife?"

"Because the gun is too heavy to carry on my runs." He chuckles silently at my shocked expression. "I'm kidding. Well, not exactly. I do have a gun, and it *is* heavy, but I only have it because of the bears."

Every muscle in my body tenses. "Bears?"

He shrugs. "They don't usually bother people. They just look for food." He nods to his fanny pack thing. "When you live in the middle of nowhere, it's good to be prepared for anything."

"I'm assuming you have a phone in there. I can't seem to find mine. Can you call a tow truck? And maybe a car rental company?"

"This is a dead zone. There's no cell service out here."

"You're kidding."

"You're the one who noticed your GPS and cell phone weren't getting signals. It's not like I'm lying."

"So what do I do?"

He holds up the knife. "For starters, how about we get you out of here?"

"Okay."

It's hard not to be nervous when a complete stranger comes at me with an eight-inch knife that he could plunge into me faster than I'd even know what was happening. But he is meticulously careful as he finds a gap in the belt and saws his way through, the blade moving away from my body.

Finally freed, I climb one-handed over the console and out the other side, happy to be out of the car, but devastated that it seems to be totaled.

"What'll I do now?"

"I have service at my cabin," he says.

I snort out a laugh. "I think I've read a thriller about this. Stranded woman goes with kind stranger who lends a hand and she's never heard from again."

"There's not much of a choice here." He looks up. "It's almost dark. And the snow is coming down harder. Not to mention, the animals will be coming out soon."

I swivel my head in every direction.

"I have a truck. I have cell service. I can either give you a ride or we can call someone."

"Or…" I put my hand on the roof of my mangled car. "I just stay in my car, and you go back to where you have cell service and call me a tow truck."

He eyes me up and down. I shiver from his appraisal, then take a deep breath to calm my nerves, but the shaking doesn't abate. I hadn't even realized how cold I was until just now. I'm wearing yoga pants, a T-shirt, a light jacket, and ballet slippers.

"You'll freeze in an hour."

"An *hour?* You think it'll take that long?"

"Longer." He points to his left. "I'm still five miles from home. Add in the time it will take to summon a tow truck and you'll be a popsicle for sure. Assuming you can walk and have something better to walk in than those flimsy shoes, coming with me is the best option. My cabin is warm. I have food, water, and cell service."

I lean against the car, weighing my choices.

Stay here and freeze. Or put faith in a complete stranger.

I am so screwed.

Chapter Three

Dallas

She leans against her car, sizing me up. One of her shoes—that obviously has zero tread—slips out from under her and when she grips onto the side mirror to keep from falling, she winces in pain.

"It's my wrist," she says, gingerly holding it against her.

She's hesitating, probably trying to decide if she wants to take her chances out here in the cold, or with a stranger who may or may not kill her for sport. I hold out the knife, sheathed in its leather casing. "Here. If it'll make you feel better, take this."

She ignores it and glances up and down the road. Surely she can see hers are the only tire tracks. Nobody travels this road unless they're camping or fishing—neither of which will be happening tonight, or anytime soon based on that sky.

I put my knife away and extend my arms out to my sides, palms facing up. "Okay, fine. But don't say I didn't warn you. I'll call for help when I make it home. But no promises. This snow is getting worse by the minute. The closest tow truck belongs to Luther O'Reilly in a town about thirty miles from here. And that assumes he's reachable and isn't pulling another half-dozen cars out of ditches. But whatever. Good luck."

With that, I put my beanie on, then my hoodie and jacket, and I start walking away.

I'm not going to just leave her here. There *are* bears and other scary shit out in the woods, especially after dark. But she doesn't know I'll walk out of sight and give her the opportunity to either call out after me or follow.

After only a few steps, I hear a deep sigh that's more like a frustrated huff. I get the idea Marti Carver does not like to give in easily.

"Fine," she says, walking up behind me. Then she grabs my elbow to steady herself when she slips on the ice once more. "Shit." She releases me when she finds her footing, her hands covering her face. "I did *not* plan for this."

"Yeah, well, shit happens. Plans get ruined. Life throws curveballs."

She studies me. "You say that like it's from experience."

I motion to her shoes. "Please tell me you have boots, or you're going to lose some toes to frostbite."

She shakes her head. "No boots. I'm from Florida, remember? But I have tennis shoes."

"They'll have to do. I'd suggest doubling or tripling up on socks. And if you don't have gloves, bring an extra pair for your hands." I take in her light jacket that can't possibly be keeping the cold away. "And layers. Florida folks still wear hoodies, don't they?"

She nods to the car. "I have a hoodie in my suitcase. Can we bring it?"

"The hoodie, yes. I'm not dragging a suitcase for five miles across snow-covered forest."

I crawl through her passenger side and pop the trunk.

She opens her suitcase and rummages through it, getting everything she can find to keep her warm. She takes off the jacket, revealing a plain pink T-shirt that shows just how cold she is based on the stiffness of her nipples. I turn away. I shouldn't be looking, for so many reasons.

When I turn back around, she's traded her yoga pants for a pair of jeans and is wearing an FSU hoodie, the hood covering her long brown hair, the string pulled tight so only her face remains visible.

"Florida State, huh? You're a Seminole?"

"That's right. And you?"

"I'm a Bulldog."

"You went to Georgia?"

I snort at the common mistake. "I'm the *other* Bulldog. Yale."

Her eyes become dinner plates. "You went to Yale?"

"It's not a big deal."

She shrugs. "At least I know you're a *smart* serial killer."

I laugh. It's super uncharacteristic of me to laugh these days and it feels… *odd.*

"Speaking of which"—she holds out her hand—"I think I'll take that knife now. You know, in case we see a bear."

"Sure thing. Just keep it in the holder." I pass it to her, handle first. "You don't want to slip and accidentally impale yourself."

Sitting on the bumper, she carefully removes her flats, puts on three pairs of socks and then squeezes into her Nikes, loosening the laces to make room for the extra layers.

I look at the sky. It's getting darker by the second. "We should get going."

"My phone. I need it. It slipped off the seat along with everything in my purse when I hit the tree."

"I'll get it."

I fish around under both seats and find it wedged between the passenger seat and the console. The screen is cracked, but it's on. I shove it, and everything else I can find on the passenger floorboard, into her purse and hand it to her.

She adds a few more things from her suitcase into her purse then closes the trunk and locks the car.

I raise a questioning brow.

She eyes the huge hole in the windshield and says, "Habit."

I thumb to the trees lining the road. "If we want to make it before dark, we'd better get a move on. Think you can keep up?"

"I ran a few 5Ks this year, so yeah."

"Good. Tell me if you need me to slow down."

She motions ahead. "Lead the way."

She's quiet as she trudges behind me. There's really not that much to say. I've gotten used to not talking to anyone, so it really doesn't bother me. After a few minutes though, I get the feeling she's more uncomfortable with the silence than I am. Either that or she thinks I'm leading her to the slaughter. We *are* walking through a darkening forest.

"How do you even know the way?" she asks. "Everything looks the same."

"I've lived here for several years. I'm always out running or hiking." I point. "The Adirondacks are that way. Great for day hikes or camping."

"As in mountains?" she asks, surprised.

"Yup. One wrong turn to the east and you'd have really been fucked."

"As if I'm not now?"

I turn and give her a hard stare. "No, actually, you're not. In fact, I'd say you're pretty lucky I heard your horn or you very well could have frozen to death."

She huffs out another frustrated breath. Why do I get the idea she does that a lot? "Fine. But I'm sure you'll understand that I'm withholding any heartfelt *thank yous* until I'm sure you aren't going to put me down a hole and make me rub lotion all over my skin."

I stop walking and double over in laughter. She really is a piece of work. "You watch too much TV, Marti Carver."

"Yeah, well, maybe you're a bit too trusting, Dallas, uh… what's your last name again?"

"Montana. And is there a reason I shouldn't trust someone who clearly needed help?"

"I suppose not. It's just, in this day and age, so many people are—" She chews the inner part of her cheek, searching for a word.

"Disingenuous?" I ask.

"Exactly." She stares straight into my eyes. "Please don't be one of those people. My life is literally in your hands."

"You're safe with me. I promise. Now, let's pick up the pace. This snow is coming down faster than I anticipated."

She looks through a break in the trees, up at the gray sky that is barely light enough for us to see where we're going. Then she shuffles forward quickly and walks by my side instead of behind me.

My life is literally in your hands. The words repeat over and over in my head. If she only knew how bad I am at saving those who need it, she might have taken her chances in her car.

Phoebe's and DJ's faces flash in front of my eyes. I blink over and over. It's just not fair that I was there to help Marti—a total stranger—and I couldn't do a goddamn thing to save my own family.

"It's not that much farther," I say, walking faster. But no matter how fast I walk, I can't seem to get away from the memories.

Chapter Four

Martina

The forest is beautiful even though I'm growing ever fearful of a coyote, wolf, or bear pouncing out from behind a tree. I've lived my entire life in Florida. I've never been in snow before. It's almost magical. I mean, if it weren't for the fact that my car is totaled, I'm still not with my son, and, oh yeah, Charles is dead.

I think of my son, Charlie, and wonder if he's even capable of understanding death. Does he know his dad isn't coming back? Or does he assume he's just at work and at any second, he'll bound through the door, scoop him into his arms as he always did and throw him into the air.

Thinking of the two of them together is so bittersweet now. Their relationship was never an issue, it was our marriage. Anita has been a godsend for Charles—or she was—stepping in as the perfect wife where I always seemed to fail. I'm not even jealous when I think of how she's become one heck of a stepmom to Charlie.

I sigh, knowing Anita must be going through hell having just lost the love of her life.

Tears brim my eyes and threaten to freeze in the falling temperature. I loved Charles. He was my best friend. Even after the divorce. We were amazing friends, just shitty spouses.

"Everything okay?" Dallas says up ahead.

I walk faster, realizing I'd slowed to a crawl. I blink away the tears, hoping he'll think they're from the piercing cold and not because I'm somewhat of an emotional wreck. Catching up to him with my head on a swivel as I scan for predators, I ask, "What did you study at Yale?"

"Finance."

"Impressive."

A shrug of his shoulder tells me he doesn't think so.

"You're not big on words, are you, Dallas Montana?"

He scoffs at my use of his full name, and I'm not sure if that means it irritates or amuses him.

"Okay, Chatty Cathy. What did you study at FSU?"

"Graphic design."

"So that would make you a…" His voice trails off.

"Graphic designer," I say with all the intended sarcasm.

"Touché." His head shakes. "And what exactly do you do?"

"All kinds of things really. Websites. Branding. I've even done some book covers. And I'm not a Chatty Cathy, by the way. It hasn't exactly been a walk in the park, you know, following you, freezing my ass off, tripping over roots and almost faceplanting into trees, all while Bigfoot may be lurking just around the corner."

"This is the forest," he quips. "There are no corners."

"Must you be so precise?"

"I'm in finance. As a group, we're nothing if not precise."

"Touché." I chuckle. "So where do you do all this financing?"

"Family business."

He really is a man of few words. I go to dig a little deeper when something comes into view. A car. No, a truck. Oh, please let it be *his* truck. As we draw closer, I notice the pile of snow accumulated on the hood. It must be close to a foot. But his truck is massive. Surely we can drive out of here.

A few steps more and I see his cabin. It's much smaller than I expected. Especially for someone who probably comes from money, having gone to Yale and all. He said he's been here for years. Surely he means he's *vacationed* here for years. This can't be his… *home.*

By the time we hit his porch, there's a small drift against his front door and I belatedly notice the wind has picked up. Being that my nose, fingers, and toes barely have feeling left, it's surprising I'm even upright.

He climbs the steps, and I stop, turning toward his truck. "Where are you going? Can't we drive to town?"

He kicks the drift away from the door and opens it, nodding back toward the vehicle. "I'm not going anywhere in the dark with this kind of accumulation. Between that and the ice underneath the snow, we're better off waiting until tomorrow. Now do you want to warm up or not?"

I glance back at the truck, wondering if he's lying and making excuses to get me to stay. The strange thing is, if the guy is some hermit who hasn't had sex in a while, he's surely not acting like he wants to get me into bed. More like I'm a nuisance.

My frozen hands can't even grip the phone I moved to my pocket. "I'll warm up while I call for help. Maybe a snowplow can come and get me."

By the look on his face, I can tell he thinks I've got lofty expectations. But he doesn't know me. He doesn't understand how determined I am to get what I want. And right now, I want to get to my son.

I feel the warmth even before I get through the door. It hits my face like a welcome breeze on a summer day. Once I step inside, I push back my hood and let the heat envelop me. As my fingers and toes begin to thaw, I vow I'll never again complain about the hot, oppressive summers in Florida.

"I don't think I've ever been this cold."

His eyes are transfixed on my forehead. "Let me clean that up for you."

I reach up and feel dried blood.

Dallas goes over to a large iron stove fireplace thing in the corner of the room, strikes a match, and lights what's inside. "This will warm you even more." He pulls one of the two kitchen chairs over near the fire. "Sit here."

He disappears behind a door—*bathroom?*—and a moment later comes out, drags the second kitchen chair over next to me, and sits. He shows me an alcohol wipe. "This may sting a bit."

"I'm a big girl."

When he touches it to my cut, I wince. He rubs gently then puts a small Band-Aid on it. Then he holds his hand out. "Let me see your wrist."

I'm actually surprised he remembered after everything that happened. I lay my arm gently on his open palm. "I'll bet all you Ivy League guys think you can pass for doctors."

He doesn't find my joke funny. "No. But it appears I'm all you've got."

I roll my eyes at his impassive expression. His soft yet strong fingers press on every bone and tendon in my hand and wrist. He manipulates each finger, then twists my wrist carefully back and forth, watching my face for signs of pain.

"It's sore, but not painful," I say.

"I think it's just bruised. I don't even see any swelling, but that might just be because we were out in the cold. We'll keep an eye on it."

He lowers to a knee and starts removing my shoes.

"Um." I pull my foot away. "What are you doing?"

"Your shoes are soaked. They need time to dry. We can put them by the fire."

"Oh." It seems I hadn't noticed my shoes at all. Or maybe I plain forgot when he started playing doctor with me.

"You can stay here and make your calls. I'm going to bring in another pile of wood so it can start drying out."

Most of my body still feeling like a popsicle, I slump forward and hold my hands out, getting them as close to the flames as I can without burning them. A glance around the cabin reveals it to be the opposite of everything I expected.

The entire side wall is covered in—I squint—*wine bottles and books?* As in there must be a hundred bottles of wine and at least triple that number of books. So I was right about him. This long-haired, Ivy League hermit is turning out to be quite the interesting character.

My eyes take a brief moment to peruse the rest of the room. It's large, kind of like a hotel suite, with a small kitchen along one wall, a love seat and coffee table along the other, and a queen size bed whose headboard is made up of one of the large bookshelves. It actually looks quite artistic.

There are two doors to the right. The bathroom he went into earlier, and what I assume to be a bedroom. I look back at the bed, wondering why it's out here if there's a bedroom behind door number two. There's another door next to the front door which must be a closet. The entire place is about the same size as the large dorm room I shared with two other girls at FSU.

The front door opens, and a gush of frigid air comes inside with Dallas, his arms loaded with wood that is still dusted with bits of snow. As he piles it in the corner, I finally get out my phone now that my fingers have regained feeling.

My bottom lip trembles when my favorites screen appears and I see Charles's name and photo underneath the cracked glass. I wonder how long it will be before I'll be able to delete it. My brother Asher's name is on the same screen, along with his daughter Bug's.

The only other name that ever reached my 'favorites' designation is Suzanne, my friend and neighbor who I often swap babysitting duties with when one of us needs to run errands. Her daughter is right around Charlie's age.

I swallow my grief for the thousandth time since Anita called me yesterday morning to give me the news. Scrolling through my contacts, I find her number and tap it. There are three beeps. I try again. The same thing happens. I look at my service bars to see there are none.

I hold my phone up when Dallas brings in his second load of wood. "I thought you said you get service here."

He doesn't speak until he's meticulously piled every last bit of wood next to the previous load. He gets his phone off the small kitchen table. "No bars." His head shakes. "My tower must be down again."

I tilt my head. "*Your* tower?"

"Sometimes when too much ice builds up, I have to climb up and knock it off. And I can't do that when it's dark. It'll have to wait until morning."

I stare him down. "Again, *your* cell tower?"

"When I bought the place a few years ago, there wasn't any cell service. I needed to be able to work remotely so I had one put up."

I belt out what must sound like a ridiculous laugh. "You just *had one put up?"*

Of course he did. Don't all Yale-educated geniuses have their own cell towers?

"Kind of convenient that *your* tower is down and there's 'too much' snow to use your truck." I use air quotes when I say *too much* to get my point across. "It's a big truck, Dallas. You can drive me out of here."

"Maybe if it were a few hours ago, but now, no way. You see the snow. You saw the ice. Hell, you almost broke your neck slipping on it. Almost lost your life when you slammed into the tree. Yeah, I have a truck. But I'm not risking your life trying to drive you the fifty miles to get—"

"You said thirty."

"It's thirty miles to Luther's auto shop. It's fifty to get to anywhere that'll do you any good. There's a hotel/restaurant/gas station that caters to tourists. Listen, I'm not going to put you in danger. Sleep with the knife. Or don't sleep at all. Whatever suits you."

I don't really have any options here but to trust the guy and hope I wake up intact and alive. "Fine," I huff and nod to the doors on my right. "But only if you let me take the bedroom and you stay out here."

He points to the bed. "Marti, this *is* the bedroom."

"What's in there?" I ask, motioning to the door next to the bathroom.

"Nothing." He turns away and I can't see his face. "A hobby room of sorts."

"Great. So you only have one bed? I'll take the couch then."

"If you want to wake up in traction," he says. "It's not nearly big enough."

"Then what do you suggest?"

He shrugs. "The bed's a decent size. You stay on your side. I'll stay on mine."

I huff. And huff. And huff some more. "You can't be serious. Oh my god, this is straight out of some twisted romantic comedy or something. If you think I'm going to share the bed with you so you can get naked and try to charm me with that… *thing* in your pants,"—I glare at him—"think again."

He looks down at his crotch. "That *thing?"* He eyes me like I'm crazy. "Listen, *Martina*, it's not like we have a choice. But if you want to give the couch a try, by all means, be my guest. But while you're ruminating over that, I'm going to whip something up for dinner." He narrows his eyes at me. "You a vegan or anything?"

"No. Why would you ask that?"

"I don't know. You look like a vegan."

"What the hell does a vegan look like?"

He shakes his head. "I just told you. *You.* Try to keep up. But maybe that's too hard for someone who went to one of the nation's top party schools."

My jaw drops. "So now I'm a vegan *and* a lush? That's pretty funny coming from a guy who's hoarding enough wine to get through the apocalypse. You really know how to treat your houseguests, Dallas."

"You're not a houseguest. You're a… lost puppy."

I stomp my foot. It echoes off the plank flooring.

He holds up his hands in surrender. "Jeez, fine. You're a strong independent woman who clearly doesn't need help from anyone, least of all the likes of me." He sticks his head inside the refrigerator. "Steaks okay with you?"

"I suppose," I pout. "After all, don't all dogs like meat?"

He turns and rolls his eyes, clearly exasperated with me. As if I had any control over the circumstances that led me to being right here. Then he grabs a hair tie and pulls back his hair, securing it at the back of his head before he starts cooking.

And despite having a hundred reasons my mind should be somewhere else, I can't help but follow his every movement as he cooks dinner.

When he catches me watching him, I get up and walk over to the decorative wall, running a finger across the sealed corks of a few wine bottles. I like to think of myself as a wine connoisseur, but only of inexpensive wine.

I find myself thinking, or perhaps fantasizing, about Dallas sitting on that bed, book in one hand, glass of wine in the other, his long hair loose and falling to one side of his face as his eyes travel across the words on the page. And suddenly… I'm jealous of a book.

Chapter Five

Dallas

I've never had a woman here, Allie and my mother notwithstanding. And now I'm making dinner for one. It feels strange, like I've entered another dimension. And it's not a feeling I like. Martina Carver should not be the woman I'm cooking for. I should be cooking for my wife.

I never did much cooking back then. Sure, I'd throw steaks on the grill on a Friday night, but Phoebe, as the stay-at-home-parent, did the lion's share. And joyfully so. Being in the kitchen was where she was happiest. Creating new and exciting dishes. Putting a spin on DJ's favorite macaroni and cheese. Always finding ways of getting him to eat vegetables. She was always creative in everything she did.

I glance up to see Marti carefully watching. She's tenacious. Mysterious in a way. And beautiful.

My mind almost stops functioning at the word. I don't think I've ever thought of another woman as beautiful. Attractive maybe, hot even. But beautiful? That was reserved for my wife. My high school sweetheart. My one and only soulmate.

My appetite disappears. I put Marti's plate of food on the table then cover mine with plastic wrap and stick it in the fridge, slamming the door of the refrigerator a little too forcefully before stalking to the front door.

"Where are you going?" she asks before I step outside.

"We need more wood."

I don't need to look back at her to know she's eyeing the large pile I already stacked in the corner. I just keep going, walk out the door, and shut it behind me. I shovel snow from the porch then I sit on the front stoop watching more snow accumulate on the steps until my ass freezes.

~ ~ ~

Not having checked the time before I went outside, I'm not sure how long I sat there. But it's almost midnight once I'm back inside. I stop in my tracks the moment I enter.

Marti is asleep on my bed. Sound asleep, as if she hasn't slept in days. All her clothes are on. Her shoes even, as if she's prepared to make a fast getaway. Why does this not surprise me about her?

My knife, still properly sheathed, lays underneath her limp hand. She's so near the side of the bed, I fear she'll fall off if she moves an inch to the right.

Seeing her that way makes me think about DJ and how I used to worry. What if he learned to pull himself up and I wasn't there? What if he fell out of his crib? If I could only go back and tell myself those are inconsequential things to worry about. If only he'd lived long enough to pull himself up. To smile up at me and call me Daddy. To grow up into the man I knew he could be.

Swallowing those thoughts, I go to the other side of the room. The kitchen is clean. Pans and dishes put away. And… damn it, my entire cabin smells of her. Vanilla, I think. I put another log on the fire hoping the smell of burning wood will somehow overtake the scent of her.

I turn down the lights—though she doesn't seem to mind them being on. She's definitely down for the count. But having slept earlier today, I'm not tired yet. I get my current technothriller read off the nightstand and dive in. Hours later, done with that book, I open my laptop, stick my AirPods in, and practice some more ASL. Luckily I downloaded the entire program. No internet necessary. It's the newest language I'm learning.

After hours of that, my eyelids are finally feeling heavy. I debate trying to sleep on the small couch, but I know getting my six-foot frame comfortable enough to sleep here would be nearly impossible.

I use the bathroom and get ready for bed, keeping on my clothes like Marti did, only choosing to forgo the shoes. I'm not sure how anyone can sleep in shoes. Carefully, I sit on the bed, keeping myself as far from her as I can, and lie down on my back, staring at the ceiling as I watch shadows dance from the flames in the fireplace.

The bed squeaks when Marti rolls toward the center. Turning to face her, I see that her eyes are still closed and the knife is no longer under her hand.

I study her, the only woman I've ever shared a bed with other than my wife, and I feel sick to my stomach. As if I'm somehow betraying Phoebe.

It strikes me how Marti looks the complete opposite of my late wife. In every way possible. Phoebe was tall, blonde, pale-skinned with high cheekbones. Marti is a brunette with a stubborn cowlick just to the left of her part. She's petite, athletic, her skin kissed by the sun.

She shouldn't be here.

Guilt crawls along my spine, stopping at every vertebra, curling its long fingers around them and squeezing until it hurts. Phoebe is the one who should be lying next to me.

People just don't get how all-consuming grief is. Even my own family has a hard time comprehending it. Mom and Allie constantly beg me to move back to Calloway Creek. My brothers aren't as insistent, but I can tell they're having a hard time with my being gone. We were always a close family. My tragedy fractured that.

They can't possibly understand. Before Phoebe and DJ died, I didn't understand it myself. The pervading nature of grief. It's always there, under the surface, in the background, a constant hum reminding me they're gone. It doesn't matter if I put on a suit, paste on a smile, and stand up at my brother's wedding, I'm still brokenhearted. And it's the kind of broken that can't be fixed. Or wished away. It's always going to be there. Phoebe makes sure of it, making almost nightly appearances in my dreams. Telling me how much she loves me. How she'll always be with me.

Fuck.

I put my AirPods back in and play music to stop the noise in my head.

My eyes unable to remain open, I drift off to sleep listening to Bon Jovi sing about riding on his steel horse. Eighties music was always Phoebe's favorite.

I float awake and drift down the aisle toward her. She's wearing her wedding dress and veil. Why is she at the altar? Shouldn't she be the one walking toward me? I can't see her face as her back is to me, but I know she's beautiful. Our wedding song is playing. But something feels wrong. Where are all the guests? Empty chairs line the aisle. Except for one. The first chair in the front is occupied by a child. He turns as I approach.

"DJ?" I say, kneeling in front of him.

He's older now. Three maybe. He has his mom's platinum-blonde hair and my dark brown eyes, a striking combination that will surely make him a lady-killer one day

Music swells, bringing my attention back to my bride. She turns and holds out her hand. I walk toward her thinking she's the most beautiful woman I've ever seen. She smiles brightly for a second, then it falls. Her face changes. She pales. Dark circles form beneath her eyes. Her arms turn frail as if they'd snap like twigs if I touched her. Her entire frame seems to wither right before my eyes. I rush to steady her as she teeters to one side.

Her sunken eyes look into mine. "You could never replace me."

"Of course I couldn't," I say, pulling her tightly against me. "I love you."

Screaming echoes in my head.

"Dallas, stop!"

When my eyes snap open, I'm staring at the eight-inch blade of a very familiar knife.

Chapter Six

Martina

"Put that fucking thing away!" he yells.

"The hell with that." I grip it tighter. "You were mauling me."

He hops out of bed looking mortified and steps as far away from me as he can. Shaking his head, he bends over and rests his hands on his knees. "Jesus, I was having a dream."

I rehome the knife. "It must have been a doozy."

He straightens. "Yeah. Sorry."

It's just beginning to get light outside. I check my phone. Still no bars. I go to the window and my heart sinks. There's twice as much snow on his truck as there was last night. When I open the front door, a powdery drift falls inside and instantly starts melting on the floor near my feet.

Feeling defeated, I close the door and shuffle toward the bathroom. Dallas must have the same idea because we almost crash into each other. I hop back and motion to the door. "Go ahead."

"It's okay, you go."

I chuckle. "I guess you're not used to having a woman around. We tend to take our time in the bathroom. I'll wait my turn."

He doesn't find my joke funny. In fact he looks upset by it. *Jeez—touchy much?*

"I'll only be a minute. Then I'm going to head out to fix the cell tower."

The door shuts. I hear the lid of the toilet echo as it hits the back of the commode. Then I hear him pee. There is definitely not much privacy here in this small cabin. The two-inch gap under the bathroom door ensures anyone out here knows exactly what anyone in there is doing. I make a mental note to be sure he's gathering wood when I need to do certain things.

He brushes his teeth, and I hear the faucet running for a while. He must be getting a drink of water. When the water shuts off, I hear him mumble, but I can't quite tell what he says.

A moment later, the door opens.

I snort. "Not one for showers?"

He sits on the couch, pulls on heavy boots, and laces them. "Marti, I'm about to climb a tower and chisel off any built-up ice from the antennas. Believe me, I'll need a shower when I return. No need to waste hot water."

He grabs his coat and is headed for the front door when I look down at my phone, surprised at what I see.

"Yes!" I scream, holding up my phone like it's a winning lottery ticket. "I have bars!"

He drops his head in relief, pivots, and sinks back down onto the couch. "That's definitely a good thing. Because after getting so little sleep, I probably shouldn't be climbing *anything*."

He didn't sleep? Because *I'm* here? I guess if you're a hermit living in the middle of nowhere, having another person around can really throw you off your game. Or maybe he has social anxiety and can't function well around others. That and a million other questions about this mysterious mountain man lurk in my head. But I push them all aside, because I have to make a call.

"I need to call my son," I say.

Dallas's face pales. He stands, pinches the bridge of his nose, then puts his coat on and goes for the door. "I'll give you some privacy then. And I'll call for a tow."

"Thanks."

First things first, I think as soon as he's outside. I need to talk to Charlie and Anita, but my bladder is screaming to be emptied. I spin around and go into the bathroom, making quick work of using the toilet and washing my hands. Seeing his toothbrush reminds me that I don't have one. I don't have anything. All my stuff is in the trunk of my car. But with any luck, the car will get towed shortly and I'll be on my way to Charlie.

I squirt some toothpaste onto my finger and rub it over my teeth then rinse. Looking in the mirror, I realize I desperately need a shower. I drove all through that first night, so it's been a minute since my last one. My gaze shifts to a shelf where there are lots of amazing hair products. My stomach flutters just thinking about him running his hands through his hair. I've never been a big fan of men with long hair, so why I'm having this visceral reaction is quite confusing.

My phone makes pinging noise after pinging noise. Texts and voicemails are finally coming through. Most are from my brother. Asher has been worried about me as I didn't arrive at Anita's, nor did I check in. One is from Bug, telling me her dad is freaking the fuck out.

I won't tell him his twelve-year-old used the word fuck. She's at that awkward tween stage where she's more than a kid but not quite an adult, and when I think about our relationship, she's more like a sister than a niece.

I scroll through my contacts and find Anita's number. I sigh. What she must be going through. I'm devastated over Charles's death. He was my best friend and my son's father. But Anita was his wife. When we last talked, early yesterday, she barely had a voice left after all the crying. Selfishly, I've wondered if she's even been able to console Charlie.

I press her number and she answers quickly. "Marti! Where are you? Everyone has been worried sick."

"Sorry about that. I'm okay. But my car isn't. It's wrapped around a tree. There was a storm and cell service was down and this guy found me and let me crash at his cabin and—"

"Wait, what? Slow down. You got in an accident? What guy?"

"I'll explain it all when I get there. We have a tow truck on the way. I should be there later tonight. More importantly, how are you? And how's Charlie?"

"Charlie's okay. He knows something's up because I'm not my usual self, but I didn't think it was my place to tell him. My parents and cousins have been keeping him busy."

"And you? How are you holding up?"

After a long moment of silence, she blows a breath into the phone. "Everyone is asking me all kinds of questions about the funeral arrangements. Marti, I have no idea what to do."

"Are you asking my advice?"

"Yes. Please. You knew him better than anyone."

There is no jealousy in her voice when she says it. She knew our history. She also knew Charles loved her way more than he ever loved me—in the romantic sense anyway.

"He wouldn't want a funeral at all, Anita. Or a gravesite where people feel obligated to visit. He wanted to be cremated. And he wanted a party to celebrate his life rather than a reception to mourn his death."

"That's what we'll do then. Will you help me plan it?"

"Of course. Anything you need."

"Marti?"

I can tell by her tone that what she's going to say next is monumental. "Yeah?"

"I'm going to move back here. There's nothing for me in Florida now. I mean, I'll miss Charlie, but I have to be around family, you know?"

Suddenly, it hits me like a ton of bricks. I'm not sure why the thought hadn't occurred to me before. I'm going to be a full-time mom.

Charles and I were co-parenting. Charlie lived half the time with him. I've always been a part-time parent. We separated before Charlie was born. From the moment he arrived, we split custody fifty-fifty. It was the right thing to do. Charlie has been loved beyond belief and has thrived being raised this way.

But now—oh my gosh—he's going to be with me one hundred percent of the time.

I love my son, and I'm happy he'll be with me, but it's going to be a huge adjustment for both of us. How am I going to tell him?

"It's the right decision," I tell her. "You need to be around family. And you'll always be welcome to visit."

"Are you ready to talk to Charlie?"

"Yes. So he knows nothing? Where does he think Charles is?"

"I'm not sure. We just change the subject or redirect his attention when he asks."

"Okay. Put him on."

"It's Mommy," I hear Anita say.

When I hear Charlie's happy squeal, my heart clenches. Is his world about to be destroyed, or is he young enough to adapt and recover without long term damage?

"Mommy!"

"Hey, buddy. Miss me?"

"Miss you lots and lots. Gwammy Jane has a pool. But it's too cold. And Nita's sister has a dog. I want a dog."

Oh, the mind of a three-year-old. "How are you, Charlie? Are you being a good boy for Nita?"

"Yes. The dog is called Joe. Isn't that a funny name? Mommy, where is Daddy?"

Oh, boy. "Did you see all the snow outside? It's why Mommy didn't get there yesterday. Lots of people are having a hard time getting where they need to be because of the snow."

"It's pwetty," he says. "Will you make snowballs with me?"

"Yeah, buddy, we can make snowballs. I'm going to see you very soon, okay?"

"Okay, bye."

Anita gets back on the line. "I don't envy you having to tell him."

"I guess I have a little more time to think about it. I'll call you when I'm on the road again. Hopefully it won't be too long. Stay strong, okay?"

"Okay."

The next call I make is to my brother.

"Where in the ever-loving hell are you, Martina?"

"Well hello to you too."

"I've been going fucking crazy. Did you fall off the face of the earth? Because if not, there is no reason you couldn't at least respond to my goddamn texts—all twenty of them."

I don't tell him he's being over-protective again. Asher is more than just my brother. After Dad died when I was twelve, he became my guardian. I swear most days he thinks he still is.

"Calm down. I'd have texted if I could. Cell service was out here."

"Where is here? Because I know you're not with Charlie."

"No. But I will be soon."

I explain everything that happened over the past day. It does nothing to tamp down his big-brother worries. "Who in the hell is this guy, and what do you know about him? Jesus, Martina, you spent the night with a stranger in the woods?"

"What would you have me do, Ash, freeze to death in my car?"

"What's his name again?"

"Dallas. Dallas Montana."

Asher is quiet for a moment. Then he says, "Holy shit. As in Dallas Montana of Montana Winery?"

I eye all the wine bottles on the wall. They make much more sense now. I laugh as I pull one from the rack and read the label. "I suppose that would be the one."

"The guy's a billionaire. Or at least his parents are."

I gaze around the meager cabin. "Seriously?"

The front door opens and Dallas walks through, looking pensive and not at all happy.

"Listen, I have to go. I'll keep you updated. There's a tow truck on the way, and I'll rent a car in the nearest town and be at Anita's parents' place by dinner."

"Stay safe, little sister."

I hang up and turn to Dallas. "So? When will it get here?"

He shakes his head. "There isn't going to be a tow truck. Not today anyway."

Chapter Seven

Dallas

"What do you mean it's not coming? You said—"

I gesture out the window, where it's already turning gray after a mostly clear morning. "You think I can control the weather?"

"I'm one little person. How hard can it be to get here?"

"That's the problem. You're one person. Snowplows and tow trucks are dispatched to places where the most people will be helped. Or to emergencies."

"This *is* an emergency. I need to get to my son."

The look on her face has a knot forming in my stomach. "Is he sick?"

"He's fine. But…" She swallows hard and gazes out the window. "His dad just died. It's why I was driving up here."

I stagger back like I was punched in the gut. My calves meet the sofa and I sit, slumping over until my forearms rest on my knees. "His dad." I look up. "Not your husband?"

Belatedly, I check her finger for a ring. In all my life, I've never been concerned with whether or not a girl was hitched. I found my one true love when I was thirteen, so why should I give a single flying fuck if this one is married or not?

"He's my ex. But he's also my very best friend." She rubs her eyes. "Or he was." She sits on the edge of the bed. "I still can't believe it."

"You said it's an emergency. Is he all by himself?"

"Charlie. His name is Charlie. And no. He's with his stepmom, Anita, and her family."

"Is he safe?"

"Yeah. They're good people."

"Okay, so it's not so much an emergency as somewhere you really need to be."

She nods.

"I'm sorry to say that doesn't make my little road the highest of priorities."

"No. I suppose not."

"Was your ex in an accident?"

As soon as the words leave my mouth, I regret them. I don't need to hear details about anyone dying.

"The doctor said it was something called an AVM. Anterior venous malformation. He had a tangle of blood vessels that irregularly connected arteries and veins. He never knew he had it but was most likely born with it. And since it was in his brain, it caused a massive stroke. It was sudden. They said he probably never felt a thing." She sniffs back tears. "The worst part is that if they had known it was there, they could have fixed it. He could have gone on to lead a normal life."

Bile rises in my throat when I think of Phoebe. I was told she might not have experienced any pain. *Might* not. Not *definitely* not. I've looked it up. Carbon monoxide can make you feel sick, cause a headache, shortness of breath, vertigo, and the list goes on. I know she had a seizure. I can only hope she didn't know what was happening to her. DJ, on the other hand, died quietly in his sleep. There's little solace in knowing that. He's still not here, and he never will be.

My phone buzzes with a text from the propane company. They won't be coming out today. Or even this week. The news just keeps getting better. "Shit."

"What is it?"

I pull up the propane meter app on my phone. "I was due for a propane delivery today. It's not coming."

She glances at the fireplace, where only embers remain. "I'm confused."

"Don't you hear the generator? The hum coming from behind the house? There isn't electricity this far out. Everything here runs off the five-hundred-gallon propane tank in the back yard. Once that's gone, the food in my fridge will spoil unless we pack it with snow. The only heat we'll get will be from the fireplace. And there will be no hot water."

"But it's not going to run out, like, *today*… is it?"

"I'm down to five percent. We're probably okay for today, but we might want to conserve where we can. I'm going to turn the heat down. And if you shower—"

She holds up a hand. "I get it, I get it, I get it. No wasting resources. It's fine. We once had to go a week without power when a hurricane plowed through the state. I think I'll survive."

"Surviving a week without power in Florida is a bit different from being in the wilderness of New York in a blizzard. Don't get too blasé about it."

"Blizzard? Who said anything about a blizzard?"

I show her my phone, the weather app displayed on the screen.

Her eyes grow huge. "Twelve more inches of snow? Are you kidding me?"

"That's just what they're predicting over the next twenty-four hours."

She falls back against the mattress and covers her face. "This is not happening."

I walk over to her. "Give me your car keys."

"Why?"

"I'm going to get your suitcase. Well, not your suitcase, but your things. I'll take an empty backpack with me and transfer your stuff into it. Easier to carry."

Her face pinks up. "I'll go with you."

"Something you don't want me to see? Devices that vibrate when activated?"

Her jaw slackens as I reprimand myself for teasing her. *What the hell has gotten into me?*

"Oh my god," she huffs. "You did not just say that." She glares at me then smirks. "Actually, so what if I did? It's really none of your business. But no, that's not what I mean. I just don't need you going through my things is all."

"Fine. Come with me then. But you'd better keep up. We'll have to go faster than yesterday with this weather moving in." I look at her shoes and her hoodie and go to the closet. "Put this coat on. I'd give you a pair of boots but you'd only trip over your own feet. Double up on your socks and bring extras in case they get wet."

"Can we at least eat first if we're going to hike ten miles?"

I open a cabinet and pull out six protein bars, tossing her one and stuffing the others in my coat pocket. Then I grab a few bottles of water and my backpack. "Daylight's wasting."

"It's not even nine o'clock in the morning."

"Yeah, and if we're not back by noon, we'll be caught out in the storm. Winds are picking up already." I hand her one of my extra beanies and a pair of gloves her small hands will swim in.

She puts on my hat and coat, stuffs extra socks in her pocket, and marches to the door, clearly irritated. As if I'm the one causing all this inconvenience. I'd say it's the other way around. She's the one inconveniencing me.

Not even ten minutes into our hike, she breaks the silence.

"Is it dangerous climbing the cell tower?"

I scoff. "We'll go a lot faster if we don't talk."

"Listen, Dallas. I'm slightly freaking out here. I'm stranded in a strange place with a strange guy, my ex just died, and I can't get to my kid. And now I find out I'm going to be trapped here for at least another day because there's a fucking blizzard coming. Sue me if I think a little conversation might be a nice distraction from my totally stressed-out thoughts right now."

I chuckle, finding I'm kind of digging this girl and her smart mouth. As soon as the feeling comes, though, it's gone.

"So the tower?" she asks, huffing along keeping pace with me.

I shrug. "It's nothing I haven't done a half-dozen times before."

"Have you always been successful?"

I hold out my arms. "I'm still here, aren't I?"

"I mean at fixing the signal?"

"Usually. But hey, thanks for the concern about my well-being."

"Sorry. Of course I'd be concerned about you. I'm just worried cell service might go out again."

"It could. I'd suggest doing whatever you need to do before the storm comes."

"Like?"

"Like calling whomever or downloading a movie. Whatever you think you'll need to pass the time."

There is a crinkle in her nose. I can tell she's making a mental list of everything she'll need to do before service goes out again. I turn away when I realize I might like that crinkle. I might like it a lot.

I walk faster.

Instead of yelling at me to slow down, she surprises me by keeping up. What surprises me more is that she's not complaining about it. I don't know Marti well, but from what I do know, the woman loves to complain.

"Charles used to like hiking. We didn't have hills in Florida, but there were always trails. You know, if you don't mind snakes and alligators."

Charles. As in Charlie's father. He was named after his dad just like DJ was named after me.

My dream is suddenly front and center as I recall an older DJ sitting in the chair looking up at me. Not a day goes by when I don't think about what he would look like. He'd have been three soon, his birthday falling in just a few days. I was hoping to be able to go to town and get a jumbo-sized bottle of tequila to help get me through the day. Now, though, I'm thinking I might be stuck with just wine.

"You really don't talk much, do you?" she asks.

"Don't have much to say." I try to think of something just to be polite. "So your son was on vacation with your ex?"

"They went up for Anita's family reunion and Thanksgiving."

Right. Thanksgiving is coming up. It's the day before DJ's birthday… just another day I no longer celebrate.

"That's nice of you letting your ex have him over the holidays."

"Charles and I split custody. Charlie lived with him exactly half the time. It worked out well, actually. And now… now I'm going to be a full-time single mom. I still can't believe it."

"Yeah, well, there are worse things."

I don't turn, but I can feel her staring a hole in the side of my head. I walk even faster. And damn if she doesn't keep pace the entire way.

Chapter Eight

Martina

Worse things?

Than being a full-time single parent? Than Charlie losing his dad?

Dallas is mysterious. Guarded even. While I've often been accused of having verbal diarrhea and spewing out every thought that crosses my mind, he seems to hold all his cards close to his chest.

Finally, I see my car come into view. It's even more mangled than I remember. Dallas was right. I'm fortunate to be alive and that a bump on the head and bruised-up wrist are my only injuries. And more than that, I'm lucky he found me.

My car is buried under a foot of snow, and when I peek inside, snow and ice cover the dash and front seats. I'd have been an icicle for sure.

I pop the trunk, open my suitcase, and motion for the backpack. "Do you mind?"

Dallas is lost somewhere in his own head. He's staring into the back seat of the car, probably wondering if I could have survived the night there.

Maybe I could have used Charlie's car seat to plug up the gaping hole in the windshield. But that wouldn't have helped with the cold. The engine is dead. I had no blankets. No hat or gloves. I shudder at how close Charlie came to losing both parents in the span of just a few days.

"Dallas?" I walk to the side of the car and put a hand on his back.

He flinches and his eyes snap to mine. "What? Oh, yeah, here." He hands me the empty backpack and I get started transferring everything I can fit into it.

I packed quickly when the phone call came. Through my tears, I stuffed clothes into a suitcase without even thinking about the enormous differences in weather between where I was coming from and where I was going.

When I pull out my undergarments, I peek around the trunk at Dallas. My cheeks heat at the thought of him touching the lace of my bra or the satin of my favorite panties. My heart pounds when a sudden image appears in my mind of him removing the garments from my body.

When he looks over and his eyes lock onto mine, he studies me, and I wonder if he knows what I'm thinking. He's not looking at me like he wants to bed me. It's more of a pensive look, as if he's trying to read me. Despite the cold, warmth spreads throughout my body, pooling in places I swear had gone dormant.

I clear my throat, look away, and go back to the task at hand.

It won't all fit into the backpack. I leave two pairs of open-toed shoes, a book, and a few toys I'd brought for Charlie. I do make sure to stuff his favorite tattered bear in with my other belongings. He was so excited to go on an airplane that he forgot to grab it. And I was so nervous about him flying, I failed to pack it.

Flying hasn't been high on my list of fun things to do. Not since Charles and I went on our honeymoon in the Bahamas and our plane almost crashed into the Atlantic.

I close the suitcase, then the trunk, and sling the backpack onto my shoulder. Then I stare at my trusty old car that I've had since I was a teenager.

"It's just a car," Dallas says with some urgency.

I turn, hands on hips. "It is not *just* a car. Betsy is full of old memories."

"Betsy?" he says, amused.

"Charles named her. It used to be his car. He won it from a friend after they made a bet over who could deadlift more weight." I laugh at the memory. "Charles's family was a lot better off than mine. I'd lost both my parents, and it was just me and my brother. So when I got my license a few weeks after he won the car, Charles gave it to me and bought a new one." I put my hand on the rear bumper. "He asked me to marry him in this car. And Charlie was almost born in Betsy."

"Sounds like someone is a little hung up on their ex."

"It's not like that. *At all.* But I'm going to miss this car."

"So, I have a question. What would the other guy have won if your ex lost the bet?"

I roll my eyes. "Me."

His face is full of surprise. And maybe anger. "What the fuck?"

I snicker. "Don't worry, he wouldn't have really gone through with it. We were kids and it was a stupid bet. Besides, Charles knew he was going to win."

"Still. He had no right." He shakes his head forcefully. "And he took the car, which means he would have 'paid up' had *he* been on the losing side." He looks up at the darkening morning sky, cursing my ex under his breath. "Anyway, we should go. Do you want another protein bar?"

I ignore the offer, still looking at Betsy.

"Well then." He takes the backpack off my shoulder, slings it onto his back, and secures the chest straps. "Let's see if we can beat the weather."

For a few long minutes as we head back, I ponder Dallas's words. *Would* Charles have given me to his friend? I mean, I'm nobody's property, but I never really thought about it. How come in seven years, I'd never bothered to ask? Maybe because he gave me the car. Still. I should have asked. Or better yet, he should never have bet me in the first place.

Dallas is perfectly content making the hike back to his cabin in total silence. It makes me think how we must be total opposites. I need conversation. I need people. I could never live out here and be one with nature and only have my thoughts to keep me company. I'd go insane.

"Tell me about this family business of yours," I say.

His gruff of displeasure is audible. He really does prefer silence.

"Come on, Dallas. It's a long walk. Humor me."

If I could see his eyes, I'm one hundred percent sure he'd be rolling them.

"I'm CFO."

"Chief Financial Officer?"

He nods, again seemingly unimpressed with his own title.

"And what exactly is your family business?" I ask as if Asher hasn't already told me.

"Wine."

"Ahhh. That explains it then. For a minute there, I thought you might have an unhealthy obsession with alcohol. I've never seen such an impressive collection. So where exactly is this family business?"

"A place I'm sure you've never heard of."

I take a dozen quick steps and poke him on the shoulder. "Listen, I don't want to be here any more than you want me to be here. But neither of us has a choice. We might as well make the best of it."

His cheeks blow out with a long exhale. "Calloway Creek."

There's pain in his eyes when he says the town name. So many questions burn in the back of my mind. But Dallas Montana doesn't seem too eager to open up to me, so I keep things cordial.

"You're right. I've never heard of it. Where is it?"

"It's just outside of New York City."

"It sounds small."

"Population twenty thousand."

"Wow, that *is* small." Maybe it's not that big of a jump for him to go from such a small town to a cabin in the woods. There were more than forty thousand students at FSU. I can't even imagine an entire town that's half the size of my alma mater's student body. "I assume you grew up there?"

"I did." He reaches into his pocket and rips open a protein bar. "I'm going to eat now."

Hmm. He ended that conversation quite abruptly. So he doesn't want to talk about this little town where he grew up. Dallas is becoming more mysterious by the minute. And I'm nothing if not curious. But I bite my tongue and fall back a few steps, because clearly he doesn't want to talk.

I let him be and make a mental list of what I need to do on my phone or laptop in case cell service goes out again. I need to make a few calls so Anita and Asher won't worry. And I should make sure all my devices are fully charged in case his propane runs out before the tow truck arrives.

I suppose I'm not the one who needs to worry about it though. He did claim we'd have enough for another day or two. I should be long gone if and when he does lose power. It makes me wonder if he'd pack up and go back to Calloway Creek. Or is the thought of going back to his hometown so daunting he'd rather freeze to death in some remote cabin?

I focus on the back of his head. Who *is* this guy?

~ ~ ~

The wind has picked up and snow is starting to fall again as we approach his cabin.

My stomach starts to rumble as we walk through the front door, but my feet take priority. I peel off my wet socks and lay them by the fire—soon to be our only heat source. "If you really think you might lose power, we should start eating anything that might spoil. Mind if I whip up some brunch?"

He puts the backpack on the floor and removes his coat. "Have at it. I'm going to take that cold shower now."

Without thinking about it, my eyes go directly to his crotch. Then my face heats up and I quickly look away when I realize I've misread the situation and am a total idiot.

"As if," I think he says under his breath as he heads toward the bathroom.

I stare after him. What the hell is that supposed to mean? An eyebrow raises. O*oooooooh, maybe he's gay*. That has to be it. Because come on, single guy in a remote cabin stranded with a pretty girl he's just saved from certain demise? That's got hot one-night stand written all over it.

And for the umpteenth time today, I find I'm practically drooling over the gorgeous puzzle of a hermit who is, at this very moment, getting naked and wet in the shower.

I scold myself when I hear my own audible sigh. I should definitely not be thinking about who may or may not remove the cobwebs between my legs at a time when my best friend's funeral is being planned.

Damn, woman, get a grip. I need to call Anita. I put her on speaker as I dice up vegetables and reheat his leftover steak from last night.

After I update Anita, check in on Charlie, and reassure him I'll be there as soon as possible, I call Asher.

"Good news, I hope?" he asks.

"Sorry, no. I'm stuck here until tomorrow. There's a lot of snow and limited resources. Getting a plow or a tow truck all the way out here is not high on their list of priorities. And it's snowing again."

"Jesus."

"What is it?"

"I'm looking at a weather map right now. Marti, it's not looking good. If you're in as remote a place as you say, it could be more than just another day. They're calling for a blizzard. Up to two more feet of snow. It's all over the news. Holy shit."

"What?" I pull up the weather on my phone and stare at the large purple blob coming this way. Purple. That's worse than red. I sit heavily on one of the kitchen chairs. "Asher, he's almost out of propane."

"What are you talking about?"

"His cabin." I sigh heavily. "It runs on propane. His delivery got pushed back due to the snow. If the weather gets as bad as forecasted, it may be delayed by a long time. He's going to lose power. And I'm… oh, God, Asher, I'm stuck here."

"Charge your phone and your backup charger. You have one of those, right? Call the authorities and let them know you're almost out of propane. That should move you up the list. I'm looking at plane tickets now and I'll—"

I look down at my phone. The call dropped. Zero bars.

My head slumps forward. How is this my life right now?

Chapter Nine

Dallas

The scent of grilled meat and sauteed veggies hits me when I emerge from the bathroom. My mouth waters as I stand in front of the fireplace. I hear the sound of cracking eggs and wonder what she's making, but after my cold shower, getting warm takes priority over my curiosity.

A few minutes later, Marti is scooping food onto plates. A lot of food.

When she notices I'm in the room, she sets them on the table and sighs. "Cell service is down again."

"Damn. I thought we'd have it longer."

"You probably should have called whoever before your shower."

I sit at the table. "Nobody to call."

I feel her staring at me. She wants to ask me something but doesn't.

Brunch is incredible. She made hash out of the leftover steak and potato. And the omelets, let's just say my taste buds are exploding. I shovel another bite in. "What did you put in these?"

"I found a can of crab meat. I hope you weren't saving it for a special occasion."

I don't bother telling her there will be no more of those. I just compliment her culinary skills and enjoy my meal.

"Can you try and climb the cell tower?" she asks.

One glance out the window confirms it's still snowing. "Not in this weather. Besides, with more snow expected, it would be wasted energy since it'll most likely go out again."

"I understand that. But Asher suggested calling the authorities to let them know you're running out of propane. That would make getting to us more of a priority."

I set down my fork, maybe a little harder than I intended. "Asher?"

The strangest feeling runs through my body. I have an inkling about what it is, but I don't like it. I don't like it one goddamn bit.

"My brother," she explains.

I ignore the fleeting feeling and say, "We're not going to freeze, Marti." I nod to the fireplace that can also serve as a stove. "I have a shit ton of wood. The cabin is small, so it'll stay warm enough. We can cook. And I have plenty of food."

"It'll spoil."

"It's freezing outside. It won't spoil. I have some coolers. We can use snow to keep everything cold."

"Or just keep the food outside."

I laugh. She knows nothing about this area. Or camping, apparently. "That's a great way to attract bears."

She slumps over until her head meets the table next to her plate. "Great. As if I needed anything else to stress over."

"Listen, this isn't my first rodeo. I ran out of propane about eighteen months ago. It was March and an ice storm came through. I was fine then, and we'll be fine now. I'm very capable of keeping you alive."

As soon as the words leave my mouth, I wince. The voice in my head tells me I should know better than to make promises I might not be able to keep.

"Oh, shit," I say, a second thought occurring.

She looks up, concerned. "What is it?"

"Abe. The only other guy who lives out here. I should check on him." I scold myself for not thinking of it before now.

"Wait. There's another guy who lives out here? And you're just telling me this *now?* He could have a vehicle that could get me out of here." She stands, hands on her hips as she glares at me, and huffs out that all-too-familiar irritated sigh. "What are we waiting for? Let's get my stuff and go."

I scoop another bite of food into my mouth. "Sit down."

"Don't tell me what to do."

"Marti, Abe Miller is ancient. He's got to be eighty-five or ninety years old. And believe me, his truck will *not* get you out of here. It may be as old as he is." I shake my head. "Damn, I should have called to check on him before I took a shower."

I glance at Marti, knowing the reason I didn't make the call. I've been… distracted.

"He has cell service too?" Her puzzled expression turns into a glare. "Oh, my god, why didn't you say anything? Maybe his is still working." She sneers at my blasé attitude. Then she actually puts a hand under one of my armpits and tries to make me stand.

I shrug her away. "Calm the fuck down, woman."

She steps back and glares daggers at me. "Dallas Montana, did your mother teach you any manners at all? You don't ever tell a woman to calm down. And you certainly don't tell one to calm *the fuck* down."

"You do when she's acting all crazy like you are now." I motion to her half-eaten plate of food. "Finish your meal and I'll tell you about Abe." She doesn't move a muscle. She's nothing if not determined. "Fine, look, Abe's tower is my tower. When I bought this place, his was the only other cabin around. I made sure the tower was erected an equal distance between us. Then I bought the old guy a cell phone."

Her face visibly softens. Then she sits, almost reluctantly, as if following my instructions means she's admitting defeat.

She takes a bite, then says, "I suppose that was a very nice thing for you to do."

I try not to smile, because that might be the closest thing to a compliment to come out of her mouth since we met.

"I'll go check on him after we eat."

"How far away is he?"

I point west with my fork. "About three miles that way."

"That's not bad. I'll go too."

"Not a good idea." I nod to her Nikes. "Those are still wet from this morning's hike. Besides—and this isn't me having poor manners—I'll make better time going alone."

I can tell she wants to argue the point. But facts are facts. I'm a more experienced hiker than she is.

"What if…" She pauses and looks around the cabin. "What if something happens and you don't come back."

I shake my head. "Not possible."

"Dallas, my ex just dropped dead from an AVM nobody knew he had. My mom died of cervical cancer before I hit my first birthday, and my dad succumbed to a massive heart attack eleven years later. And, well… it *is* possible. It just is." A pained look crosses her face.

Fuck. This woman has been through a lot. I stare at her, thinking she's more like me than I thought.

"You're right. Bad shit happens all the time. But nothing is going to happen to me."

"You can't possibly know that for sure. Lots of things can kill you. Bears, trees… not to mention it's freezing out there."

I hold up a hand to stop her. "Okay, okay, fine." I take a deep breath. "Wait, trees? How can trees kill me?"

"I don't know. You could trip on a root. Or a branch could fall on you. It could happen."

I shake my head at her paranoia. "If I don't come back, my wood pile is over behind the truck, my keys are in the drawer by the bed, and you're welcome to all the wine. Just wait for the snow to melt and cell service will return. You'll be fine, Marti. I promise."

Don't promise, my subconscious reminds me. But it's too late, I already did.

"How long do you think it will take?"

"A couple hours. Three tops."

She looks at the time. "And if you're not back in four?"

I stand, walk over to the wine rack, and pull out a bottle. "If I'm not back in four, open this. I guarantee it'll take your mind off things. It's my best one." I point to a cabinet. "Glasses are over there."

Finished with my food, I do the dishes. Then I bundle up, put a few things in my backpack, and head for the door.

"Dallas?"

I turn. Her expression morphs from her usual one of stubborn determination into one I've never seen before. Her hazel eyes bore into me with an intensity I've never experienced. "Yeah?"

"Please don't make me open the wine."

I don't say anything. The way she's looking at me. The pleading in her alluring eyes. The helplessness in her enchanting gaze. The pure fucking beauty of her entire being. I don't say anything because I can't. The only thing I'm capable of doing is giving her a slight nod and walking out the door.

And damn it if I don't spend the entire hike to Abe's thinking of the pretty brunette sitting back in my cabin.

Chapter Ten

Martina

I take the fastest cold shower in the history of mankind, washing only the most important areas. I figure I can stretch it a few more days before I have to shampoo my hair. Hopefully, it won't be too long, and I'll be out of here and able to take a warm bath. Not to mention give Charlie a big hug. I smile at the thought.

Still wrapped in the large fluffy towel, I race out into the other room and warm myself by the fire. I rotate, letting the heat hit every part of me.

It's strange being alone here. On one hand, I'm scared of being in the middle of nowhere during a snowstorm. On the other, I'm not sure I could be in more capable hands than the man who just left to check on his elderly neighbor.

It makes me wonder if Dallas will still be here when he's Abe's age. And more—why is he even here in the first place? It's a question I've been dying to get to the bottom of, but every time I see an opening, he changes the subject.

Warm enough now, I shed the towel and get dressed. Pulling my one-and-only hoodie over my head has me thinking—when the propane runs out, I won't be able to use the washing machine. Hand washing laundry is on the same list as flying. I hate it.

Going off the assumption that I may end up here for another day or two, I eye his stackable washer/dryer unit off to the far side of the kitchen. How much propane would it take for one load? Maybe if I do a quick wash cycle, then hang my clothes near the fireplace to dry, it won't use too much.

Remembering the laundry hamper in the bathroom, I collect Dallas's dirty clothes, along with my damp towel, and head to the washing machine. It's just big enough to fit everything. I'm not sure what comes over me when I pull one of his shirts to my nose and inhale. I almost don't want to wash it. It smells heavenly—a mixture of the body wash I just used along with a sharp outdoorsy scent of wood, smoke, and citrus that evokes a visceral reaction in the center of my body.

I quickly stuff the shirt into the machine knowing it's pointless to lust after a guy who is only around me because he's forced to be. One who will be rid of me as soon as he's able. And one who, for all I know, is gay.

He's not.

Something in the back of my mind tells me it's not possible. That if he were gay, we wouldn't banter like we have been. Nor would he look at me the way he does when he thinks I'm not aware.

I remove my hoodie and stuff it in on top of the load then add soap and start the machine, hoping he won't be mad that I used up a little propane. But I only have so many pairs of underwear.

Being an unexpected visitor, I try to be a good houseguest and clean up whatever I can. I sweep the floor. Wipe the counters. Organize his cupboards. But I can't help looking at the door next to the bathroom. He said it's a hobby room. He never explicitly said I couldn't go in there. But somehow I get the feeling it's not something he'd be too keen on. Still, it calls out to me, preying on my curious nature.

To pass the time, if not distract myself from the other room, I peruse his book collection. The books he has are not ones I would generally read. Mostly autobiographies, finance books, mysteries, and thrillers. I pick one up, recognizing the title, then quickly put it away, deciding I do not, in fact, need to be reading a Stephen King novel about being trapped with a psychopath in a remote location during a blizzard.

I decide on the Matthew Perry autobiography as I've always been a fan of *Friends*.

A while later, I'm startled awake by a loud noise. I must have drifted off while reading. I hop out of bed to investigate, hoping it's Dallas coming back. Sadly, it's not. A tree branch snapped under the weight of the snow, only missing the front of his truck by mere inches.

This does nothing to tamp down my nervousness over all the things that could go wrong with Dallas being out in the storm. This is one time I hate being right. Branches *can* fall and kill you.

Instead of dwelling on all the ways he could be injured, I empty the washer and drape the clothes over the makeshift laundry line I strung from the side of his refrigerator to the bathroom door. I can rotate the clothes periodically, so they all get equal time by the warm fireplace.

When I put a pair of his boxer briefs on the line, another tingle shoots through me. Choosing not to ignore the intense feeling this time, I grab a pair of my panties and hang them right next to his boxers so they're just touching, figuring it's the closest I'll ever get to being in his underwear. I back away, admiring the proximity of our respective undies, and laugh at my adolescent antics.

A sound in the distance has my heart beating wildly. This time it has to be him. I dart to the window and peer out, but the falling snow prevents me from seeing beyond his truck.

I hear it again—the distinct sound of a bark. *Oh, God.* Is it a wolf? Or a coyote? *Do* wolves and coyotes bark? For a moment, I picture myself stuck inside this cabin, a pack of hungry animals standing guard outside just waiting for their next meal to emerge.

Then I see movement. Dallas comes into view carrying something that looks heavy on his shoulder, and there's a dog by his side. My chest heaves in deep relief.

I hurry to the door, throwing it open, knowing the smile on my face tells him just how pleased I am that he's back. But his face doesn't reflect my bliss. In fact, his expression is sullen and distant as he climbs the stairs to the cabin.

The dog sees me and trots ahead of him. I squat and am rewarded with a cold nose against mine. "Hey, buddy. Were you lost?" I look up at Dallas. "Did you find him in the woods?"

Dallas shakes his head and I just know what he says next isn't going to be good.

He walks past me, shuts the door, and drops a forty-pound bag of dog food on the floor, stretching his arms out over his head.

I stand upright, stare at the food and look at the dog. "Don't tell me your neighbor fled from the storm and abandoned his dog. Because I will hunt him down and—"

"He didn't abandon him." He pulls out a chair, its legs scraping on the hardwood floor. He rubs a hand across his scruff and sits. "Marti, Abe is dead."

A hand flies to my mouth. "Oh my god! What happened?"

I don't know this Abe. Heck, I just found out about him hours ago, but the thought of anyone dying is exponentially sad. The dog stands next to me and nudges my leg. I sink to the floor and pull him into my arms—which isn't easy to do considering he's a Husky.

"He likes you," Dallas says. "His name is Bex."

"Spelled B-E-X? Or B-E-C-K-S?"

His brows sling low. "What does it matter?"

I shrug. "I just don't want to get it wrong."

"Well, I have no idea."

I look into the dog's eyes. His big, icy-blue, sad eyes. "I think you're Bex with an X. It has more character. And I think you have a lot of character."

"Bex with an X it is," Dallas says.

"So what happened to Abe?"

"Best as I can tell, heart attack. And I'm pretty sure it instantly killed him. His whittling knife and a piece of wood he was working on were on the ground under the snow, and his glasses were still perched on his nose."

"Did you try and resuscitate him?" I say, having trouble getting out the words because I know all too well how horrible it is to be the one to find someone, or *someones*, after they have passed.

His face carves into tormented lines. "He'd obviously been there for some time. A snow drift was halfway up his legs. He was basically covered in snow except for—" he stops talking and looks away, emotion having clogged his words.

"Except for what?"

Dallas swallows hard and can barely speak. "There was a melted spot on his thigh in the shape of Bex's head. The dog must have been sitting there for… I don't know, days even, just waiting for Abe to wake up."

Tears spill down my cheeks and I hug Bex tighter. "We have a lot in common, you and me," I say. I run my hand along his gorgeous dark coat. He leans into me as if he needs someone as much as I do. I rub his white underbelly as I tell Dallas, "I'm the one who found my, um… dad. No one else was home. I did exactly what Bex did. I wrapped myself around my dad and prayed for him to wake up. Even at twelve years old, I knew he wasn't going to, but I stayed by his side for hours, wishing it to be true anyway."

He closes his eyes. "Damn. That's messed up."

He has no idea just how much. "You're telling me. It took more than fifteen years of therapy for me to figure my shit out."

He cocks his head. "So you're older than twenty-seven? I'd have guessed you're younger."

"I'm twenty-four."

"But you said your dad died when you were twelve. That doesn't add up—" He stops talking and nods slowly. "Oh, got it. Still broken."

Broken. Yeah, that's me. I stare up at Dallas, wondering if it takes one to know one.

"Not all therapy is as easy as snuggling a good dog," I mumble into Bex's lavish coat. "You're the bestest boy." I turn to Dallas. "Will you keep him?"

"Hadn't really thought about it. But I wasn't going to leave him there." He shrugs his backpack off. "I brought some bones and chew toys."

"You should keep him. I'll bet he's great company. So I guess you really need to fix that tower now. You'll want to tell the authorities about Abe."

"They'd be in no hurry to recover the body of a deceased elderly man, Marti."

"But, what if the snow stops and he… thaws." I barely get the word out as it's a horrifying notion.

His face pales a bit, mirroring my emotions. "I moved him inside. Animals won't be able to get to him. I turned off his heater so it'll stay cold and better preserve him until they can get up here and take his body."

"Did he have anyone? I mean besides Bex?"

"I don't really know. It's not like we talked a lot."

"Right. Because you mountain men all come up here to get away from that sort of thing."

"You said your mom died when you were little," he says, completely dodging my musing. "Does that mean you and your brother went into foster care after your dad passed?"

"Asher raised me."

Dallas looks almost as curious about that as I am about *his* past. "Really?"

"He's fifteen years older than I am. My parents were on the older side when I was born. I was an *oopsie*. My mom was diagnosed with cervical cancer when she was pregnant with me. She could have been treated, but she'd have lost the pregnancy. She chose me over her own life. I don't remember anything about her, but Asher does. He tells me stories about her a lot and that makes me feel closer to her."

He nods. I can tell he wants to ask more, but he doesn't. He's not one to pry. And somehow that makes me think he's also not one to *be* pried. So I don't even try.

Belatedly, he looks over my head, scrunches his brow, and asks, "Um, Marti, what are your panties and my boxer briefs doing hanging on fishing line?"

I laugh and get up to rotate them around, my heart frolicking slightly when I touch his boxers. "I hope you don't mind I did a load.

I wanted to make sure we had clean clothes before the power went out."

His eyes graze over the Yale sweatshirt I forgot I was wearing. "Is that why you're wearing my hoodie?"

Heat erupts from my chest to my face.

"Yeah. Sorry. Mine was in the wash. I got cold."

I start to remove it, but he stops me. "Leave it on. It's only going to get colder in here."

"About that. Can we use Abe's propane?"

"I had the same thought. But he was almost out as well. I assume we're on the same delivery schedule." He stands and goes for the door.

"You're leaving again?"

"I'm going to chop some more wood."

"I've seen the pile, Dallas. You have enough to last weeks, I'd say."

"You can never have too much. Besides, I saw the tree branch that almost hit the truck. I need to use the chainsaw to cut it and move it out of the way for when the weather clears."

"And exactly when do you think that might happen?"

"I don't know. But it's not looking too good." He opens the door and pauses. "Good thinking about the laundry. See you later."

He says it like he's not going to see me for a while. Considering he was just outside for hours, it stings a bit to know he's choosing to go out in the weather again versus being stuck inside with me. Maybe I was reading too much into those 'looks' I thought he was giving me. I guess going as long as I have without dating has made me seriously question my ability to read men.

Through the window, Bex and I watch Dallas diligently chainsaw through the massive tree limb, then cut it up into small pieces, adding it to his ever-growing pile.

I get the idea he uses chopping wood as exercise.

Or an escape. But an escape from what, exactly?

My eyes fall upon the door of his hobby room, and I wonder if all the answers lie behind that old, wood plank door.

I'm not sure how long I sit on the couch and gaze out the window. I lose all track of time and become entranced watching Dallas as Bex lies contently next to me, his head on my thigh as he's a most happy recipient of all my petting attention.

Dallas stands straight up, stretches his back, and wipes sweat from his brow. He looks over, catching me staring at him. Our eyes meet. He's at least thirty feet away, but he might as well be right in front of me with how our gazes seem to connect. I don't blink. I don't move. I don't breathe. Something passes between us. Something profound. It's like desperation, sorrow, and… passion. An odd combination. But nothing about this situation has been normal, why should the way we look at each other be?

He turns away sharply, as if remembering something, and goes back to chopping wood.

"Come on, Bex," I say, patting his head. "Let's make dinner."

~ ~ ~

Ninety minutes later, I'm putting away the last of the clean dishes.

We ate in relative silence, the only sounds being the hum of the generator and the occasional grunt from Bex as he implored us to drop scraps off the table.

Maybe Dallas was worn out from all the hiking and wood chopping. Maybe he was thinking about Abe, or what he's going to do with Bex. Or maybe he was wondering how long he's going to be stuck with me.

By the time darkness falls, I've convinced myself that nothing passed between us earlier and I was reading far too much into what was probably only a few-second glance and not some deep connection between our souls.

Bex is staring at the front door. I pull on the coat Dallas loaned me earlier. "I'm going to take him out."

Dallas looks up from his laptop. "I'll do it."

"You've been outside all day. I don't mind, really."

"Don't go far."

His eyes hold mine for a moment and the feeling from earlier comes rushing back. I wasn't imagining things. There *is* something passing between us.

Then suddenly, he averts his eyes, slams the lid to his laptop, and walks across the room, hand on the doorknob to his hobby room. "Don't wait up," he says, then he disappears behind the door.

"What was that?" I ask Bex.

He doesn't answer. He just nudges my hand with his snout.

"Okay, boy. Let's go."

Hours later, I feel Dallas get into bed. I keep my eyes closed and try not to move. The urge to look at him is strong, though I don't know how much I'd be able to see by the dim light of the fire. I lay still and pretend I'm sleeping until I don't feel any movement or hear any rustling of covers.

How long has it been? Five minutes? Ten?

When I open my eyes, my breath hitches. Dallas is lying three feet away, his head on his pillow, and he's staring directly at me. Flames from the fire dance in his eyes. Warmth spreads throughout my entire body as if it were ninety degrees in here instead of sixty.

If circumstances were different, and we weren't being forced to be together in this small cabin and in this sole bed, I might scoot over and snuggle into him. Let him know I was open to whatever seems to be happening between us. But we aren't here by choice, only by necessity. And that changes things.

Maybe he can't tell I'm awake. The fire is behind me. It's possible he can't see me staring back at him.

I'm frozen, lost in his eyes. His sad, sexy, dark, intriguing eyes.

Those eyes move away from my face and focus on my chest. Last night I slept in all my clothes. But it was far from comfortable. Tonight, being more confident that I'm not going to be murdered, I put on my normal sleep pants and cami and snuggled under his thick blankets. Those blankets must have fallen away, my shoulders and neck now exposed to the cool cabin air.

The bed creaks slightly as the mattress shifts and Bex appears. I guess the floor was getting cold. He walks in a circle in the large gap between Dallas and me, then settles in next to me. When I reach out to put an arm around him, Dallas's eyes slam shut. I swear I see him utter the word 'fuck,' but it's dark, so I can't be sure.

What I *am* sure of is that he turns his back to me, not giving me another look for the rest of the night. And the reason I know this, is because for most of the night, I'm staring at the back of his head, snuggling a large furry dog, when I know I'd much rather be in the arms of the mercurial man three feet away.

Chapter Eleven

Martina

I must have eventually fallen asleep, because when I wake up it's light out, and Dallas is gone.

Bex, however, is still nestled next to me. I don't blame him. It's getting colder. I wonder if the propane has run out or if Dallas merely turned down the heat even more to conserve it. I listen for a second and hear the sound of the generator. With a sigh of relief, I steel myself to get up and make breakfast before it does run out.

I pull on socks that I left by the side of the bed, then put on the Yale sweatshirt that still smells like Dallas even though I wore it yesterday, and head to the bathroom. When I emerge, Bex is staring at the front door.

"You have to go too?" I ask.

I pull on my tennis shoes and take a beanie off the coat rack by the door. I don't bother with a coat. We won't be out long.

Footprints in the snow indicate the direction Dallas went. The depressions are already filling up with more fluffy white powder, dashing my hopes for a rescue once again. Yet, I find I'm not that upset at the thought of having to stay another day. I miss Charlie, and I want to be with him, but the idea of having to tell him his father has died is more than daunting. He's in good hands. Anita and her family love him. There is nothing I can do to bring Charles back. And I'll be with Charlie soon enough.

A familiar cracking noise lets me know exactly what Dallas is doing. He's chopping more wood. Surely he doesn't chop this much firewood regularly. If so, he'd have a much larger pile. He's only doing it because I'm here. But… why?

He looks up briefly when he catches movement in my direction. I wave. He lifts his chin. I point at Bex. He goes back to splitting the huge log.

"Well, good morning to you, too," I mutter, following Bex's trail in the snow.

Bex sniffs around the base of a few trees. I've always wondered what exactly dogs smell for, and why they choose the spots they do. Seemingly satisfied with the pine tree around the backside of the cabin, he lifts his leg, coloring the snow-packed roots of the tree. He wanders around to the very rear of the cabin and does more of his 'business' along what normally would be a thick, lush hedge, but is currently a huge mound of ice and snow.

I praise him for doing well and picking an out-of-the-way spot we're unlikely to step in.

He prances around, likely feeling good now that he's ready for the day, and he mouths a small stick that's fallen from a tree above.

I laugh at the tiny twig in his large mouth. "You need something bigger than that."

I scan the area, looking for any other sticks atop the fresh snow. I see a great one about thirty feet behind the cabin. The snow fascinates me as I head out to retrieve the much larger stick. I'm twenty-four years old and this is the first time I've seen it in person.

Dad never took us on vacations. After Mom died, he was both single parent and sole provider, putting his retirement plans on hold so he could give us the best life possible. That life didn't include luxuries like vacations, but it did consist of a roof over our heads, decent enough clothes, and plentiful food.

Sure, we'd take day trips to Ichetucknee Springs and float down the river on innertubes. Or we'd pack a picnic lunch and go to the beach. But getting on a plane or loading up the car for a drive this far north was just never in the cards.

And after he died, it was even less likely, being that my twenty-seven-year-old brother was suddenly responsible for not only his hormonal twelve-year-old sister, but he had just found out he was going to be a father.

I lean down to pick up the stick, pleased that it seems the perfect size for Bex. When I turn and wind up my arm, Bex barks excitedly. This obviously isn't his first rodeo. I launch the stick into the air, hurling it as far as I can with my amateur arm.

Laughing as he happily prances through the snow after the stick, I take a step toward him and hear a loud crack right before the ground falls away from my feet.

For a minute, my heart pounds until my feet once again hit the ground. But when they do, I'm standing in water up past my knees. *Shit.* I must have walked out onto a pond. It's going to take forever for my shoes to dry after this. I step up onto the ice, my legs already stiff from the freezing water, and I hear another crack. This time, my feet don't meet solid ground but come out from under me and my whole body submerges into the frigid pond. *Damn, it's cold!*

I try to control my breathing as the water stabs my skin. Normally, I would laugh at my clumsiness, but not now. Now I'm trying not to panic as I attempt to claw my way out. Each time I clutch the edge of the ice, another piece breaks off in my hand. And the more the ice breaks, the more I get pulled under. I can't scream or I'll take in water. Completely submerged now, in water *and* sheer terror, all I feel when I reach up is a solid sheet of ice.

My hands flail around frantically, searching for the hole I fell through. But it's not there. I can't see anything through the murky water and snow-covered ice above me. I hear a muffled sound. I think Bex is barking. He was watching me. Is he realizing the same thing I am? That I'm trapped. I'm trapped under the ice.

Everything is numb. My arms, my legs, even my mind seems to be shutting down as everything gets hazy. I can't move. All I can do is hold my breath and pray for this to be over.

I can't tell if seconds have gone by, or minutes, when my thoughts shift from praying to get out of this mess, to wishing for death. Because even though I know it will gut Charlie, and even though this will make him an orphan like me, I can't take this paralyzing numbness another second.

I'm sorry, is the last thought that goes through my mind before I stop struggling and succumb to my frigid tomb.

Chapter Twelve

Dallas

Bex is barking. I look up, wondering why they're still outside, when Bex comes tearing around the corner like a rabid dog.

My heart lodges in my throat as warning bells go off. "Marti?" I yell, glancing around. "Where are you?"

When there's no response and he's still barking his head off, I say, "Take me to her."

Bex runs in the other direction, looking back at me to make sure I'm following him.

Dread crawls up my spine when he leads me to the pond. *Oh, Jesus Christ, there's a hole in the ice.*

I race to the edge and fall to my knees, scraping the foot or so of snow away as I carefully navigate my way out. The pond isn't deep, maybe four feet at the center, more like two or so where the hole is. "Marti!" I scream, staring at the hole while frantically brushing away more snow.

Then I see a patch of darkness through the ice and a tornado of fear rips through me. *No, no, no, no, no.* It's my navy-blue sweatshirt.

I stand up, move to the left, and jump high, bringing all my weight down on the ice. I do it three times and then it cracks. I move chunks of inch-thick ice out of the way and fish my way to her, my chest throbbing violently.

When I reach her and pull her toward me, I'm devastated to see her blue lips and still body. Nightmares bombard me. I close my eyes and see Phoebe's blank eyes staring into mine as her lips curve down. DJ reaches toward me, then his arm falls to his side as they both drift away. This cannot be happening again.

"Save her!" a voice screams in my head, shaking me from my nightmare. *"You have to save her!"*

It's not my voice, however. It's… Phoebe's.

I put my arms under Marti and hoist her out of the freezing water, ignoring the stabbing, numbing pain in my legs. When her hand moves and her eyes open, I cry out, releasing a strangled breath.

Her gaze fixates on me. Does she even know what's happening to her?

Carefully, with her in my arms, I break more ice, moving it out of the way while I trudge the last ten feet to shore. "Hold on, Marti. I've got you."

Her sunken, hollow eyes stare up at me as I run to the cabin, Bex still barking behind me. I swing open the door then kick it shut behind us, put her down on the floor, then haul my mattress off the bed and over by the fireplace. I pick up her limp body, carry her onto the mattress, and start removing her clothes.

Holy God she's cold. She's not shivering. That can't be good. Her eyes drift closed.

"No!" I pull and tug and maybe even rip the soaked Yale sweatshirt off her. I tear away the tank top underneath, and then her sleep pants, yanking off her shoes and tossing them aside.

I grab as many blankets as I have and cover her. "Marti, don't go to sleep. Open your eyes."

She makes a noise. "Nnnnnnn." Then her entire body starts shivering.

I have to bring her body temp up. I get next to her and pull her close, but all I'm doing is making the blankets wet. Hastily, I stand and rip my own clothes off, then I get under the blankets with her and use my body heat to warm her. I run my hands along her frozen arms and back, rubbing with so much friction I worry I'm hurting her, but she has to get warm. She *has* to. This… this can't happen again.

"S-s-s-s-o c-c-c-cold," she mumbles.

"Shh, it's okay. I've got you. You're going to be okay."

I tuck a blanket around her wet hair then go back to cuddling her body as close to me as I can.

Minutes pass. Her uncontrolled shivering lessens but doesn't abate.

"You're doing great," I tell her. "You'll be warm and toasty in no time. Think warm thoughts. Chicken soup. Steaming coffee."

"H-hot ch-chocolate?" she asks.

I laugh, mostly out of relief. "I think that can be arranged."

"I've n-never b-been so c-cold in m-my l-life," she stutters.

"Things could be worse," I say. "You could be as cold as old Abe."

It's a horrible, awful, tasteless joke, I know, but I'm not exactly thinking straight.

Her gentle laugh tickles my arm. "Oh, my g-god. You d-did not just say th-that."

My shoulders shake in silent laughter. "You sure do like to tell me that a lot."

She cranes her head slightly, looking at me the best she can when my front is to her back. "Y-you say a lot of inappropriate th-things."

"I suppose I do. Now shush. Save your energy. Just lay here and get warm."

Slowly, over the period of what must be an hour, I feel her body temperature return to normal. In fact, I think she's fallen asleep. Which is fine, now that she's out of the woods and I'm still pressed against her hard enough to feel her heartbeat.

Her foot caresses mine. "Thank you for saving me."

"My pleasure."

She shimmies her butt. "Is that Bex's god-awful stick poking my backside, or are you happy to see me?"

I pull away slightly, knowing she's got not only her wit back, but all her feeling. "Well let's see, I'm lying next to a naked woman who's been basically vibrating against me for the last hour. Shoot me for having a completely natural physiological reaction." I sigh. "And please never refer to a man's penis as god-awful. I may develop an inferiority complex."

"My apologies." She snickers and turns to face me. "But are you… naked?"

"It was the fastest way to warm you up. You almost died, Marti." I scrub my hand across my eyes and down my face. "You scared the shit out of me."

She grimaces. "Not on this mattress I hope."

Bursts of air shoot from my nose. I'm laughing when I should be crying. But this girl. This woman.

I take the blanket off her head and let heat from the fire further dry her hair.

"In all seriousness, I thought you were dead. When I found you trapped under the ice, eyes closed and not moving, I was sure you were gone."

I feel sick to my stomach just thinking of it. It's an all too familiar feeling. One I hoped I'd never experience again.

Tears roll down the sides of her face. "I wanted to die. Not at first. But, Dallas, I was so cold. I couldn't move. I couldn't think. There was so much pain, like a thousand knives were piercing my skin. I just wanted it over." She starts full-on sobbing. "I thought about Charlie and how he was going to be an orphan like me. I know Asher would have stepped up, but my son would have lost both parents in less than a week. How could I have given up so easily? Why didn't I fight?"

"You did fight, Marti. There were claw marks all over the ice."

She brings her hands up in front of her face. "My nails are all broken."

"You fought for as long as you could. No one can blame you for giving up. I can't begin to imagine what it's like to be trapped underneath ice."

Except, in a way, I can. I feel it's where I've been trapped for years. Yes, I can breathe. I can exist. But that's about all. And a lot of days, I *do* think about giving up.

"It was horrible. I was so scared." She leans close and cries into my shoulder. I let her. I let her cry and sob and get it all out. She had a brush with death. *Again.* Only this time, she was on its damn doorstep. And she nearly crossed the threshold. That's got to mess with a person.

"I know. I know." I rub her shoulder. "You're safe here. I promise."

There's that word again. *Promise.* The word I shouldn't be saying to anyone.

You saved her.

It doesn't matter. Phoebe and DJ—the ones I *couldn't* save—are still dead. Rescuing someone else can't simply erase that reality. I could save a hundred people and it still wouldn't matter. The ones who really count aren't here.

Now tears are collecting in *my* eyes.

She sees them and reaches out. "I'm sorry. I didn't know there was a pond back there. I was trying to get a good stick for Bex." She stiffens. "Bex! Is he okay?"

Hearing his name, Bex trots over and puts his head near hers. She gives him a pat. "Thank goodness. That must have been horrible for him. For both of you."

I drive out a harsh sigh. "Like you can't imagine."

She's crying again. Her crying makes me cry, albeit more quietly and less snotty. We lie here and stare at each other, tears of both stress and relief erupting from both of us.

Without thinking, I lean in and press my lips to hers. They're cold, but not too cold. Perfectly soft and supple. And despite having been in the murky pond, she tastes like toothpaste.

My emotions running amok, I deepen the kiss when she doesn't resist. But not only doesn't she resist, she snakes her arms up and around my neck. At the feel of her touch, there's a hunger deep in my soul I can no longer deny. A restless throb of desire besieges me as I bury my fingers in the damp tangles of her hair.

It's probably not a good idea to do what we're doing, but at the moment, it seems nothing if not right. So I take it further and put my hands on only the second pair of breasts I've ever felt in my life. And despite the fact that a mere hour ago, she probably had a body temp in the eighties, she responds immediately, arching her chest into my hands, groaning in pleasure.

It's those groans that have me wanting more. So I take more. I take whatever she wants to give.

Chapter Thirteen

Martina

His lips devour mine in an almost feral way. Like it's been a while since he's been kissed. Like maybe he's gone as long as I have.

Kissing must have changed, I think as my body ignites with tingles, because I don't remember it being like this. His lips are strong and demanding, yet soft and playful. They exude both confidence and gentleness.

His hands on my body make me entirely forget about the last few hours of my life and how I almost died. Because this right here, is the most alive I've felt in a very long time. My heart jumps wildly against my rib cage. Every last one of my nerve endings bristles as his hands explore my breasts and his fingers brush against my nipples. A shiver runs through my body, this time not because I'm cold.

When his lips stray from mine and travel across my neck, my head falls back against the mattress and I get lost in the feeling. Everywhere his mouth touches my skin is instantly on fire. I want his mouth on every inch of me. I groan when he lightly pinches a nipple, my hand gripping his large, toned bicep.

My hand travels up a broad shoulder. My fingertips skim across his chest, down his ribcage, and along his rippling abs. I'm soaked between my legs, having never touched such a fine sculpt of muscle.

His hand snakes down from my breast to my thigh. He caresses it tentatively, as if testing the waters. I almost shout at him that the water's fine, perfect, in fact, and he should dive right in—headfirst.

I look at him and our gazes lock. His hand falls away and his chest caves with an exhale. *No!*

Panic grips me. I fear if I let this moment slip away, it may never return. I run my hand across his lower abs, tracing his muscles with a finger. When the tip of my finger grazes his erection, he sucks in a quick breath. His eyes close and he murmurs something I can't understand. *Is he cursing at himself?*

"Dallas," I whisper, as I let my fingers fully wrap around his penis.

He lets out an almost pained, guttural cry right before he flips me onto my back and hovers over me, staring down at me, eyes burning into me like flames from the fire. I'm not sure exactly what I'm seeing in them, though, and it's confusing. I don't think it's want or passion behind them. It's more like anger. He's suddenly dark and dangerous, a war going on within him that I can't possibly imagine or understand.

Is he thinking he'd be taking advantage of me—the helpless woman he just saved from certain demise?

"It's okay," I say. "I want this."

Determined to show him how I'm anything but helpless, I reach for his erection again. He stops me, moving both of my hands up, trapping them on either side of my head. He stares down at me once more, putting all his weight on me as his breath falls heavy on my neck.

I fear there really is a war going on inside him, and that I may end up on the losing side.

I wiggle one of my hands free, put it on the back of his head and force his face toward mine. This is one girl who's not going down without a fight. Even if this only happens once. Even if the snow stops and I'm rescued, never to see him again. Even if I'll wake up and regret it tomorrow. In this moment, I want this more than anything. And somehow, I get the feeling that, even if he doesn't want it, he may need it.

Resisting at first, finally, he gives in and lets me pull his head until our lips meet. It's an explosion of want and need. And maybe desperation. Our lips feast on each other, our tongues tangling in ways that have pulses shooting through me like a meteor shower.

When he reaches between us and runs a finger through my wetness, I moan so loud Bex comes over and puts his head on my arm. I brush him away. My hand lands on Dallas's ass and I squeeze the soft, muscular globe.

A finger plunges inside me and I cry out. He adds another and I almost detonate as shocks of pleasure rob me of the air in my lungs. *So long*, I think. It's been so long since a man's hands have done this to me. Was it always like this? Hell, was it *ever* like this? I know it wasn't. This is different. *He* is different.

My entire body shudders when he rolls off me and toys with my clit. He groans his appreciation at my response, and without warning, his tongue replaces his finger. Ten seconds later, I'm shouting his name as he brings me to climax faster than I've ever been able to get there.

Oh. My. God.

Before the tingles can subside, he's hovering over me, erection poking my entrance, staring at me with that same pained, distraught look. Maybe this is just his sex face. "It's okay. I want to," I assure him.

He shakes his head but doesn't move away. His cock is dancing against my sensitive clit, and I wonder if it's possible to have another orgasm so quickly.

"I don't have any condoms," he says.

"I'm on the pill."

He doesn't look convinced. Maybe he's worried about my sexual past.

I grab his butt cheeks hard. "Dallas, I assure you I'm on the pill. And I'm good. I haven't even been with anyone since…" I don't say his name. Because I'm lying here with another man on top of me, and well, now is not the time to think of my dead ex-husband. *Sooo* not the time.

His gaze lingers on my face in a visual caress before he buries his head into my shoulder. I think he's going to roll off me, but instead, he pushes inside me. In one thrust, he sinks to the very end of me, complementing me in the very way men and women were made to fit together. He stills. I swallow, tears dancing in the back of my throat at the feeling of having a man inside me again. It feels amazing. Exquisite. So incredibly right.

I lift my hips in encouragement, and he begins moving. Sliding out of me almost completely and then back in. Again and again, teasing me with the threat of pulling out, then thrusting inside so we're joined together as solidly as two people can be.

Holy crap! If I thought *kissing* had changed, this is… I can't even find the words.

It could be this place. The remoteness. The blizzard. My brush with death. All of that could be making this experience unlike any other.

It's him.

My insides are on fire, a far cry from how they were just a short time ago. My muscles tighten and *that feeling* builds, starting in my stomach, and spreading down to my thighs.

Dallas's thrusts come quickly now, as do his breaths. Knowing he's close to coming brings *me* even closer. It's going to happen imminently. It's starting—a freight train I have no way of controlling. "Oh, God," I sigh explosively into his shoulder.

He thrusts once, twice, a third time, grunting loudly as both of us erupt in simultaneous pleasure, my hips bucking wildly underneath him as he stills and pulsates inside me.

He collapses down on top of me, sweat from our slick bodies squishing between us.

I don't know why, but I start laughing. I've been such a fool. Why haven't I been doing this all along? I've wasted so much time thinking that whatever man I decided to date had to be a great role model for my son. If I couldn't confirm they were potential husband material, I'd just be wasting my time. It had me rejecting them at every text, phone call, or coffee date. All this time I could have just been having fun. I'm only twenty-four, after all. As soon as I get back home, I promise not to shut myself off from the dating world.

My jubilant demeanor disappears. *Home.* Two thousand miles away from where I am now. I close my eyes, the weight of the situation dawning on me. I don't want to go back into the dating pool. I don't want texts, calls, coffee dates, or even kisses from other men.

I just want *this man.*

He rolls to the side, opening his eyes and looking at me in the oddest manner. As if I'm a stranger. Or maybe he was put off by my laughing.

For a long moment, he's quiet, an unreadable mask of emotion clouding his expression. Then he rolls away from me, grabs one of the blankets, and stands up. "I have to get out of here," he says, his back to me.

Without even bothering to hit the bathroom, he's dressed and out the door in less than a minute.

I sit up and pull the blankets around me, wondering what just happened.

Bex climbs onto the mattress, sniffing around inquisitively. I ruffle the fur atop his head. "Why are boys so incredibly hard to read?"

He circles the mattress and finds a spot to lie down.

My nose starts running and I swipe a finger under it. When I notice blood, I'm not surprised. The air up here is much drier than I'm used to, even with all this snow. I pinch my nostrils between my fingers and glance around for a tissue. Not seeing any, I get up and pull open the top drawer of the nightstand. My stomach lurches into my throat and I absently release my nose. And then… then droplets of blood splatter down next to a framed photo of Dallas. Only it's not just a photo of Dallas. It's a photo of Dallas next to a beautiful woman. A woman with a baby in her arms.

Chapter Fourteen

Dallas

"Fuck!" I scream to the trees. I lean over, hands on my knees. "Fuck, fuck, fuck!"

I've been out here for over an hour, slogging through the deep snow, wondering why the hell I did it.

What was I thinking?

I put as much distance between myself and my cabin as I can. It doesn't seem to matter, though, because *she's* still there. Marti. And I can't get her face out of my mind. Her cold, wet, lifeless face. And then, her moans, groans, and sexy as fuck noises.

Her soft-as-sin skin. Her shapely, athletic legs. Her breasts. Jesus, her perfectly sized breasts that felt amazing underneath me.

I've hiked at a breakneck pace for miles, yet my pants are tightening with a hard-on.

I sit on a tree stump, getting one of the protein bars left in my jacket. I eat it and think about how horribly things could have turned out today. Nobody was coming to help. What if she had died under that ice? Abe dying was bad enough, but Marti? The woman staying in my house? The single mom whose son just lost his father. I'm not sure how I'd have dealt with that big a blow.

Marti and I are too similar. We're both surrounded by death. I muse that Bex has now joined the club, the three of us making one unlikely trio.

I glance up at the sky, wondering if today is the day it will clear up. Trying to decide if I want it to.

Of course I do. Things need to get back to normal so I can get on with my life.

Normal. It's a word that hasn't existed in my vocabulary in well over two years. And getting on with my life—who am I kidding? I don't lead much of one.

Maybe I'll keep the dog. He's obviously a good and loyal companion. It's kind of been nice having him around.

Just him?

I shove the rest of my snack in my mouth and stand up, ready to add more miles to my hike, wondering just how much distance would make me feel, I don't know… *untethered.*

Thunder sounds in the distance. It's rare, but thunder snow does happen. I take it as a sign that this storm isn't done with us yet, and I head back, figuring fate has been tempted enough for one day.

It's well after noon by the time I return. I can gauge the fresh snowfall by looking at my own footprints from hours ago, or lack thereof. The snow today is amazing. Soft and fluffy, not like the wet snow that's fallen the past two days.

Approaching the cabin, I stop and duck behind a tree. Marti is outside, twirling around like a schoolgirl, looking up at the sky with her mouth open as if she's trying to catch snowflakes on her tongue. Bex is watching her like a hawk from his perch on the steps. Somehow I get the idea he'll never again leave her side. A pang of guilt twists my gut. I abandoned her. The goddamn dog is more loyal a creature than I am.

I almost bolt out of the trees when Marti falls back onto the snow. But I don't. Because she doesn't appear to be in distress. And what happens next takes my breath away.

She stretches out her arms and legs, moving them up and down, in and out. She's making a snow angel.

I can see her satisfied smile all the way from here. I stand and watch in fascination, sure I haven't ever seen such a beautiful sight. The smile on her face. The joy she's allowing herself despite everything she's gone through. Is *still* going through.

The thought that snow could bring such happiness to her is an unconscionable notion. It surrounds me four months of the year. There's nothing special about it. In fact, it's more annoying to me than anything else. For a moment, though, I'm reminded of its beauty. Its innocence. Its imperfect perfection.

I blow out a deep sigh, wondering if the snow is really what I'm thinking of.

Knowing I can't hide forever, I step out and make my way over. Bex wags his tail and barks once, as if alerting Marti to my arrival.

She turns her head, still lying flat on the ground, and looks up. "You," she sneers, her entire demeanor changing from giddy schoolgirl to scorned lover.

I walk right past her, up the steps, and into the cabin. If she's about to chew me out for sleeping with her then bolting, I'm at least going to warm up while she does it.

A second after I'm inside, I hear her stomping up the porch steps. For a small woman, her feet sure can make a ruckus. She rips off her coat and gives me a death stare worthy of Darth Vader. "You," she says again, wagging her index finger like a pissed off nun at Catholic school.

"You already said that."

She huffs, the irritated trademark noise of hers coming out even sharper and more forceful than ever. She stomps across the room and gets something off the nightstand. I stiffen like a board when she holds out the last family picture that was ever taken of Phoebe, DJ, and me. "Tell me you did not just make me a dirty mistress." She tosses the picture frame onto the mattress, which I just now realize is back on the bedframe, fresh sheets and all. Her hands rest on her hips and she booms, "Are you some douchebag adulterer who keeps this remote cabin as your fuck pad?"

I gawk and try not to laugh. I swear, if I weren't so physically and emotionally drained, I'd find her spunky attitude a little endearing. But my amusement fades quickly. Because I know in order to answer her question, I have to utter the words I try to avoid at all costs.

"I didn't make you a dirty mistress."

She visibly relaxes, her hands falling to her sides. She sits on the bed and picks up the picture. "So she's your ex?"

A knot of air catches in my chest. "I'm not divorced."

She looks between me and the picture, confused. "But she has a wedding ring on, and if you didn't cheat on—" Her words stop immediately and she looks up at me, guilt souring all her features. "Oh, no. Really?"

"Really," I say flatly.

She stares at the picture. "So, you're a single dad?"

I swallow, because it's becoming harder and harder to hide my emotions. "I'm not anyone's dad. Not anymore."

Her eyes snap up to mine. Tears instantly coat her lashes. "Dallas, no."

I turn my back to her and open the refrigerator. "I'm going to make some food. Mind putting the photo away?"

I stare into the fridge, not looking for anything in particular. In fact, not looking for anything at all. I just had to stop looking at *her*.

I hear her shuffle behind me as she puts it back where she found it.

"I'm so sorry," she says.

"Yup. Me too." I close the fridge and open the freezer. "Pork chops for dinner?"

"Sounds good. What can I do?"

Go away? Get out of my head? Stop invading my every fucking thought? "Nothing. You should rest. You've had a big day."

"We both have."

I turn and her burrowing gaze meets mine. Is she talking about her falling through the ice, or what happened after? Looking into her eyes, it's hard to tell. She's looking at me the way everyone does when they find out my family died.

She clears her throat uncomfortably. "I think I'll take Bex outside for a while and let you cook."

"Wait," I say, throwing the meat on the counter to start thawing. I put my coat back on and motion for her to follow. "Come with me." I walk her around the back of my cabin, traverse the yard, and show her exactly where the edges of the pond are.

I go to the wood pile and get an armload of wood, dropping pieces every few yards to delineate the water from the shore. I should have done this earlier. I can't be trusted to keep anyone safe. She could be dead because of me. *Just like they are.*

Bex comes to my side as if he's read my thoughts. Is he missing Abe? I'm reminded once again just how much the dog and I have in common. We're both alone, left by the only ones who truly loved us. Yeah, I think maybe I *will* keep him.

I thumb toward the house. "I'll go make that dinner."

Bex stays behind. He's not about to leave her alone like I am. But I have to. Being around her is wrong. It's messy and noisy and torturously tempting.

So then, why, when I turn the corner to the front of the house, do I look back at her once more, my heart battering my ribs when I think of how spectacularly she fell apart beneath me?

Chapter Fifteen

Martina

He's a widower. And he lost his child.

Ever since he told me, emotions I haven't felt in a while surface all over again and I've found it hard to breathe.

No wonder he's here. How long ago did it happen? I think he said he's been here a few years. That's the reason he left Calloway Creek. He's running. Running from memories of *them*.

He really does live here. This isn't just a fishing cabin he comes to a few times a year.

I can't imagine being that alone. For me, after my losses, the only thing that helped was being around people. When I wasn't, and I had only my thoughts for company, life was depressing. Talking with people who knew and loved them, remembering the good times—that's what got me through. But Dallas seems to have nobody. Was that a choice? Or did it happen by default?

He has a job. And I guess he has parents. After all, someone has to run the family winery.

If I had access to the internet, I could probably find out how his family died. A car accident most likely. My heart pounds. Oh, God. How he totally freaked out when he saw the car seat after my accident, it all makes sense now. Did he lose his own child that way? It's a horrible and unsettling thought.

The internet would also give me information on his job and family. I wonder what it's like to own and work for a winery. It must be fascinating. But I wouldn't know. He hasn't talked about his past, where he's from, or… anything really.

For the next half hour, I watch Bex chase a lone squirrel braving the cold to look for food. He skitters up a tree and Bex dutifully circles the trunk over and over hoping the critter will come back down.

When I can't stand the cold anymore, I call Bex and head back inside.

Bex settles by my side on the couch as I try to read more of the autobiography I started yesterday. I'm not successful, however, as I find myself reading the same paragraph over and over, distracted by Dallas's movements as he prepares dinner.

I can't help but admire his light-blue jeans when he bends to get a pot from a low cabinet. The right rear pocket has the frayed outline of a wallet that isn't even there. I suppose when one lives in a place like this, carrying around a wallet isn't needed. But it speaks to the age of the jeans. Maybe guys are like women, having that one old, comfortable pair that fits so nicely you just can't get rid of them. And, *wow*, they do fit him nicely.

His maroon, long-sleeved thermal fleece hugs his torso in all the right places. His strong arms. His tight abs. My insides quiver because I know exactly what those abs feel like. They're hard as a rock, testament to all the physical labor he does around here. I long to run my hands down them again. But I fear it might not happen.

He ran away. Is it because he thinks what we did was a mistake? My jaw slackens and I cover my mouth in surprise. Am I the first woman he's slept with since his wife died?

I sigh. Well, that'd be another thing we have in common. He's the first man I've been with since Charles. And the only other man I've ever been with.

A million questions linger in my mind as I continue to follow his every movement, my eyes growing heavier and heavier.

"Marti." My eyes snap open. Dallas hovers over me. "Dinner's ready."

"I… sorry. I must have dozed off."

He throws a log on the fire on his way to the table. "I hope you like asparagus. I'm trying to use up the fresh vegetables instead of the canned ones."

"Good idea. And I love asparagus. Thank you for making dinner. I'll cook tomorrow."

He motions for me to sit, then he does the same. "We might not have power tomorrow."

"How much is left?"

He picks up his phone and looks at his app, which surely isn't updating without service. "I have no idea. It never went below five percent. Maybe that's as low as it goes. Either the sensor can't detect smaller amounts, or the people who programmed the app didn't think anyone would be stupid enough to let their tanks run out."

"So you have no idea when the power will go out?"

He shakes his head.

"But tomorrow is Thanksgiving."

A slow breath eases out of him. "I'm aware."

"You have a lot of food here. I saw a tenderloin in your freezer. And you have apples and all the staples I'd need to make a pie. Do you mind if I try to throw something together?"

"Like I said, we might not have power."

"Assuming we do, what would you like? Are there any favorite dishes? Something your mom used to make?"

He shrugs, uninterested. "It's just another day. But do what you have to do."

"There's something you should know about me," I say, cutting into my juicy pork chop. "I'm a pretty good cook."

"Great. Go for it then."

The tone of his words tells me he's anything but excited. But it's Thanksgiving. We can't just do nothing.

During our mostly quiet dinner, I make a mental list of possibilities. I know he's got potatoes. I should be able to whip up gravy. I try to remember what vegetables he has in the refrigerator. If I were at home, I'd make homemade macaroni and cheese. It's not a traditional Thanksgiving side dish, but one Asher and I insisted on growing up. So Dad always made sure to have some.

I'm going to miss Dad tomorrow. And Charles. And, well… lots of people. Charles and I would spend most holidays together so Charlie would have both parents around. This was going to be the first one Charlie would have to spend without me. And now he's going to have to spend it without both of us. Will they even make a turkey?

I know firsthand how hard it is to celebrate the holidays after a death. Dad died only weeks before Christmas. I was in no mood. But Asher insisted. He did everything—put up the tree, strung lights outside, bought Christmas presents, even cooked. And though it was the hardest holiday I'd experienced up until then, I was glad he'd done all those things. Because sitting around feeling sorry for myself was no way to spend Christmas.

I glance at Dallas. Is that how he spends his holidays? Up here, alone?

Bex is lying at our feet, no doubt hoping something will drop from the table.

"Have you decided anything about Bex?" I ask.

He nods. "I'm thinking of keeping him."

Relieved, I smile. "I think he'll love that."

"Why's that?"

"You mean besides the fact that he won't have to starve to death?" I chuckle. "Because you're good for each other. You've both been through stuff. He probably understands you like others can't."

Dallas stops chewing and stares at me.

My words replay in my head, and I wonder if he's thinking what I am, that *I* might just understand him in a way others can't.

If he only knew.

He looks away and takes another bite.

I take a sip of water then say, "I was thinking it's funny how the world works."

"How so?"

"Well, I'd be dead if Abe hadn't died."

He studies me pensively.

"Bex saved me. You wouldn't have known I'd fallen in the pond if he wasn't here. And he wouldn't have been here if Abe hadn't died."

"You could also reason that if Abe hadn't died, Bex wouldn't be here. Therefore, you wouldn't have walked on the pond to find a stick for him."

My brows crash together. "Oh my god, you're so right. It's interesting how one thing changing can set off other events you didn't anticipate."

"The butterfly effect," he says.

"What?"

"Chaos theory argues that even the smallest change in one nonlinear system can result in large differences on a broader scale."

"In English please."

"So there's a metaphorical example having something to do with the formation and path of a tornado somehow being influenced by minor perturbations such as a distant butterfly flapping its wings. Today, we use the expression in a context outside of weather, as in one small change to anything anywhere has the potential to influence larger consequences or even a chain of events."

I shake my head. "And you think *I* watch too much TV."

He motions around. "Do you see a television? I read, Marti."

"Yeah." I glance at his massive book collection. "I can see that. What else do you do? Besides read, hike, and chop wood?"

He shrugs. "I have hobbies."

I can't help but look at the door to his 'hobby room' and wonder what lies beyond it. "What kind of hobbies?"

"Languages. I learn them."

"As in you teach yourself?"

"As in, I buy programs that teach me. And books."

I laugh. "Of course books. What languages have you learned?"

"French. Russian. Portuguese. I'm learning American Sign Language at the moment."

My brows shoot up. "Really? That's interesting. Why would you choose that one?"

"I have a deaf niece. And my brother's new wife is deaf, too."

I smile. Finally, he's revealing some personal details. "Fascinating. Will you sign something?"

He sets down his fork and moves his hands around quickly, doing all sorts of signs.

Before Dad died and we moved into an apartment in another school district, I had a deaf friend in middle school. I learned a little

ASL back then. But I'm super rusty. Still, as he talks with his hands, I pick up a few signs. I could swear one of them is *beautiful.*

"What did you say?" I ask.

He blinks then looks down at his food. "That it's snowing and cold and no tow truck is coming for at least another few days especially since it's going to be a holiday."

He's lying. I'd bet my right arm that's not what he signed at all.

There's no more eye contact while we finish up our meal. No conversation either.

When he's done, he picks up a book and sits with Bex on the same couch I was sitting on when he was cooking. I concentrate on doing the dishes, having to keep myself from turning to see if he's watching me the way I was watching him. I swear I can *feel* that he is. My whole body is flushing and tingling. Hell, it's practically humming as I wonder if he's thinking about earlier. How he ran his tongue down my body. How he pushed his fingers inside me. How he made me come twice—something Charles was never able to do.

Okay, so Dallas wouldn't exactly know *that* little tidbit. But I do. And it does nothing to lessen the ache in my belly that longs for it to happen again.

By the time I'm done with the dishes, Dallas has fallen asleep on the couch, just like I had. His arm is resting on Bex's back. His head is cocked to the side, leaning on the high couch cushion. I step closer, taking a moment to admire him. I love his hair. His long, thick, unruly hair. What's more, I love the way my hands felt weaving through it.

Bex's eyes fly open. He watches me as if he knows what I'm thinking. I roll my eyes at him and go change for bed. It's still early, but it's been a long day. I don't bother waking Dallas. If I did, he'd probably disappear into his hobby room or go outside. It's only been a few days, but if I know anything about him, I know he doesn't like sleeping.

I turn out all the lights and settle into bed, watching the dancing shadows from the fireplace on the ceiling. They mesmerize me and pull me closer to sleep.

~ ~ ~

The bed squeaks and I wake. But I don't move. I remain still and listen. He's facing me. I can tell by the sound of his breathing. I almost flinch when something brushes against my face. I think he's moving my hair behind my shoulder. My heart pounds fiercely, so much so that I'm sure he can hear it.

He exhales a long, slow, drawn-out breath.

I can't stand it anymore, so I open my eyes. He's staring right at me. Neither of us speak. Is he going to make love to me again? His eyes tell me that's what he wants. But he doesn't move a muscle.

"Are we going to talk about it?" I whisper.

He blinks. There's no need to explain what *it* is. We both know what I'm referring to. The elephant that's been in the room all day. The one that's taking up so much air it's becoming harder to breathe.

He says a single word. "No."

"Is it going to happen again?"

His head shakes slowly. "I don't think so."

Hoping I don't sound like a desperate, horny, crazy lady, I say, "It can. I won't hold you to anything. I'll be gone in a few days anyway."

"It wouldn't be fair to you."

"Why? I said it's okay."

He sighs again. It's deep and slow and straight from the pit of his stomach. "Because I'm not sure it would be you I'd be making love to."

Tears sting my eyes. Because I'm positive I've never heard a more honest answer. Or a more heartbreaking one.

Chapter Sixteen

Dallas

Without a word, she rolls over. Her reaction is exactly what I expected.

Bex jumps up on the bed. He sniffs around, looks at me, then stretches out protectively next to Marti. I want to call him a traitor for being drawn to her more than he is to me, his savior, but it's not like I can blame him. She's much prettier than I am. And she smells a whole lot better too.

I inhale deeply, her vanilla scent swirling around me as I try to sleep, knowing I might be the biggest jackass to have ever lived. How could I have said what I did to her? Every damn word was a lie. But it's easier to have her believe what I said than try to explain how I feel like I'm betraying a woman who isn't even here anymore.

~ ~ ~

"Last quarter's financials," I say, handing a piece of paper to Dad.

Normally, I'd just send them in an email, but with as well as we did, I couldn't help going old school.

He glances at the numbers, eyes widening.

I've been working as the CFO for the winery since graduation a few years ago, but it's taken me a while to get my footing. Dad has been more than patient with me, allowing me to make mistakes and learn from them.

The pride on his face as he grips my shoulder is palpable. "Amazing," he says, beaming. "I knew you could do it, son."

Son. It's a word he's always used with me and my brothers when we've done something that pleases him. It used to be a competition between the three of us growing up, who could get the most 'sons' out of him.

"You've come a long way, Dallas. You're proving yourself worthy of this job."

"I've got to make sure there's something left of the business for DJ to run one day."

He smiles at the mention of his only grandchild. "That you do."

"He's sitting up now."

Dad's eyes sparkle with delight. "That's wonderful. You should bring him by the house this weekend."

"Can't. It's our fourth anniversary. I rented us a house on Martha's Vineyard."

"How could I forget?" He looks at his calendar. "Are your mother and I babysitting?"

I shake my head. "DJ is coming too. Phoebe doesn't want to go a whole weekend without him. She's still nursing him."

"She's an incredible mother."

"The best." I chuckle. "Do you know she's already tossing around the idea of having another?"

"Doesn't surprise me. Your wife was born to be a mom. DJ is one lucky kid."

"I'm the lucky one."

"We're all lucky," he says, sparing a glance at the multi-generational family portrait he commissioned shortly after DJ was born.

"I won't argue with that." I check the time. It's after five thirty. "If there's nothing else, I'm going to head out."

"Go ahead. The latest cash-flow forecast I requested via email can wait until tomorrow."

"I didn't see that email. I can get on it right now."

"You don't have to, Dallas. I know how hard you work. Go enjoy dinner with your family."

"It's okay, Dad. It won't take long. Say hi to Mom."

"Will do."

I leave his office, go back to mine, and read the email.

What he said was true, it could have waited until tomorrow. But I truly enjoy pleasing my father and proving myself to him, so I stay and put in an extra hour.

Crunching some numbers, I grin at the photo of Phoebe and DJ on my desk. Everything I do is for them. I work my ass off so the winery will one day make my son as rich as my father. No, richer. Because that little boy deserves the world. And I damn well plan to give it to him.

I'm vaguely aware of Dad, Lucas, and the others leaving as I concentrate on finishing up. I lose track of time and curse myself when I see it's nearly seven. I hate to be late for dinner, which Phoebe always plans for seven-thirty. I'd better get a move on.

There's movement in my doorway as I shut my laptop. It's Dad. And he looks… off.

"I thought you left already," I say.

"I was on my way home when I got a call." He swallows, a greenish hue to his skin.

"A call from who?"

"It was… Patrick Kelsey."

The hesitation with which he says it has dread pooling inside me like poison. Patrick Kelsey is a firefighter/paramedic. He's a lieutenant in the Calloway Creek Fire Department. Dread turns into outright panic when I see the look on Dad's face. He looks almost… broken.

Patrick called him. He turned around and came back. That means whatever he's here to tell me, he had to say it in person.

I bolt out of my chair. "What is it? Is it DJ? Phoebe?"

Tears flood his eyes. His forehead creases with heavy lines. What he's about to tell me is going to destroy me.

"Sit, Dallas."

"I don't want to fucking sit. Tell me."

He swipes a thumb under his eyes then wipes his nose. "It's… both of them. There's been an accident."

My gut twists into one large knot. "An accident? In a car? Are they in the hospital?" I check my phone. "Why didn't anyone call me? Why'd he call you?"

When he doesn't say anything, I begin to understand. The rug is pulled out from underneath me. I stumble to the wall and slide down until my ass hits the floor.

Nobody called me because they wanted to be sure someone was with me when I heard the news. Nobody called me because there's nothing I can do. Nobody called me because… because… I look up and ask the question that will ruin the rest of my goddamn life. "Are they dead?"

My father blinks. I can tell he's trying to hold it together. He's trying to hold it together because he knows I'm about to completely fall apart. He sniffs then sighs heavily. "Yes, son. They are."

All the air in my lungs vanishes. My stomach clenches. Bile riles in my throat. I turn and hurl all over the floor of my office. On hands and knees, I retch and heave until there's nothing left and my throat is burning and raw.

Arms come around me, holding me tight. "Dallas. Baby, I'm s-so s-sorry."

My mother's words try to soothe me. When did she get here? Pained cries, almost as loud as my own, echo in the doorway. My sister Allie is here. Snot runs down her face as she sobs into Lucas's shoulder. Dad stands stoically to the side, his body shaking as he attempts to keep from falling apart like the rest of us.

"No!" I get off the floor, unsteady on my feet, and head for the door. "It's not true. It can't be. They would have been at home. She's always cooking dinner right now. Someone got the facts wrong. I have to go find them."

Dad holds me back as I try to pass. "Dallas, they were at home."

I shrug his hands off me. "What are you talking about? You said there was an accident."

"There was, but not in a car."

"Quit being so goddamn cryptic and tell me what the fuck happened."

"Patrick said it was carbon monoxide."

"No," I say forcefully. "No." Fully in denial now, I try to push past my father and siblings. "You've got it wrong. Everyone has it wrong."

Dad grips me tightly. "Son, they're gone. I'm sorry. To the depths of my soul, I'm sorry. But they're gone."

I crumble into him as his words sink in for the second time. He supports my weight as my mother, Allie, and Lucas come up behind me. They form a circle around me, hugging me and holding me up from every angle as sobs bellow out from all of us. The only one missing is Blake. He's at school. But I know the instant he finds out, he'll be here too.

"It's going to be okay, son," Dad says. "We're going to get you through this."

It's not going to be okay. It's never going to be okay. I'm twenty-six years old and I might as well have died with them, because nothing is ever going to be okay again. Not for a goddamn day in whatever remains of my miserable life.

"I have to see for myself."

"Dallas, no," Mom says. "You don't want to do that."

I break away from them. "I have to," I demand. "Don't you understand none of this seems real? I have to see them."

"I'll take you," Dad says.

"Chris," Mom sobs. "What good could possibly come of it?"

"I get it, Sarah. If it were you, I'd have to see for myself." Dad takes my elbow as if he thinks I might fall over. "Come on, son. If you need to do this, I'll be right there with you."

I nod and blindly follow, my body numb.

The only thought I have during the ride is that I'm alone in this world. I have my parents. My siblings. But I might as well be a man on an island, because I'll never again have the woman who made me whole. And DJ—my stomach rolls—he never had a chance to become the little boy I dreamed of. The man I hoped he'd one day be.

Not even sure how we got here, we enter the hospital. Each person we pass has the same look on their face. They all know me. It's a small town. Word has probably spread quickly. I stop looking at people as I'm escorted down a flight of stairs. I stare at the plaque on the wall.

MORGUE.

What a horrible fucking word.

"Right this way, Mr. Montana," someone says. I have no idea who. I stopped caring about anything anyone said as soon as my entire life went up in flames.

"Are you sure, son?" Dad says, still by my side.

"Can you… not call me that?"

He nods, probably thinking it's because of DJ. It's not. It went from being a token of achievement, to the endearment used to announce I'd lost everything.

I'm escorted into a room with two clinical steel tables. My throat almost swells shut at the small shape underneath one of the stark white sheets. Oh, Jesus, this can't be happening.

My chin quivers uncontrollably as I approach the small bundle. I pray so hard that this is all a bad dream and when I peel back the cover, it won't be him. I reach for the sheet but pull away. I can't do it. I can't stand here and look at my dead son. He's only been here for six short months. I watched him come into the world. I held him before anyone else did. I looked into his eyes and instantly knew he was my purpose.

I can't see him like this. I just fucking can't.

But I have to see her. *The girl who moved to town when we were kids. The girl who, from the moment we met, I knew was going to be mine. The girl who shot me down when I started asking her out when we were thirteen, and who finally said yes four years later. The girl who made me a husband, a father, and the happiest motherfucker who ever lived.*

Balls of tears stream down my cheeks when I pull back the sheet covering Phoebe's face. I let out a gut-wrenching shriek that turns into messy, slobbery sobs as I slump over her ashen body and cling to her. If only I could crawl inside so that even in death, we can be together.

I'm not sure how long I stay like this. Time has ceased to exist. Everything ceased to exist the second they *did. Life no longer matters. I no longer matter. Because who am I if I'm not her husband. His father.*

"Dallas." Dad clears his throat. "It's time to go."

I can barely lift myself off her. Miraculously, I do. And I say one last goodbye to the first and last girl I'll ever love. Leaning down, I place one final kiss on her forehead. Another on her blue lips. I straighten and go to pull the sheet up when she opens her eyes and looks directly at me. "How come you saved her?" *she asks. "What about us?"*

I scream.

Something wakes me. It's Bex. He's licking my neck. Probably because I'm lying here in a pool of sweat.

"You okay?" Marti asks.

"Yeah. Go back to sleep."

She turns away, understandably upset by my earlier declaration.

I push Bex away, get out of bed, get dressed, and go for a hike.

Chapter Seventeen

Martina

No way am I going back to sleep. That scream. It was the most guttural, painful sound I've ever heard.

Was he dreaming about them?

I try not to think of my own demons. About the times I, too, had horrible, gut-wrenching nightmares. When fear kept me awake and sitting next to Charlie's crib just to keep watch and make sure he was breathing.

I get up, knowing it's not even dawn. But it doesn't matter. I'm fully awake. The hum of the generator and the relative warmth of the cabin tell me we haven't lost power yet, so I get dressed and start on a pie.

For a bachelor living in the middle of nowhere, Dallas has a lot of basic staples. Flour, two kinds of sugar, baking soda, vanilla extract, and a stock of canned goods that could rival any mom-and-pop grocery store.

Finding some pumpkin pie filling among the cans, I decide to make *two* pies. I stare at the can and wonder why a guy who doesn't celebrate Thanksgiving has a can of pumpkin pie filling. The near-expired date on the can clues me in on the fact that he had no intention of ever using it. It makes me wonder if anyone else ever comes up here and buys him groceries. His mother perhaps.

With the pies in the oven, I get to peeling potatoes. I make extra of everything knowing that when the power goes out it will be easier to eat leftovers than to cook a brand-new meal. I walk to the fireplace, studying the flat cooking surfaces on the top. There are two of them. A careful touch for barely a second proves it's super-hot. I'm sure we can even boil water on it if necessary. He thought of everything when he got this place.

When Dallas still isn't back by the time the pies are out of the oven, I start to worry. It's freezing outside, and the snow is wetter than before. How can he stay out in the cold so long?

I guess it's true that you acclimate to your surroundings. In Florida, we get used to the oppressive heat and humidity. Here, Dallas has gotten used to the cold. I'm sure his collection of boots and outerwear helps.

When I think of him, I try not to get too hung up on what he said last night. The words that stung me to my very core. The guy is obviously battling some major demons. I, more than anyone, know he needs patience and understanding.

Instead of dwelling on why I know that, I busy myself with other things. I make sure my phone and laptop are plugged in for when we lose power. I clean up the potato peelings and the spilled flour. I play with Bex. I browse Dallas's collection of books.

I do everything I can think of to keep my mind off the one thing I really want to do—go in that damn room.

I glance at the door then at Bex, who's lazing in front of the fireplace.

"He didn't specifically say I couldn't go in there," I say aloud.

Bex's tail thumps at the sound of my voice.

"What do you think? Should I?"

He momentarily lifts his head off the floor, making eye contact as if scolding me.

"Oh, what do you know? You're just a dog."

I pout, staring at the stupid door.

"Screw it. I'm doing it," I say, pushing off the couch.

I peek out the window to see if there's any sign of Dallas, which in itself tells me I shouldn't be doing what I'm about to do. But I justify it by surmising it's his own fault. If he wouldn't up and leave every ten minutes, I wouldn't be here by myself, going bored out of my mind.

I half expect the door to his hobby room to be locked. It's not. And I'm not sure why my heart rate shoots through the roof when I open it, but it does.

Because you shouldn't be in here.

Once inside, I look around, confused. This is it? Maybe I built it up too much in my mind, expecting this room to be some sort of sacred ground filled with pictures of his wife and son. But it's not. It really is what he said it was—a hobby room.

It's filled with art projects. Sculptures. Paintings. Paper Mache and other small crafts.

Damn, the guy is multi-talented for sure. I guess he does have a lot of hobbies other than learning languages.

I pick up a few crafts and study them. It seems he prefers abstract art as they don't really resemble anything. But they're beautiful all the same. The paintings are the most interesting to me. Again, abstract, using a myriad of colors to create almost a visual language of shapes, lines, and forms.

Movement outside the lone window in the corner startles me. I rush to make sure everything is how I found it, but in my haste, I knock something over. "Shit." I place it upright, close the door, then race back to the kitchen.

Bex's nails click against the floor as he scurries over to greet Dallas.

"Hey, bud. Have you been out?" he asks the dog.

I crane my neck around the side of the refrigerator. "Twice."

He removes his hat, coat, and boots. His nose is bright red. He must be freezing. I pour him what's left of the coffee I made hours ago.

"Drink this by the fire. You shouldn't stay outside that long. You'll get frostbite."

"I'm fine."

"Tell that to your nose. It looks ready to fall off your face."

He pulls a kitchen chair close to the fire and sips his coffee, looking over at the cooling pies. "You were serious about this Thanksgiving thing?"

"Of course. Just because we're stuck here, doesn't mean we can't celebrate."

"I'm not stuck here."

"Okay, fine. Just because *I'm* stuck here."

He stands and comes over, looking at the massive pile of peeled potatoes resting in a pot of water. "Expecting company?"

"I wanted leftovers. It'll be easier to reheat them than to whip up something new."

"Smart." He puts his cup in the sink. "I'm going to shower, then…" He looks at the hobby room.

You're going to hide some more? I almost blurt.

"Dinner will be ready around two."

He nods, then without another word, he's behind another closed door.

Closing doors. Yes, that's exactly what Dallas Montana does best. He closes doors and runs and hides. I stare at the bathroom and wonder just what he's running and hiding from. His memories. Or me.

Chapter Eighteen

Dallas

Incredible smells have been drifting into this room for hours.

I feel like a major dick, being in here while she's out there slaving over a dinner I'm not even going to enjoy.

Looking down at my book, I realize I haven't turned a page in… well, maybe since I sat down. I slam it shut knowing I can't get the captivating brunette on the other side of that door out of my goddamn head.

When I glance at my surroundings, it makes me feel all kinds of guilty. I pick up one of my favorite sculptures and trace my finger along the edge.

A knock on the door has it slipping out of my hands. It almost hits the floor, but I scoop it up right at the last second, my heart pounding at the thought of how close it came to being a shattered mess.

"Dinner's ready," Marti sing-songs through the door.

I blow out a relieved breath, place the sculpture back where it belongs, then straighten a painting that's tipping awkwardly off the end of an easel. I study it for a half-second before leaving the room.

Instantly I'm bombarded with the mouth-watering scent of fresh bread, cooked meat, and all kinds of other amazing foods my palate hasn't experienced in a long, long time. Out of nowhere, I find myself looking forward to a meal.

As saliva flows across my tongue, I momentarily wonder if it's the meal I'm looking forward to—or the company.

I glance at the table, all done up with fancy napkins and shit. "Where did you get all this?"

"Don't you know Amazon delivers everywhere?" She laughs and I look at her like she's nuts. "You don't do much spring cleaning around here, do you? You had this stuff in the bottom drawer of that hutch."

"My mother must have put it there when she and my dad brought up some of my belongings."

Her head cocks to the side. She's going to ask me something.

"Smells great," I say quickly to avert any questioning. "I can't believe you threw all this together at the last minute."

I peruse the spread of food on the counter. Homemade stuffing. Green bean casserole. Sliced beef tenderloin. Even mashed potatoes and gravy.

"Do you want to pick a bottle of wine?" she asks.

I hesitate. Wine would make this feel like it's something it's not. Sure, I drink it with meals all the time. But alone. Not with someone else. And definitely not with a woman. Because this isn't a date.

But she's gone through all this trouble. It's the least I can do.

"Not the special occasion bottle," she adds. "Just your ordinary everyday wine will do. Hell, give me a glass of Barefoot and I'm good."

I cringe. "You won't find anything like that in this house."

"No. I suppose I won't. I am looking forward to tasting what you have, though. You'll forgive me if I don't sniff it, swish it, and talk about things like body and acidity. I'm just a girl who likes what she likes." She shrugs. "Or spits out what she doesn't."

"Spit out my wine and you'll be sleeping outside tonight."

A smile reaches her stunning hazel eyes that dance with laughter. I question why she's even doing this. Doesn't she hate me after what I said last night? You'd think she'd be pissed off at me, not cooking me dinner.

When her cheeks pink, I realize I've been staring. It's the first time today I've really looked at her. There's a tug in my gut, like a tractor beam holding me hostage to her. Sheepishly, she tucks an errant hair behind her ear. She bites her lower lip, chewing on it anxiously. Her feet shuffle. She does all those things, but the one thing she doesn't do is look away.

A crackle of raw energy passes between us. The attraction is palpable. Our eyes are locked onto each other. A pang of excitement has me stirring below the belt and some foreign emotion cascades through me. It's a longing I haven't felt in eons. One I never thought I'd feel again. And the way it sneaks up on me and pounces, like a lion finding a meal, knocks the wind right out of me.

That longing gives way to guilt, and finally I break the stare and turn to fetch the wine.

Behind me, she lets out a deep, audible exhalation that I try to ignore as I select a bottle. I take far longer to pick one than I should, needing time for my erection to abate.

While I open the bottle, she dishes food onto our plates and brings them to the table.

She sits and puts her napkin in her lap, waiting for me to join her. Our eyes connect again, and then…

The lights go out, leaving us shrouded in darkness and silence. The propane has finally run out, the only light coming from the fire.

Instantly, I know it's not even the power I'll miss. It's the noise. The constant drone of the generator that's always there in the background. It's gone. The silence is almost deafening, leaving nothing where there once was something. Like that ever-present hum of grief that lives in my head, it's been a source of comfort almost. The white noise that keeps me from overthinking shit.

It's gone now. And I miss it.

Marti is most definitely not having the same reaction. In fact, she's laughing.

"Wow." She giggles heartily. "That couldn't have been better timing."

I set the opened bottle on the table and put a few more logs on the fire. It's midday, but the sky is gray, offering little in the way of light.

Marti gets a few candles from a cabinet. I watch her every move, trying to decide if I'm disturbed by how well she knows her way around my cabin after such a short time.

She takes them to the fireplace and lights them, then places them on the table. Then she sits, looking over at me expectantly.

Dinner. Wine. Candlelight. It's all a little too romantic for me. I've half a mind to turn and go back outside and chop wood until the woman sitting at my table gets the fuck out of my head.

But my mother would have my balls on a platter if she knew Marti had gone through all this trouble and I bailed. She raised her sons better than that. So I sit. Despite the warning sirens in my head.

"I wonder if Anita's family is doing anything for Thanksgiving," Marti says, staring at her plate of food. "I think it's important to keep up some semblance of normal when life spins out of control." She sighs. "I guess I'm missing Charlie a lot today." She looks up from the table, guilt in her eyes. "I'm sorry. I shouldn't have said that."

I shake my head, pick up the wine bottle, and fill our glasses. "You don't need to filter yourself for my sake. You have a kid. It's natural for you to talk about him."

"Yeah, but…" Her words trail off.

"Marti, it's fine. Really."

I go to dig into my food when she puts a hand on mine, halting the motion. "Wait. My family has this tradition. It's something we've done as far back as I can remember. My father would make us say one thing we were thankful for. He'd say no matter how bad life was, there always had to be something, however small. After he died, we kept up the tradition."

"Sorry. Not playing."

Her hand falls away, disappointment in her eyes.

"Fine. I'll go." She chews that bottom lip again, deep in thought. "I'm thankful for snow. Snow angels, snowballs, snowmen. All of it. Even if I haven't done the latter two. But maybe…" She looks at me hopefully. Then her body shivers. "But not ice. I'm definitely not thankful for ice. Which reminds me, I'm also thankful for you. You saved me. Twice." She looks at me, her gaze soft and inviting. "C'mon, there has to be *something*."

I push food around on my plate.

"One thing," she says. "Anything."

I shuffle my foot. It runs into something soft. Bex is under the table. "Bex," I say. "I'm thankful for Bex."

I don't elaborate and tell her why. That if he hadn't barked his head off and led me to her, she'd be dead. And I'd be stuck here, trapped, with no way to escape. Visions of her under the ice cloud my mind. Her limp body. Her blue lips. Then the limp body becomes Phoebe's. Her cold, lifeless, blue body lying on the steel gurney at the morgue. Panic crawls up my spine and I can feel the wine glass shake in my grasp.

For the second time, a soft hand lands on mine. "Well, there you go." She picks up her fork. "Let's dig in."

One touch. That's all it took. One touch from her to keep me from spiraling.

My heart rate slows. I gulp down some wine. Then I eat the best meal I've had in years.

Chapter Nineteen

Martina

I can't stand eating in silence. So I talk. I talk about Charlie, but not too much. And Asher and Charles. I also tell him about my niece.

"Why do you call her Bug?" he asks.

"Her real name is Darla. Asher named her after our mom. Ever since she was little, she's been fascinated with insects. She's a real lifesaver when there's a roach or spider in the house, which happens a lot in Florida. I'm petrified of bugs, but she has no problem with them."

"And Bug's mother? Is she in the picture?"

I shake my head. "She gave up all parental rights. In fact, she wanted to have an abortion. Asher talked her out of it. He said he wanted to raise the baby all on his own. He was twenty-seven and our dad had just died. I think he was secretly hoping for a boy since he was already stuck with me. But the moment she was born, he was entranced. He loves that kid so—" It dawns on me what I've been rambling about. "Aw, dang it, there I go again. Sorry."

He waves off my concern. "You don't have to walk on eggshells around me."

I almost spit out my wine. "Are you kidding? Dallas, I absolutely have to walk on eggshells around you. You're the most mysterious, closed-off, confusing man I've ever met. You live in a remote cabin with a secret room. You have a tragic past. A cell tower you installed so you could work up here for, what… *ever?*"

Without a single display of emotion, he pours himself another glass of wine and tops mine off. "So about that secret room." He looks at me like a parent scolding a child. "You've been in it."

Guilt washes through me at the invasion of privacy. "Yes. I'm sorry. I was bored with you being gone half the time. But in my defense, you never explicitly said I couldn't go in there. And, might I say, you're one super talented dude. Your artwork is amazing."

He glances over at the door. "Nothing in there is mine."

"Not yours? Then who—" When realization dawns, I stop cold, not needing to put my foot in my mouth any more than I already have.

I sit back in my chair, feeling ten shades of regret. All those sculptures and paintings were created by *her*. His dead wife. The woman in the picture whose name I still don't know.

"I'm… jeez, wow. I didn't mean to invade your privacy like that."

"It's fine." He stands, taking our empty plates to the sink and starts washing.

I turn. "The water still works?"

"Water and toilet. I'm on well and septic, and the water pump has a battery backup. It'll work just fine. It just won't get hot."

"Well, that's a relief. On both counts. For a second I thought we'd have to go outside to do our business like Bex."

His shoulders shake in silent laughter. They do that a lot. I get the idea he doesn't like to laugh, but that sometimes it just happens spontaneously.

After he cleans up and I package the leftovers, I stare at the massive amount of food. "What should we do with it now that the fridge is out?"

He goes into the hobby room and comes out with two large coolers. "We'll put all the refrigerated stuff in here and then fill them with snow. We'll just have to keep doing it a few times a day and drain out the water. As long as we don't open the freezer, everything in it will keep for a few days. You never know, maybe the weather will break and I'll get my propane delivery by then."

Sudden sadness washes over me. If the weather breaks, that Luther guy will be up here with a tow truck. He'll take me into town, I'll rent a car, and that'll be it.

Will Dallas even think about me when I'm gone? Or will he just regret me?

"You okay?" he asks.

I swallow. "Yeah."

He hands me one of the coolers. "You want to fill this up halfway with fresh snow? Ice would be better, but I don't want you anywhere near the pond."

I try not to smile. He's worried about me. He's protecting me.

While scooping snow into the cooler, I take note of its consistency. It's heavy and wet and seems to clump in my hands. My cold lips curl up into a sinister grin. I pack snow tightly between my hands, forming a snowball, then I place it on top of the rest of the snow inside the cooler. I take it back inside, set the cooler down, open the lid, take my weapon out and launch it at Dallas, hitting him square in the back.

He spins and looks down at the chunks of snow, amused. "Did you just throw a snowball at me?"

"I did indeed," I say, with zero regrets. "And you now have the distinct honor of being the first person I've ever hit with one." A thought occurs. "Hey, why don't we go outside and work off some of those calories? We can have a snowball fight."

He thinks about it then turns away. "I'll pass."

I walk the cooler over to him, set it down, then put on the warmest clothes I can find, which consist of another one of his sweatshirts, his beanie cap, and the coat I keep borrowing. "Suit yourself. I'm going out."

"To have a snowball fight with yourself?" he asks over his shoulder.

I roll my eyes. "You're a party pooper, Dallas Montana." I pat my thigh. "Come on, Bex. Let's you and me go have some fun."

He barks once and trots after me. At least someone is as excited to play in the snow as I am.

I make a large snowball and throw it at the front door in spite, watching it clump to the ground. I'd like to say it came to rest on a welcome mat, but there isn't one. Dallas isn't exactly the roll-out-the-red-carpet kind of guy.

I get it. He wants his space. He wants to stay up here and chop wood and read and learn a gazillion languages and, what… stare at all his wife's creations? Is that what he was doing in there for hours? How depressing. I mean, I know the feeling. After my own losses, I'd sleep with a shirt or a blanket that smelled of them. I was devastated when the scents began to fade. I wanted to keep the memories alive. Over the years, my therapist—and quite frankly, Asher—have taught me how to do it in a much healthier way.

I look back at the house, wondering if he's ever sought out therapy. I doubt it. Not if he's been living out here ever since. But I know one thing, if anyone was ever in need of a therapist, it's him.

Movement flashes in the window and I catch Dallas watching me. I'm not even sure he's aware that I see him even though I'm looking right at him. Is he daydreaming? Zoning out? Wishing me gone?

I push the thoughts aside and go back to making another snowball, but instead of tossing it at the window—no need to tempt fate and risk breaking it now that we're without power—I keep adding more snow and it gets bigger and bigger.

I've never made a snowman before, but I assume this is how it starts. Too large to hold in my hands now, I put the snowball on the ground and then use my hands to scoop the surrounding snow onto the snowball. But all I end up doing is making it look like a lame, asymmetrical blob. Come on, how hard can it be to build a snowman? Kids do it.

It makes me wonder if Charlie has been playing in the snow. He's not that far from me. A few hours at most. Surely it's been snowing there too. He must be even more mesmerized by it than I am. I hope someone has taken him out, maybe even built a snowman with him. I know he'd love it.

But Anita is grieving. Is my son sitting in a corner, forgotten, as his stepmom mourns his father?

My need to get to him is strong. But knowing there are many relatives to care for him does offer me comfort. Surely someone will step up and make sure he's being well taken care of. Most of her family didn't even know Charles. They won't be as distraught as Anita. This gives me confidence that he'll be alright. My kid is resilient. Adaptable. He'll be okay. I just wish I could talk to him, assure him I'm here and close and will be with him as soon as I possibly can.

A war rages inside me. I love my son. More than anything. But going to him means leaving here. And over the past days, despite everything that's gone wrong, I've found it to be magical. I've found *him* to be magical. I glance back at the window to see he's still standing behind it.

Why is that? Why am I drawn to a man who has shut himself off from the world? One who clearly doesn't want a relationship. One who deals with a houseguest by not being in the house a lot of the time. One who isn't interested in the future, only in holding onto the past.

Maybe because he reminds me a little too much of the person I once was.

The door opens. "You call that a snowman?"

"Hey!" I bark. "If you're not going to help out a girl whose only experience to draw on is building sandcastles, then you don't get an opinion."

He's still for a moment. I can tell he's thinking about it. *Come on*, I implore with my mind.

When he shuts the door, my heart sinks. But I don't let it deter me. I'm going to build this godforsaken snowman if my hands freeze off in the process.

A minute later, however, I have company. Dallas has outfitted himself like he's ready to go into the Siberian tundra. I chuckle, having never seen him in a scarf, but he's got one wrapped around his neck and mouth, and tucked into the back of his coat.

He holds a second scarf out to me.

I try to wrap it around my neck as he has his, but it's a futile effort.

"Jeez," he pouts. "Do you southerners not know how to do *anything?*"

"Hey, now, that's hardly fair. I'd like to see you try and put on a wetsuit and go surfing."

He throws his head back, laughing. "*You* surf." He waves a hand up and down my body. "*You.*"

"Stop it," I say, batting away his hand. "Anyone can surf. I've even started Charlie in lessons. My friend's dad has a condo in Cocoa Beach. She has a daughter Charlie's age. We take the kids there one weekend a month."

He drapes the scarf around my neck, pulls it snug, and wraps it a second time. Our faces are close. Our breath mingles. He stares down into my eyes. "Seems dangerous."

I momentarily wonder if he's talking about surfing, or… *us*.

"It's not. Believe me, there are plenty of instructors and lifeguards."

"Can he even swim?"

"Since he was eighteen months."

His head bobs up and down. "Smart." He lowers to his knees. "You're doing it all wrong. You don't bring the snow to the base of the snowman, you need to roll the snow, picking up more along the way." He packs the snow tightly and shows me.

It's not an unwelcome sight watching his backside as he leans over and pushes the ever-growing snowball around the yard until he's happy with the size. He rolls it back to me. "I'll make the middle and you make the head."

"Sounds like a plan."

I move over near the side of the house to make sure I'm getting fresh snow.

"Marti!"

I look up.

"Don't go around back."

I want to tell him I'm a big girl. I know the boundaries. How could I not since he put the logs there yesterday? And since, he's added even more as if he thinks I'm incapable of getting the point. He doesn't have to worry. After what I went through, I'm not going near the pond ever again. Yet, there's a warmth that flows through me knowing he's trying to keep me safe.

It could be for his benefit more than mine, however. The last thing he needs is another dead person on his hands. I think of poor Abe, sitting frozen in his cabin. What did Dallas feel when he saw him? I probably would have had a panic attack. I'm glad I didn't go.

"Is this big enough?" I ask, carrying back a… snowman head?

He laughs. "Did you ever see the movie Beetlejuice?"

"Um, a million years ago, why?"

He holds out his hand. "Give me that."

I hand it over and he places it on top of the middle section. And then I understand. This snowman has the smallest head in the history of snowmen. I stomp over, remove the head, and return to the side of the house to make it bigger.

"Here," I say when I'm done. "Mr. Snowman architect."

Rolling his eyes, he takes it from me and secures it to the top. "Not bad."

I smile triumphantly. "Can you find some sticks for his arms?"

"On it."

While he's doing that, I go into the house, rummage through a cooler, and pull out a carrot stick for our snowman's nose, trying to remember what typically gets used for eyes. I'm not sure I ever knew.

I come outside holding the carrot. He sees it when I approach. "Just make sure you put that in the right spot."

Heat crosses my face when I comprehend his insinuation. Dallas doesn't crack many jokes, so when he does, it hits me in all the right places. Especially when said joke is accompanied by a wink.

Then I see he's used rocks and small pebbles for eyes and a mouth. "Good thinking," I say, right before jamming the carrot in the middle of the snowman's face.

I pull out my phone. "I have to get a picture of this."

"You sure you want to waste battery?"

Holding my ground, I insist, "Dallas, this is my first snowman. As in ever. I'm not going to let this momentous occasion go by without photographic evidence of its existence. Now get over here. I'm great at selfies."

"I think I should just take one of you."

"But you helped make it. Seriously, get on that side of him before you realize what a bitch I can be if I don't get my way."

He holds up his hands. "Wouldn't want to see that." He takes his place by the snowman, who is about a foot shorter than I am.

"Smile," I say, holding out my right hand to snap the photo while doing bunny ears behind the snowman's head.

I look down at the picture to make sure it's in focus. Dallas isn't smiling. He's not even looking at the camera. He's looking at me. And the intensity of his gaze definitely came through the lens. Despite the fact that he ran out after we had sex. And regardless of the unpleasant words he uttered last night, his eyes paint an entirely different picture.

He wants me.

Whether or not he can admit it, his eyes don't lie.

So regardless of who he thinks he'll be making love to—I decide I want it just as badly. Because despite Charles's death, or maybe because of it, I've found myself never feeling quite so alive.

Chapter Twenty

Dallas

"He needs a name," Marti says, admiring our creation. She tilts her head left then right, thinking. "How about Abe?"

I raise a brow.

"You know," she continues, "because he's frozen."

Shocked by her words, I'm not sure whether to laugh or cringe.

"Sorry." She stifles a laugh. "Bad joke. But honestly, *you* made a bad joke about him first."

"You remember that?"

She nods. "I remember *everything* about that."

The way she says it, I know we're not talking about Abe anymore.

"He's missing something," she says.

"A hat?"

"No, that's not it."

"Yes, it is. All snowmen have hats, Marti. You know, one of those top hat thingies."

"Mmm," she ponders. "There has to be something we can—"

Marti stops talking and tugs on her scarf until it loosens and comes free. She wraps the scarf around the snowman's neck and ties it. When she pulls to secure it, she pulls too tightly and the head wobbles to one side.

We both watch as it falls off and slides down the body, tumbling to the ground in a messy clump, the carrot sticking up toward the sky. We look at each other and start laughing. *Hard.*

"Poor Abe," she says. "We should say a few words."

I roll my eyes.

"Abe was…" She chews that bottom lip. "Abe was a jolly happy soul," she deadpans. "He didn't have a corncob pipe, a button nose, or two eyes made of coal. *Oh, right… coal,"* she says looking somewhat like a lightbulb went off.

"Abe could be cold at times," she continues somberly. "And he didn't talk much. But for those ten glorious minutes that he graced the world with his presence, he brought joy and happiness to everyone around him. Sadly, though, he lost his head. The murderer is still at large, however, so if you see a frozen crazy lady without a scarf, please detain her for questioning." She pats his back. "We'll miss you, old pal."

My body shakes with laughter. This girl. This *woman.* She pulls emotions out of me without even trying.

When she's done with the eulogy, she picks up what's left of Abe's head, packs it tightly, takes a few steps back and hurls the snowball at me.

I look down at the remnants of snow on my coat and the mushy pile at my feet. "That's twice you did that."

Her eyes narrow into a challenging glare. "What are you going to do about it?"

I punch my hand into Abe's gut and come out with enough snow to make one hell of a snowball. Marti shrieks and races away, taking cover behind a tree before I launch it at her, narrowly missing her head and slamming into the tree trunk.

"You're toast," she says, leaning down to gather more snow.

I run behind my truck and take cover when she darts one at me. I sink down and begin on my arsenal, making snowball after snowball, piling them together for easy access. Peeking around the front bumper, I see that she's busy doing the very same thing behind the tree.

Bex stands almost halfway between us, his head on a swivel, probably wondering what the hell we're doing.

When I've made a dozen or so, I get up, carefully glancing out from behind my shelter. A snowball splats against the front window, missing me by a good yard. I grab one of mine and toss it at her. It misses by a mile.

You can do better than that, Montana.

I get another one before she has a chance to retaliate. Squinting at my target, I wind up like I'm Stryker Taylor from the Nighthawks, and launch it across the yard. It hits her square in the chest and she goes down.

My breath catches. *Shit.* I race out from behind the truck and sprint toward her, Bex at my side. But before I get there, she pops up and throws a snowball right at me, hitting me in my goddamn face.

She got me. She got me good. Still running, I wipe off the wet snow as best I can, and tackle her back to the ground.

"Ooof!" she exclaims when her back hits the snow and I land on top of her.

I brace myself with extended arms so she's not bearing the full brunt of my weight. As I hover over her, snow that was lodged in my cap falls down onto her and slides off the side of her face. I shake my glove off and wipe her cheek.

She looks up at me with those gorgeous eyes as we breathe heavily onto each other, the clouds from our warm breath swirling around our heads. Her tongue darts out, laying moisture along her lips. Without a second thought, I lower myself until my mouth is on hers. Her lips are cold, soft, and inviting, opening immediately so I can plunge my tongue into her mouth.

Marti's frozen hands work their way up under my scarf, her frigid fingers wrapping around the back of my neck, securing me against her. Despite everything around us being cold, warmth spreads through me as we make out like teenagers in a snow fort.

My lips, warm now, travel down across her cold neck, but I can't go any further without exposing her to potential frostbite. So I roll to the side, gather her in my arms, and pick her up.

She doesn't say a single word. She just presses her head against my chest as I carry her into the cabin. I hold the door open only long enough for Bex to follow. He shakes snow off his coat and settles by the fire.

I set Marti down. She takes off my beanie, then pulls my scarf from around my neck. I remove her hat and toss it to the floor. Our arms tangle as we attempt to unzip each other's coats at the same time. She giggles, then looks up, lower lip pulled into her mouth, gauging my reaction. I get the idea she's afraid to do something that will pull me out of… *this.*

What she isn't aware of, however, is that not even a goddamn freight train running at full speed down a hill could stop me from what comes next. And her laugh—her soft, feminine, enchanting laugh—is just fuel on the fire.

I don't waste another second, ridding her of her clothes as quickly as I can, then doing the same with mine until we're both standing totally naked. Naked and shivering, thanks to the fact that we no longer have power.

I pull back the covers and she climbs into bed. I hurry in behind her and pull her against me, basking in the feeling of her body against mine.

She cranes her neck to look at me, a tease glinting her eyes. "The last time you cuddled me like this, you had just saved my life."

I flip her over and thrust my erection against her hip. "It's different this time."

Before she can ask how, I lean down and capture her lips once again. *Three days.* For three days she's all I've thought about. The way she smells. Her dazzling, angelic eyes. How she flips her hair when she's annoyed. How she bites her lip when she's shy. How she takes care of Bex. Hell, how she takes care of *me*. Even after the way I've treated her.

Marti is the whole goddamn package.

I wonder if she knows it. How caring and nurturing and forgiving she is. How she brings light to the darkness. Humor to the sadness.

I deepen the kiss, exploring her tongue, her lips, her every stilted breath. When I've drawn all I can from her mouth, I journey to her chest, kissing and licking my way down, tasting every delicious nuance of her skin along the way. Reaching her nipples, they harden into small tight points when I suck one into my mouth and toy with the other using my thumb and fingers. She likes it when I do this. I already know her left nipple is more sensitive than her right, so I concentrate most of my efforts on that one.

She arches into me, a moan escaping her that only encourages me to try for more. To drive her higher and farther. To make her come so damn hard that no other orgasm after this, *after me*, will ever suffice.

I push aside the thought. Because the ramifications of it are too much.

When I dip a finger inside her, she murmurs my name, and holy fuck it's sexy.

She tries to grab my cock, but I push her hand away as my mouth travels even lower. I'll come instantly if she touches me. I'm not ready to come. Not until I make her see God.

Instead of grabbing me, she fists the bed sheet, tearing it from the sides of the bed when I drag my tongue over her swollen clit. She tries to buck her hips, but I hold her down, not letting her move against me. With my hands, I hold her thighs apart, trapping them to the bed. She can't move her lower body, and I know that's going to heighten everything she's feeling.

She releases the sheets and claws at my shoulders. She may even draw blood. But I couldn't care less. She's completely and utterly falling to pieces underneath me. And I'm drunk on the power.

"Dallas! Oh, God!"

Her screams bounce off the walls. My fingers get squeezed inside her as she pulsates over and over. My fucking balls tighten and threaten to release my load, my body ready to convulse with sexual energy.

Holy fucking shit.

Before she's even done climaxing, I climb on top of her. Her eyes fly open. I look down into them, swimming in those hazel pools.

Then, as I push myself inside her, I close my eyes, hoping I don't drown.

Chapter Twenty-one

Martina

His face contorts with both pain and pleasure when he comes.

But he comes so quickly, it makes me wonder what he could have possibly gotten out of it. Me, though… I blow a long slow breath out of pursed lips. I've never had such amazing sexual experiences in my life.

He rests his forehead on my shoulder, panting heavily.

I try not to think of what he said last night. Because for all I know, he *was* making love to her, not me.

Does that make me a doormat? Or just someone who is horny enough not to care.

Except, I do care.

I run a hand down his strong arm, wondering what will happen in two minutes. Two hours. Two days.

The two-minute answer comes when he rolls to the side. A squishy, bubbling noise when he pulls out of me has my face reddening. I'm glad it's dim in here so he can't clearly see my level of embarrassment.

"Let me get you a tissue," he says.

When he opens the drawer in the nightstand, his entire body stiffens, making me remember what lies inside.

Without turning back to me, he holds a few tissues out and goes to get up off the bed. He's going to run again. Maybe quite literally.

I hastily pop over to his side and put my hands on his shoulders. "Don't run away. Please. Just stay and sit with it for a while."

He sighs. "Sit with what?"

"Whatever is going through your head." I rub my hand along his back. "Dallas, please. It's cold. Lay back down. We'll just lie here and get warm. We don't have to talk."

I can hear him swallow. It's loud and telling. It's the only noise in the room other than the occasional crackle from the fire.

Feeling he's going to bolt despite my pleas, I reach behind the bed and pull a book from the shelf. I open it and start reading aloud. It's hard because it's so dim in here. I tilt the book so light from the fire illuminates the pages.

He doesn't move, which I take as a good sign. He's not leaving. But he's not exactly staying either. He appears to be debating what to do about me. Trying to decide if what we just did was a mistake. Or most likely, whether or not he should race out the door.

I move away, prop a pillow up, lean back, and pull the covers around me. I keep reading. The story grips me from the first page and I wonder if it's one he's read before.

On the third page, he grabs the battery-powered lantern on the nightstand, handing it to me. Then finally, he lies back, not right next to me, there is space between us, but not as much as if he'd left. It's a tiny yet monumental step. I don't acknowledge it for fear I'll jinx it. I just keep reading.

I read for hours. My throat is dry, and my voice is hoarse, but I don't stop. Because Dallas is sleeping. His chest is moving up and down slowly. His face is relaxed. He looks peaceful. And I keep reading because I get the idea this doesn't happen often.

Bex trots over, lays his head on the bed, and stares at me. The poor guy is probably crossing his legs. I heard him drink his entire bowl of water an hour ago.

The last thing I want to do is stop reading and risk Dallas waking. But even less desirable than that is cleaning up dog mess. I put the book down and get out of bed as carefully as I can. Quietly, I gather up my clothes and visit the bathroom, hoping the flush from the toilet and the sound of running water doesn't wake him.

I cringe when the front door creaks then look back at the bed, grateful to see Dallas not moving.

Outside, after Bex takes care of business, I spend a few minutes throwing a stick to him. Then I make Abe a new head, replacing the carrot and pebbles on his face, this time not decapitating him with the scarf I gently tie around his neck.

Snow is falling. I'm not sure it ever stopped.

At this point, I'm not sure I ever want it to.

Feeling a sudden pang of loneliness, I take Bex back inside, fully expecting Dallas to be either putting on hiking clothes or hiding out in the hobby room. But he's exactly where I left him. He hasn't moved one iota. His lips are slightly parted. A soft, sexy snore escapes him, and a wallop of desire warms me. I'm drawn to him like a moth to a flame. I walk over and gaze down at him. He's beautiful.

I've never thought of men as beautiful. But *he* is. Through all his burliness, protectiveness, and standoffishness, he's beautiful, inside and out.

For a moment, I'm jealous. I'm jealous of the woman he loved so much, even in death, that he left his entire life behind.

Will anyone ever love me like that? It's almost inconceivable.

I startle when his body shifts. But he doesn't open his eyes. He's still asleep, deeply asleep. Why? What changed?

The book rests on the edge of the bed, still opened to the page I stopped on. Could it be my voice? My chest tightens at the idea that listening to me read to him allowed him to relax enough to sleep. And sleep peacefully.

I put two more logs on the fire, get a glass of water, then strip down, crawl into bed, and pick up right where I left off, vowing to read as long as the man next to me needs me to.

Chapter Twenty-two

Martina

I wake before he does. Which is strange on so many levels. It's early, because we fell asleep before dark, and it's cold. Bone-chilling cold. I wrap a blanket around myself and stoke the fire that has burned down to embers. Then I let Bex out, opening the front door just enough for him to squeeze through. I shiver at the gush of frigid air that slaps me in the face.

Standing at the window, shifting my weight from one cold foot to the other, I wait for Bex to do his thing and come back. When he comes through the door, he looks at me expectantly.

I lower down, pat him on the head, and whisper, "Don't worry, buddy. We'll play later."

After pulling on sweatpants, a hoodie, and three pairs of socks, I sift through the coolers. The snow in them has melted, but the water is still very cold. Refilling them with fresh snow can wait until later.

I decide on eggs and pancakes—both of which I should easily be able to cook in the cast iron skillets that fit perfectly on top of his fireplace stove.

It's nearly impossible not to make noise. And when I glance over at the bed, I see Dallas sitting up, staring at me, looking way out of sorts.

"What is it?" I nod to the pans on the stove. "You don't mind if I cook breakfast, do you?"

"It's not that. I slept like the fucking dead." He runs his fingers through his long hair. "Strange."

I smile, because I'm pretty sure I know why. I read for hours and hours. I must have gotten halfway through the book. My throat feels raw today because of it. "Yeah." I nod. "Strange."

He disappears into the bathroom for a bit, returning just as I put breakfast on the table.

"You don't owe me anything," he says sharply. "I'm perfectly capable of cooking."

"Wow," I say dramatically. "Despite all that sleep, you're extra grumpy today."

He doesn't say anything. He just picks up his fork and shovels food into his mouth.

"You can stop beating yourself up," I say. "You told me how things were, and I still let it happen. That's on me, not you."

His head shakes and he looks all kinds of guilty. "That's not it."

That's not it? So he's not being a grouch because he regrets last night? I finish my breakfast without another word, wait for him to clean his plate, then I get up to do the dishes. Dallas takes them from me. "I've got it."

This man. He doesn't talk much, but that doesn't mean he isn't speaking volumes. His eyes, the way he moves, even the way he breathes reveals he wants nothing to do with me. It's the polar opposite of how he looked at me yesterday.

He wipes his hands on a dishrag and turns, catching me watching him. "I'm sorry," he says, looking at the floor. "I'm not going to be very good company today."

I grab the throw blanket off the back of the couch and pull it around my shoulders, almost as if it can offer me protection from more than just the cold. "Today?" I raise a brow. "Or *all* days?"

I'm not sure why I ask the question. Because in all honesty, I'm afraid of the answer. But I'm a silly, silly girl searching for validation. I'm foolish to think I can find it in this cabin, with him. But over the past few days, no matter how much I've tried to deny it, I've fallen for him. Fallen for a man who is unattainable. Unreachable. And for all I know, unlovable.

"Forget I asked," I say after a very pregnant pause tells me everything I need to know.

"Today is…" He scrubs a hand across his jaw and closes his eyes. "I mean, today *would have been* DJ's birthday."

My heart tumbles into my stomach. "DJ is your son."

He nods, heartbreak weighing down his features.

DJ. Dallas Junior. His son was named after him just like we named Charlie after his father.

"I'm so sorry." Tears clog my throat. I know how hard these occasions can be. "Can I… can I ask how long ago it happened?"

"Two years. Six months. Three days."

Wow. That's… *specific.* And when I do the math, it seems we both suffered unimaginable tragedies within months of each other.

He puts on his boots. His coat. His hat and gloves. "Thanks for breakfast." He goes to the door. "Come on boy," he calls to Bex. "Let's go chop some wood." Then, after a moment of hesitation, he looks back at me, his eyes hollow. "He would have been three."

He walks through the door and closes it.

My hand flies up to cover my mouth. I stifle a pained cry. His son would be three. *My* son is three. No wonder he looks at me the way he does. I must represent everything he lost. And me talking about Charlie—I never should have done that. I can't imagine how he must have felt every time I said his name.

I open the nightstand drawer and gaze down at the picture. DJ was just a baby. If he'd be three today and he died two-and-a-half years ago, he'd have died shortly after this photo was taken. My heart breaks into a million pieces. Because I know all too well how he feels.

I look at the other person in the photo. The tall, blonde, beautiful woman. She looks so happy. Dallas looks happy. They're the perfect family.

And he lost it all. He lost even more than I did. He lost everything.

I put the picture away and go to the bathroom, sobbing at how cruel life can be.

~ ~ ~

After taking a shower that felt like icicles stabbing my entire body, I park myself in front of the fire, drying my hair with a towel. I'm wearing the Yale hoodie again. Yes, it's ripped, and yes, it's the hoodie I was wearing when I fell in the pond. But somehow, when I wear it, I feel better. Like I'm wrapped in him. Even though it no longer smells like him after it was in the pond and then washed.

I wonder if he'll mind if I take it when I go. It's damaged. He'd probably throw it out anyway. I might just stuff it in with the rest of my things without telling him. As a souvenir. Something by which to remember my adventure.

My fingers run across my lips knowing I'll never forget these past days even if I leave here with nothing but my memories.

My heart is being torn in two different directions. I desperately need to get to Charlie. To tell him about his dad. To console him like only a mother can. To figure out how life is going to be when I'm a full-time single parent.

On the other hand, getting to Charlie means leaving this place. This magical, surreal cabin, and this mercurial man I seem to have fallen for. Hard.

And deep in my soul I know there's no way these two worlds can coexist.

I swallow my feelings and head for the kitchen cabinets, doing the one thing I know how to do when days like this hit.

Chapter Twenty-three

Dallas

It's been hours. I've walked the dog. Shoveled the porch. Chopped wood. Patrolled the pond for more breaches in the ice. I even snuck back in the cabin and refilled the coolers with snow when she was in the shower.

Marti probably thinks I'm avoiding her. Punishing her for what happened yesterday. She'd be wrong. I'd have worked my fingers to the bone whether or not she was here. It's the only way to keep the thoughts at bay.

But the thing is—it's not working. Every swing of the ax has me seeing DJ's face. Every crack of the wood has me hearing his laughter. Every goddamn tear that freezes on my cheek reminds me of the years I've spent without him.

Bex went inside long ago. He's smart like that. Me—not so much. My fingers are so cold I can't even wrap them around the ax anymore. I sit on my chopping stump and look back at my cabin, watching the trail of smoke plume from the fireplace vent in the roof.

I sniff, and the smell of baked goods permeates my nostrils. She's *baking?* But the oven doesn't work.

My thoughts shift, and I remember last night. She read to me. No one has ever read to me. I mean, I'm sure Mom did when I was little. But that's different. Hearing Marti's soothing voice as she read one of my favorite thrillers—is *that* what caused me to sleep so well?

I cock my head. I don't even remember dreaming. *Did I?* Not a night has gone by in the past few years without me dreaming of Phoebe or DJ. It's crazy to think that Marti reading to me was better than any sleeping pill I've ever taken.

As I ponder this, I see movement in the window. Marti is standing there in my Yale hoodie. She smiles and waves. Why isn't she pissed at me? She has every right to be. I was basically a dick to her this morning. I seem to be excelling at that lately.

I wave back, my fingers stinging under my thick gloves. But I don't smile. Today is not a day for smiling.

She sits on the sill, sipping something from a mug. It must be something warm and I momentarily imagine that warmth spreading throughout her body.

I shake my head, disgusted with myself that I'm thinking such thoughts on today of all days. I turn, pull my keys from my pocket, and get in my truck. I start the engine and blast the heater. I'll sit here until my fingers thaw. Can't chop wood with frozen fingers. But with the way the truck is facing, I can't help but look toward the cabin. At her. Perched on my windowsill. I'm a good thirty feet away, but things pass between us. Things I haven't felt in—

I cut the engine, get out of the truck, and slam the door way too hard, causing snow to come loose and cover my boots. In an attempt at even more avoidance, I busy myself scraping the few feet of snow off the hood even though it'll likely get covered again. I look at the drift that surrounds the truck, wondering just how long it'll be before Luther or a snowplow will reach us. Wondering just how I feel about it.

Being back in the cold has my fingers hurting again. Knowing I shouldn't stay out here any longer, I gather an armful of wood and carry it inside.

Upon opening the door, I'm hit with a gush of warm-ish air along with the overwhelming scent of… *cake?*

I pile the wood in the corner and glance at the kitchen. Marti is biting that lower lip again—this time in apparent nervousness—and her focus is all over the place, except on me. She's sitting at the table. The table that is, in fact, holding a cake.

A cake with *three* candles.

I power over and sneer at her. "Is this some sort of sick joke? What the fuck, Marti?"

She holds her hands up. "I know how this must look. But please let me explain. Then, if you want me to throw it out in the snow, I'll do it."

"What the hell is there to explain? You made a birthday cake for my dead son."

She nods. "Yeah. I did."

Sickness grips my stomach. "Why?"

"Sit." She motions to the other chair. "Please."

I do, albeit reluctantly. I cringe at the thought of looking at the cake though, but my eyes go there anyway, no matter how much I don't want them to. Three fucking candles. Jesus.

"After my, um… losses," she says, "I wasn't sure I'd ever be able to celebrate any holiday or birthday again. But Asher, he was far wiser than I gave him credit for. He forced me to acknowledge those important days. It was hard that first year, I'm not going to lie. It's still hard, even years later. It's difficult celebrating anything knowing they're not with me."

She picks at a spot on the table, holding a lighter in the other hand. At least she didn't light the candles. That would just be… wrong.

"On March fifth, when I was thirteen, Asher came home from work with a cake, and I almost threw it at him. He got so mad at me, upset that I didn't want to acknowledge our father's birthday and celebrate him for everything he was to us and all he did for us." She nods at the cake. "So from then on, we celebrated his birthday and those of others we'd lost. We'd eat the entire cake, the whole time sharing stories about our loved ones. On our dad's birthday, we talk about what we loved about him, and sometimes what we hated, like when he made us pull weeds. When we celebrate Mom's birthday, I listen to Asher recall his memories of her. It's a way for us to remember. To feel close to them. To honor them. To honor *everyone.*

"If you think it's stupid, I'll throw it out. But, Dallas, it would be great if you could try. Just a little. Even if you don't say it out loud, maybe you could think of a happy memory of DJ. And if you wanted, you could light the candles and wish him a happy heavenly birthday. It'll be hard. But one thing I promise you—it'll also be cathartic." She quiets for a moment. "What do you say?"

I stare at the cake. The cake for my son. The one that should have been baked by my wife. One that DJ would blow out the candles on as he stood up on a chair, leaning over the table.

I can almost see it—DJ at three years old, falling face first into the cake to get a bite as I record it on my phone for all of eternity. Or maybe he would reach out with his bare hands and squish a fistful between his fingers, licking it off while telling me how much he likes the sugary icing.

Prickly tears run down the back of my throat. I swallow hard and close my eyes. "He… he had just learned how to sit up. We would prop him up with pillows, terrified he'd fall over. And when he did"—my voice cracks with emotion—"he would laugh. He thought falling over was the funniest thing."

I get up quickly and pace the room, my chest tightening with each step. I spare a glance at Marti, and she offers me an encouraging nod and a sad smile. Why am I going along with this? It's not making me feel any better. It's only dredging up memories that died along with them.

I draw in a stabbing lungful of air and continue. "He wasn't crawling yet. But he'd do this thing when he was on his stomach. His butt would go in the air and he'd inchworm his way across the room." A picture of him doing it appears in my head and I chuckle. Then I cry out in pain because it hurts so bad.

Arms come around me in a warm embrace, holding me tight. I sob into the side of her head. She cries with me, somehow sharing a pain I doubt she could even possibly imagine. I don't know how long she holds me like this, or how many tears I cry, but afterwards I realize I feel… *better.*

Feeling like a blubbering idiot, I pull away and cock my head. "How did you bake a cake without an oven?"

"It wasn't that hard," she says, wiping the remainder of her tears. "You had two skillets of the same size. I whipped up some batter and took a chance. I have no idea if it'll be any good though. I didn't have the benefit of searching the internet for a recipe."

"What kind of cake is it?"

"Carrot."

"DJ hated carrots. He'd spit them out all over the floor and we'd have to clean up a slobbery orange mess."

The sweet laughter on Marti's lips makes me smile. She holds out the lighter. "Do you want to do the honors?"

It feels strange lighting candles on a birthday cake for a boy who isn't here to blow them out. If you'd have told me yesterday that I'd be doing this, I'd have called you crazy with a capital C. But here I am, doing it. I close my eyes, visions of DJ dancing in my head. What he might look like. How he'd call me Daddy.

"Happy birthday, little man," I squeak out through the lump in my throat.

"Happy birthday, DJ," Marti whispers respectfully.

I blow out the candles then look across the table. "Thank you."

She smiles and picks up a knife, cutting us each an oversized slice. "Will you tell me about him? I'm all ears. And we have a lot of cake to get through. It's tradition, Dallas. We have to eat the entire thing."

We spend the next hour eating, talking, and crying our way through his cake.

Marti's eyes sparkle with tears when I take the very last bite. And ... *fuck me*, she was right. This feeling I have. It's more than cathartic. It's everything.

Chapter Twenty-four

Martina

There was a shift in Dallas yesterday. With each memory of DJ that he shared, he seemed a little lighter. With every bite of cake, he looked more at peace. It was a huge risk I took. It could have easily backfired and become a disaster. He could have totally refused and spent the night chopping wood. But sometimes you have to take big risks for the people you… *love?*

I draw in a sharp breath. I've only known him for six days. I barely know anything about him. Is it possible to fall in love that quickly? I've read it in books. Seen it in movies. But that insta-love is usually something that goes both ways. Whatever this is, it's definitely one-sided. But it's also incredibly intense. I'm experiencing feelings I've never had before. Sure, Charles and I were in love. But it was a slow love, the kind that develops through years of friendship. It wasn't the punch-you-in-the-chest, hit-by-a-ton-of-bricks kind of love, it was more like waking up one day and realizing it was more than just friendship. Like, yeah, of course we're in love, haven't we always been?

Or maybe it was everyone and their dog telling us we belonged together.

This, though, is different. It's like one day I was this part-time single mom making a half-decent living branding people's websites, not even thinking about my next orgasm, and the next thing I know, I'm falling for the reclusive mountain man who literally rescued me from the grips of death.

That's got to be it. Dallas rescued me. I'm the patient who falls for her doctor. The princess who falls for the white knight. The horny single mom who falls for the first guy to bed her in years.

"Hey, there. Everything okay?"

Dallas's voice startles me back from wherever I'd gone. He's wondering why I stopped reading.

Yes, it's the middle of the day. But it's cold, and there isn't much to do, so we're sitting in bed, blankets tucked around us, Bex at my feet, and I'm reading the book aloud. And somehow, over the course of the hour, his head ended up in my lap.

I look down. "Sorry."

"Where'd you go?"

"I… honestly, I was thinking about Charles."

Okay, honestly, *I was thinking about* you *and how different my heart feels when I'm around you compared to how it felt being with him.* Honestly, *I'm sitting here trying to talk myself out of falling for a guy who's totally and emotionally unavailable.* Honestly, *I'm secretly hoping that the weather keeps me here just a little bit longer, because I'm not ready to leave this fantasy.*

"Tell me about him."

His request surprises me. He's never asked me any personal questions. Maybe after yesterday and the sharing he did about DJ, he feels comfortable asking.

"We met in middle school gym class shortly after my dad died and Asher and I moved to a new school district. His parents had just relocated from Indiana. I was the awkward girl in glasses with no athletic ability whatsoever."

He narrows his eyes. "Are we talking nerdy coke bottle glasses or sexy librarian glasses?"

When I laugh, his head bounces up and down on my lap. "I was twelve, believe me, there was nothing sexy about me."

"Mmm," he mumbles.

Somehow, that makes me smile.

"Charles was the brainy math geek who had zero idea he was hotter than the entire starting lineup of the baseball team. Being the new kids, it was natural for us to gravitate together. Especially since we were on the same bus route, albeit he was dropped at the upper-middle-class neighborhood a mile away from my apartment complex."

With the book at my side, and nothing to do with my hands, I find one gravitating to his hair. My fingers drift through his locks, lightly massaging his scalp.

"Was he your first boyfriend?" he asks.

"First and only."

His brow wrinkles. "Only?"

I nod. His eyes bore into mine, searching them for the answer to his unspoken question.

Yes, Dallas, I answer with my mind. *You're the only other man I've slept with.*

I expect him to be a little more surprised than he is. I am twenty-four after all. And single. His lack of surprise has me wondering if he too had a 'first and only.'

My heart is pounding against my chest wall at the intensity of his gaze. And the sexy smile ruffling his lips clues me in to the fact that he may be patting himself on the back right now.

"We didn't get together for years," I tell him. "In fact, we called people absurd when they said we were perfect for each other. To us, we felt like brother and sister. It wasn't until one drunken night sophomore year when we kissed on a dare. I guess we both liked it enough to take it as a sign. From then on, it was us against the world. We became inseparable. We got married the day after graduation. Even went to college together. But I dropped out when I got pregnant."

"But you still went on to be a graphic designer."

"Yeah. You don't technically need a degree for that, just a lot of experience and great references."

"So you built your own business."

"I did."

"Is it lucrative?"

I chuckle. "You saw my car, you tell me."

"But it pays the bills?"

"It pays them well enough."

He tilts his head, even as my fingers rummage through his hair, and studies me. Maybe a guy from his background has no idea how people can survive making the kind of money I do.

"Did Charles pay child support?"

"Every month. Never late. Even though we split custody, since he made considerably more than I did, he paid for most of Charlie's needs. Even more than our divorce arbiter suggested."

"Why do you think it ended between you two?"

I'm trying hard not to show my amusement at his interest in my private life. He really has changed over the past day.

I shrug. "We didn't adult well together."

"Care to elaborate?"

"As we grew older, we just didn't work as a couple. He was super intelligent, much smarter than me. He took college courses when he was a sophomore in high school. When he went to FSU, he had so many credits, he graduated in two years. By the time I was pregnant with Charlie, he'd gotten a job at a bank and was already moving up the corporate ladder. We drifted apart and separated even before Charlie was born. The fact that neither of us was that upset about it means it was the right thing to do. We're much better as friends."

My chest seizes up and my heart stills. "Or, we were." I lean back against the pillow. "Sometimes I forget he's dead." My ill-chosen words echo in my head. "Oh, gosh, I didn't mean—"

"Stop it." He puts a finger to my lips. "I said you didn't have to bite your tongue around me."

"I just… never know what to say."

"Say whatever you want. And, Marti—don't ever refer to yourself as not smart." He picks up the book. "How about you just read?"

I take it from him, find my place, and continue, never letting my left hand stray from his hair.

~ ~ ~

Dallas wakes me.

I look around to see it's still light out. "How long was I asleep?"

"A few hours." His head shakes as if he's trying to comprehend something. "I was out too. It's crazy."

"What is?"

"The past few nights. Today. I've never slept so well."

Satisfaction dances within me, and I find it hard not to smile.

He hops up. "I'm going to see if I can fix the cell tower."

My eyes widen. "You are?"

"The snow stopped." He goes to the window and gazes out. "The sky looks better. Maybe we're out of the woods… so to speak."

I pull my knees to my chest. "If you're going, I'm going with you."

"It's still cold as shit out there."

"I've walked to the car and back. The tower isn't farther than that, is it?"

"It's about a mile and a half. But why come when you could stay here in front of a warm fire?"

"Why?" I wave my hand around. "Because I'm not staying here while you risk your life. What if you fall and break your neck? What if you get lost?"

He scoffs. "One, I won't get lost. Believe me. Two, I've climbed up there a half-dozen times. Haven't we gone over this?"

"How high is it?"

"Not as high as you'd think. Some cell towers can be two-hundred feet tall. Mine's only fifty."

I huff out a breath. "*Only* fifty? Are you crazy?"

"Depends who you ask," he says with a wink.

I don't even have time to process the fact that Dallas Montana just winked at me, because all I can do is envision him falling and leaving me a heartbroken mess. Because even though Charles was my son's father and my best friend, losing Dallas would hit differently. It would pierce my heart in such a way that I'm not sure I'd recover. And once again, I'm asking myself *how* I could feel like this in just a few short days.

"Are you coming?" he asks, lacing up his boots as I stare at him from the bed.

I trade my yoga pants for jeans. I don't bother going into the bathroom to change. It's not like he hasn't seen every inch of me. When I turn back around, he's watching me pensively. Is he thinking how casual I'm becoming with him? How comfortable? And further, if he *is* thinking those things, is he okay with it?

"We'd, uh, better go." He thumbs to the door. "Come on, Bex."

On his way, he stops at the closet and pulls out a tool belt. He straps it around his waist then hoists a rope and harness over his shoulder. Thank God for that. At least he's not totally insane.

I look up at the sky along the way. It's still overcast, but much lighter than before. These clouds don't look like they'll bring any more snow. I glance over at Dallas, not sure how I feel about that.

The entire walk, I think of Charlie. I'm used to being away from him, having shared custody since his birth, so this really isn't much different, with the major distinction of him not being with his father. But I have to believe he's doing okay. It's the only way to get through this.

I still don't know how to tell Charlie about his father's death. It's what keeps me up at night. Well, that and the unknown consequences of the guy sleeping next to me.

"There it is." He points ahead to a clearing.

It's the only clearing in the woods, and I marvel at the crisp, white, pristine snow that blankets the ground. I stop and take it all in knowing this may be the only time I get to see something as awe-inspiring. For as far as my eye can see, nothing disturbs the terrain. There aren't even any animal tracks—for which I'm grateful.

My hand covers my heart. "It's beautiful."

"It is," Dallas says from behind.

But when I turn, he's not even looking out across the impressive white landscape. He's looking at *me.*

My heart stops and then restarts. Our eyes hold each other's gaze. Our feet are frozen in place. I've never wanted to be kissed more than I do in this instant. In this very place. Surrounded by this incredible scenery.

Bex barks and prances toward a distant tree, seemingly to chase a squirrel or bird. I try not to be too mad at him, he is, after all, just a dog. But the moment between Dallas and me has passed, and he slogs through the untouched snow, blazing a path for me to follow as we make our way to the tower.

The closer we get, the more anxiety I feel. The tower gets taller and taller with every step I take toward it.

When we reach the base, he puts on the harness and steps on the ladder.

"Wait!" I say, gripping his arm.

He turns. "What is it?"

"Just… don't… don't…"

Die, I say only in my head.

"I won't," he says confidently, his grin skewed.

While the smile is reassuring, especially because he doesn't often do it, I still hold my breath as he climbs, only releasing it to draw in another and hold it some more. His foot slips off a rung about twenty feet up and I scream, blood rushing in my ears.

He regains his footing and yells down, "Being a little over-dramatic, aren't we?"

"Over-dramatic?" My hands land defiantly on my hips as I shout, "You're the one who said not to worry, Mr. I've-done-this-before! So how about you don't give me a heart attack watching you fall to your death?"

Laughter spews from his lungs as he continues his climb.

"Would you fucking concentrate?" I bellow.

He shoots me an irritated look over his shoulder. I scold myself for talking. Every time I do, he looks down, putting himself in danger. I vow to remain silent and let him do what he needs to do.

Every five feet or so, he hooks a carabiner onto the side of the ladder. Though it offers me a modicum of reassurance, I question the ability of the small clips to hold his weight should he fall. Dallas is tall and sturdy. Two hundred pounds of solid muscle.

When he makes it to the top and secures himself, relief takes hold. We're halfway there.

He brushes snow off one of the panels. Some ice must remain because he pulls a tool off his belt and starts chipping away. He moves to the next panel, and then the third, doing the same thing.

"Okay, try it now!" he shouts, looking down at me from above.

"Try what now?" I ask.

"Your phone."

I hold my hands out. "I don't have it with me."

Of course I didn't bring my phone. I haven't carried it with me in days. Why would I? I guess if I'd thought more about what we were doing, I'd have brought it. But all my thoughts were centered on his safety.

"Are you fucking serious?"

"Listen, buddy!" I yell. "You didn't exactly tell me to bring it. If it was so critical, why the hell didn't you bring yours? You're the one who's done this before."

His head shakes in annoyance. He's got no place to argue. This is his show.

"We'll just have to—"

His foot slips. My heart jackhammers and my lungs hold my breath hostage as I watch in slow motion as he falls backward, arms flailing, searching for something to grip.

"Dallas!" I scream, fear blistering my stomach.

I close my eyes, because I can't watch the man I quite possibly love plummet to his death. A million things go through my head all at once. Will the snow cushion his fall? What if he breaks a leg, or worse, his back? Do I remember how to do CPR? What if I lose him before I even get a chance to *have* him?

"Hello-o?"

His loud and clearly sarcastic voice instantly relieves me and alerts me to two things: he's not dead, and he's not down.

My eyes fly open and scan the tower, my hand covering my mouth when I see him hanging upside down, his foot trapped between the ladder and the main tower structure, the rest of him dangling dangerously. "Oh my god!"

He tries in vain to pull himself up and free his foot. After a few unsuccessful minutes, his body goes limp and he looks down. "A little help?"

"Me? How can I help?"

"My foot is stuck. Really stuck. I can't turn and position myself to pull up and release it."

Dread, fear, and crippling anxiety crawl up my spine, because I absolutely know what he's going to say next.

"Marti, sweetheart, I'm sorry, but you have to climb up here and help free me."

Terror rips through me like a brick dropping through my core. My brain doesn't even register what he just called me. My only thoughts are of me, or worse, him *and* me, falling to our deaths because of my intense fear of heights.

"Do you think your wrist can handle it?" he asks.

It's not my wrist I'm worried about. "There's something you should know," I yell.

"Please, by all means, let's have a long, drawn-out, personal conversation while all the blood is rushing to my head."

"Will you shut up, Dallas Montana?"

"Fine. What should I know?"

I swallow. "I'm insanely scared of heights."

"Breathe, Marti. Because I'm afraid you coming up here is the only way I'm getting out of this."

I have no harness. No rope. No safety net should I fall. Bex seems to understand this, because when I take the first step onto the bottom rung, he prances over and barks.

"I'll be okay, buddy. I think. But if something happens and we fall, or if I don't come down, promise me you'll run and get help like you did when I fell through the ice."

He nudges my calf. I'll take that as a promise.

When I can't get a good grip on the rung, I realize my gloves have to go. My hands might just freeze before I get to the top, but if I wear the gloves, I'll slip for sure. I tuck them into my pocket, take a few deep breaths, and start climbing.

"You're doing great," I hear from above. "Just don't look down."

"Thanks, Captain Obvious, for reminding me what I'm terrifyingly afraid of."

I hear him laugh, which is ridiculous considering the situation.

"Almost here. You're amazing, Marti."

His voice is closer now. He isn't yelling anymore. I keep my eyes trained on only the rung in front of me, fearful that if I look up or down, I'll freak out and fall.

"Four more. Keep going. Three. Two. Okay, reach up with your right hand."

"I can't." I tighten my death grip on the ladder.

"Marti, I need you to do this."

I still don't look up, but I reach up like he asked. When I do, he shoves a length of rope into my hand.

"Tie this around your waist."

I close my eyes, gripping the ladder with all my might. "And how exactly do you suggest I do that?"

"Wrap your elbow around the ladder to secure yourself. That will free up your hand to tie the rope."

"Oh my god, this is not happening."

As I say the words, it's like déjà vu, because I swear I've said or thought the very same thing at least a dozen times this week.

It takes three tries, and I drop the rope repeatedly. Thankfully, *he* never lets go of it, and I keep at it until I've got it secured. But I'm no expert. I have no idea if the knot I tied is good enough or tight enough to hold me should I fall. I've no choice but to believe it will.

"Amazing," he says reassuringly. "Now climb up a few more rungs. I'll be on your left."

I do what he asks, my mouth bone dry and my stomach churning at the thought of what happens if I don't succeed.

"Okay, great. Now look at me."

I shake my head, acid eating my insides.

"Marti, I'm right here. Look at me."

When I open my eyes, he's on my left. He's upside down. His face is bright red, but his lips dance with a crooked smile.

He reaches out and grips my arm. "I guess we'll be even after this."

"No we won't be. You'll still be one up on me. And I'd like to keep it that way if you don't mind."

He chuckles. "Okay. You can do this. My foot is wedged pretty tightly. The problem is I can't lift myself up to free it. I need you to get directly under me so I can use your body as leverage. You're going to have to hold on tight, with everything you have. Most of my weight will be on you."

"What if I—"

"Look at me. Sweetheart, you can do this. *We* can do this. Together."

He gives me clear instructions about where to anchor my hands and feet, wedging myself into a hunched position so he can push himself up using my back.

"Okay. I'm ready."

Before he puts any weight on me, he reaches out and secures my knot, making sure it's not going to give should either of us fall.

"Hold on. I'll try to do this as quickly and safely as I can."

"Do it, Dallas."

He grunts as he uses his ab muscles to lift his body as far as he can until his back is resting on my back. He's heavy. My arms shake and burn as I hold on as tightly as I can.

"Almost there," he says.

My foot slips and I scream. I regain my footing, tears streaming down my face. "I'm okay."

"Jesus," he says, his voice laced with fear.

"Go. I'm good."

Putting even more of his weight on me, I try to keep myself from being pushed down. I gather up all my strength and hold myself steady, ignoring the intense pain of my arms practically ripping from their sockets.

Suddenly, his weight is gone. Just as I start to panic, he says, "I'm free."

The breath I take is what it must feel like when a baby is born and they get their first lungful of air.

More tears streak my face, this time from relief.

"Hold tight," he says. "I'm going to climb around you."

I keep my eyes closed, feeling his body work around mine.

"Okay, I'm right behind you. We're going down together."

"I hope you mean on the ladder."

He presses into me and whispers close to my ear, "It's nice to know you haven't lost your sarcastic wit."

"It's nice to know you haven't stopped eating your Wheaties. What do you weigh, three hundred pounds?"

Laughter bellows out of him. "One-ninety. But that still makes you a hero in my book. Now, come on. Let's get you to solid ground."

We climb down slowly, him staying behind me, caging me against the ladder with his body. I'm terrified, but at the same time, I've never felt so secure.

"Ten more feet," he says. "Almost there."

I feel myself start to fall apart with relief.

When his body moves away and he's no longer surrounding me, I know we've reached the ground. As I go to step off the last rung, my head swirls in circles, my ears ring, and finally, I fall. I fall right into blackness.

Chapter Twenty-five

Dallas

I catch her and fall to the ground, bundling her in my arms, still in awe of what we just accomplished. What *she* accomplished.

Throwing my right glove off, I touch her cheek. It's cold and wet with tears. Hair sticking out from under her wool cap is stuck to the side of her face. I swipe it away then rub my thumb across her lips.

"Marti?"

Her eyes flutter open as if waking from a dream.

"You're okay," I say "We did it. *You* did it."

She blinks repeatedly, looking around. "What happened?"

Bex wags his tail and licks her face. He must like the salty taste of her tears. I push him back. "Easy, boy. Give her some room." Marti makes no attempt to extricate herself from my arms, and I'm not in a hurry for her to leave them. "You fainted. My guess is, you had a ton of adrenaline going through you, but once we reached the ground, you let it go and succumbed to the fear."

Her lips press together, and she cranes her neck to look at the tower. "What if that had happened up there?"

"It didn't. You did exactly what you needed to." I lean down. "Thanks for that," I say, right before I kiss her.

Her lips are salty and sweet, but before I can really enjoy them, she surprises me by pushing away.

"What in the hell were you thinking?" Her eyes flood with tears. "What if you were alone out here?" She hits my chest over and over. "You can't take risks like that. Dallas, oh my god, if you'd gotten stuck up there." She hits me a few more times, then fists my coat, draws near and sobs into me.

I wrap my arms tightly around her and let her emotions play out. It's only now that it sinks in what a colossal risk she took climbing the tower without any safety gear.

"I'm so sorry," I say quietly and close to her ear. "I shouldn't have made you do that. It was an idiotic idea. I should have told you to go back to my place and call for help."

She looks up at me with red-rimmed eyes. "And leave you hanging upside down? You'd have passed out, or worse. Your face was already red. What if no one could get here? Or what if the cell signal still wasn't working? What then? I *had* to do it." She glances up again. I do too. The tower looks extra tall when you're sitting at the base of it. "Holy shit, I can't believe I did that."

"You're a badass, Martina Carver." I narrow my eyes. "What's your middle name?"

She hesitates, almost uneasily. "Why?"

I shrug. "I just thought the badass statement deserved the addition of a middle name."

"It's Alexandra," she says with an almost imperceptible hitch.

"No shit?"

"Yeah, why?"

"Alexandra is my sister's name. We call her Allie."

"You have a sister?" She squints at me.

I guess I haven't exactly been an open book of information. "And two brothers."

"Older? Younger?"

"Lucas is the oldest. I was next. Then Allie. Blake is the baby. He's the one with the deaf wife and daughter."

"Dallas?"

"What?"

"How old are you?"

"Twenty-eight."

"Dallas?"

"Hmm?"

For a moment, based on all the other information I've divulged, I think she's going to ask me about Phoebe. I've told her a little about DJ. But she doesn't even know Phoebe's name. Do I *want* to tell her? It's only natural for her to be curious about my wife. And though I could swear it hangs in the air between us, the question never comes.

She holds up a hand. "I can't feel my fingers. Can we go home?"

Home. She called my cabin home.

I know she didn't mean it like it came out, but for a fraction of a second, I want it to be true. But only a fraction of a second, because like every other thought I have about Martina Alexandra Carver, it gets overshadowed by memories that creep in and devour any pleasant feelings.

Getting to my feet first, I offer her my hand to help her up. Damn. She's right, she is cold. Her fingers are pale. "Where are your gloves?"

She unzips a pocket and gets them out. "I couldn't climb the ladder with them on."

I look at my own super-durable work gloves with grip and feel horrible all over again. She climbed the tower unassisted, nearly got frostbite in the process, and she fucking saved me. All through what must have been crippling fear.

"Good thinking. Let's go. I'll make you a gallon of hot chocolate when we get back."

She smirks. "After what we just did, I think I'm going to need something a little stronger than hot chocolate."

I laugh and turn to Bex, patting my thigh. "Come on, boy. Let's go home."

~ ~ ~

Luckily, the cabin isn't freezing when we return. But the fire has burned down to almost nothing. Still, the place is small enough that even embers radiate warmth.

Marti looks like a popsicle. I move a chair in front of the fire, pile more wood in, and wrap her in blankets. Then I put a pot of water on.

I check my phone. Three bars. Good enough. I find where she left hers and hand it to her. "Do you want me to leave when you make calls? I can step outside."

"I think we've both been outside enough for today. It's fine. I need to check in with Asher and Anita."

"While you do that, I'll try Luther again and see if I can get a weather update."

"Do you think"—her eyes meet the floor—"they'll be able to get someone up here soon?"

"That's the hope," I say, unsure if I really mean it.

By the look on her face, it may not be the answer she wanted. And that both excites and scares me.

She calls her brother first. I try not to eavesdrop, but in this small space, it's hard not to listen. She has to calm him down and assure him she's okay. I completely understand. If Allie ever went off the grid like Marti did, I'd go ballistic along with the rest of my family.

It sounds like she also talks to her niece, but not for long. She tells her she has to call Anita and Charlie. Then, I watch her closely as she stares at her phone, hesitating before she dials. Because I'm here listening? Or because she doesn't know what she's going to say?

"I'm good. I'm good," she says. "We lost phone service and power. But everything is fine. I'm still not sure when the roads will be clear enough for me to get out of here, but Asher said the airports are up and running again so he's going to catch a flight."

She listens for a while. I wish I could see her face. But I'm imposing too much already by listening to her private conversation.

"Oh, Anita. I'm so sorry you had to do that. I wish I could have been there with you. But I understand why you had to tell Charlie. Do you think…" She glances back at me. I rummage through a cabinet, trying to pretend like I'm not listening. "Do you think he knows he's gone? Like forever gone?"

Her words hit me square in the chest. She's talking about her son. And his dead father.

"Okay, put him on the phone." She blows out a deep sigh. "Hey, buddy… Yes, it's me… I miss you too." Her shoulders slump. "Yes, Charlie. I know about Daddy. I'm so so sorry. You know he loved you and didn't leave you on purpose… Oh, buddy, no, he isn't coming back… No, he's not in Florida." She sniffs and I can tell she's holding back tears. "I'll be there as soon as I can. Have you played in the snow?... A snowman? I made one too. I called him Abe. What did you name yours?" She laughs. "That's a perfect snowman name. I can't wait to see Frosty… Yes, buddy, I'll make snowballs with you. I promise… Yes, Grumpy is with me. I'll bring him too. I love you, Charlie, and I'll see you soon. Hopefully it'll only be a few more sleeps… Yes, put Anita back on the phone now." She makes kissing noises, then talks to Anita again.

They discuss plans for a funeral, or not a funeral, something else. That's when I tap out and go outside, finding it all too close to home for me to deal with. I take the coolers with me and refill them with snow.

Still not ready to go back in, I call Luther, the tow truck driver.

"Mr. Montana, how're things lookin' up there?"

"Cold. I ran out of propane two days ago."

"Damn. Good thing you got plenty of wood."

"Good thing. So where are we at this point?"

"They're working on Route 13. It's bad, man. Two families got trapped in their cars. One old lady expired before they could get to them."

I think of Abe, still sitting in his cabin. "I'm sorry to hear that. Do you have any idea when the snowplows will get out this way?"

"Depends on the weather. It looks promising. They say there's less chance for snow over the next few days. But I'm not gonna lie, there's a lot to be cleared before they get to your road. We've only got one plow working all of Tug Hill. *One*. Everything else has been commandeered to work the more populated areas."

"Best guess?"

"If everything goes as planned, and there's no more snow, I'd say four days."

"Four?" I blurt, surprised.

"They say this is worse than the blizzard of '78. But I reckon you weren't even alive back then to remember."

"No. No I wasn't. Hey, you have my number. Please keep me updated if things change."

"You got it. You ain't runnin' out of food, are you?"

"No."

"And the lady? She okay?"

"Yes."

"Good. I'll keep in touch. Don't know what else I can do from here, but let me know if you need anything."

"Will do. Thanks, Luther."

I call the local police and tell them about Abe. They pretty much tell me what I told Marti, that it isn't a priority, but I'd done right to move him inside and keep him cold.

I spend the next few minutes answering texts from family, assuring them I'm alive and okay. I crack the front door and listen. When I don't hear Marti's voice, I step back in, coolers in tow.

She cranes her head around when she hears me enter. "I think I'll take that drink now."

I scoop a large helping of dog food into Bex's food bowl then nod to the water warming on the stove. "Coffee? Hot Chocolate? Or…"

"Wine. Lots and lots of it."

I open a bottle and pour her a glass, then pour one for myself. Setting another chair next to hers, I sit down and pull her feet up onto my lap, keeping them off the cold floor.

She shakes her head over and over, clearly tormented.

"Your boy must be pretty torn up," I say.

"No. I mean, yes, of course he's sad. But I'm not sure he understands the finality of it. That's not why I'm so upset." She shoves her phone at me. "Look. I googled it. Did you know that a person can only survive hanging upside down for a few hours? *Hours*, Dallas. You would have been dead if I hadn't been there. And you would have died had you sent me back here to call for help."

I take a drink, then set down my glass, rubbing her feet through her thick socks. "Well, it's a good thing neither of those things happened."

Concern pinches her forehead. "You need people, Dallas."

"People?" I ask, watching Bex circle around the base of the fireplace, finding a spot to sleep after his meal.

"Yes. People. You know, friends or family you can count on if you ever say… find yourself hanging upside down from a cell tower."

"Do *you* have people?"

"I do. I have"—she closes her eyes—"*had* Charles. I have Asher. I have Bug. Who do you have all the way out here in the middle of nowhere? Don't try to sit here and tell me you have your siblings or your parents. They aren't here. Who's going to help you the next time you climb the tower? You don't have anyone."

I squeeze her toes. "I have you."

She tilts her head, her gaze homing in on me. *"Do you?"*

I swallow. I shouldn't have said the words. It's too much too soon. I try to brush it off. "You want to know the truth? That wasn't even the most precarious place I've ever found myself. Once, Blake and I got trapped upside down on a roller coaster. It took a long time for them to rescue us." I nod to her phone. "I guess now I know why they sent about a dozen fire trucks. I had no idea you couldn't hang upside down for that long."

She eyes me strangely. She knows I'm dodging her question. But she doesn't push. She sips her wine, watching over the rim of her glass as my hands massage her feet.

"I can't seem to get warm," she says, tugging the blanket around her.

"Same."

"What do you suggest we do?"

My eyes dart to the bed. "What do *you* suggest we do?"

The intense depth of her gaze lets me know we're on the same page. I take the glass from her, put it on the ground, then gather her in my arms and carry her over. Laying her on the bed, trying hard to keep the blanket around her, I peel off her clothes. Then I undress and climb in next to her. "Thanks for saving my ass today."

She smiles playfully as her fingers wrap around my lengthening cock. "It wasn't just your ass I was saving."

We make love for hours. My total loss of control around her is as unexpected as it is unbelievable. We work up a sweat until neither of us are the least bit cold. I give her four orgasms. She graces me with three.

Eventually, completely satiated and worn out, neither of us having the energy to cook dinner, we lay side by side, our fingers entwined.

"I have an important question," I say. "One that's been burning inside me all afternoon."

She looks worried. Or excited. Or maybe intrigued is the better word. Sometimes I can't read her at all. Other times it's as if we're connected telepathically.

"What's the question?"

"Who's Grumpy?"

She cocks her head.

"Earlier on the phone, when you were talking with Charlie, you said Grumpy was with you. I thought it was possible you were talking about me."

She giggles. "I could have been. You *are* pretty prickly at times. But no, Grumpy is his favorite stuffed animal."

"That makes a lot more sense."

A part of me wonders if Charlie will ever know about me. Or if *anyone* will. About the week she spent in the wilderness with someone who went from complete stranger to lover to…

I close my eyes and shut off my brain, unable to finish the thought.

She picks up on my unease, leans over me, and grabs our book from the nightstand. "Want me to read a bit?"

"That would be great."

I lay my head in her lap hoping she'll massage it like before. She does. Her small fingers work through my hair, running rhythmically over my scalp, my temples, my neck. Instantly I relax as I listen to the soothing cadence of her voice and enjoy her gentle touch.

I'm fading fast, my eyelids heavy. Before I go to sleep, there's one thing I feel the need to say. "Marti?"

She stops reading and rests her eyes on me. "Mmm?"

"Phoebe. Her name was Phoebe."

She smiles sadly, nods, then picks up the book and begins again.

Chapter Twenty-six

Martina

I wake before Dallas. Again, he looks to be sleeping peacefully. It makes me happy to think I have something to do with it. But at the same time, I'm gutted that he's been battling demons for years.

Was last night a turning point? He told me her name. He told me even though I didn't ask.

I have the sudden urge to know everything about him. I eye my phone on the nightstand. I'd bet my right arm there is information on the internet. About him. His family. His childhood. Maybe even about how Phoebe and DJ died.

The temptation to google all things Dallas Montana fades when his eyes open, he sees me watching him, and he grins. No—the only way I want to learn about Dallas is from the man himself.

He runs a hand down my arm, sending shivers throughout my body.

I turn on my side, prop up on my elbow and say, "Tell me some weird random fact about yourself."

"Okaaaaaaay. Let's see…" His lips shuffle from side to side. "I played the saxophone in middle school."

"Just middle school?"

"Gave it up right before ninth grade when I thought it was uncool." He touches my hand. "Now you."

"That's easy. I used to eat my hair."

He blinks. "What?"

"It's called trichophagia. They think it was due to stress from my dad's death. Nobody knew about it until I felt constantly nauseous and Asher took me to the doctor. They found a sixteen-millimeter hairball in my stomach. Had to put a scope down my throat to get it out. If it had been much bigger, it would have required surgery. Your turn."

"I ate grass."

I turn up my nose. "From the ground?"

"I guess. I don't really remember, but my parents told me about it."

"I didn't wear underwear until I was thirteen."

His brows creep toward his hairline. "Uh… why exactly?"

"I'm not completely sure. Asher theorized it was because my dad was late to potty train me. My mom had trained Asher. I guess my dad just didn't know how to do it. I think I was five before I was completely out of diapers. And then… I guess I just didn't want *anything* down there." I laugh. "My poor dad. He was a wreck every time I wore a dress. He didn't want to tell me no, but he was terrified I'd flash my bits."

"So, why thirteen?" he asks.

"Necessity." I say no more, and he eventually gets it.

"I did a lot of things that drove my mom crazy. I cracked my knuckles constantly. And I would suck on my shirts in school. I didn't even know I was doing it. I ruined all my collars."

Instantly, Charlie is in my thoughts. "I actually know someone who sucks on his shirts. And it *is* annoying."

"Charlie?"

I nod.

"I'm sure my mom could give you tips on how to stop it."

For a second, my heart flutters. Is that some sort of invitation?

"I, uh," —he stutters nervously— "also used to eat butter. Sticks of it. Plain butter."

Okay, so not an invitation. "I ate pizza crust."

"What's so weird about that?" he asks.

"Because I only ate the crust, not the rest of the pizza."

"Jesus, you really *are* a freak."

"Oh, you have no idea."

"I have *some* idea. I mean you do talk in your sleep."

A blush ambushes my chest as I wonder what I could have said. "Really?"

His eyes dance with a smile. "Okay, that was a lie." He scoots closer. "More."

I try not to read too much into the fact that he's enjoying this game. He likes learning about me as much as I do him. That has to mean something.

"None of the food on my plate could touch or I wouldn't eat it."

His head bobs sideways. "You are aware it touches as soon as it's in your stomach, right?"

"You're asking this as if a girl who ate her hair was normal."

"Right." He chuckles. "I would put ketchup on everything. Even cereal. And when my mother made tacos, I'd deconstruct them, eating the shells first and then the contents."

I cringe. "Ketchup on cereal. You've totally crossed the line. I'm not sure we can be friends." I pretend I'm going to get out of bed.

He pulls me back, pushes me into the mattress, and climbs on top of me. He takes a chunk of my hair and works it between his fingers. "I'm glad you don't eat your hair anymore. It would be a shame. You have such nice hair."

I reach up and run my fingers through his. "Have you always had long hair?"

His eyes go dark. "Not always."

Damn. I inadvertently brought up something touchy. He moves to get off me, but I grip his shoulders. "Kiss me. Kiss me right now. Kiss me everywhere, Dallas."

My demand surprises me. I've never been one to be sexually forward. But the words just came out. I didn't want to lose the connection we were having.

"Challenge accepted," he says as his erection grows between us.

Then, as his tongue travels every inch of my body, going way above and beyond my highest expectations, I shoo Bex away when he whines at the edge of the bed, and get lost in this amazing shirt-sucking, ketchup-eating, knuckle-cracking man.

Chapter Twenty-seven

Dallas

We've barely left the bed for twenty-four hours. When we get hungry, we bring food to bed. If Bex needs to go outside, we let him out quickly with a promise to play later.

There are three empty bottles of wine, multiple food wrappers and dishes, and a pile of books sitting on the nightstand.

Every muscle in my body is sore. It doesn't matter that I spend hours a day hiking or chopping wood, apparently those aren't the same muscles one uses for marathon sex.

I lost track after the fifth time. I chuckle softly when I think we should have kept count.

"What's so funny?" she asks with a yawn.

Marti's head lies on my chest where she's been, unmoving, for the last hour. I wasn't even aware she was awake.

"I was just wondering if we should have kept a tally. Because maybe Guinness has a category for that."

She giggles and tickles my ribs. "We'd win that world record for sure. But I'm pretty sure in order for it to be official, there have to be witnesses."

Now we're both laughing.

She maneuvers off me and lays her head on her pillow.

Her pillow, I think momentarily. Somehow, over the past week, there is a pillow that's come to be hers. She has a side of the bed. Even a designated chair at the table.

We lie facing each other.

"It was for sure my PR," she says. She stretches her neck. "And I swear to God I used muscles I didn't even know I had."

"Me too," I say, reaching up to rub one of her shoulders. "So, personal record, huh?"

She nods. "Charles and I were a one-and-done kind of couple. Even when we were teens."

"So he's the only one you…"

"Yeah."

"Mmmm." I close my eyes briefly. "Same for me."

She doesn't look surprised. It's as if she already suspected. We look at each other, probably thinking the same thing. We both married our high school sweethearts. Our first loves. Our best friends. Our only lovers. And now they're both gone.

I ask the question that's been bouncing around in my head since yesterday. "Marti, how come you didn't ask me about the tow truck the other day?"

She averts her gaze, staring at the ceiling through a deep sigh. Then she looks back, tucking her hand beneath her head, under her pillow. Her eyes capture mine. "How come you didn't tell me?"

We stare at each other. Hell, we stare *into* each other. I'm not sure either of us needs to verbalize an answer. We both know why.

I take a chunk of her hair and rub it between my fingers. "He said it would probably be four days. Well, two now."

"Two days," she repeats, glumly.

When she says the words, and I see the emotions on her face, I swear a countdown clock appears in my head. Two days. Two more days with her. It seems surreal at this point, only a week after I found her wrecked car in a ditch, that on that first day, I couldn't wait to get her out of my cabin. But now… now I believe that when she leaves, the cabin will feel empty.

And I fear the cabin isn't the only thing that'll feel that way.

Bex jumps up on the bed and worms his way between us. He licks my hand over and over. I can hardly blame him. Based on where my hand has spent most of the last day, it must taste damn good. "Okay, okay, I get the hint." I sit up and pull on my sweatpants. "I'm going to take a quick shower and then take him outside for some exercise. Can I make you some coffee?"

Marti's arms stretch above her head then she pulls the covers tightly around her. "Coffee would be amazing."

I put the water on and let it boil while I take a shower, washing off the distinct smell of sex that now permeates every pore of my skin. I brush my teeth, the whole time looking at Marti's toothbrush wondering just how I'll feel a few days from now when it's no longer here. But then I look in the mirror, aided only by the light filtering through the window. Looking at my reflection is not something I do often, because every time I do, I see DJ. He had my eyes. My nose. The shape of my chin. I see what he might have looked like had he grown up. And I see the empty space next to me. The space that should be occupied by Phoebe.

Guilt courses through me at the idea that she might know everything about what I've been doing. My actions. My thoughts. Is she somehow watching me, feeling betrayed at how easily I jumped into bed with Marti?

Fuck.

I sit on the closed toilet waiting for the feeling to pass.

It doesn't.

After staying in the bathroom far longer than necessary, I go out, get properly dressed, then pour hot water into a mug, mixing it with my emergency stash of instant coffee.

When I hand it to Marti, she looks at me inquisitively. "Everything okay?"

"Yes," I lie and gesture to Bex. "I just really need to get this guy outside."

"You know where I'll be." She chuckles, sinking deeper into the covers. "I suppose I'll get up and shower eventually, but right now, the thought of it is even more unappealing than staying all sticky."

"Alright then. I'll see you later."

She tilts her head, staring at me oddly. I turn and call to Bex as he excitedly races to the door.

~ ~ ~

Three hours later and half frozen, I go back inside, having let the dog in long ago. Bex is sleeping in front of the fire, and Marti is still in bed working on her laptop.

She shuts the lid quickly.

I lift an amused brow. "Don't tell me you were watching porn."

She guffaws. "Of course not."

"It's okay if you were."

She rolls her eyes. "I do not watch porn, Dallas. Do you?"

I shrug. "It's been a while." I take my coat off and warm my hands by the fire. "So why the secrecy then? You slammed that thing shut so fast I'm surprised you didn't break it."

"I was… just trying to get a little work done."

I narrow my eyes at her. "You're lying."

Her arms fold across her body defensively. "I am not."

"You want to know how I know you're lying?" I stride over and pull her lower lip from her teeth. "You bite your lip when you lie. You also bite it when you're shy. And horny. But after the last twenty-four hours, I doubt you're either of those. So, tell me, Martina Alexandra Carver, what exactly is it you don't want me to see? Because I'm not moving until you tell me."

I try to push away the guilt that niggles at the edge of my consciousness. Half of my time outside was spent convincing myself I was going to keep my distance. Put up a wall between us. Put a stop to… whatever seems to be happening here. But the moment I walked back in and saw her, my resolve instantly began crumbling.

And now she has a secret. Something she doesn't want me to see. It's not a bad secret, based on the look on her face. But maybe an embarrassing one. If curiosity killed the cat, I'm as dead as a feline surrounded by a pack of wild dogs.

I sit on the edge of the bed, knee up on the mattress, facing her. "Come on, show me. How bad could it be?"

An eruption of pink crosses her cheeks. "Okay, but please understand I was just fooling around. It's not anything serious."

She opens her laptop, types in the passcode, shifts the screen so I can see it, and closes her eyes.

My jaw hits the mattress as my brain wraps around what I'm seeing. The screen is split. On the right is our website: Montana Winery. On the left is a bunch of graphics I've never seen before.

Graphics that include the business name, wine labels, logos, and all kinds of other branding stuff.

I'm completely dumbfounded. "How long was I out there?"

Her eyes open. "I told you, I was just messing around. I was bored and didn't feel like doing any real work."

I point to the logo. "Can you zoom in on that?"

She clicks and the large logo fills the screen. It's similar to our current one, only crisper, more vibrant. And a hell of a lot more interesting. It's hard to even put my finger on what's different. The texture? The depth of the background? The subtle difference in shading and color?

"Holy shit. This is amazing, Marti."

She draws in a breath, then releases it. "You really think so?"

"Yes, I do. You're super talented. You should show these to Lucas. He runs our marketing. He'd go nuts over these."

Her quiet laughter sprinkles the air. "Dallas, I was just playing around. I'm not going to show anyone anything."

"I'm just saying you should. He'd flip. We've had the same old tired branding for years."

"Branding is how you're recognized. You don't want to go changing it."

"We wouldn't be. Not really. See what you've done here? It's the same but different. Better. A lot better."

At the compliment, another shot of color splashes across her face. She closes the laptop.

I touch the lid. "I want those. All of them. What's your usual price?"

Her eyebrows melt together. "I'm not going to sell them to you. I didn't even do that much. You can have them."

"That's bullshit, Marti. Don't ever underestimate or devalue yourself like that. You've got genuine skill." I carefully fish my wallet out of the nightstand, making sure my fingers don't touch anything they shouldn't. Then I hand her my business card. "Email them to me. Please. I'll show them to Lucas and if he wants to use them, we'll pay you fairly and generously."

She takes my card and tucks it inside her laptop. "Whatever. You don't have to patronize me." She gives me a hard stare. "And if by some miracle, he does want them, you'll pay my normal fee and nothing more, or else I'll know the graphics aren't really what I'm being paid for."

Guilt is back in full force. But for a very different reason. I don't like what she's insinuating. I don't like it one goddamn bit. But I bite my tongue.

The air between us is filled with awkwardness.

She wraps the spare blanket around her shoulders. "I need to shower. Desperately. I'm just having a hard time convincing myself to get out of this cocoon and go become an icicle. What I wouldn't do for a warm bath."

I glance over at the hot water on the stove and get an idea. "Give me a half hour."

"What for?"

"I'm going to draw you that warm bath."

Chapter Twenty-eight

Martina

He gets out two massive pots, fills them with water, sets them on the stove, then disappears into the bathroom where I hear him filling the tub.

It's hard not to smile knowing what a kind, chivalrous deed he's doing.

When he comes back into the room after adding the two boiling pots of water to what must have been a dauntingly cold tub, I start to get up.

"Not yet," he says, refilling the pots at the kitchen sink. "It's going to take at least two more rounds."

"I'm sure it's fine now, Dallas. You really don't need to go through all the trouble."

"Stay." He points a finger at me. "Go big or go home, right?"

I settle back on my pillow. "Whatever you say."

A little while later, he emerges with a smile. "It's ready now. And I don't mind saying I'm a little jealous. It's a shame my tub isn't big enough for two." He sees I'm ready to put up an argument. "Shhh. Not a word. It's all for you swe—uh, Marti."

He was going to call me sweetheart. Just like he did up on the tower. Only this time, he caught himself. I try not to read too much into it, pretending I didn't notice as I toss off the covers. "You have no idea how excited I am."

On the way to the bathroom, I shed the clothes I put on when he was outside, leaving a trail of sleep pants, his Yale hoodie, a T-shirt, my socks and, lastly, my undies. At the bathroom door, I turn to see if he was watching. He most definitely was. I pop my right foot up behind me before stepping through the door.

I leave it open, hoping maybe he'll join me after all, but when I study the tub, I know he's right. No way will it fit both of us. Two small people, maybe. But not someone as tall and broad as he is.

When I step in with one foot, my eyes roll to the back of my head. It's warmer than I expected. There's even steam rising from the water. I sink down into it, reveling in the feeling as every inch of my skin touches the water. It's pure heaven.

I waste no time grabbing his loofah and squirting body wash on it. I meticulously wash every part of my body, knowing this is the cleanest I've been in a week. When I wash between my legs, I realize how raw I am. Flashbacks of the last day bombard me. The way his stubble felt between my thighs. How his fingers worked inside me. And his tongue… oh, Lord, his amazingly skilled tongue. I'd be surprised if he didn't sprain it with how many times he used it to make me come.

My eyes open to catch him leaning against the doorway, watching. He's changed out of his jeans and into sweatpants, making his erection clearly visible to anyone looking. And, yes, I'm looking. But I hold a hand up in a 'stop' motion. "No way, buddy. This coochie needs a minute to recover."

He laughs heartily. It's an easy laugh. A carefree laugh. One I've never heard before but warms my heart even more than the water does.

"How about a glass of wine?" he asks.

"That would be heavenly."

He disappears for far longer than it would take to get a glass of wine. When he returns, he has a glass in one hand, and one of the large pots—the one with a carry handle on top—in the other. He hands me the glass and sets the pot near the tub. "I thought we could use this to rinse out your hair."

"We?" I raise an eyebrow.

He kneels on the rug next to the tub, squirts shampoo into his hands, and washes my hair.

I've had many people wash my hair before. Hairdressers. Not hot burly men who chop wood, climb towers, and rescue women. And definitely not hot burly men who have given me countless orgasms.

I practically have another as he gently works his hands through my hair and massages my scalp. I even groan in pleasure once or twice. I never want it to end. But the water turns tepid and I know my time in here is short.

His hands disappear.

I miss them more than I can say. My eyes close knowing it's just a precursor of things to come.

"Look up," he says, picking up the bucket. "And keep your eyes closed. I've never done this before."

His statement makes butterflies dance in my stomach. Am I the first woman to have her hair washed by him? Or perhaps just the first to have water dumped on her head. Either way, it's comforting to know that maybe, just maybe, when I'm gone, he'll think of this… think of *me*… without the memory being clouded by her.

Before any other thoughts of *when I'm gone* can ruin this moment, warm water splashes against my forehead, cascading down my back as it flushes out the shampoo. I moan at the feeling. My mouth relaxes open and I murmur, "Oh, god."

"Will you stop doing that?" he says, placing the bucket on the floor before squeezing excess water from my hair.

"Doing what?"

"Making sex noises."

My lips smash together in a thin line, holding in my laughter. I peek at his crotch, which is in almost perfect alignment with my head, and my eyes widen at the massive bulge. "Put that thing away, mister. I told you, I'm temporarily closed for business."

"Temporarily." He ponders the word. "So, just, you know, ballpark, when might we expect your, um… *doors* to be open again?"

Just to add fire to the flames, I reach down and put a hand between my thighs as if I'm checking for soreness. I'm not. I'm teasing him. And it's working exactly as intended. His eyes lock onto my hand as I move a finger between my folds.

"Jesus," he whispers.

Without warning, his hands go under my armpits, and I'm being hauled out of the tub. He wraps me in a fluffy towel, puts another one in my hands, presumably for my hair, and then he pushes me toward the door.

"I need the room," he says once I'm through. Then the door closes, leaving me dripping wet and confused.

Making my way to the fireplace, it dawns on me why he *needs the room.*

Tingles shoot through my body when I think of what he's doing behind the door. Wetness, that's not from bath water, coats the area between my legs. I sit on the edge of the bed, unable to keep my fingers from wandering beneath the towel.

I draw the wetness up to my clit, careful to avoid any kind of insertion or friction against my raw parts. My clit, however, seems perfectly fine. I run circles on it as my mind paints a picture of Dallas gripping his cock and bringing himself to orgasm, making himself come to thoughts of me.

Is he standing, one hand braced against the wall as the other pumps his rigid length? Or is he sitting down, neck extended, eyes closed, face toward the ceiling as he thrusts into his palm over and over?

When I hear a muffled grunt, I come instantly, as if we're connected somehow even though we're separated by twenty feet and a large wooden door.

I lie back on the bed—that totally smells of sex—and listen as the tub drains and the shower starts.

The chill of the room starts getting to me, so I dry off, wrap my head in a towel, and get dressed.

Cringing at the smell of the bed, I strip the sheets off and wash them in the kitchen sink. Then I string my laundry line across the room and hang them to dry.

Dallas runs right into one when he emerges from the bathroom. "What the heck?"

I peek out from behind a sheet, drying my hair by the fire. "Had to wash the sheets. It smelled like a brothel in here."

"Guess we gave them a bit of a workout, huh?"

"We got a bit of a workout ourselves." I bite my lower lip for emphasis. "Then *and* now."

He narrows his eyes.

"While you were—you know—*in there*. I was—you know—*out here*."

His shocked expression almost makes me laugh. "I thought your coochie was broken."

"What I did had nothing to do with my coochie and everything to do with a little area north of there that may or may not rhyme with Delores."

He runs a hand through his long, wet hair. "Woman, you're going to fucking kill me."

Chapter Twenty-nine

Martina

I sit on the couch with my laptop, Bex at my feet, and try to get some work done. But it's hard. Especially because I can't take my eyes off Dallas. He's working too. And I've never seen this side of him. He paces around, talking to whoever is on the other end of the phone, stopping to jot down an occasional note. He sounds so professional talking about financial reports, forecasts, and a new tax law that could affect the winery.

He's all businesslike, and so different from the reclusive mountain man I've come to know. I can almost picture him sitting behind a desk wearing khakis and a button down.

My flesh comes alive with goosebumps as I imagine him making love to me in an office. I fantasize about him sweeping everything from his desktop, hoisting me up onto the edge, and burying his face in the valley between my thighs.

Dallas's amused eyes swing my way, his lips twitching with a smile as he continues his call.

Was I gaping at him?

I close the lid of my laptop, work being a futile effort at this point, and I make my way to the coolers in search of something to make for lunch.

When he's done with his call, I light a few candles and take plates to the table, then we sit side-by-side to eat the last of the Thanksgiving food.

When he gets up to fetch a bottle of wine, I dish a heaping spoonful of potatoes onto his plate. "Tomorrow is December. Can you believe it? Where did the time go? I haven't even started buying gifts."

"Mmm," he grumbles, pouring us each a glass.

I want to ask if he even celebrates Christmas anymore. But I don't. He doesn't need me bringing up painful memories. He had one single Christmas with DJ. *One.* He would have been four weeks old at the time. Dallas was probably dreaming of the next year when his son would be toddling around, tearing into his new toys, smiling, laughing, calling him Daddy.

My heart hurts so much for him it overshadows my own painful memories.

Dallas sips his wine. "There's something I've been wanting to ask."

My heart flutters. Is he going to ask me to stay? To be his girlfriend? To have some sort of long-distance friends-with-benefits thing?

Staying isn't an option. No matter how much I'd like to hide out here forever and live this surreal life with my mountain man, Charlie is my number one priority. Being Dallas's girlfriend would be nice, but there are so many logistics we'd have to work out. And would I even *want* a no-strings, see-you-when-I-see-you relationship?

"Marti?"

I shake away the thoughts. "What? Oh, yeah, ask away."

"How come you didn't fly to New York?"

Letting out the breath I was holding, I'm not sure if I'm sad or relieved he didn't make one of the aforementioned propositions. "Because I don't fly."

"Ever?"

"I flew once. I won't again."

"What happened?"

I take a long drink of wine to tamp down the anxiety that grips me as I think of it. "Six years ago, Charles and I went to the Bahamas for our honeymoon. I told you we got married right after high school, right?" He nods and I continue. "Okay, so I was super excited. I'd never flown before. It was a short flight in a small plane, not one of those massive 747s. This one had those propeller things.

"Halfway into the flight, I was mesmerized looking down into nothing but blue ocean. I'd been to dozens of beaches but had never seen the ocean from above. It was amazing. Almost like the first time I saw snow up here."

He sits back in his chair, not eating, eyes glued on me as if he's hanging on my every word.

"Then everything went south. The plane started shaking violently. People were screaming. Belongings fell out of the overhead bins. Those oxygen mask things came down. It was terrifying."

Dallas puts a hand on my arm, running his thumb in circles. It soothes me and calms my pounding heart as I recall the horrific experience.

"Charles told me it lasted less than a minute, but to me it felt like an eternity. I swear I saw my life flash before my eyes. They say we went through a change in atmosphere—something to do with thermals—and it was just bad turbulence. Anyway, that was my first and last experience in an airplane."

"So they turned around and went back to Florida?"

"No, we landed thirty minutes later on the island of Great Exuma and had the most amazing time."

He tilts his head. "But you said that was your first and last flight. You must have gone on the return flight. How'd that one go?"

"I didn't. I wasn't lying when I said it was the only flight I've ever been on. While the vacation was great, the one and only thing Charles and I fought about the entire week was my refusal to get on another plane."

"Did you charter a boat?"

I laugh. "Only a gazillionaire would ask that question. No, Mr. Moneybags, we did not charter a boat. But we did take a ferry. It extended our vacation by five days because we basically ferried between Bahamian islands one at a time until we got to Bimini, the closest island to Florida. From there it was only a two-hour ride on yet another ferry. It was rough. A lot of people got seasick, but I didn't care. At least I wasn't thousands of feet in the air. Thank goodness Charles's dad offered to pay for our extra hotel nights and ferry charges. I'm not sure what I'd have done if he hadn't helped. I'd probably still be living in the Bahamas."

"That must have been some turbulence." He picks up his fork and shovels potatoes into his mouth. "And for the record, I'm not a gazillionaire."

"Okay, billionaire."

He shakes his head. "Not that either."

"Millionaire?" I ask, head cocked.

He shrugs.

"Wow. So you actually have like a million dollars sitting in a bank account?"

"Money isn't everything, Marti. And it's only because my parents made something of the winery. I had nothing to do with it. I've never been one to live large."

I snicker and wave my hand around. "Obviously."

"Besides, it's my parents who are the billionaires, not me."

"I'll bet you have one hell of a trust fund though."

He narrows his eyes. "Is money important to you?"

I don't like the way he asks it. And I feel guilty for pressing him on the subject. I throw my hands over my eyes. "I'm such an idiot. No, Dallas, of course not. I mean, yeah, sure, who doesn't want money and the security of not living paycheck to paycheck, but I swear money has nothing to do with the way I feel about you, or—"

I stop talking. Because there it is. Accidentally, I put it out there. We haven't talked about feelings. Not one time in the past eight days has either one of us even alluded to it. Sure, there have been looks, gestures, insinuations even. But no words. Never words.

"I mean—" I sigh and pick at my food. "You know what I mean. Forget it."

Out of the corner of my eye, I detect the hint of a smile.

"So you really don't think you'll ever fly again?" he asks.

I shake my head vehemently. "It would take an act of God."

"Hmmm. Even now? Are you upset you didn't fly, knowing what you could have avoided?"

What I could have avoided. *The accident? The snow? Him?*

I look him straight in the eyes. "No. I'm not upset. Not even a little bit." I swallow. "Are you? Understandably, your life would have been a whole lot easier if I'd have simply flown."

"No. I'm not upset," he says, holding my gaze. "Not even a little bit."

A million butterflies pirouette in my stomach. And I momentarily wonder if the flapping of their wings will change anything—as in the course of my life.

~ ~ ~

I stare out the window as Dallas chops wood. There is a pattern developing. Every time we get too close emotionally, he leaves physically. He puts distance between us. Erects proverbial walls. He's not upset that I'm here, obviously. It's evident by the amount of time we've spent in bed. But men aren't like women. They can separate sex from feelings.

Still, every time he looks at me, I can see it in his eyes. He feels something. Maybe he even feels *more* than something.

I push the thoughts aside and make my daily call to Charlie, delighted that he seems to be taking things in stride.

Then, just as I'm getting engrossed in the autobiography again, Asher calls.

"I just landed in Syracuse. I'm renting a car and should be with Charlie in a matter of hours."

I sigh. "I can't tell you how relieved I am to know you're going to be there for him. Is Bug with you?"

"She's staying with her friend Mel until I get back. She said it would be too depressing. Any word on when you might be joining us?"

"Two days, maybe."

"Damn. You must really be in the boonies. The interstates and other major roads seemed clear based on what I could see from the air, but there are still blankets of snow covering a lot of the state. You doing okay?"

"I'm fine."

"Fine? Martina, what aren't you telling me? Has that rich asshole tried anything? I swear to God I'll drive through ten feet of snow to kick his ass if he so much as touches you."

My eyes roll at his over-protectiveness. "Calm down, Asher. I said I'm fine. Just missing Charlie."

I decide not to tell him about falling through the ice. Climbing the tower. And the dozens of orgasms the *rich asshole* has so diligently provided me.

"You sure?"

"Yes. I'm sure," I say with as much conviction as I can muster. "Don't worry about me. Just get to Charlie."

"I'll call you when I get there. Are you staying warm?"

I glance out at the ever-growing wood pile and the man adding to it. "Yes, there's plenty of wood." I hold in my snicker at the double-entendre.

"Okay, they're calling me over to pick up my car. Talk to you later."

"Bye."

As soon as I'm back to reading my book, Dallas's phone rings. I look up, surprised. I haven't heard it ring since I've been here. Either he's had it silenced this whole time, or he just doesn't get many calls.

I ignore it and it rolls to voicemail.

A few minutes later, it rings again.

When it rings a third time within another few minutes, I begin to worry. I glance outside and don't see Dallas, so I spring off the couch and go to his phone. The screen reads "Allie," and the picture of a beautiful girl is in the background.

Allie. *His sister.* What if this is an emergency?

Without giving it another thought, I swipe to answer. "Dallas Montana's phone, can I help you?"

"Um… uh… are you sure this is Dallas's phone? Is he okay?"

"Yes, it's his phone, and yes, he's okay. Can I help you?"

Puffs of air that I'm quite sure are laughter, come through the phone. "And you are?"

"The woman stranded at his cabin after my car ran off the road last week."

"Last *week?*"

"There's been a blizzard and I've been unable to get a tow truck."

More laughter coming from the other end of the line assures me there is not, in fact, any sort of emergency. "I'm Allie. His sister."

"I'm Marti."

"Well, nice to meet you, Marti. *Really, really* nice to meet you."

I can practically feel her smile. And the insinuation behind her words is as deep as the snow drifts out back.

"I don't normally answer his phone, by the way. He's outside right now. But it was ringing so much I thought it might be something urgent."

"It isn't. I just know my brother. He doesn't answer his phone. Texts either. Not unless it's work related."

"You work for the winery too?" I ask.

"I do. I'm the events coordinator."

"That sounds fun. Is there a message you'd like me to relay?"

"An invitation is more like it, to Lucas's birthday party."

"Your oldest brother? That's nice. When is the party?"

I could swear I hear her say 'wow,' but I'm pretty sure the word wasn't meant for me. "It's Saturday."

Saturday. Five days from today. It's like a punch in the chest to think that by then, all this will be a memory, and we'll be back to living our own lives.

"I'll be sure to tell him."

"You could come too."

"Thanks, but once I get to my son we'll be heading back to Florida."

"You have a son?"

"Yes. He's three. His name is Charlie."

"He's three?" she asks, shocked. "Does Dallas know about him?"

I sigh. "Yeah. He does. I try not to talk about him much out of respect for DJ though."

Silence. So much silence I think the connection has dropped. I glance at the phone, worried the tower might be down again, but I see full bars.

"Allie? Are you there?"

"I'm here. I'm just… stunned."

"Why?"

"Let's just say Dallas isn't one to talk about himself or his past."

"Well, I don't know much, just what he's told me about the winery, and you guys, and that Phoebe and DJ died two and a half years ago."

"Okay, wow. Marti, you must be some kind of man whisperer, because if I'm not mistaken, that's the most personal my brother has gotten with anyone since it happened."

"Would you mind…" I glance outside to see Dallas swinging the ax again and decide I might be waiting forever if I wait for *him* to tell me. "Could you tell me how it happened? How they died? I don't mean to be insensitive, but—"

"You're curious. It's only natural. And it's no big secret. They died at home. It was carbon monoxide. It happened while Dallas was at work. In fact, he was working late, which is why he blames himself."

"Oh my god, that's horrible." My hand flies to my mouth recalling my own devastating memories. "And he found them?"

"No. It was a delivery driver. Through a window, he saw Phoebe having a seizure on the floor. By the time anyone got there, they couldn't be saved. DJ was in his crib. They said he died peacefully. They couldn't be so sure about her."

Tears stream down my face as I watch Dallas swing over and over. It's inhuman how long he can keep that up. Is he somehow punishing himself? Because of them? Because of… *me?*

"Poor Dallas," I say as my voice cracks. "I've lost people in my life as well." *Too many of them.* "Just last week, my son's father, who was also my best friend, died. That's why I'm here. I was driving up to get Charlie who was spending the holiday with him and his new wife."

"I'm sorry, Marti. It sounds like you and my brother have a lot in common."

More than either of you know.

"I don't know about that. He lives in the middle of nowhere. I could never do that."

"He doesn't live there because he wants to. He's running away."

I blow out a long breath. "I kind of had a feeling."

"So you're going back to Florida, huh? That's a shame."

"How so?"

"Because, Marti, I believe my brother has opened up to you more than he's opened up to anyone, and that's a huge step in the right direction."

I let her words sink in as I stare out the window at the man we're discussing. I hope she's right. Because Dallas needs huge steps—in *any* direction.

It's a lot to process, so I retreat to more comfortable information. "Well, the weather has been clearing. It looks like I'll be able to get out of here in a matter of days. But I'll be sure to pass along the message about the party."

"Thank you. And Marti, the invitation stands. You know, in case you find yourself in Calloway Creek."

"Thanks," I say, not adding how unlikely that is. "Goodbye, Allie."

I stare at the blank screen, all of my suspicions having been confirmed by his sister. He's not up here because he wants to be at one with nature or some existential crap like that. He's here because he's trying to run from his past. Or avoid dealing with it. I'm not sure which. I glance over at the hobby room door. I'm drawn to it more now than ever.

I peek outside to make sure he's still working, and then I pick up the lantern, walk over, and open the door.

It's odd being in here now. The last time I was in this room, I thought Dallas had created everything. It makes me look at things in a different light. Upon closer look, the paintings all have initials in the lower right corner. PKM. Was this her profession, I wonder, or just a hobby?

My eyes fall on something I didn't see last time. Dallas got those two large coolers from this room, maybe they were hiding what sits in the corner. Tears cloud my vision when I see the Moses basket. Inside it is a blanket, a stuffed elephant, and a pacifier.

This room *is* a shrine to his family.

"What are you doing in here?"

I jump at his words. I turn and see him in the doorway, not happy that I'm in his private space.

"I'm sorry. Allie called and I—"

"Allie? What do you mean Allie called? She called *you?* My family doesn't know who you are or even that you're here."

I hold out his phone. "She called you. The phone kept ringing over and over and I thought it might be an emergency, or your tow truck guy calling with news."

He takes the phone from me a little too hastily. "You answered my phone? You're just full of surprises today. What's next, you want to go through my laptop? Do a deep dive on the internet?"

"Dallas, it's not like that."

"Please tell me what it's like then."

"How about you tell me?" I snap, suddenly fed up with his attitude. "Tell me why you came up here supposedly to live this reclusive life and get away from losing your wife and son. But the reality is you brought *them* with you. I mean, there's keeping mementos of your loved ones, and then there's this." I motion to all the artwork. "It's like she's still here and will walk in at any minute and pick up a sketch pad or paint brush. This is unhealthy, Dallas. You need to let people in. And you have to stop bottling it up inside. The pain isn't going to go away until you face it. Until you talk about it."

"What the hell do you know about my pain? Yeah, I get you've lost people. But until you lose the love of your goddamn life, and worse, your own flesh and blood child, you have no right to give me advice or even think you have any idea what I've been going through."

"You think you have a corner on this market, Dallas Montana? You think nobody could ever understand the pain of losing a child? An infant?" I step forward and jab him in the chest with my finger. "Well, fuck you and your high horse, because guess what? I *have* lost a child. Her name was Alex. She was pink and perfect with ten fingers and ten toes, and I had eight incredible days with her. Eight days…" I swipe a tear from under my eye and suck in a deep breath. "On the ninth day, I woke up at seven in the morning and realized I'd slept all night. She hadn't woken to eat. Before I even looked over in the bassinet, I knew what I was going to find. Week-old babies don't sleep ten hours straight." I wipe snot on the sleeve of his Yale sweatshirt. "It hurt. It hurt like hell, but I got through it. You know how? With the help of Charles and Asher and Bug and even Charlie. Being around people helped. Celebrating her birthday *still* helps."

He leans against the door jamb as if it's the only thing holding him upright. "Why didn't you say anything?"

"Because you're still where I was. Two and a half years later, you're where I was right after it happened." I perch against the table. "After I lost Alex, my therapist told me that when you're in hell, you just have to keep going until you find the exit. And with her help, I learned the only way out is through. But you… Dallas, you seemed to have set up camp in your purgatory."

He pulls out the sole chair in the room and sits, shaking his head over and over.

"You'll never find your exit if you continue to let fear have such a grip on you. What if I'd let fear keep me from climbing the tower? What if you'd let it stop you from jumping in the pond? Fear keeps you locked in a prison. *This cabin* is your prison."

I feel the stab of his glare as he looks up at me. "You think I'm here because I'm afraid?"

"Of course you are. You think you came here to get away from them? Their memories? You did exactly the opposite. You brought them with you. Fear made you leave the town and the family you love. And fear is what keeps you from going back."

"Okay, Ms. Psychoanalyst," he huffs, clearly pissed. "What the hell do you think I'm afraid of?"

I hold my arms out to my side. "Me."

He looks dumbfounded. "You?"

"Or someone like me. You're afraid to open yourself up again, to feel what you felt for them. You're afraid of getting hurt and losing people. Maybe like I was, you're afraid that somehow you may have been responsible for their deaths. Maybe you're punishing yourself by not letting anyone be a part of your life. Whatever it is, it all comes down to fear."

He shakes his head, looking like he's going to bite my entire head off. Tell me I've got it all wrong. Maybe even tell me to get the fuck out of his cabin and his life. But someone needed to say something.

He points to the door. "Get out of this room. And don't come back."

I nod and pass him, tears streaking my face. He doesn't look at me. He just slams the door shut behind me. I'm surprised it stays on the hinges. I run over and flop down onto the bed, burying my head in a pillow as muffled sobs bellow out of me. I'm crying for him. For DJ. For Alex. I'm crying for everyone either of us have ever lost. But most of all, I'm crying because I know for sure, if there was any sliver of hope of us having a future, I just squashed it. By answering the call. Going in the room. Accusing him of things I had no right to say.

Sometime later, I hear him exit the room. He goes outside. Of course he goes outside. He chops wood even faster this time, grunting loudly with every pained swing.

I wipe my eyes. "Way to go, Marti."

And for the first time in eight long days, I wish I *had* flown. Because then my heart wouldn't be breaking over a man I love but who is incapable of loving another. A man who, in just a few days' time, I'll leave forever.

A man who will always reside inside me to the depths of my very soul.

Chapter Thirty

Dallas

"God damn it!" I come down hard with the ax, missing the wood and almost chopping my foot off.

Who the hell does she think she is, psychoanalyzing me like that? Like I don't know what I'm doing and why I'm here. She had no right to answer my phone. No business going back in the room after she knew good and well what was in there. No place to try and compare the level of grief we might be feeling.

"Shit." I turn my back to the cabin, sit on my chopping stump, take my gloves off, and rub my hands across my face.

She lost a child. She lost a child too. *How long ago?*

That ever-present hum in the back of my mind—the one that reminds me of Phoebe and DJ over and over again—it's as loud as a fucking chainsaw right now.

I wish she'd never come here. She's ruining everything.

Snow begins falling. I look up at the sky and wonder if I want it to continue or not.

Not. I shake my head. *Definitely not.*

Things need to go back to the way they were before this tornado of a woman crashed into my life. I'm perfectly fine being out here by myself. I could stay here forever if I need to.

My thoughts turn to Abe. Only this time, when I picture him, dead and frozen, I see myself. Long hair, burly beard, old… and alone. I close my eyes knowing that's not how I want to go out of this world, but also knowing it may be how I deserve to.

"I thought you might need some coffee."

My eyes snap open to see Marti, all bundled up, holding out a steaming mug.

She shrugs. "Consider it a peace offering. I… I'm sorry, Dallas. I crossed the line. It wasn't my place to say those things. People grieve in different ways, and I shouldn't have tried to compare—"

She stops talking when my eyes completely bulge out of my head and I look beyond her.

"Dallas?"

"Marti, listen to me. Do not scream. Do not run. Do exactly as I say."

"Wh-what do you mean?" she asks, stiffening into a statue.

"No sudden movements." I stand slowly, my heart splintering up my throat. "Walk toward me slowly and casually. Get right behind me."

She turns her head to see what I'm focusing on. When she sees the black bear standing only twenty feet behind her, the coffee cup falls to the ground, liquid darkening the snow by her feet, and she stifles a cry.

"Marti, get behind me," I implore through gritted teeth.

She's visibly shaking, but not from the cold. And she's frozen in place, unable to move.

Visions flash before me. Her screaming. The bear attacking. Me unable to stop him from mauling her body. Her laying lifeless on the ground, blood slowly turning the snow red like a sick, twisted version of a snow cone.

You can't lose her.

You can't lose her too.

My knowledge of black bears and what to do when confronted by one kicks in. I carefully stand up on the stump, making myself look as large as possible. "Now, Marti. Get behind me. No sudden movements."

I keep the tone of my voice low and casual knowing you shouldn't be loud around black bears, not unless an attack is imminent. Right now, I think he's just curious.

That knowledge doesn't help much, though, when Marti is standing between him and me and the entire last eight days flash through my mind.

"I don't think I can move," she says in a pained whisper, fear hindering her voice.

I hold my hand out and down. "Step forward. Two steps and I'll have you. Slowly. You can do it." I avert my eyes from the bear and focus on her. Tears cascade down her cheeks. "You've got this, sweetheart. I'm not going to let anything happen to you. I promise."

There's that word again. *Promise*. Only this time, I swear on my own life that I mean it. I'm not going to let anything hurt her. I won't let anything hurt her *ever*.

Her left foot shuffles forward.

"That's it," I say. "Just another few steps."

She shuts her eyes, takes a deep breath, and closes the few feet between us.

I grasp her cold, trembling hand in mine. "Good. Now get behind me." I turn to the bear. "Hey, bud. There's nothing to see here," I say calmly. "We don't have any food. You might as well be on your way."

"You're… *talking to him?"* Marti asks from behind.

"Bear Encounters 101," I tell her. "If you speak to them, they know you're human and not another animal. And see how he's standing on his hind legs? That means he's curious, not threatening."

"How come that doesn't make me feel better?"

I laugh quietly, because at this moment I'm shitting my pants too.

I've seen bears over the years. Plenty of them. Mostly from afar. They aren't aggressive like grizzlies, but that doesn't mean we should be inviting him for dinner. *Oh, shit, food.* I have a granola bar in my pocket. I always keep a stash there for when I'm working outside. Can he smell it? I don't dare give it to him. It would be like feeding a stray cat—he'd never leave.

I run different scenarios in my head. We could slowly back away and go for the cabin. But it's thirty feet in the other direction. What if he follows us? I should stay here and send Marti by herself. That way I could distract the bear from watching or going after her. But she'd have to walk around the truck, and what if he—

The truck. It's right behind us. And it's unlocked.

"Marti, I want you to get into the truck. It's behind you and to the right. If you back up ten steps, you should be at the front bumper. Don't waste time going around to the other side. And don't go to the cabin. The truck is unlocked. Get in and you'll be safe. Lock the door. Bears know how to open them."

"If bears know how to open them, why do you leave it unlocked?"

I turn my head and look at her. *"That's* what you want to argue about? Jesus, Marti, just get in the goddamn truck. I need you safe."

"What about you?"

"I'm bigger than he is up here. He won't attack." *I think*. "Now go."

Keeping an eye on the bear, I watch her in my periphery as she backs away, reaches the truck and gets inside. The relief that floods through me is palpable.

Okay, now what? Will he come closer if I get off the stump and go toward the truck? Do I just stay here until he leaves? I lift my arms over my head, trying to make myself look even bigger. "There's nothing here for you, dude."

A sound startles me. *Oh, shit, it's Bex.* He's seen the bear from inside and is barking his head off.

The bear gets down on all fours. *This is not good.* He starts slowly walking toward me. Does he think *I'm* making the noise? I am directly in between him and the cabin. *Shit. Shit. Shit.*

My heart thunders in my chest, pounding so hard I fear it will explode.

I hear another noise behind me. The distinct sound of the door to my truck opening. *No!*

"Get in!" Marti whisper-shouts.

I risk glancing over. She's got the door wide open. Ten steps. If I jump down and run over, I might be able to get in before the bear registers what's happening.

When I look back at the bear, *he's* now looking at the open door to the truck.

"Oh, no you don't," I say, then leap off the stump, covering at least half the distance in the air. When I hit the ground, I sprint the last few steps and dive into the back seat, reaching back to close and lock the door behind me just as the bear's face appears on the other side of the glass.

With my heart still beating out of my chest, arms wrap around me from behind, squeezing me tightly. I turn and embrace her, air swelling my lungs in a cleansing breath.

She pulls away and starts pounding on my chest. "You son of a bitch!" she yells. "You could have died. What would I have done?" Her eyes glisten with tears. "You could have died. I can't… I can't… do this without you."

I tug her close and envelop her in my arms. "Shhh. It's okay. We're okay. We're safe."

"For now. What about later? What if he comes back? What if cell service goes out and you have to climb the tower? What if you're alone and need help? Dallas, what if—"

I do the only thing I can think of to shut her up. I kiss her. I pull her onto my lap and kiss her as hard as I ever have. I tell her with my lips, my mouth, my tongue, that everything is going to be okay. And she tells me with hers that everything she said is true. That she worries about me. That she wants to protect me as much as I want to protect her. That she… *loves me?*

I draw back and look deep into her eyes, searching for the answer to the question while at the same time wondering what I really want it to be.

No matter what the answer is, one thing I know to be true is that I'm not capable of love. I can't give her what she needs. What she deserves. She deserves everything. She deserves so much more than I could ever offer her. But I can offer her this, here, now.

The ticking clock in my head makes another appearance. *Two days*, my inner voice echoes. Two more days I have her. And I vow to make every minute of those days count. Because all those minutes, they might have to last me a lifetime.

Chapter Thirty-one

Dallas

No matter how much I'd like to strip her naked and have her right here in the back seat of my truck, it's just too damn cold. Besides, Bex is still barking, and the bear hasn't left the vicinity. In fact, he's standing on my front porch.

Marti's attention has shifted from me to the bear. Her hands press against the window as she watches his every move. "Can bears open house doors too?" she asks, shooting me a look over her shoulder.

"Probably. But let's hope not. There's a lot of food in there. Not to mention Bex."

Her hand flies to her mouth. "Oh God. Even if he can't open a door, he can easily break a window. Dallas, we have to do something."

She's right. I climb into the driver's seat and press down on the steering wheel, blasting the horn over and over.

Marti sticks her head between the front seats. "I thought you said not to scream. This is so much louder."

"Loud noises are fine as long as we're protected. Noise could potentially scare him away. But the bear could also think a scream is a prey animal's sound. It wasn't worth the risk. Believe me, if he'd attacked us, I'd have yelled my fucking head off."

"Look!" Marti cries when the bear turns our way.

We watch him, still on the front porch but looking at the truck now. I could swear it's like he's trying to decide if getting into the cabin is worth the trouble anymore. After what seems like minutes, but is probably only seconds, he gets down on all fours and scurries down the porch stairs and out into the woods.

I keep honking the horn for several minutes, hoping it will drive him farther away.

Marti gets in the passenger seat. "Do you think he'll come back?"

I shrug. "Hard to say. There are bears all over Tug Hill. This was their habitat long before people came around."

"How do you do it? How do you go on hikes and stay outside all the time when things like that are out there?"

"Bears tend to stay away from people for the most part. You're much more likely to die from exposure or an accident up here than a bear attack."

Her eyes close tightly. "You're not making me feel any better. Especially knowing you're alone."

I take her cold hand in mine. "I'm not alone now."

The countdown clock appears in my head again, reminding me of just how soon I will be.

She nods sadly, making me wonder if the same clock is in *her* head.

"Come on. I think the coast is clear. Just wait here for a second."

I get out, retrieve my gloves and the coffee mug, then go around to her side, keeping an eye on the woods. I open her door and she hops out, darting across the snow to the cabin, flinging open the door and waving impatiently for me to hurry up.

She slams the door behind me and locks it. She falls to her knees and gives Bex a hug. "You better not have to go out for a long time, buddy." She looks up. "And you. I hope we have enough wood in here for two days, because I'm not letting you go back out there."

"Not *letting* me?" I grin, my eyes traveling over her heavily clothed body as she stands. "Whatever will we do to pass the time?" I close the gap between us and finger the zipper on her coat.

She looks up at me, fire in her eyes. "Whatever you want."

Instantly my dick springs to life. Because when it comes to Martina Alexandra Carver, I want a hell of a lot.

"Does that mean you're open for business?" I ask.

She giggles. "We might have to test the waters and see."

I wrap her in my arms and lean down to kiss her. Hell, I lean down to *claim* her. For a few minutes out there, when Marti was between me and the bear, I was scared shitless. Not of the bear itself, but of losing her. Of losing someone else that I… that I…

I deepen the kiss instead of completing the thought. Because with all the brushes with death we've had over the past week, right now, we just need to feel alive. And kissing her, touching her, making love to her—those are the things that give me life. Those are what make my life worth living.

Her arms try to snake around me, but the bulk of our coats gets in the way. I step back and remove mine. Then she removes hers. I lean over, unlace my boots, and kick them off. She toes off her sneakers. I take off my shirt. She does the same. We follow this routine until we're standing before each other, totally naked, our eyes panning the landscapes of each other's bodies.

Neither of us seem bothered by the fact that it can't be more than sixty degrees in here as we stare at each other, hunger in our eyes, knowing what lies in store.

She puts a hand on my chest, pushing me backward toward the bed until I fall over onto it. She climbs on top of me. I pull the covers around us until we're in a cocoon. The warmth from our bodies is welcoming. The heat of our stare is intoxicating. The feeling of her on top of me is fucking everything.

She leans down and kisses me. I hold her tightly against me, my cock dancing between us as if it's been a hundred years since we've done this and not twelve hours. She presses her hips into me, moving her slick center across my stiff erection. The friction is purely divine. I could push inside her right now and give my greedy cock what it wants.

But she has other ideas. She kisses down my body, starting at my neck, then across my chest, teasing my nipples in the same way I like to tease hers. She disappears beneath the covers as her tongue blazes a trail down my abs. Holy shit, that's sexy. Just when I think she might sit up and ride me, she does something she hasn't done before.

I feel her tongue flit out and touch the tip of my dick. Surprise—and let's face it, excitement—has me throwing off the covers so I can watch.

She glances up at me, her cheeks flushing as if she's embarrassed to have me looking. But she isn't deterred. She licks her lips and leans closer. I feel her breath against my sensitive skin. The anticipation of what she's going to do has me about to explode even before her mouth is on me.

Then it happens, she seals her lips around me. They are wet and gentle and moving down my shaft torturously slow. She withdraws, leaving my slick cock cold and lonely. Then her mouth surrounds me again, more forcefully this time. Sliding on. Sliding off. Sliding back on. It's enchanting. Mesmerizing. It's mysterious, wet, and warm.

I feel a tickling sensation. It's her tongue slowly, gently, purposefully working its magic. I almost blow my load instantly, but I concentrate hard on holding it, wanting to feel this incredible sensation for a few more moments. Because the feel of her lips on me is heaven on earth. Ecstasy in its purest form. God… this is better than porn.

Her head bobs up and down, her hair bouncing around with each dip. I brush it aside to get a better view. Her mouth comes off me with a *pop*, then her tongue is on my balls. Her finger caresses the smooth area between my sac and my butthole, sending waves of pleasure pulsing throughout my body. When her mouth envelops me again, I try to keep myself from thrusting up into her. It's fucking hard. I fist the sheets and bite my lip as I watch her drive me totally insane, one inch at a time.

Damn, there's nothing in this world as good as a blow job. Especially from someone who seems genuinely happy to be giving it. It's like great sex minus all the work. And while it feels amazing, I know a lot of it is in my head. It's why I had to uncover her and watch. Because seeing someone do something so selfless just for my pleasure, while having such direct control over me, is a recipe of sensations that blend together into the most intense cocktail.

My resolve crumbles when she moans, the vibrations bouncing off my dick. Detonation is imminent. It's happening now no matter how much I want to prolong this life-altering experience. My head slams back against the bed and I shout into the ether, coming harder and stronger than I ever have in my entire fucking life.

I can't move. I'm completely spent. My breathing is hard and fast as if I've just run a race.

The mattress shifts next to me, and she lays her head on my chest.

"You just wait," I say when I recover the ability to speak. "Give me a minute and my payback will be tenfold. I'm going to make you come so hard and scream so loud we might attract every goddamn animal in the forest."

She giggles. Then she snuggles into me. It's now when I realize just how much I like her near me. How much I *want* her near me. Maybe how much I even *need* her near me. But I push those dangerous thoughts aside for now. Because I have a job to do. A very important one.

I disappear beneath the covers, making her come not once, but three times before I finally sink myself inside her and once again find that feeling that men sometimes search their whole lives for.

Chapter Thirty-two

Martina

I lay in his arms by the light of the fire. He plays with my hair. I run my hand along his abs. I have no idea what time it is, only that it's late. Neither of us sleeps. *Because we know we don't have but one or two sleeps left?*

On his chest, I perch up on a hand. "I have a confession to make."

His breathing stops. Does he think I'm going to admit my true feelings for him? I'm not. I'm not sure I ever can, no matter how substantial the pull is between us. We're in two different places. Emotionally and physically. And the bottom line is… he's just not ready.

"Relax." I tickle his ribs to lighten the mood. "I was just going to tell you I've never done that before."

"That?" He squints. "What are you talking about? We've been doing *that* for days."

"I mean what I did to you."

His eyes widen like saucers. "Never?"

I shake my head, embarrassed. "Charles wasn't circumcised. He was self-conscious about it and I guess I just never pressed the issue. And he didn't, um… want to do it to me either."

His mouth opens in surprise. "Seriously? So I was the first on both counts?"

When I nod, I swear there's a look of pride that overtakes him.

I wrinkle my nose. "I guess that makes me kind of a freak, huh?"

He caresses the side of my cheek with his thumb. "You're anything but a freak."

"So it was… okay?"

"Are you kidding? Marti, it was sensational. How in the hell does someone who's never given head do it so expertly?"

My face heats up and I just know I'm blushing. "I read a lot."

"Well, thank the Lord for books," he says, laughing.

"Speaking of books. Are you ready for me to read?"

I'm not sure how many hours of the day I spend reading to him, but it's definitely become our thing. How I'm going to miss it. How I'm going to miss *him*.

"Not yet," he says. "I was thinking you could tell me about Alex. If it's not too difficult, that is."

I close my eyes and see her angelic face. "I'm happy to. I love talking about her. She was one of the highlights of my life. Those eight days I had with her were some of the best I've ever had. It was amazing how much she looked like Charlie. I think she would have had his eyes. *My* eyes." I reach up and touch my hair, just left of my part. "She definitely had my cowlick. Just like Charlie does. In fact she was born with a full head of hair."

"Wait. This was after you had Charlie? I thought you said Charles was the only man you'd been with."

"He was. Alex was his. The pregnancy was accidental. Charlie was six months old. We'd been separated since before he was born. We were friends who were blissfully co-parenting. It was the day the divorce papers came. Charles brought his over along with a bottle of tequila. He said we started it together, we were going to end it together. One thing led to another and nine months later, Alex was born. The plan was to eventually share custody like we did with Charlie, but since I was breastfeeding, she stayed primarily with me. Charles would come over every day to spend time with her. And Charlie… oh my gosh did he love having a baby sister."

A picture forms in my head. One with Charlie holding Alex, me by his side carefully holding her head as Charles snapped the photo. It's my favorite picture, and to this day it has a place of pride on my nightstand. It makes me think of Dallas's photo in the drawer. I wonder why he keeps it there, hidden away. Before I can ask the question, though, he beats me to it with one of his own.

"Why didn't you tell me about Alex when I first told you about DJ?"

"It was DJ's birthday. It was about your grief, not mine. You needed to feel what you were feeling without anyone, I don't know, one-upping you."

"So if my calculations are correct, your loss is even more recent than mine."

"She died two years and two months ago. What bothered me the most is that they couldn't find a reason. Crib death, or SIDS, they called it. When an infant just stops breathing for no explicable reason. I thought it was my fault, of course. Was it something I'd eaten that she'd gotten through my breast milk? Was it something I'd done during pregnancy? I was a wreck for months after. Every night Charlie was with me I'd sit by his crib and check his breathing.

He was fifteen months old, but I was sure the same thing was going to happen to him."

Dallas's eyes are glassy with unshed tears. He may be the only person I know who can truly understand what I've gone through. "How do you deal with it? How are you so… normal?"

"You think I'm normal?" I laugh. "Half the time I'm barely holding it together. One minute I'm fine, laughing and playing with Charlie. The next, I'm in tears because Alex's face flashes before my eyes, transposed onto his. What would she look like? What would her laugh sound like? What would she have been like as an adult? I think she'd have done something incredible with her life, like cure cancer."

"DJ would have helped run the winery. Maybe he'd even have become CEO."

I glance up. "Is it unhealthy to dream about how they would have been?"

He shrugs. "What does your shrink say?"

"She says everyone grieves differently and that there isn't a script." I shift uncomfortably. "Which is why I feel so guilty about yesterday and how I acted in the hobby room. I should never have said those things. I'm so sorry."

"It's okay. I get it. And Marti, those things you said are probably right."

"Grief sucks."

His chin dips in agreement. "It does."

"People don't understand that there isn't a timeline in which you magically get over someone. They don't get that you don't just lose someone once. It happens over and over. In our dreams. In the faces of others. In a simple word, gesture, or memory. They don't get that there isn't an end to the loss. That there isn't a cure for the daily shock you feel when you suddenly realize they're gone. Again."

He squeezes me. He squeezes me tightly because he knows every word I said is true.

I look up at him, tears coating my lashes. "And most importantly, what they don't understand is that while it might be true that in time, the wound may heal, we will forever have a scar."

"Jesus," he whispers, eyes closed, tears escaping and rolling down the sides of his face.

I wipe the wetness away. "I'm sorry. I didn't mean to be such a downer."

His eyes open and he stares directly into me. "You're not. Believe me." He runs a finger along my jaw. "I think Alex would have had your kind heart."

I rest my head back on his chest. "DJ would be strong like you."

"She'd be a badass like her mom. Climbing towers to save the day."

"He'd save damsels in distress."

"She would be snarky. And funny. And"—he lifts my head so I have to look at him—"totally fucking beautiful."

My heart explodes in my chest, spreading love and warmth throughout my entire body, all the way to every finger and toe. And I know for sure, in this moment, that I'm in love with him. Deep, profound, all-consuming love. The kind that won't go away when you aren't together. The kind I never thought I'd experience. The kind I know I'll never get over for the rest of my life.

I crawl up so we're face to face, mere inches between our lips. I inhale a long breath. "I… I…"

Love you.

But I can only say it in my head.

"… need you to kiss me."

He sighs, visibly relieved I didn't declare my love for him. It breaks my heart to be in love with a man who can't love me back.

Or won't. But I see it in his eyes. The emotion. The desperation. The desire to regain something he once had. The intense fear of what that might do to him.

When his lips collide with mine, I get lost in them. In him. In the world I can only temporarily belong to. So I enjoy every feeling. Remember every touch. Relish every second.

And I ignore the ticking clock that's counting down to just another moment in time that will destroy me.

Chapter Thirty-three

Dallas

Dawn breaks outside and light streaks through the windows, casting bright lines across the floor. I stare at Marti as she sleeps, careful not to wake her. She's only been out for a few hours. We've been having sex almost nonstop since we talked about her daughter the night before last, only pausing for food, bathroom breaks, reading marathons, and naps.

It's like we're both counting down the hours until the snowplow and tow truck arrive.

Will it be today?

I try to wrap my head around how I feel about that. This time with her has almost felt like a dream. One I'm about to wake from but don't want to. But I know better. Even if deep down this is something I truly want, it's not anything I can have.

There were a few times there when I could swear she was going to say things. Things like she doesn't want to leave. Things like she's in love with me. It's ridiculous to even think it. We've only known each other for ten days.

I'm glad she didn't say it, even if there's no way it could be true. I know myself. I'd have run right out of the cabin door and kept going for miles. I'd have tried to run her, this, everything, right out of my head. The problem is, I'm not sure there are enough trails in all of New York to make that happen.

No matter how much I try to tell myself it's not happening, it is. I'm falling for her. Despite every cell in my body screaming that it's wrong. That I can't. That going through it all again would wreck me.

Because shit happens. Look at our lives. It's almost unbelievable the tragedies that have touched us both. She's lost both parents, a child, and now, Charles.

Maybe that's why she didn't say it. Because she too knows that love only leads to heartbreak.

If you don't have anything, you have nothing to lose.

My phone vibrates with a text. I get it off the nightstand. It's from Luther.

I close my eyes and let my head fall back onto the pillow as all kinds of emotions worm their way through me. Disappointment. Sadness. Pain.

"What is it?" Marti whispers.

I put my phone down and turn toward her. I swipe a piece of hair behind her ear and try to look happy. "Good news. My road is going to be plowed today. Luther said he can tow your car later."

Her chin quivers. She tries to blink away tears. She looks on the outside how I feel on the inside.

"Th-that's great," she stutters, unconvincingly.

"You'll finally get to Charlie. You must be so happy."

She nods. She nods even though tears stream down the side of her face.

"Oh my god." She covers her eyes. "I'm being so dramatic. Of course I want to see my son. It's just… just…"

I pull her toward me and wrap her in a hug. "I know."

We embrace for a long time, neither of us moving. Because we both know it's over. That when we get out of bed, the world changes. It goes back to what it once was.

She leaves.

I stay.

Finally, I pull away and cup her chin. "Your son needs you."

Sniffing, she says, "Why does all of this feel like a dream? One I'm just now waking up from?"

I laugh sadly, because she stole the words right out of my mouth.

"I mean, it's crazy to think that over the last ten days, I almost died four times. I survived a car accident, a frozen pond, a cell tower, and a bear. That's like a lifetime's worth of near-death experiences. Not to mention you may have given me a lifetime's worth of orgasms."

I chuckle.

But I don't respond. I don't tell her that what she's given me over this past week and a half is a lifetime's worth of memories. Memories that will make me happy and not sad. Memories that may even get me through the dark times. Good memories that are almost as loud as the bad ones.

She swipes a finger across my lower lip. "Promise me you'll celebrate their birthdays. You'll make a cake and remember all the things you loved about them. You'll eat the entire thing, even if it's only you." She offers a sad smile. "I'm sure Bex will be happy to help."

I nod reassuringly. "I promise."

"And holidays. You need to celebrate them. Spend them with Allie and your brothers. Your parents. You need people, Dallas. They miss you so much. I know they do. Promise me you'll go back to Calloway Creek, even just for the day. Or invite them here. There's so much more life left in you. I don't want you to waste it."

I shrug. "Maybe I'll go home for Christmas."

"That would make them very happy. Not that it matters, but it would make *me* very happy."

I hold her stare. "It matters. And what about you? What'll you do for Christmas?"

"I'll spend it with Asher, Bug, and Charlie. It'll be hard without Charles, but we'll get through it. We'll get through it because we have each other. And we'll remember everyone who's not with us. I'll remember Dad, Mom, Charles. I'll remember Alex." An errant tear rolls down her cheek. "I'll remember you."

My throat thickens. I have to wait a moment to speak. "I'll remember you too."

She snuggles close. "I know we have to get up. But I don't want to."

"We have a minute."

I lift her chin. Our lips come together. We kiss so thoroughly and possessively, I know this will be the one I remember most. I let my hands wander every inch of her soft curves. When her fingers explore my abs, my skin crackles with heat and anticipation thickens the air in my lungs.

Despite how many times we've done this, I'm hardening quickly. I groan in raw appreciation when she encircles my cock with her hand. I latch tightly to my control, using every ounce of willpower to keep from coming. Because our time is short, and I do not plan on wasting my final orgasm in her hand.

Just before the point of no return, I arch away from her, take a few seconds, then use my fingers and tongue on every crevice of her body, making her come twice before sinking myself into her one last time.

Our eyes connect, right along with the rest of us, conveying a million unspoken words neither of us will say. We bathe in each other's electrified stare as I maintain a slow steady rhythm. Her palms flatten against my back, holding me close. Her breath whispers across my neck when she groans my name. I chronicle every moan. Every quiver. Every thrust of her hips. I burn all of it into my memory, putting it inside a box that I can open after she's gone.

We orgasm together, pleasure ripping me apart as if my body knows this will be the last one we share. I collapse down on top of her, burying my face into her shoulder. The words almost come out. I'm dangerously close to asking her to stay. But that would be selfish. Not to mention impossible.

She has a life. A son. An existence I could never fit into.

Still… I almost ask. I almost ask because it's a want as strong as any want I've ever had.

I roll to the side. Without words, she sits up, wraps a blanket around her, gathers her clothes, and heads to the bathroom. She pauses before closing the door and looks over her shoulder, tears glistening in her eyes. "I'm going to miss you, Dallas Montana."

She smiles, even through her tears, as if I've given her something she needed. As if even though we aren't going to see each other again, she's grateful for the time we had. As if she wouldn't take it back, even knowing how it would end up.

The door closes.

My head falls back onto my pillow.

"Fuck."

~ ~ ~

When she comes out of the bathroom, she stops cold and looks out the window. That's when I hear it—the distant rumble of the snowplow clearing my street.

We look at each other, neither of us saying anything. What is there to say?

She's all business. She packs her clothes into my backpack. I don't say a word when she stuffs my Yale hoodie in and zips it up tight. She plays with Bex. She makes lunch. I look down at the plates somehow feeling this is like The Last Supper.

I get out a bottle of wine. *The* bottle.

Her brows leap skyward. "You are not opening that one."

I stab the cork with the screw. "Too late." I pour her a glass, then me. I hold my glass high. "To a hell of a ten days."

She taps hers to mine. "There's no one I'd rather have been snowed in with."

We stare at each other over the rims of our glasses as we drink the most expensive bottle Montana Winery produces.

"Oh. My. God." Her eyes roll into the back of her head, and she makes the same noises she makes when she comes. "This is without a doubt the best thing I've ever had in my mouth." Then she shakes her head and laughs. "Okay, maybe second best."

Now I laugh, too. Only Martina Alexandra Carver could make me laugh when she's moments away from walking out of my life.

She's walking out of my life. The words sting like a thousand bees. So much so that I can't stop what comes out of my mouth next. "I think I should drive you to Anita's."

Marti's eyes snap to mine and she all but chokes on a bite of food. "Um… what?"

"I'll drive you. It's ridiculous for you to rent a car to drive ninety minutes when I have a perfectly capable one."

"You want to drive me."

It's not a question. More of a musing.

I shrug. "It's not a big deal, Marti. It'll be good for me to get out of this cold cabin for a while."

"You want to drive me," she says again, in disbelief. "To Anita's. To where Charlie is. And my brother." She chuckles. "Talk about going before the firing squad. Asher told me he'd drive through ten feet of snow to kick your ass if you touched me."

I furrow my brow, ignoring the part about her son—because honestly, I hadn't really contemplated that—and focus on the kicking-my-ass comment. "Why would he want to kick my ass? What did you tell him?"

"I think he assumed that any guy who has a cabin in the middle of nowhere would try and take advantage of a stranded woman."

"And you didn't set him straight? Wait… *do* you think I took advantage of you?" I stand up and pace, running a hand through my hair as I feel sick to my stomach. "Oh, shit. *Did I?* I mean you had just fallen through the ice. I'd saved you. You weren't in your right mind. You were vulnerable. Holy fuck, I *did* take advantage of you."

Marti stands, troops over, and puts her hands on my shoulders, looking straight into my eyes. "You did no such thing. I swear you didn't. In fact, I wanted it to happen even before I fell through the ice."

"You did?"

I try to think back and remember if I did as well. All I recall is that one minute I was irritated by all her snarkiness and wit, and the next we were going at it on a wet mattress in front of the fireplace.

Her lips turn up to form a grin. "Have you seen yourself? You're smoking hot. That body. This hair. If you hadn't kissed me, I'd have shamelessly thrown myself at you."

Relief comes in one gigantic wave. "So just how big is your brother?"

She giggles. Her demeanor has changed. Mine has too. We have more time. More minutes. More hours. Maybe even more memories.

But things *are* changing. It won't be just us anymore. We'll be driving away from our snowy fortress and into the real world. The world with brothers and dead ex-husbands.

One with three-year-old sons.

Maybe it's a mistake. Maybe I should have left well enough alone.

"He's all bark and no bite, I assure you. A big teddy bear. Kind of like you."

I pick her up and scoop her into my arms. "I'll show you how I can bite."

Her eyes light up, the fire behind them intense. Why can't I get enough of her? Is it because I know this is over?

A knock on the door halts my plan to have her one final time.

Cursing, I set her down and go to answer it, Bex at my heels. It's Luther.

"Hey, Mr. Montana. You doin' alright?"

"Never better."

"I passed the lady's car on the way up. She's lucky you were around."

Marti comes up behind me, touching my back gently, but not in a way that's obvious to Luther. She holds her other hand out to shake his. "Marti Carver. And yes, I am lucky. Thank you for towing my car. I'll get you the keys."

Luther looks at her oddly. "You're not comin'? Thought I was drivin' you to town."

Last chance, I think. If I want out, I'd better say so now.

"I don't need a rental after all," she says happily. "Dallas is driving me the rest of the way."

"Is that so?" Luther asks, raising a brow in my direction.

I make a smacking sound with my lips. "Guess I am."

Marti hands over her keys then fishes through her purse. "How much do I owe you for the tow? Do you take credit?"

I push her wallet back toward her. "I'll take care of it."

"Dallas, I can't ask you to do that."

"You didn't ask. I offered. And it's settled." I turn back to Luther. "Text me when you find out the state of the car. I think it's totaled, but I'm not exactly a mechanic."

"I'm guessin' it'll be scrap metal. But I'll let you know."

"Let me grab a few things and we'll follow you out. We need to get her suitcase from the trunk."

"Sure thing. See you there in a few." He tips his hat to Marti. "Nice meetin' you, ma'am."

I close the door behind him and turn to Marti. We both know this is the last time we'll be in this cabin together.

She thumbs to the bathroom, looking sad. "I'm going to freshen up and then we can go."

"I'll put your things in the truck."

Once she's gone, I say to Bex, "Hope you don't get car sick. We're going for a ride."

He barks once, wags his tail, and paws at the front door. He must have understood. He's a smart little fucker. I'm glad I decided to keep him.

I re-cork the bottle of wine, clean up lunch, then gather up a few things for Bex. I load everything in the truck and look back at the cabin just as Marti comes out the front door.

Sadness on a level I don't expect kicks me square in the gut as it hits me once again.

She's leaving. I'll be alone.

And I know when I return, things will never be the same.

Chapter Thirty-four

Martina

We haven't talked much on the ride. Is he thinking what I am? That once he drops me off, that'll be it? Maybe it would've been easier to part ways at his cabin. At least then I could have had a good cry in a rental car with nobody around to see. I could have gotten it out of my system so all my energy could go toward Charlie.

I glance over at Dallas, knowing the truth—he'll never be out of my system.

His knuckles are practically turning white as hard as he's gripping the wheel. The roads have been cleared, so it can't be that. "You okay?" I ask.

He relaxes his hands, as if he just now realized the death grip he had on the steering wheel. "Fine. Why wouldn't I be?"

Because our time together is coming to an end.

Because you'll meet my big brother.

Because… Charlie.

I almost tell him I'm proud of him for doing this. He's going way outside his comfort zone. It could be a step in the right direction for him. But I keep my mouth shut.

My shoulders slump when the GPS voice alerts us that our destination is ahead. How can a person be so incredibly happy yet insanely sad at the same time? I'm about to see Charlie. I've never gone this long without seeing him. But seeing him means leaving the past ten days behind.

Dallas pulls up in front of the hotel, underneath the massive brick awning.

My heart hurts as much as it did when I got that horrible call from Anita. *How do I say goodbye?*

I turn to him, unable to keep the tears from welling in my eyes. "I…"

He puts a hand on my arm. Our eyes connect, revealing in total silence there are still things we want to say but can't.

What does *he* want to say? I'd give anything to know the answer.

What I want to say would scare him, send him bolting out of this parking lot faster than I could complete the three words.

Wouldn't it?

I stare into his eyes, almost willing to risk it, because I swear his dark, expressive, sad eyes are saying the same things mine are.

A knock on the window has me turning.

"Mommy!"

Charlie's smiling face is on the other side of the glass. Asher is holding him. They knew we'd be arriving any minute as I've been in constant contact with them.

I swing open the door, hop out, and pull my son into my arms, closing my eyes at the feeling of his little limbs tangling around me, hugging me as tightly as he can.

Rubbing my face over the top of his hair, I inhale his scent. This little man is my entire world. "I've missed you so much, buddy."

"There's a pool," he says excitedly. "Unca Asher let me swim."

"That's great, Charlie. I'll watch you swim later. After we go talk to Nita."

"Nita is sad."

"Yes, buddy, she is."

"Are you sad?"

I nod. "I'm very sad. I miss your daddy very much."

"Where did he go?"

"He went to heaven. Remember? He didn't want to go. He wanted to stay and be your daddy forever and ever. But he couldn't. You can still love him forever, though. He's with Alex now. You remember Alex, right?"

I know he doesn't actually remember her, but I do talk about her, and I have pictures. So he nods. "Sissy."

"Yes, Daddy is with your sister, Alex."

He looks at me inquisitively. "Is there a pool where he is?"

Oh, how I love his innocent mind. "Yes, buddy. I think there is a pool."

Asher pulls me in for a hug and I thank him for coming. Then he moves me aside, almost forcefully, and leans into the truck. "Asher Anderson," he says, holding out his hand to Dallas.

Dallas shakes it. "Dallas Montana."

"Yeah. I know exactly who you are."

I nudge Asher with my elbow, silently telling him to take it easy.

Asher gives me a dismissive head nod that only a brother can give, then turns back to Dallas. "I understand thanks are in order for saving my sister from certain death."

"Well, your sister is kind of a badass. The accident, the pond, the tower, and the bear hardly even phased her."

My overprotective brother turns to me, a new expression on his face. I know this one. He's scolding me for not telling him about my three other brushes with death. "What the fu—, uh… what haven't you told me?"

I laugh. "I didn't want to worry you, Ash. Everything is fine. I'll tell you all about it later."

"I'd actually like to hear about it from *him*." He leans into the truck again. "How about you stay for a drink? Or dinner even. Marti will want to go talk to Anita. I'll be stuck here. The hotel has a great restaurant."

Dallas looks at me over Asher's shoulder. He looks at me, then he looks at Charlie, a host of emotions crisscrossing his face. "I… um…"—he thumbs to the road—"should probably get going."

"Come on," Asher urges. "One drink. Maybe a sandwich. You'll be out of here by seven."

Dallas blows out a long, drawn-out breath. "Alright. I'll just go park."

I could kill Asher for strong-arming him into staying. But I could also kiss him, because it means we don't have to say goodbye quite yet.

"Be nice," I tell Asher as the truck pulls away.

"Why wouldn't I be?" He stares me down. "Any reason in particular?"

I shrug. "There are just… things." I glance at Charlie. "I'll tell you later."

"Things. Right." He shakes his head. "Listen, I saw the way you two were looking at each other. It's pretty obvious what happened in that cabin."

"Please don't be hard on him, Asher. He's lost a lot. Much more than you and I have."

He cocks his head. "*More* than you have, Marti?"

"His wife and son died a few years ago. It's just him now. And his son would be Charlie's age, so give the guy a break, okay?"

"Damn." He watches Dallas as he approaches, rolling my suitcase behind him, Bex on a leash at his side.

I elbow Asher in the ribs. "Do *not* say anything about it."

"I'm not an insensitive prick, Martina."

"Mommy! A doggy!"

I set a squirming Charlie down on his feet. "This is Bex," I say. "He's very nice. Hold out your hand so he can sniff you."

Charlie does what I ask, and Bex licks his hand, much to my son's amusement.

My eyes swing to Dallas's when Charlie giggles in delight. Dallas is watching the interaction as if he's looking at an accident. He doesn't want to see what's happening, but he just can't look away.

After Charlie has his few moments with Bex, the question I've been dreading arrives.

"Mommy," Charlie says looking up at Dallas. "Who's that?"

My heart lurches, because I'm about to introduce my son to the man who lost his.

"Charlie, this is Mr. Montana. Mommy's friend."

"Dallas," he says. "It's just Dallas." He looks at my son, his eyes gutted with pain. "Nice to meet you, Charlie."

It was almost imperceptible—the hitch in his voice—but I noticed it. And it wrecks me.

"Can I play with Bex?" Charlie asks.

"Later," I say. "We need to go to Anita's for a while." I turn to Dallas. "Will you be here when I get back?" Then I mouth the word, *please.*

He nods, albeit hesitantly.

Asher takes my suitcase from Dallas and hands me a set of car keys. "It's the silver Camry over there. There's a car seat inside. The address is programmed into the GPS." He gives me a hotel key card. "Your room number is 417. You have a connecting room to where Charlie and I have been staying."

"Thank you for coming." I give Asher a hug. "I want to stay," I say, blinking over at Dallas. "But I have to see Anita. How's she doing?"

"As well as can be expected. She's got family around. You as well as anyone know what a comfort that can be. I've kept my distance though. I'm here for Charlie. You're more of a friend to her than I am. I don't even know her all that well."

I lock eyes with Dallas. "So, I'll see you later?"

Maybe asking that a second time makes me sound desperate, but if this is the last I will ever see of Dallas Montana, I have to know.

"I guess you will." His gaze flits to Charlie. "You did promise him playtime with Bex."

The urge to reach for him is strong. But knowing he'll be here later, and we'll have at least a little more time together, has me reaching for Charlie's hand instead. "Come on, buddy. Let's go talk to Nita. Bex will be here when we get back."

"Can he swim with me?"

I laugh. "No, Charlie. Dogs won't be allowed in the pool. But maybe we can find a nice stick and throw it to him out here."

Dallas's eyes cut to me as his face relaxes into a smile. We're both thinking of the stick, the pond, and what came after.

My feet are cemented in place. It takes a nudge from Asher to get me moving. "You'd better get going."

"Right. Well, I'll see you guys later."

Taking Charlie to the car, I strap him in the seat and look back at the hotel entrance where Dallas is watching me. I wave. He lifts his chin.

I duck inside the car, my chin quivering, knowing so much has gone unsaid, hoping that somehow, some way, I'll get to say it.

Chapter Thirty-five

Dallas

"You think the hotel will have a problem with Bex?"

Asher shakes his head. "It's pet friendly. But I'm not sure about the restaurant. Will he be okay if we leave him in the room?"

"I think so."

"You *think* so?"

I shrug. "Bex has only been mine for about a week. But he seems like a great dog, so I assume he'll be fine. I'll pay for the damage if he causes any."

"A week, huh? I'm guessing there's a story there." He tilts his head, studying me. "I'm guessing there are a *lot* of stories there."

"She really didn't tell you anything?"

"Marti thinks I'm overprotective."

"And you're *not?* Listen, I have a younger sister. It's not like I raised her like you did Marti, but I'd sure as hell want to know shit if she'd found herself in Marti's situation."

"So you get why I asked you to stay."

"I do."

"And I gather you must be an honorable guy for accepting my invitation."

I snort air through my nose. "We'll see if you still feel that way in an hour."

He laughs. I kind of like the guy. He's quite a bit older than I am, pushing forty if I remember correctly, but he seems like someone I might have hung out with back in the day.

Bex gets lots of attention from some kids on our way up the elevator. *Teens.* Not little kids, for which I'm grateful. Because, Jesus, when I first laid eyes on Charlie, all I could see was DJ.

Just one more reason Marti and I could never work in the real world. An isolated cabin with nobody else around, sure, but not here. Not like this. And to be honest, even if she didn't have Charlie, I'm not sure it could work. I had my one true love. There just isn't any room in my life for another.

My subconscious shakes his finger at me, saying something about me being in denial. I promptly shut him the hell up.

As we enter the room, I get a text from Luther. "Damn," I say. "Marti's car is totaled."

"Totaled." Asher scrubs both hands across his jaw. "Fuck. It's a good thing you were there. I can't even imagine what would have happened if you hadn't been. Poor Charlie would have lost two parents within a week." Guilt crosses his face. "Ah, shit. I didn't mean to bring up any bad memories."

"So she told you."

He nods sadly. "I'm really sorry, man."

"I'm sorry for your losses as well. Marti's too."

"Did she tell you about Alex?"

"Yes."

"I'm not surprised. My sister isn't one to keep things bottled up."

"As she tells it, she has you to thank for that."

His eyes widen. "Really?"

"My son's birthday was last week. She made me celebrate it." I shake my head, still unable to believe how that went down. "She said you're the one who started that tradition."

"I guess I was. I hope she wasn't too pushy."

"Oh, she was." We both laugh. "But it was a push I was desperately in need of."

"So, you think Bex will be okay here?"

I pull a few things from my backpack. Bex's water and food bowls. A baggie of kibble. A chew toy. "I imagine so."

"Good. Because I can't wait to hear how you ended up with a dog during a blizzard."

~ ~ ~

Two hours later, Asher stares in disbelief, still processing the information I just dumped on him. Marti's brushes with death. Abe. Losing power. Marti climbing the tower to save me. And though I omitted other… *details*… I'm sure he can put two and two together.

"Just… holy crap," he says, downing his third beer to my one. "That's a lot of fucking shit to unpack."

"It was a hell of a time."

"Alright, listen." He sets down his beer and gives me a stern look. "I'm her big brother, so I gotta ask, what are your intentions here?"

A hundred answers go through my head. But I settle on the one that has another finger wagging in my head. "I just wanted to get her here safely. After all she went through, she didn't need any more hassles. I figured after that, you could take it from there."

"I could *take it from there?* What exactly does that mean?"

"Exactly what you think it does."

"That you had your fun with my sister and now you're done with her?"

I hoist a shoulder. "I'm not sure what you want me to say, man. No promises were made. We both knew the score."

"The score?" He pushes away his half-eaten cheeseburger. "As in you were fuck buddies to pass the time, and now you're dumping her?"

"I'm not dumping anyone. She was never mine to dump." I lean back in my chair, my eyes meeting the table. "I don't expect you to understand. Being with her, with anyone, is not something I'm capable of. And she knows it."

"Are you sure about that?"

I nod. "Yeah. I am."

He huffs in irritation, confirming to me that's where Marti picked up the same habit. "Doesn't mean she won't be nursing a broken heart."

"I'm aware."

"Are you?"

Thankfully, the waiter brings the check, saving me from having to answer. I take a hundred from my wallet and throw it on the table. "I'd better go check on Bex."

Asher doesn't follow me. In fact, I hear him order another drink. It's a lot to process for a big brother, so I can hardly blame him.

Once off the elevator and approaching the room, I realize my mistake. I don't have a room key. Turns out I don't need it, as I hear laughter coming from the other side of the door. A *child's* laughter.

I stop and lean against the wall, processing a thousand emotions all bombarding me at the same time.

There are two people behind that door. One represents everything I lost. The other gave me a taste of hope… of a future I thought wasn't in the cards… of simply living again.

The one hurdle—the one thing I can't get past—is that the two people behind this door come as a package deal. But I fear that package could never give me what I crave. What I need. What I now know I want.

Inner fucking peace.

Chapter Thirty-six

Martina

There's a knock on the door and I race over, because it has to be Dallas. Asher would have used the key.

Relief swells through me when I see his face.

"What?" he says. "Did you think I was going to leave Bex stranded here?"

I bite my lip. "So you just came back for the dog?"

He doesn't answer. Because with the way we're looking at each other, he doesn't need to. My heart pounds not knowing if I have two more minutes or two more hours with him.

"How's Anita?" he asks, crossing the threshold.

"Drugged up on Valium. She's having a hard time. I'm not sure if my being there helped or just brought up more memories she couldn't deal with. There was no point in our staying after she'd gone down, so we ate at McDonalds and then came back here. Charlie's been playing with Bex for about twenty minutes. I think he's in love."

He's not the only one, the voice in my head screams. *Tell him!*

Charlie squeals gleefully behind us. Bex has all but pinned him to the floor and is licking his face, the dog's large tongue almost the size of Charlie's cheek.

Dallas strides over. "Easy, boy." Bex sits dutifully at Dallas's side. "I don't think he realizes he's as big as you are."

"I'll be bigger," Charlie exclaims. "Mommy says I'm a weed."

Dallas chuckles and my whole world flips upside down. He's talking with my son. *And* he's laughing. My heart couldn't be fuller.

"You'll be bigger than him in no time, I'm sure," Dallas says.

"Dallas?" Charlie says, sounding as cute as ever as his three-year-old lisp makes Dallas's name sound more like *Dallith.*

Dallas sits on the bed. I can tell he's hesitant, but at least he's not running out the door. "What is it, Charlie?"

"Will you swim with me?"

"I'm sorry. I don't have a swimsuit."

"Unca Asher took me to the big store. He can take you too. Then you can swim."

"I think the store might be closed," I say, coming up with an excuse for Dallas. The last thing he needs right now is my son asking to jump into his arms off the side of a pool. While every fiber of my being longs for it to happen, I know it's simply not possible. Not today. Possibly not ever.

"You watch me, okay?" Charlie asks. "Pwease, pwease, pwease?"

I sit down next to Dallas. "Charlie, I don't think—"

Dallas puts a hand on my shoulder. "It's okay. I can watch you swim for a few minutes, okay? Then I have to go back home."

"Mommy says you have a cabin and there's bears. Does Bex like bears?"

Dallas chuckles again. So do I. "No," he says. "Bex definitely doesn't like bears. But speaking of Bex, I do need to take him outside. Why don't you get ready for the pool while I do that?"

Asher comes in from the connecting room. The door was open, and it makes me wonder how long he was over there listening. "I'll get Charlie ready," he says. "Why don't the two of you walk Bex and we'll meet you at the pool."

Dallas clips a leash on Bex. "Sounds good." He nods to my coat—or rather *his* coat that he loaned me. "Better put that on, it's cold out."

The two of us walk in silence to the elevator. Once inside, he does something that makes my heart soar. He holds my hand. It's silly to think that such a small gesture means anything after all the sex we've had, but it has my pulse racing.

It doesn't mean anything. It doesn't mean anything.

Except that it means *everything.*

He runs slow circles across my finger with his thumb. It's the first time we've touched in hours, and I feel like an addict who just got her fix. He's become the drug I need to survive. I just hope I don't have to go cold turkey.

It's an idiotic fantasy, thinking something can become of this. Deep down I know how unlikely it is. But that doesn't keep my mind from wanting it. My heart from craving it. My body from demanding it.

"Marti?"

I look up at him.

"Your death grip is about to break a few of my fingers."

"Oh, sorry."

I try to pull my hand away, but he doesn't let me.

We walk through the lobby and out the front door. Snow flurries dance around us when we clear the awning. I crane my neck and let them fall onto my face. Memories flood my mind: the snowball fight, the snowman, our trek to the tower.

"You think you'll miss the snow?" he asks.

"A thousand percent, yes."

Bex leads us over to an area with bushes and trees and starts sniffing.

Dallas gives my hand a squeeze. "Will you miss anything else?"

I turn to him and throw his words back at him. "Will you?"

He glances over his shoulder, then pulls me behind the nearest tree, dragging Bex along with us. He presses me against the large trunk, gazes down into my eyes, and lowers his lips to within an inch of mine. Just before they touch, he whispers, "What do you think?"

"I think—"

I'm not able to continue as his lips claim mine. They claim mine in a way that tells me this could very well be the last kiss we ever share. That thought has me returning the kiss with just as much desperation and fervor as I'm feeling from him. Because if this is the last kiss we ever have, it needs to be memorable. Intense. Utterly mind-blowing. I want it to be a moment I can look back on without any regrets. A goodbye that overshadows all others. A parting neither of us forgets.

My head swims as our mouths devour each other. Our breath mingles and our hands grasp for purchase, moans erupting from both of us, sounding different than before. These are filled with anguish, torture, and despair. Neither of us wants this kiss to end, but we know it will. It has to. Our days of being snowed in are over. *This* is over. We're just trying to hang on to one last moment.

When we're both breathless, he pulls me against him and buries his head down on my shoulder. I'd give anything to know what he's thinking at this very second.

I take a lock of his hair and run it between my fingers. "This is my favorite part of you."

He chuckles and thrusts his hips into mine. "Some of my other parts are offended." He pulls away and winks.

"No. I mean, when I look back on our time together, I think it's your hair I'll remember the most. The way it felt when I'd run my fingers through it as I read to you. How it fell around my face when we made love."

His eyes close briefly. He's going to miss those things too.

Tell him.

This is your only chance.

"Dallas?"

His shoulders stiffen as he looks at me, his face a veil of uncertainty knowing good and well what I want to say. Shifting ever so slightly on his feet, he lightly scratches his forehead. He's afraid of the words that sit on the tip of my tongue.

Which is why I don't say them. "I think I left my bracelet at your cabin. It's the silver one with my initials on it."

Chicken.

He heaves a chestful of air, looking both relieved and disappointed. "I'll look for it when I get back."

"Um… Dallas?" I say, my heart a pattery mess.

"Mmm?"

My arms twine around him in a bruising embrace, afraid of what my forthcoming words will do to him. But I have to say something. I'll regret it if I don't.

"I can't remember the exact quote, where I read it, or who said it—probably some famous philosopher—but the words stuck with me." I take a deep breath and blow it out, the cloud of it swirling around us. "Love is the only thing that can be divided endlessly and still not diminish."

He doesn't say anything. He just stares at me, his forehead a map of wrinkles. It's the first time I can't read his eyes.

"Do you understand what that means?" I grip his shoulders. "It means you can still love them, but you can love others too. You could even love… *us*. You don't have to choose. Both can exist, and that doesn't mean either will be any less."

"I…" He swallows hard, rips his eyes from mine, and stares at the tree behind me. Is he contemplating the words? Getting ready to run? About to tell me I've read him all wrong? "We should probably go back. Your boy is waiting."

My lungs deflate with defeat. "Okay." I start to walk away when he surprises me by taking my hand once again. I'm relieved I didn't run him off. But at the same time, I'm worried I may have ruined what could be our last private moment together.

I didn't tell him exactly what I wanted to say. But I told him enough. He can read between the lines. He can see it on my face. Feel it in my kiss. Hear it in my voice. I'm hopelessly, stupidly, maybe even recklessly in love with him.

~ ~ ~

I grab my purse and a towel for Charlie. We leave Bex in the room once again and head down to the pool.

I'm not used to indoor pools. There's no need for them in Florida. This one is massive. The hotel is built around it, and the dome above is a glass roof that offers a view of the tall ceiling beyond. One end of the pool is a kids' area with water toys and small slides. This is where we set up camp.

After Charlie goes down a slide, he calls for Asher to go in the pool with him.

"Watch me!" he shouts over when he climbs out and jumps back in, right into Asher's arms. Then he swims to the edge, climbs out again, and sloshes over to Dallas. "Did you see? I hold my bweath and go under."

"I did see," Dallas says. "You're a great swimmer, buddy."

Buddy. My heart swells.

"Show me how far you can swim. Can you kick your feet?"

At Dallas's challenge, he races back to the pool, jumps in and demonstrates his capabilities.

Dallas turns to me. "You weren't kidding when you said he could swim. Impressive."

"This is nothing. You should see him surf."

As soon as the words are out of my mouth, I regret them. Dallas retreats into a shell. It wasn't an invitation, just something that popped out.

"I mean… not that you should… it was just…" I cover my face with my hands. "Dallas, I don't know how to do this. What exactly is going on here?"

"What's going on here is that I'm keeping my promise to watch Charlie swim."

I pick at the pool towel. "And after that?"

"After that, I'll get in my truck and go back to my cabin."

"And after that?"

It's the million-dollar question. The one I haven't asked but has been on my mind for a week. I finally did it. I asked the 'what about me?' question like a pathetic love-sick girl.

Asher drops into the seat next to Dallas. *Talk about bad timing.*

"He was invited by those kids to play on the splash pad," Asher says, drying off.

I look over his shoulder to see Charlie playing with four other kids about his age. I watch for a moment, thinking how this must seem like just a vacation to him. He still doesn't fully grasp that his father has died and won't be coming back. I know it's a conversation that we'll have over and over again until he's older and can understand the finality of death.

I narrow my brow and gaze at Dallas as he talks with Asher, wondering if my son isn't the only one who doesn't comprehend it.

Asher orders us a round of drinks, but Dallas barely touches his, all the more indication that he'll be leaving sooner rather than later.

We all keep an eye on Charlie as we talk. I notice that Dallas does so even more vigilantly than I do. It's like he can't bear to be around him, but he has a need to protect him all the same.

"Something's wrong!" Dallas says. He sprints out of his chair and dashes over to the splash pad.

My stomach churns at the tone of his words and how quickly he moves.

I dart after him until we reach the pod of children.

Charlie looks up at me, distressed. "Mommy, my mouth feels funny."

My heart beats wildly. Did he just swallow too much chlorine, or… I look up. "My son has a severe peanut allergy. Did he ingest anything?"

A woman steps forward, holding out a packet of cookies. "My son was eating these." She turns to him. "Sam, did you give this boy any of your snack?"

The boy, who can't be more than four, looks scared, like he doesn't want to be punished. He shakes his head.

I sink to his level. "Sam, it's really important. You're not in trouble, but Charlie may need help. Did you share your snack with him? Please tell me."

His lip quivers. He's afraid of all the commotion going on around us. He nods slowly.

I read the ingredients of the package. Peanuts are third on the list. *Oh, dear God.*

Asher shoves my purse into my hands. I pour out the contents onto the wet splash pad, searching for the EpiPen I never leave home without. "Where is it?" I rifle through everything. It has to be here. I look up at Asher, terrified. "It's not here!"

He gets on his knees, helping me sift through everything. He checks every nook and cranny of my purse.

When realization dawns, it's like a stab to the heart. My eyes connect with Dallas's. "The accident. Everything spilled out of my purse. Oh my god. I don't have it." I stand up and yell, "Does anyone have an EpiPen?"

"I'm calling 911," Asher says behind me.

I vaguely hear him telling the operator that we have a child going into anaphylaxis and we need epinephrine immediately.

"Charlie, help is on the way. It's going to be okay."

I'm on my knees, holding him close, knowing that this is going to get very bad very quickly. Just as soon as I think it, I see his lips swelling up and then he collapses. But before I can catch him, Dallas swoops in and scoops him into his arms. "We'll meet the ambulance out front."

Why didn't I think of that? Seconds count when my son's throat is closing a little more with every tick of the clock.

People are yelling, still trying to find an EpiPen. Kids are crying. A woman comes over, steps in front of us, and shoves a packet of Benadryl pills in my face. "Give him this."

"He can't take pills." I push it away. "Besides, it won't work in time."

"I read that—"

"It won't work!" I look at my son, limp in Dallas's arms. His face is ballooning, and his lips are already turning blue. "He needs epinephrine," I cry. I look at Dallas. "Dallas, oh my god."

"No!" he shouts and continues toward the front of the hotel. "This is not happening."

Tears are streaming down his face. He's shaking. Yet he's holding my son as if he's a China doll, taking care to support his head against his chest, while at the same time keeping it extended to give him the best chance at getting air.

In the back of my mind, I curse the hotel for being so large and for having the kids' pool area at the very back of the massive indoor structure.

Asher runs up behind us. "They're on the way. Two minutes."

Two minutes. How long has it already been? Does he *have* two minutes?

I cry out a guttural sob, running beside Dallas until we get to the lobby, plowing through the curious onlookers who have gathered to see what the emergency is.

"Stay back!" Asher barks as he escorts us through the front doors.

Sirens sound. They aren't close enough.

"Baby, it's okay," I say, putting my lips to Charlie's forehead. I squeeze him gently. "You're going to be okay. M-mommy's here. I'm right here." I look up at Dallas. He looks as destroyed as I feel. "Th-this c-can't h-happen."

"It's not going to." He sniffs sharply, tears still falling. "No way. He's going to be okay. He's got to be."

He's not looking at me. He's only looking at Charlie. There's not even room in my mind to think of what Dallas might be going through at this very moment. Because all I can think of is my son and how incredibly helpless I feel standing here doing nothing.

Lights flash. The siren is piercingly loud. The ambulance pulls up under the awning and two paramedics dart out.

I'm too distraught to even speak at this point. Asher explains. One of the paramedics takes Charlie and carefully places him on the ground while the other administers epinephrine.

In an instant, Charlie takes a huge breath, coughs a few times, then starts crying. His lips pink up. A moment later, his facial swelling starts to abate.

My whole world swirls and I fall into Dallas's waiting arms.

When I come to, it must have only been seconds that passed, because Charlie is being put on a gurney and loaded into the back of the ambulance. Covered in blankets now, he has an oxygen mask over his face and he's calling for me.

"We need to bring him in for observation. There's always a chance of a rebound reaction," the paramedic says, looking between Dallas and me. "We can only take one of you."

"Me. I'm going."

"We'll follow," Asher says. "Go."

"Ma'am," the paramedic asks. "Are you okay?"

"She's perfectly fine," Dallas insists. "She's good and she's going with him."

I look over at Dallas as I make my way to the back of the rig. "Thank you," I say, my eyes pools of relieved tears.

He's visibly trembling as he nods.

The last thing I see before the large rear doors close is Dallas running over to vomit into a nearby bush.

And somehow, deep down, I know it's the last memory I'll ever have of Dallas Montana.

Chapter Thirty-seven

Dallas

Asher and I head upstairs. He has to change, and I have to… get the fuck out of here.

"He'll be okay, you know," Asher says. "He was little when we found out about his peanut allergy. This is the third time it's happened. Marti always has an EpiPen with her. Always."

"It's my fault. All her shit spilled out of her purse during the accident. When I went to look for her phone, I just stuffed whatever I could find back into her purse." I lean into the corner of the elevator, feeling the walls close in on me. "Jesus, he could have died."

"Stop right there, man. I'm guessing you had no idea about his allergy. There is zero chance you would have known to look around her floorboard for an EpiPen. If it's anyone's fault, it's mine. I didn't even think to ask Anita for the one they would have had when I picked him up and brought him back here. You want to blame someone, blame me."

I steady myself on the wall, shaking my head over and over. I hear what he's saying, but it doesn't help one goddamn bit. The boy had hives all around his mouth. His face was swollen. His fucking lips were turning bluer with every step I took. It's all I could do not to go bat-shit crazy.

When we reach the rooms, he lets me into Marti's. "You're not coming to the hospital, are you?"

"I think Bex and I need to head home."

"She'll be gutted."

"Charlie is okay, that's what matters. It's the *only* thing that matters."

"If that's what you really think, you're not as smart as I gave you credit for."

I put Bex's leash on and gather his things. "Tell her… tell her I'm glad he's okay. Charlie seems like one hell of a kid."

"He is."

I hold out my hand. "It's been a day."

He shakes, disappointment all over his face. "It's been nice meeting you, Dallas. Even if you're being a stupid motherfucker."

"That I am," I tell him as I lead Bex out of the room. I close the door and look back at it one last time. "That I am."

~ ~ ~

The drive back to my cabin takes longer than the drive out. Not because of the weather, but because I have two panic attacks on the way home. I have to pull over and let them pass.

I've never had a panic attack before. When the first one hit, I was sure I was having a heart attack. I was close to calling 911, but figured what would be the point? I've just walked away from the only good thing in my life in two-and-a-half years. To what—go back to my pathetic existence?

Pulling up to my cabin, I turn off the engine and stare out the windshield. The place looks different somehow. Smaller. Emptier.

Stepping inside, my eyes go straight to the bed. It's still unmade, and I'll bet it smells of her. Her and sex. I walk over to see the bracelet right where she thought she left it. I run my finger across the initials, contemplating putting it in my pocket. But I don't. It'll still be here tomorrow.

I look at the kitchen and see her making a meal. At the table, I can picture her laughing.

The couch reminds me of the hours and hours she'd read to me.

I don't even have to enter the bathroom to imagine her taking a bath and touching herself.

She's everywhere.

And I know I can't stay.

Before, this place was my solace. The spot I needed to hide away and exist in all the nothingness. But then Marti happened. And I no longer want the nothingness. She's right. I need people.

It's too cold in here, and not just because the power is out.

I load as much wood as I can into the fireplace to keep the cabin at an acceptable temperature until the propane comes, then I slam the small wrought iron door shut with my foot. *Hard.* I'm not sure why I'm pissed at it specifically, but I'm pissed at *something.*

I stuff some clothes into my backpack, get Bex's bag of food, and go back to the truck where Bex awaits, still inside, as if I already knew I wouldn't be staying.

Before starting the engine, I look at Abe the snowman. He still wears the scarf I gave to Marti. He probably always will. That is until he's a pile of mush and the piece of fabric lies on the dirt.

I'm glad I won't be here to see him melt. It would be like seeing… *ah, hell, I need to get the fuck out of my head.*

I drive another fifty miles to the only hotel around, get a room for Bex and me, then walk next door and buy a bottle of tequila. When the bottle is half empty, I lie on the bed and stare at the ceiling. Bex jumps up and stretches out next to me. I give him a pat when he puts his head on my chest.

"It's just not the same, buddy." I close my eyes and let sleep pull me under.

~ ~ ~

I float down the flower-lined aisle toward the altar. Phoebe's back is to me, but she's still beautiful. Her gown is all buttons and lace and fits her like a glove. I can't wait to peel her out of it later. A veil covers her head, but I just know her hair is down and flowing over her shoulders, just the way she knows I like it.

Why is nobody here? Am I that early? As I approach, however, I see one person occupying a chair in the front. It's DJ. He's got a huge smile on his face.

"You look handsome, Dad."

I cock my head and study him. When did he get so darned old? Kids grow up so fast these days. It seems like just yesterday he was six months old and I was bouncing him on my knee.

I reach Phoebe. She turns to me, but I still can't see her through the mesh of the veil.

She takes my hands in hers. "You saved me. You saved him."

DJ hops off the chair and runs over, hugging us both.

But when I look down, it's not DJ. This boy has hazel eyes and dark hair with a cowlick on one side.

"I'm so happy, Dad."

Confused, I look up at Phoebe, who's no longer wearing her veil. In fact she's not wearing a wedding dress at all. She's in a Yale hoodie. And… she's not Phoebe. She's Marti.

"Wait... no," I say, backing away from them. "This isn't how it's supposed to be."

When I turn to run, Phoebe is sitting in the front pew holding our infant son, running a soothing hand over his platinum-blond hair.

She looks up at me. "You can love them," she says. "You can love them and *us. That's the great thing about love. There is an endless well of it in your heart. An infinite capacity. It can never become too full." She stands, DJ in her arms, and she walks away from me. There's a cloud behind her. A light that resembles the glow of a fire. Before she walks into it, she turns once more. "The well will never run dry, Dallas."*

I step toward them. "But... you said I could never replace you. You asked why I saved her and not you."

"No. That was you. You *said those things. It was all you, Dallas. We have to go now. And you need to let us."*

"I can't. I can never let you go."

She smiles brightly, as luminescent as the fiery hue behind her. "We'll see you again. On DJ's birthday. On mine. Until then, my love, go fill your well. Fill it as full as you can and then fill it some more."

She turns, DJ in her arms, and they both disappear into a wall of flames.

I spin back to the altar, but it's gone too. My arms grow heavy. When I look down, I'm holding DJ, but he's older. No, not DJ. Charlie.

"I love you, Dad," he says.

I jolt awake, sweat running off my temple. Because...

What. The. Fuck.

Chapter Thirty-eight

Martina

Bright light shines from overhead. I swing an arm over my eyes to keep it out.

Wait… light? The power is back on?

I move my arm, open my eyes, and see the ceiling tiles of the hospital room. It all comes back in one huge wave. Charles's death. The accident. The ten glorious days with Dallas. *Charlie.* I bolt straight up when I remember what brought us to the hospital.

The nurse across the room smiles and gives me the 'ok' sign. She comes over and quietly tells me, "He's doing great. There was no rebound reaction overnight. The doctor will clear him for discharge this morning."

She shoves a dozen pamphlets at me concerning kids and peanut allergies. It's nothing I don't know, and it's a futile attempt to try and tell her that I know at least as much about it as she does, but a string of unfortunate events put me in a situation of not having the EpiPen.

I know *all* the tips. It was a stupid mistake. Why didn't I say anything at the pool? It's usually the first thing I do when around new people. *Hello, I'm Marti. My son Charlie has a severe peanut allergy, please don't give him any food or have any peanuts around or even eat them when he's near.* His preschool won't even allow peanuts through the front doors as he's one of three kids there with an allergy.

I feel incredibly guilty over not having my son's life-saving medicine. Everyone probably assumes I'm a horrible mother. Maybe I am. I should have checked to make sure it was in my purse when I first went to Dallas's cabin.

I swear on my life that I'll never be without an EpiPen ever again. I'll have one stapled to my hip if that's what it takes. I won't lose him.

For a moment, I can imagine what it's like for Dallas. To feel so broken and alone. Losing Alex was impossibly hard, but if I lost Charlie, it would be the last straw. I couldn't recover. *Is that what it's like for him?*

When the nurse leaves, I tiptoe over to Charlie's bed and gaze down on him, feeling all kinds of lucky despite everything that went horribly wrong.

It's hard to get the picture of Dallas holding Charlie and carrying him to meet the ambulance out of my head. *Dallas.* Not me. Not Asher. *He* was the one who acted so swiftly. Who knows what those precious moments saved Charlie from. Brain damage? Death?

I shudder to think of it.

And once again, Dallas Montana becomes a savior. A hero. I know it's not a distinction he cares about, but he's earned it nonetheless.

Last night, they wouldn't let anyone else up here. It was after visiting hours. Asher texted and said he'd pick us up in the morning when Charlie got released. *He'd* pick us up. Not Dallas.

I saw his visceral reaction last night once Charlie was safe and in the ambulance. His face was as white as a ghost. He was shaking so hard I thought *he* might need medical attention. And then he got sick.

Dallas isn't coming. Not today. Probably not ever.

There's a soft knock on the door, then Asher's head pops in.

I wave him inside.

He walks around the side of the bed and puts an arm around me, kissing my temple. "That kid scared the shit out of me," he whispers.

I nod, trying to keep the tears at bay.

The first time Charlie had an anaphylactic reaction to peanuts, he was fourteen months old. We were at a theme park, and luckily they had their own paramedics who carried EpiPens. After that day, I was vigilant about having one on me at all times.

The second time it happened, we were at Suzanne's daughter's birthday party. By this time, everyone I knew understood they couldn't have peanuts anywhere near Charlie. But one of the toddler party-goers had eaten a peanut butter sandwich just before coming, his parents unaware that even residue on his mouth, face, and hands could potentially kill my son. Luckily, I was there with the EpiPen. He never got anywhere near as bad as he was last night.

Charlie stirs. His eyes open, and he looks up at me. I lean over the bed and pull him into a huge hug. "Hey, buddy. You gave us a scare, but you're fine now."

"The big bad food?" he asks, returning my hug with fervor.

"Yes. The big bad food. But, Charlie, you need to start calling it peanuts. Other people don't know what the big bad food is. You're a big boy now and you need to be able to tell people you can't have peanuts. And you can never never accept snacks without asking me or Uncle Asher."

"Okay, Mommy. I'll say penus."

Asher and I chuckle at the way it comes out. Asher whispers, "People will think he's allergic to dick."

I swat his arm. "Stop it."

Asher and Charlie play games on Ash's phone while I fill out Charlie's discharge paperwork. "I wonder how much *this* is gonna cost me," I mumble.

The nurse must have overheard me. "Word is the bill has already been paid." She places an EpiPen on the table. "Including the cost of this."

I look up. "What are you talking about?"

"One of the night-shift nurses said a man called to get an update on your son. No information could be released of course, but he insisted on paying the bill. Rather vehemently, as I heard it. We don't deal with billing, but he was directed to the people who do." She tosses a look to Charlie. "Looks like your son has a guardian angel."

She raises a brow at Asher. He holds up a defensive hand. "Don't look at *me*. I had nothing to do with it."

"I can't believe he did that," I say once the nurse leaves.

Asher puts away his phone and steps closer. "About Dallas…"

"You don't have to tell me. I know he's gone."

A wrinkle cuts across his forehead. "He called you?"

"No. I just know."

He scoops Charlie into his arms. "Come on, bud. Let's get you back to the hotel. Today, we're swimming all day long. We're going to be in the water so much, we might turn into fish."

"Like Nemo?" Charlie asks.

"Yes, just like Nemo."

Asher turns to me. "I called Anita last night and told her what happened. Or I told her mom anyway. Anita was sleeping. Jane said the remembrance service has been planned for tomorrow. Charles's mom and sister are flying in later today. So, that means we're free to go home on Saturday." He punctures me with a glare. "Should I make airline reservations for three?"

I cackle. "With all the bad luck I've had lately, no thank you. You go ahead. Charlie and I will drive."

"You know driving is—"

I wave a hand around. "More dangerous. Whatever. I'm not flying, Ash."

He huffs in frustration. "Fine. I'll go with you."

"You've already been here for days. Bug needs you."

"Bug is having a great time with Mel. Believe me, she's fine. You and Charlie are my priorities this week."

I wrap my arms around him and Charlie. "I love you, big brother."

"You'd better. Now let's get out of here. Charlie and I have some swimming to do while you help Anita's family plan for tomorrow."

I hand him the EpiPen. "Do not let this out of your sight."

"Never. I'm sorry I didn't have one. It was stupid of me not to ask for Anita's when I picked him up. She wasn't in the right mind to remember. I feel awful."

"Ash, stop. I'm the one who should have had it."

"Can we not play the blame game here? He's good, and we'll never be in that position again. Agreed?"

"Agreed."

He lowers Charlie to the ground, and we leave the hospital, Charlie between us, each of us holding one of his hands. And a sudden wave of sadness overtakes me that Dallas isn't the man holding Charlie's other hand.

Chapter Thirty-nine

Dallas

I sit on a bench and stare at the grave marker. The one I've never seen before. The one that has the names of my wife and son, buried together for all of eternity.

There are still some wet teddy bears nestled near the headstone, brought by my family no doubt for DJ's birthday last week.

After having the same goddamn dream two nights in a row, I drove down early this morning, drawn here by some inexplicable force of nature. It's been two-and-a-half years, and this is the very first time I've sat in this spot and looked upon this grave.

The sun has melted most of the snow from the blizzard. Only piles on the side of the road made by snowplows remain. What a difference a few days can make.

When my mind drifts back to the past week with thoughts of Marti and Charlie, guilt begins to consume me. The mother and child I should be thinking about are right here, practically under my feet. What was up with that strange dream? And why did I have it twice? *The exact fucking dream.* I can't get it out of my head. In the dream,

Phoebe said it was all me, that all those words she's said in my previous dreams were my words, not hers. But then how can I believe the words in last night's dream were hers? It's all one huge clusterfuck inside my head right now.

"Dallas?"

My head swivels. To my surprise, Allie is approaching, bundled in her cold weather running clothes.

"How in the hell did you know I was here?" I ask.

"I didn't. I jog by the cemetery almost every day. When I saw someone sitting over here, I had to come see who it was." She bends over, hands on hips, as if she's had a long run. Then she gives Bex a pat on the head. "Since when do you have a dog?"

"Long story."

She shoves me aside and I make room for her on the bench. "But one you'll tell me, right?" she asks.

I shrug.

She elbows me. "I didn't even know you came here."

"I don't. I mean, I didn't. Until now."

One of her brows rises in curiosity. "Reeeeeealy?"

"What the fuck does that mean?"

She shrugs innocently. "Just that some mysterious woman shows up in your life, gets stranded at your cabin for a week, and suddenly, you're here."

"It was ten days. And one doesn't necessarily have anything to do with the other."

"Whatever you say."

I shake my head. She's as tenacious as Marti.

And there's the guilt again. My eyes rake over Phoebe's name on the headstone and I silently apologize.

"You're staying for Lucas's party tomorrow, aren't you?" she asks.

"I might make an appearance. But I have to head back to my cabin first."

She flashes me a set of crazy eyes. "Dallas, why? You're here now. Why would you drive four hours there and then four more back tomorrow?"

"There are things I need to take care of." I stand and hold out Bex's leash. "Can you take Bex until I get back? He's been in the truck long enough. And I might need the room."

"Need the room for what?"

"Stuff."

Her eyes widen like dinner plates. "Dallas, are you—"

"Don't get too excited. I'm not sure what I'm doing. Will you watch him or not?"

She takes the leash. "Sure."

"Come on. I'll give you a ride home. I've got some of his stuff in my truck."

We ride in silence, mostly because I refuse to be a part of the Spanish Inquisition. When I pull up to Mom and Dad's house, I ask, "Are you ever moving out?"

"Tried once last year when Mia and I got an apartment together. But honestly? Why would I give all this up? Montana Manor has everything, including an apartment for me with a separate entrance over the garage. And at over twelve-thousand square feet, I never even have to see Mom and Dad if I don't want to. Not that I don't want to."

"So, what, you're going to live here forever?"

"Until I have a reason to move, yeah."

"What would that reason be?"

"The perfect man I suppose."

I laugh. "You'll be living here until the day you die, little sister. You should know. It's what you thought about Jason. The two of you were together for years and then one day you decided on a whim to take that internship in Australia, and then it was just over."

She gulps, getting that sullen look on her face anytime anyone mentions her ex. Then she shores herself up with a giant breath.

"The perfect man *is* out there," she says. "Anyway, how can you be so cynical? *You* were the perfect man yourself once upon a time. You could be again if you'd just let it happen."

I shove the backpack at her. "I'm not talking about this."

"Well, you should. Because Marti is perfect for you. And you for her. I know you have feelings. She's a single mom. Charlie needs a father figure. You could fill that void. And you have a pretty big fucking void yourself that the two of them could fill."

"What the fuck, Allie? You think I'm looking to replace my wife and kid?"

"No, of course not. All I'm saying is that it just makes sense. They need you and you need them."

I narrow my eyes. "Have you been talking to her?"

"Just the one conversation when she answered your phone. I'm very good at reading between the lines."

"Well, it could never work."

"How do you know?"

"I just do."

She sighs loudly. "Dallas, if you don't even try, you may never forgive yourself."

"He almost died in my fucking arms, Al."

She looks confused. "DJ?"

"Charlie. Her kid. He's allergic to peanuts and a kid gave him a cookie and there wasn't an EpiPen because I stupidly didn't find it in her car after her accident. And… Jesus, his face. His lips. His throat was closing." A warm tear runs down my cheek. "He almost died in my arms as I ran him to meet the paramedics."

"Oh my god." A hand covers her mouth. "But he's okay?"

"I called the hospital. They wouldn't tell me anything. But I'm pretty sure he is. The ambulance got to him just in time. He was already breathing normally just a few seconds after they gave him the medicine." I rub the back of my neck. "But if they'd have been just another minute…" I wipe my nose on my coat sleeve. "I can't go through that again. I won't lose anyone else."

"And you think not being with them is the answer? If a tree falls in the woods and no one hears it… it still falls. What if you *hadn't* been there? Charlie still would have been exposed to peanuts, but you wouldn't have rushed him to meet the ambulance. He was in *your* arms. Do you think you're somehow keeping them safe by staying away? Because I'd say it's just the opposite. Especially when it's written all over your face how you feel about Marti."

I reach over and open her door, dismissing her with a wave of my hand. "You're free to go."

"Fine," she pouts. "Don't admit it to me. But do me a favor and at least admit it to yourself."

She gets Bex from the back and then yells at me through the window, "Party's at eight at Donovan's. Be there!"

I give a thumb's up along with a snarky, defiant sneer. Then I pull out of the long, circular driveway and head out of town, careful to avoid the one street I never plan to drive down again.

Chapter Forty

Martina

After a busy two days of planning, supporting, remembering, and crying, we're finally on our way back to Florida.

Charlie is secured in his seat, holding Grumpy in one hand, and a juice box in the other. I'm lucky my son likes car trips, because this is going to be a long one. We plan on breaking it into three days, finding parks and playgrounds for him to let off energy along the way.

It gets hot in the car with the heat blasting, so I take off my coat. Well, not *my* coat. Dallas's coat. I sigh heavily as I reach over and put it in the back seat.

Asher takes his eyes off the road momentarily, looking sorry for me. "Some people are just damaged beyond repair, Marti." He pats my knee. "I'm really sorry."

I stare out the window, holding tears at bay. "I don't think anyone is that damaged. Sure, he's broken in a way. I am too. But what if…" I look at him as if he has all the answers. "What if it takes one broken person to fix another? Like maybe two broken people can make each other whole somehow. Fill in each other's cracks."

"If that's true, what are you doing here while he's God knows where?"

"What happened at the hotel had to be terrifying for him. I should know. I've lost a child, too. We've both been through it. We've lived it. And he thought it was happening again."

"You had brushes with death when you were with him, Marti. He didn't bail then."

"He couldn't, Ash. We were stranded. And he kind of did bail in a way. He'd run away. Literally. As in he'd go out in the forest and run. Or he'd chop wood. It didn't matter if we'd had a bad moment or a good one, they all seemed to bring back memories of what he was hiding from. But he was changing. I could see it. I could feel it. He celebrated DJ's birthday. That was a huge step for him. And after we'd… well, you don't want the details—"

"God, please, no."

"After he ran out the first time, he began to heal. He stopped pulling away as much. He was opening up to me and sharing some of his past." I look wistfully out the window. "If we'd only had more time together."

We pass a sign that marks the western edge of the Tug Hill Region. Asher points to it. "So show up. Go to his cabin and see what happens. Lay it all out for him."

I shake my head. "I can't do that."

"Why not?"

"Sometimes it's better to just walk away with the good memories. If I showed up on his doorstep and he rejected me, it would negate those ten days. Right now, I can hold onto them. Asher, I know it sounds strange because Charles had just died and I couldn't get to Charlie, but those ten days were some of the best of my life." I sigh. "Besides, even if I wanted to, I'd have no idea how to find his cabin. It's not like I can just google it. It's in the middle of nowhere. I doubt it even has an address."

He pats my knee again. "I'm sorry, Marti. I wish there was something I could do to help."

"You have helped. You were there for Charlie. And you're here for me. That's enough."

Even though it's just mid-afternoon, my eyes grow heavy after a few hours on the road. I grab the coat from the back seat and use it as a pillow, balling it up and wedging it between my head and the window. I inhale sharply, hoping it still smells like him. It doesn't. I've worn it so long, his scent is gone, and that saddens me to no end. "I guess I'll have to send the coat to him somehow," I muse aloud. "I could mail it to the winery I suppose."

"Mmm," Asher mumbles, and turns the music on low.

I fall asleep to Taylor Swift singing about her broken heart, wondering if writing a song would help me get over this crippling hurt that has taken up residence inside me.

~ ~ ~

I'm shaken slightly. "Martina, we're here."

I rub my eyes. "How long did I sleep? We're in Pennsylvania? But it's not even that dark yet."

"We're not in Pennsylvania."

I look out my window. "So why aren't we on the highway anymore?"

"Small detour." He points ahead to a large sign on the side of the road.

Montana Winery.

I stiffen. "Asher! What are you doing?"

He shrugs. "You said you wanted to return the coat to the winery. Well, let's return the coat to the winery. It was only fifteen minutes out of the way."

My mouth hangs open.

Fully awake now, I'm picturing a million ways this could turn out. None of them good. "Turn around."

"Too late. Road's too narrow." He pulls onto a long winding road where endless rows of dormant grapevines go on as far as the eye can see. It's mesmerizing. It's a piece of Dallas I never thought I'd get to see. A part of his life I didn't think I'd ever experience.

I quit protesting. Because even though he's not here, I feel closer to him.

"It's the weekend," I say. "The place will probably be closed." I look down at the coat and feel a sudden pang of loss knowing just how much I wanted to see its owner no matter how unlikely it is that he'd be here. "We can just leave it by the door with a note."

As the car approaches the front and several large buildings come into view, I'm hit with disappointment upon seeing the empty parking lot.

I'm not sure what Asher thought he was going to accomplish by making this detour. But my guess is it has nothing to do with returning the coat.

Asher parks right next to the entrance, not even bothering to pull into a spot.

I ask, "Did you even like him?"

He laughs half-heartedly. "I didn't expect to. In fact, I expected to hate him. But the truth is, I did. Which is all kinds of crazy despite some crap he said. But the guy is oddly charming."

"Tell me about it." I narrow my eyes. "What *crap* did he say?"

"It's not important."

"Asher, you don't have to protect me. I'm a big girl."

I'm startled by a knock on the window and I whirl around in my seat to see a beautiful woman. When I recognize her from the picture on Dallas's phone, I quickly roll down the window.

"Can I help you?" she asks, pulling a sweater tightly around her. "Are you lost?"

My heart pounds for no explicable reason. It's not him, after all. "I'm Marti."

Her eyes double in size and a huge smile splits her face. "Oh my gosh. Fantastic! What are you doing in there? Get out here so I can give you a proper hug." I open the door and slip out. She wastes no time squeezing me. Hard. "I'm so glad you came."

Confusion sets in. "Um…" I reach back inside and get the coat. "I just needed to return this. We're on our way back to Florida."

Now *she's* the one who looks confused. "You aren't here for Lucas's party?"

"The party." I pretty much deflate on the spot. "I'd forgotten all about it. No. We were just passing by Calloway Creek on I-95 and took a detour." I offer her the coat. "Cheaper than sending it."

She pushes it back at me. "It's cold, Marti. You should be wearing it. And as long as you're here, you should definitely come to the party. We had a wine tasting today." She jiggles a set of keys. "I was just getting ready to go home and change for the party when I saw you drive up." She stops talking and looks around me into the car.

"Sorry," I say. "I didn't mean to be rude. Allie, this is my brother, Asher Anderson."

Allie's face lights up a second time. She all but hops into the front seat, stretching out her arm. "Asher Anderson," she muses as she puts her hand into his. "Sounds very presidential."

He laughs. "Nice to meet you, Allie Montana."

I raise a brow, noticing a slight change in his voice. It's sturdier. More masculine. My eyes bounce back and forth between them when I realize they haven't let go of each other's hands. She giggles, practically preening, and my brother's eyes are laser focused on her. "You should come too, Asher. And Charlie." Her gaze finally breaks from his and she looks at my sleeping son in the back seat. "Damn he's cute."

Finally, after far too long a handshake, she pulls away and backs out of the front seat.

"What do you say?" she asks me. "Will you come?"

"No." I shake my head vehemently. "No way."

Her hands land on her hips. I take it she's a woman who's used to getting what she wants.

"For one, we don't even know Lucas. And then there's the fact that Dallas will be there. That would probably be a bit too awkward."

"My brother is a complete idiot. He needs a nudge is all. Maybe this party is just the thing to—" Allie's phone rings. "Excuse me for a sec." She retrieves it from her pocket. "Well, speak of the devil." She swipes her finger across the screen as my heartbeat accelerates. "Hey, Dallas. You'll never guess who's standing in front of me right now."

I step forward and get her attention, waving a hand wildly then doing the cutthroat sign.

"It's um… um… Mia's brother, Dax. He wants an invite to the party. Think I should extend one?"

She laughs at whatever his response is.

Then her jubilant demeanor changes. "Aw, no, really?" Her eyes settle on me. "Are you sure?" She shifts her stance, pouting. "Well, whatever. If it can't be avoided. Guess I'll see you when I see you." She tucks her phone away. "Problem solved. He's not coming.

Something to do with the authorities wanting to talk to him about some old dead guy."

"Abe," I say, feeling sad about the man I never met all over again.

She rubs her cold hands together. "So? Will you come?"

"We won't know anyone."

"That will be remedied about thirty seconds after we go through the door."

"Marti," Asher says, leaning over the console. "It could be fun. We've had a lot of depressing situations in the past few days. A party might be just what we need."

I shoot him a *'you're not helping'* glare.

"Mommy?" Charlie says from his car seat, awake now. "Is there a party?"

"There sure is," Allie says. "And there will be lots of kids there. Wouldn't you like to come and eat great food and play? There will be cake."

"Mommy! Can we?"

These three. They're teaming up on me.

"I don't know, buddy." I turn to Allie. "We'd have no place to stay. Is there even a hotel here? I know the town is small."

"We have two, actually, but there's no need. You can stay with me. There's plenty of room."

"I don't know."

"Mommy, pwease?" Charlie begs.

I look at Asher, who's innocently holding up his hands. I feel I don't have a choice. I sigh. "Fine."

Allie jumps up and claps. "Great. Let me lock up. My car is around back. You can follow me home and we'll all freshen up."

She runs off before I have another chance to protest.

I get back in the car and point a finger at Asher. "You." I shake my head. "I can't believe you backed me into a corner on this. This wasn't in the plans. It'll set us back a day."

"So we'll drive an extra few hours tomorrow. It's no big deal, Marti. Geesh, when did you become such a stick in the mud?"

I close my eyes, lean back into the headrest, and surmise it was two days ago when I became said stick. The day the man I'm in love with walked away with my heart in his pocket.

~ ~ ~

My jaw is in my lap as I look at the massive house we're pulling up to. The house goes on forever. It looks like a governor's mansion or something. Sprawling grounds. Walls of windows. Dormers and peaks and angles and garages… oh, so many garages.

It's all decked out for the holidays. Huge decorative Christmas ornaments hang from trees. Wooden reindeer displays dot the landscape. There are wreaths in every window, and a massive red bow adorns the front door.

I grab Asher's arm. "This can't be her house. She's only twenty-seven."

A classy-looking couple steps out of the front door and walks toward the car. We park behind Allie in the large circular drive and get out. The woman, who looks to be in her fifties, with hair the color of Dallas's and a welcoming smile, says, "Welcome to our home, Marti and Asher. I'm Sarah Montana, and this is my husband, Chris." She peeks in the back. "And that must be Charlie." When she sees the odd look on my face, she adds, "Allie called from the car. She said we'd be having guests for the evening."

"I… I thought we were staying at Allie's place."

Chris chuckles. "This *is* Allie's place." He points to the windows over the four-car-garage on the left—one of two four-car garages connected to the house. "Or that is anyway."

"I only wanted to return Dallas's coat. This"—I wave a hand around—"is not what I intended."

Sarah's eyes crinkle with a smile. "Sometimes the best things in life come when we least expect them." She holds my gaze and it makes me wonder just how much his family knows of our snowy escapades.

"But you don't even know us. We really don't want to impose."

Sarah scolds me with her eyes. "You're not from a small town, are you?"

I shake my head. "Orlando."

She laughs. "Well, we do things differently here. Everyone is family. Come, get your bags and I'll show you to the guest rooms."

"Mrs. Montana, are you sure?"

She puts a hand on my shoulder. "It's Sarah. And I'm positive."

A familiar furry friend emerges from the house, surging toward my son, tail wagging.

"Bex!" Charlie exclaims.

I quickly turn to Allie. "I thought you said he wasn't here."

"I'm dog sitting for a few days."

"Oh."

I want to ask her so many questions. Like how did Bex get here? Did Dallas bring him? Why just a few days? But I don't have a chance to ask because Sarah takes my elbow and escorts me inside.

Ten minutes later, after being shown our rooms, not to mention a tour of the house that is like Disneyland to Charlie, we're changing for the party.

Charlie and I are in a room connected to Asher's by a large bathroom.

I sit on the bed and look around, wondering if this used to be one of their boys' bedrooms. Maybe even Dallas's. I run my hand along the bedspread, trying to *feel* him as if his aura is still here.

Asher walks through the bathroom and peeks his head inside our room. "You could do much worse."

I roll my eyes. "I'm not *doing* anything, Ash. Can we just get through the next few hours please?"

When we're as ready as we can get, since I didn't exactly pack party clothes, we head to the living room. It's hard not to look at the pictures on the wall. There are so many of them. And the people—there must be dozens. I imagine Dallas growing up with tons of cousins, aunts, uncles, and grandparents. I'm envious of all the love he must have had surrounding him.

I glanced at the photos during the tour, but I can really study them now. I'm fascinated by one in particular. It's the four Montana children standing in the middle of a vineyard right before sunset. I immediately know which one Dallas is even though he must be only ten or so. Those eyes are exactly the same. His face was fuller and his hair shorter, but he was a cute kid.

Another photo captures my attention. It's a photo of the entire family. Chris, Sarah, their four kids… and Phoebe and DJ.

Sarah comes up behind me. She looks between me and the picture on the wall. "Does this bother you?"

"Not at all." I lean against the wall. "Out of curiosity, what do you… know?"

There's a glint in her eye that tells me she might just know more than I think. "My son isn't one to share details about his life. Especially since he lost them. Allie filled us in with what little she knows. We all read between the lines." Her face turns soft, her eyes inviting. "Marti, it seems you've been the breath of fresh air my son has needed for a long time."

I curse myself when tears come to my eyes, rendering me unable to respond.

"He visited their graves yesterday." She takes my elbow and guides me to the sofa. "That might not seem all that significant, except for the fact that it's the very first time he's done it."

My eyes snap up to hers.

She nods, another bright smile crinkling her beautiful complexion. "Whatever happened between the two of you up in that cabin has changed him." She pats my hand in that motherly way—the way I imagine my own mother would have. "But it took two-and-a-half years, Marti. It might just take him another minute to digest everything. All we can do is be patient with him. But I'll tell you this, I think you and that little boy of yours might be just what he needs."

I shake my head and stare at the massive two-story Christmas tree in front of the windows that overlook the extensive property. "I don't think so. I had hoped, but with Charlie I don't know if it's possible. I think it's just too much with the both of us." I look at Sarah. "But now I have hope that he will find the one he needs. And I'm so happy he'll have that."

"Mmm. I guess we'll see." She stands. "Shall we go to the party? I think you might enjoy our little town."

Charlie races into the room and points out back. "Mommy, they have a pool!"

"And you can come swim in it anytime you want," Allie says. She turns to my brother and winks. "That goes for you too."

I don't tell her she's being ridiculous. And far more hopeful than I could ever dare to be.

"Car's warmed up and ready to go," Chris says. "No need to grab your car seat, we already have one for our granddaughter, Maisy."

I've only known these people for a half hour, yet they're treating me like family, even though they already have a massive one. Sarah is treating me like a daughter. And Allie, a sister. I'm sad that tomorrow we'll be leaving, and it'll go back to being just the four of us—Asher, me, Charlie, and Bug. No extended family. No grandparents. No second and third cousins. No village in which to raise our children.

And despite all the tragedy Dallas has endured, I hope he understands what a lucky, lucky man he is.

Chapter Forty-one

Martina

When we enter the party at a place called Donovan's Pub, people immediately swarm to meet the strangers. We're introduced to Lucas, Blake and his wife, then Allie's aunt, uncle, and cousins, and so many Calloways I can't keep them all straight. And every single one of them is warm and welcoming.

I feel like I'm in the twilight zone.

There are several children here, but Charlie is particularly fascinated by Maisy, Dallas's deaf niece. He doesn't fully understand that she can't hear him, so he talks to her normally, which Allie informs me is just how he should.

"This is Cooper and Serenity," Allie says when an attractive couple walk over. "They run the place. Ren and I have been friends since we were kids."

They both shake my hand.

"It's very nice to meet you," I say, caught up in the surreal experience of meeting what seems like everyone in Dallas's world. Or his *old* world anyway.

Cooper says, "We're peanut-free here. Have been since a friend of our son had a bad reaction a few years ago. We do cook with peanut oil, but I'm told that's okay."

I nod and smile, curious as to how they even know about Charlie's allergy. "Yes, that's okay. And thank you, that's good to know."

Allie elbows me like an old friend. "One anaphylactic reaction this week is enough, eh?"

I'm positive my shock is written all over me. "He told you?"

"Yeah. Pretty crazy, right? Not about the peanuts, but about Dallas actually revealing something personal about his life." She gets a look on her face. "I'm telling you…"

Arms wrap around her. She turns and squeals as she and another beautiful woman embrace.

"Is this her?" the woman asks when she sees me.

"Marti, this is my other friend, Mia."

"It's a pleasure," I say. "Are you a Montana or a Calloway?"

"Neither," she laughs. "I'm a Cruz." A finger settles in front of her lips. "Shhh, don't tell anyone. I'm the enemy in this territory."

I narrow my eyes.

"There are a lot of family rivalries in this town," Allie explains. "The McQuaids hate the Calloways. The Cruzes hate the Montanas. And the list goes on."

"So how did you and Mia and Serenity end up friends?"

"Because men are stupid," Allie says. "And we're *so* much smarter. They're the ones who hold the grudges."

We sit in a booth, me keeping an eye on Charlie as Sarah supervises him and Maisy at a table with some coloring books. Drinks get delivered to the table and I hear the abridged story of this town, right down to how it got its name and why there are so many feuding families.

"So you're a single mom?" Mia asks.

"I am." I glance at Charlie, still thinking how unbelievable it is that I'll be his sole parent from here on out.

"And you have a little boy?"

I point to him. "Charlie is three."

"Does he have any brothers or sisters?"

Sorrow blazes a trail to my heart. "I had a daughter, but she passed away when she was a week old."

Instantly, Allie's eyes fill with tears as she has some sort of visceral reaction to my admission. Mia takes her hand and I swear something passes between them. Both seem very empathetic. I can't help thinking the three of us would be great friends. If circumstances were different, that is.

"I'm so sorry," Mia says, reaching over to put her other hand on mine.

"I've made my peace with it. But I still miss her every day."

Allie stares at me, wiping a tear. "You're even more perfect for Dallas than I thought."

I sigh. "Would you mind if we don't talk about him?"

"Hold the fucking phone," Mia exclaims, digging her fingers into Allie's forearm. "Who in the ever-loving hotness is that?"

Allie's and my eyes follow the direction of her gaze to where Asher is standing at the bar talking to Lucas and one of the Calloway brothers, cousins, or… I don't even know.

"Don't even think about it," Allie says. "I saw him first."

"Really?" I say, giving them both a look.

"It's a small town," Allie says. "It's not often we get fresh meat here."

I almost choke on my lemonade. "Oh my god, can you please not refer to my brother as fresh meat?"

"Your brother?" Mia asks, her eyes finally back inside her head and looking at me now.

"Okay, Marti, give us the rundown," Allie says. "I didn't see a ring. And based on the look he gave me in the car earlier, he's either totally eligible, or he's a cheating snake."

Mia bounces excitedly in her seat. "Did he give you fuck-me eyes? Oh, please tell me you're going to have a hot one-nighter with the gorgeous older stranger." She turns to me. "How old is he anyway?"

I shake my head. My brother is handsome—that I know. And more times than I can count, I've been asked to facilitate an introduction or even a blind date. But come on, he's not *that* hot. Not *Dallas* hot.

Is he?

Ewwww… just no. I can't even look at him that way. He's the guy who used to hold me down and fart on my face. But that was back when times were easier, long before Dad died and Asher became much more than my brother. He became my guardian. My protector.

And now I'm thinking of the *other* man who has taken on that title. Geesh, can I not go two minutes without thinking of Dallas Montana?

"Asher is thirty-nine," I say. "He's not married. He has a daughter."

"This keeps getting better and better," Allie says. "Hot single dad. Older guy. And very eligible."

I rub and hand across my brow because I *so* do not want to be talking about this.

"Widowed or divorced?" Mia asks.

"Neither. Bug—that's what we call her, her real name is Darla—never had a mom in the picture. The woman who gave birth to her didn't want her and signed away her rights. Asher had a real battle on his hands trying to keep her from terminating the pregnancy."

The two women across from me each put a hand to their hearts.

I roll my eyes at all the swooning. "He *was* married once, though. But she had five miscarriages, and it really did a number on both of them, so much so that they couldn't make it work."

Mia frowns. "How sad. So he lives in Florida, too?"

It surprises me how much people seem to know about me when Dallas isn't one to talk. "Just outside of Orlando."

It hits me that Allie hasn't stopped drooling over Asher since the moment they met in the car. "How old is your niece?" she asks.

"She's twelve."

Allie sighs. Hard. "And he raised her almost all by himself? Impressive."

"He basically raised me too." I go on to tell them about how my dad died and he became my guardian.

"Wow, he really is the whole package, isn't he?" Allie says. "I think I love him already."

I want to scold her. Tell her it's impossible to fall for someone you don't even know. But really, who am I to talk? Not after how hard I've fallen for *her* brother.

"Oh my god, here he comes," Mia shrieks like we're freshmen in the school cafeteria and the varsity quarterback is on his way to our table.

"Ladies," he says to them then turns to me. "Lucas was wondering if he could have a word."

I point to myself. "With *me?*"

"That's what he said. Why don't I keep these lovely women company while you go talk to him?"

Allie and Mia look more than a little ecstatic at his offer.

I find Lucas perched on a barstool and take the empty one to his left. "Asher said you wanted to talk to me?"

"I did. I like what I've seen and I'd like to make you an offer."

"Um… what *kind* of offer?" I ask hesitantly, considering what I know about this guy's history with women.

He laughs heartily. "I guess I should have started with the fact that what I've seen refers to your profession."

"Oh." I feel my cheeks redden with embarrassment.

"But it's nice to know my reputation precedes me."

"I'm sorry. I wasn't aware Dallas had shown you anything."

"He showed me all right, and I think they're fantastic. In fact, I believe it's exactly what we need to take us to the next level. I've been wanting to shake things up for a while now. See if we can compete with the big dogs like Mondavi, Gallo, and Frères. With your incredible vision for our branding, I think we'll be off to a good start."

I'm sure my mouth is hanging open, but I can't seem to close it. I'm trying to wrap my mind around what he's saying.

"Marti?"

"Yeah, I… um, so you want to buy those graphics? I was just fooling around, Lucas. If you're serious, I'm sure I can do much better."

He chuckles. "If that was you fooling around, I can't wait to see what else you come up with. And, Marti, I want to do more than buy the graphics. I want to commission you for a total rebrand including website, on-site signage, label design, and ongoing advertising."

My momentary feeling of jubilance wanes. "I'm not going to be anyone's charity case, Lucas."

"You think I'm taking pity on you because my brother is a total twat bag who doesn't know a good thing when it's standing right in front of him?" He laughs sadly. "I'm all too familiar with that, Marti.

But, no, that's not why I'm interested. I'm interested because you've impressed the hell out of me. I've spent a few days getting my hands on everything I can find out there with your name on it. I'm interested because I'm quite sure if I don't snag you, it won't be long before you're so busy, you won't have time for any new clients. I'm interested because no matter what happens between you and my brother, I think your designs are fucking amazing."

"Stop it." I blush. "You'll give me a big head."

He laughs and calls over the bartender. "So what's it going to be, Marti? Are we ordering celebratory shots or aren't we?"

I look into his eyes, eyes that are similar to those of the man I love, and try to assess the genuineness of his offer. I haven't heard a lot about Lucas from his brother, but the one thing I did pick up on is that Lucas is one hell of a businessman. It makes me relatively confident he wouldn't do this because he feels sorry for me, or as some kind of favor to Dallas.

"Tequila," I say. "I'm a big fan."

Lucas slaps the bar happily then turns to the bartender. "Two shots of Don Julio 1942 please."

The bartender unlocks a cabinet, retrieves the tall brown bottle, and pours us each a shot.

Lucas raises his glass. "I'll email you the details of our offer on Monday."

"Monday?" I put down the glass. "Lucas, I have a lot going on right now. I just became a full-time single mom. I've been asked to take care of my ex's things down in Orlando since his widow doesn't want to deal with it. My plate is about to be pretty full, and it's a lot to process. I'm not sure I'd be any good working for anyone right now."

He shrugs nonchalantly, like nothing I said matters whatsoever. "I'll wait a week or two then. Give you time to acclimate to your new life. But just so you know, whatever we offer—you should ask for more."

I smile, clink my glass to his, and take a shot of the best tequila that has ever crossed these lips.

~ ~ ~

When I wake up, I'm disoriented. I've been so many different places over the past few weeks, it takes me a minute to recognize where I am.

My eyes come to rest on a Montana family photo on the desk and my heart flutters. Then it falls when reality assures me I'll never be in a picture like that one.

Turning over, I reach out and discover the other side of the bed is empty. "Charlie?"

When I don't get a response, I pull on a hoodie and pad out to the living room. It's not long before I hear Charlie's laughter. I make a right turn and head for the kitchen.

Standing in the doorway, I like what I see. Charlie is sitting on a barstool 'helping' Sarah make breakfast. He's making more of a mess of it than actually providing help, but Sarah doesn't seem to mind in the least.

"Mommy!" he calls out when he notices me. "Pancakes and eggs."

"Yummy. I can't wait." I walk to the counter. "How can I help?"

"Charlie and I have everything covered." She nods to another long counter at the other side of the gigantic kitchen. "There's fresh coffee."

"Perfect."

I pour myself a cup then top off Sarah's. I sit on the barstool next to Charlie and watch, holding back tears because he never got to do such things with my mother. Heck, *I* never got to do such things with my mother. And Charles's mom—a widow now—is always traveling. It's a rare occasion when Charlie sees her and, as such, he never remembers who she is. It's always made me so sad that my son hasn't grown up with a big family. I've always wished for him to have more than I had. But maybe it's just not going to happen.

A noise behind me has me turning.

Asher is coming down the back staircase. The one I know is the rear entrance to the apartment over the garage.

"Good morning, everyone," he says, reaching into a bowl of blueberries then popping one into his mouth. "We should try to hit the road by nine if we want to make up for lost time."

I'm mortified that he's doing the walk of shame right here in front of Sarah.

"Of course," I say. "I'll save you some breakfast if you want to go shower."

I shoot him a hard stare. The last thing Allie's mother needs is to eat breakfast with a guy who smells like sex after being with her one and only daughter.

He ruffles Charlie's hair then shoots me a half-smile over his shoulder on his way out.

"It seems your brother and my daughter got along quite well last night," Sarah says, not even missing a beat cracking eggs into a bowl.

I cover my face, embarrassed to high heaven. "Sarah, I'm so sorry you had to see that. I apologize on behalf of my insensitive brother. He had no right to disrespect you in your own home."

"It's okay, Marti. Allie is a grown woman. It's her house, too. And she's got a good head on her shoulders, which means your brother must be a decent man."

"He is. In fact it's very unlike him to—" My eyes flit to the back stairway.

She chuckles. "As far as I know, it's very unlike my daughter to—" She swings a hand at the ceiling. "I have to say I see the appeal. He's quite charming."

Allie comes bounding down the stairs, hair wet from a shower, sporting a smile a mile wide.

"Sleep well, honey?" Sarah asks, her voice dripping with sarcasm.

Allie giggles. "If you call what I did sleeping, then yes, I did it *very* well."

Sarah stops what she's doing. "Must you?"

"Sorry." She ruffles Charlie's hair just like Asher did. "Hey, sport. Looks like you're being a big help."

"Makin' eggs and pancakes," he says with a full-on grin that reminds me of Charles.

"Sounds heavenly. I'm super hungry." Allie winks at me. "Really worked up an appetite."

She giggles again as Sarah scolds her with her eyes.

How I envy the two of them, having such a close relationship.

Chris joins us for breakfast and tells me how excited he is for me to be joining their team. The five of us sit and eat like this isn't anything special. Like they have big family breakfasts every morning. I can't keep the longing from my thoughts. Maybe they do.

I plate some food for Asher and help Sarah clean the kitchen while Allie lets Charlie play in the elevator.

Thirty minutes later, we're rolling our suitcases out the front door.

"Chris, Sarah, I can't thank you enough for being such gracious hosts. I'll never forget your hospitality."

Sarah wraps me in a hug. "You're always welcome here." She crouches down. "You too, Charlie. You're the best pancake maker I've ever seen. Nobody can put in blueberries like you can."

Charlie's face breaks into a glowing smile.

Asher pulls Allie to the side, and they speak quietly, still flirting and laughing. I'm sure I'll get the whole story later. Asher and I have always been pretty open when it comes to each other's business.

With the suitcases in the trunk, and Charlie strapped in the back, we say our goodbyes.

Allie surprises me by coming over to my window instead of Asher's.

"Just to let you know, Dallas wasn't just coming back for the party. He was coming back to Calloway Creek for good."

My jaw goes slack.

"He's an idiot for running away like he did, Marti. You're an amazing person. And Charlie—*Gah!*—I could just eat him up."

I'm still wrapping my head around what she said. "He's moving back *here?* Out of the cabin?"

"He's changed. *You* changed him. Don't give up on him quite yet."

"I'll be two thousand miles away, Allie. Not much I can do from there. But I'm glad he's going to be around his family. I hope he gets everything he wants." I try not to choke up. "He deserves it."

She leans through the window and gives me a hug. "He's not the only one."

When Allie pulls away, she shares a long, intense look with Asher. Then she waves, and we're gone.

I look behind us, watching the three Montanas get smaller and smaller, sad beyond belief that I'll never see them again. But then I think of Lucas and what his offer might entail. Will he want me to come to the winery?

My stomach tightens at the possibility of seeing Dallas again.

It wouldn't feel right, however, showing up in a professional manner when we're not together. What if he has a girlfriend by then? He's moving back to Calloway Creek. That must mean he's ready to get on with his life. Meeting someone new would be a natural part of that. I'm not sure I could bear it.

I slump down in my seat, thinking about how happy I was to be getting an offer from such a prestigious company. Now, however, I believe the only right move is turning it down.

On the way out of town, we pass Donovan's Pub. All the memories of the party come rushing back. The people here, they're all so nice.

I've always thought living in a small town would be boring. Now it's something I crave.

I turn one last time as we head out onto the road that leads back to I-95, and I say a silent goodbye to what must certainly be the best place anyone could ever live.

Chapter Forty-two

Dallas

A heavy plume of smoke wafts into the sky as my truck makes the winding drive back to my cabin. Where's it coming from?

I haven't stayed here since the day I drove Marti to see her family. I've been back, sure, but I slept at the motor lodge in town, making daily runs to stoke the fire so the thousands of dollars of wine inside wouldn't freeze and turn to vinegar.

Staying there… sleeping there… wouldn't be the same. Not after everything that happened. Not after every inch of the cabin reminds me of her—Marti, not Phoebe. Even the damn hobby room where we had our first real argument.

The plan was to load the truck and leave yesterday, but the local police wanted to talk to me about Abe. It was just one more excuse to put off the inevitable: me packing up and moving back to Calloway Creek.

Part of me knows it's just another way of running. Only this time, it's Marti's memory I'm running from, not Phoebe's. Oh, the irony.

Getting closer now, something just isn't right. The smoke is dark and thick and much denser than what my one small fireplace should produce. When I make the final turn and drive over the small hill that brings my cabin into view, I slam on the brakes. Because what's in front of me isn't my cabin. It's a smoldering mess of what used to be my cabin.

It's… gone.

It's just fucking gone. Burned to the damn ground.

I get out of the truck, approaching slowly. Heat still emanates, warming my face the closer I get. The ground is all rock and dirt for at least thirty feet in all directions, the snow having melted from the heat of the fire.

Water is visible in the pond out back, the ice now gone on the side closest to what was my home. And I can see the pond because there's nothing standing between me and the rear of the property. Nothing but the godforsaken wrought-iron stove—the sole remaining relic and the likely culprit.

I sink to the ground. *Did I do this?*

When I kicked the stove the other day, did I somehow breach its integrity?

I contemplate calling the fire department, but what would be the point? The fire is out. There aren't any flames. Just embers, smoke, and ash.

Still stunned, and with nothing else to do, I sit on the chopping stump and watch the smoke do its dance as it floats up and away from the burned remains.

Staring at the corner of the lot where the hobby room once stood, my heart sinks. All of her creations, all of their things, are gone. I look over to where the wall of wine and books should be. There's nothing. Just… nothing.

Disappointment courses through me when I glance over near the woods and don't see Snowman Abe. He, too, was a casualty.

I don't know whether to laugh or cry. Because now, I don't have a choice. I *have* to leave. Until this very moment, there was a question that lingered in the back of my mind of will I or won't I. Now the decision has been made for me. The only difference is that I can't take anything with me. I can't take the only things that really mattered.

Hours later, after most of the smoke has cleared, I finally feel it's safe enough to approach. I stay on the ground around the perimeter, not risking melting my shoes or falling on hidden embers. Not one of my over a hundred wine bottles are discernable. They must have all exploded, then melted, leaving reformed clumps of indistinguishable glass.

The charred remains of my kitchen appliances sit among the rubble, only recognizable because I know what and where they were. Some cookware and a few kitchen utensils are still clearly visible, though covered with soot, as I sift through the ash with a long stick.

The fireplace really is the only survivor, its intact iron chimney looking odd as it stands tall in the same way it had before, snaking up and through the rafters and roof that no longer exist.

Around the far corner of the lot, something catches my eye. I stride over, using the stick to move away the rubble, and find a ceramic sculpture. It's a vase. Phoebe's one and only attempt at ceramics. It's sooty and gray. I touch it lightly to make sure it's not too hot, then take it to the pond and dunk it below the surface, wiping all its edges. It emerges virtually unscathed, and I turn it over to see her initials still branded onto the bottom.

An engine behind me steals my attention and I turn to see the propane truck pulling up. The driver's eyes go wide when he sees the state of things. The young guy gets out, looking between me and what's left of the cabin. "So, I'm guessing you don't need the refill?"

I don't think it was meant as a joke, but I can't help laughing at the irony of it. Of *all* of it.

"Dude, are you okay?" the driver asks at my unusual behavior.

"I'm fine," I say, sitting back on my stump. "And no, I won't be needing propane. Ever."

"I'll let the company know." He hesitates, probably not knowing what to say. "I'm sorry."

With that, he climbs back in his truck, circles around my truck, and leaves.

Belatedly, I think I should have told the guy not to bother with Abe's delivery either. But it was the last thing on my mind.

I hold the vase and let my eyes rake over the complete and total destruction of everything. The ash that represents the past few years of my life. But when I look down at the vase, only one thought occurs—I wish I'd found something of Marti's too. The book we were reading. The last bottle of wine we shared. *Ah, fuck…* the bracelet she left.

All of a sudden, I remember the dream. The dream that plagued me for two nights. The one where Phoebe and DJ walked into the fire. *Jesus, that's…* I scrub a hand across my jaw… *that's fucked up.*

I make my way back to the truck with only the vase in my hands, not bothering to look back.

There's nothing left for me here.

It's a fact I think I knew even before I drove up here four hours ago.

~ ~ ~

Nobody's home when I arrive, but I know the code to the front door. I doubt my parents will care very much if I crash here for a while. In fact, I'm fairly sure they'll be happy about it.

Bex greets me as soon as I walk in.

"Hey, buddy. Where is everyone?"

When he doesn't answer, I go back to the room that used to be mine. I sit on the bed thinking how it's changed. Long gone are the race car posters that once lined these walls. The signed swimsuit photo of Gigi Hadid that, as a fifteen-year-old, was my most prized possession. The binders of Pokémon cards I used to trade with my grade school friends. Everything about this room is different. I lie back and close my eyes.

They snap open when a familiar vanilla scent swirls around me. I sit up and look around, half expecting Marti to be standing in the room, wondering if I even want her to be. *Knowing* I do.

But she's not here. Just the ghosts of my childhood fill the room… and vanilla. I swear I can smell her. My nose is playing tricks on me.

I lay back and close my eyes again, but the silence is disrupted by the rumble in my stomach. Why didn't I stop for lunch? Or breakfast for that matter? Thinking back, I haven't eaten a thing since yesterday and it's almost dinnertime.

Bex runs into my calves when I stop abruptly in the kitchen doorway. My coat is hanging on the back of a kitchen chair. And not the coat I was wearing when I arrived. It's the one I loaned to Marti. The one she never returned.

Again, I look around as if she'll appear out of thin air.

My heart stops when someone comes around the corner. It restarts again when I see it's just Allie.

"You're home!" She runs over and wraps me in a hug.

I pat her on the back. "Yeah, well, I didn't really have a choice."

"What does that mean?"

I shake my head, not wanting to delve into it quite yet. "Where is everyone? And how in the hell did this coat get here."

A sinister smile grows up her face. "Marti brought it."

Thump thump thump.

"She's *here?*"

"Was. Not anymore. Left this morning."

"Um… what… why?"

"If you don't know why then you're not as smart as I thought you were, Dallas. That girl is obviously in love with you. She came under the guise of returning the coat."

I nod. "She thought I'd be at the party."

"She said she completely forgot about the party. But she did end up going. Along with Charlie and… Asher." She sighs like a schoolgirl with a big-time crush.

I cock my head and give her the side-eye. "What aren't you telling me?"

She smacks her lips. "Promise you won't go all big brother on me?"

"No."

Her eyes roll. "I may have hooked up with him last night."

"Marti's brother? Are you fucking crazy?"

She gives me a hard stare. "Says the pot to the kettle."

I hold out my hands. "Fine. Fine. But they went to the party? And they stayed… here?"

It makes total sense now, why my old room smells like her.

My mind reels over what might have happened had I been here. Had the police not needed to talk to me and I'd come home to find her here. In my old house. In my old *room.*

Would it have changed anything?

Or was the police interview some sort of divine intervention that kept me from coming home earlier?

Allie shoves her phone in my face. "We got some great pictures. You missed a heck of a party."

I push it away, not wanting to see any reminders of *her*. Of *them*.

"You're an idiot," she declares.

"Never said I wasn't." I grab the coat. "I'm going to go lie down."

~ ~ ~

A hand rubbing my arm wakes me. For a moment, my heart pounds. *Is it her?*

My mother looks down on me with a sad smile. "You okay, honey?"

"Yes. No." I sit up. "To be honest, I have no idea."

"You've been through a lot in the past few weeks. Asher and Marti told us everything. It's understandable you'd be shaken up. Especially after what happened with Charlie."

"So he's okay?"

"He's more than okay. He's a very special little boy," she says, getting that look in her eye.

"Mom, don't start on me too. It's been a long day."

She sits on the edge of the bed just like she used to when I was a kid. "I'm here for you no matter what."

My head slumps and I rub my eyes over and over. "It's gone. It's all gone."

"Oh, honey, you haven't lost—"

"I mean my cabin. It's gone. Burned to the ground along with everything in it."

Her eyes widen in horror. "Are you injured?"

"I wasn't there. I couldn't go back after… Well, I just couldn't. I was staying at a hotel in town. When I showed up this morning to pack my stuff, it was all smoke and ash." I nod to the vase on the desk. "That's literally the only thing left."

She scoots up onto the bed and wraps her arm around my shoulder. "Thank God you weren't there. I'm so sorry about the cabin, Dallas, but maybe in some strange way it's for the best. You needed to move on. You're like the Phoenix rising from the ashes." She touches my heart. "And the only memories you really need are safe in here."

I don't respond. Because I can't. Everything I want to say is tied up in a ball of fucking phlegm in my throat.

"Take some time," she says, sweeping a piece of hair out of my eyes. "Figure out what you want."

"And then what?"

"And then maybe go after it."

"It?" I look up.

"Therein lies the problem," she says with a shrug. "You're the only one who can figure out what *it* is."

She kisses my forehead and exits the room, leaving me and the vase swirling in a pool of vanilla.

Chapter Forty-three

Dallas

Lucas walks into my office, Blake trailing behind him. He puts three shot glasses on my desk and fills them with my favorite tequila.

I look strangely at the liquor. It's only noon after all.

"What exactly are we celebrating?" I ask.

"It's Christmas Eve," Blake says. "We're celebrating another great year of building our legacy here at the winery."

I tilt my head. "Shouldn't we do that on New Year's Eve instead?"

Blake shakes his head. "Ellie, Maisy, and I are leaving for Hawaii the day after tomorrow. We'll be ringing in the new year on Kauai."

I find it interesting that he tends to sign when he speaks, even when his wife and daughter aren't around. Sometimes I wonder if he even knows he's doing it.

"Ah." I pick up a glass and wait for one of them to toast.

"To an amazing year," Lucas says. "Despite our ups and downs, it's great to have you back where you belong, brother."

They touch their glasses to mine as Blake says, "I'll drink to that."

We down our shots and they take the two seats opposite my desk.

Lucas kicks back and rests his feet up on the edge. "It's been nice having you back in the office, Dallas, but you work too damn much."

I shrug. "Nothing else to do."

"That's of your own doing," Blake says.

I give him a hard stare. "Must we go over this again?"

"Yes, actually. I think we should. Because despite appearances, you're miserable here, and I'll bet my left nut she's miserable down there. I get that it's scary as fuck. Do you think I knew my ass from a hole in the ground when Maisy showed up on my doorstep? No. But you know what? I stepped the fuck up, and now look at me."

Lucas takes a swipe at the back of Blake's head. "Yeah, now look at him. You can't wipe the stupid-ass grin off his face."

"Because I'm happy." Blake points at Lucas and me. "Something neither of you seem to be able to accomplish even when it's staring you in the goddamn face."

"He's right." Lucas lowers his feet to the floor and leans his forearms on his knees. "I screwed up the best thing that ever happened to me." He shakes his head. "Four freaking times. The point? Don't be like me, little brother."

"Are you done? Because I have work to do."

"Jesus Christ, Dal, it's Christmas Eve. Go home."

I shoot eye daggers at Blake. "*You* go the fuck home. It's a hell of a lot easier when you've got something to go home to."

"Okay. I'm sick of this shit," Lucas says. "We've all been tiptoeing around you for weeks. Hell, for years if I'm being honest. It's time for you to grow some fucking balls, Dallas."

I point to the door. "Get out."

He doesn't move an inch. "We sent her the offer last week."

I try to look uninterested.

"Seriously?" he says, shaking his head in disgust. "I know you want to know."

"You don't know dick."

"She turned it down."

My eyes snap up. I'm sure I misheard him. No way in a million years did I think she'd turn it down. I saw the offer. It was a lot of money. And a better offer than we've ever laid out for any contract employee.

"Shocking, right?" he says. "Or maybe not so much. Because everyone here knows she turned it down because of you."

"She told you that?"

"She didn't have to. Why in the hell else wouldn't she take it? It's not like she had to move here. She works remotely. It was a killer offer, as you well know. She could have put her kid in private school. Hell, she could have fired all her other clients and still come out ahead. Who in their right mind would turn down a deal like that?"

His head shakes. Disappointment oozes from his every pore. "Brother, are you fucking stupid? You see what I did. Time after time I've been such an idiot. And with Lissa especially. I was sure she was my soulmate, man, and I still screwed it up. I have to live with that. Marti is amazing. Beautiful, smart, a great mother. She's the whole package."

"*Mother.* What do you not get about that being the part of the package I can't deal with?"

"She told me what you did when Charlie went into anaphylaxis. You stepped up. What you did might have saved him from brain damage. You're twenty-eight years old, Dallas. Are you going to avoid kids for the rest of your life? Because news flash, you already have one niece, and I damn well plan on having kids one day."

"There's a big difference between being an uncle and being a… dad." I still have a hard time forming the word.

"Charlie's pretty damn amazing. I spent some time with him at the party."

"He was great with Maisy," Blake says. "Super smart for a three-year-old."

"Three-and-a-half," I say, prompting the two of them to share a look.

"You'll change your mind one day. Maybe it'll be in a month, or maybe a year." Lucas stands, puts his palms on my desk and leans close. "But one day you'll be ready, and she'll be someone else's girlfriend or wife. Will you be able to handle that?"

"Again, get out, Luke."

"Do you love her?"

"Get. The. Fuck. Out."

"Do you fucking love her, Dallas?" he shouts in my face.

"Yeah!" I shout back. "I do. Is that what you want to hear? That I'm in love with someone I can never be with. That it fucking hurts every time I think about her? That it hurts almost as bad as the void Phoebe and DJ left? But there's not a goddamn thing I can do about it."

"There is, you idiot. Go fill the damn void, Dallas."

I throw him a look. "Have you and Allie been conspiring?"

"The whole family has been conspiring, man. We all want you to win this one. Don't you think you deserve it?"

I stand and pace behind my desk. "What if I *can't* win? What if I join the race and fail miserably and never make it to the finish line?" My hands run through my hair in frustration. "What if I fill the void you're all so eager for me to fill and something happens to take it all away?"

Lucas's face softens. "So *that's* what this is all about? Fear of losing what you have?"

"Hell yes, it is," Blake says. "Earlier this year, when I told him about Ellie and Maisy, he said something about it being easier not to have anyone because then you have nothing to lose."

Lucas sits again. "Jesus, Dal. You can't spend the rest of your life fearful of losing people you love. You'll die miserable and alone."

I stare right at him. "Says the guy who pushes away every woman he's ever loved."

He huffs loudly, reminding me of how Marti would do it. "This is definitely a case of do as I say and not as I do. I'm a fool. I admit it. You've always been the smart one. The stable one. The most rational. Now's the time to live up to those expectations, brother."

"Anyone with eyes and ears"—Blake laughs—"hell, even those who *can't* hear know how you feel about her and her you. We only spent one night with Marti. Hours even. And everyone knew she was the one. Why can't you pull your head out of your ass and just admit it?"

"You love her," Lucas says. "So get on a fucking plane already and go get her."

It's something I've contemplated at least a dozen times in as many days. But she hasn't so much as called, texted, or emailed. What if she wants nothing to do with me?

I grab my coat. "Fuck it. It's Christmas."

I'm pretty sure my brothers high-five behind me.

"Tell Mom not to hold Christmas dinner," I say, already halfway down the hall.

Blake calls out, "I'm sure this is one holiday she'll be happy to celebrate without you."

In the truck, I scroll through my contacts until I find Quinn Thompson's name. Quinn has been the Montanas' private helicopter pilot for years, working not only for my immediate family, but my uncle's. As usual, he answers quickly.

"Dallas Montana! Well that's a name that hasn't popped up on my phone in a good while. How're they hangin'?"

"Good. Hey, listen, I need a favor."

He hesitates. I understand why. He's got a family. It's Christmas Eve.

"I don't need you to fly," I say. "But I was hoping you could use one of your contacts to charter me a plane."

"I could do that. For when and where?"

"Well… now. I can fly out of the city or White Plains. Destination is Orlando."

"I see." There is a hesitation in his voice.

"You don't think it'll be doable?"

"Oh, it's doable. But it's going to cost you."

"See, this is one of those times when being rich as shit comes in super handy. Whatever it takes. I can be ready in a few hours. I just have a few errands to run."

"I'm on it. I'll text you with the details as soon as I have them. Maybe now you'll talk your daddy into investing in a private plane?"

I laugh. "My father has never been that flashy. A helicopter he shares with his brother—yes. An entire airplane—he'd rather eat dirt and donate what he would have spent to starving children."

"Chris Montana is a good man. Orlando, eh? Looks like his son is a good man, too."

"I see you've been keeping up with the rumor mill."

"Word travels fast around here."

"Okay, gotta go. Get me that flight."

"You bet I will."

I place a few more phone calls and make several necessary stops. Before I can even go home to pack a bag, Quinn texts me.

Quinn T: Can you be at White Plains airport in an hour? I found a team to fly you, but they want to be home by midnight. It's a three-hour flight. Drop off only. They'll turn around immediately and fly back.

I check the time. Perfect. I'll be in Orlando by seven.

Me: On my way. I owe you.

Quinn T: No man, but you'll owe them. A fucking lot.

Me: Not a problem. Thanks. And Merry Christmas.

Quinn T: To you as well. Hope you find what you're looking for.

I don't answer, but I sure as hell hope so too.

~ ~ ~

After putting a small dent in my bank account and renting one of the few remaining—and ridiculously overpriced—cars at the Orlando airport, I'm well on my way to Marti's apartment.

Traffic is horrendous. Not New York City bad, but terrible all the same. Don't these people have somewhere to be, like with their families?

Family. The word hangs in my head, bouncing around as I try it on for size. Am I really ready for this? Honestly, I don't know. But if I don't at least try, I think it's something I might regret for the rest of my life.

"Your destination is ahead," the car announces, causing my heart rate to skyrocket.

What if she doesn't want this? What if Martina Alexandra Carver is one of those women who moves on quickly—out of sight, out of mind and all that?

What if I just spent sixty grand for nothing? Not including all the other shit I bought earlier.

I'm a bit surprised, but not unhappy that she lives in a gated community. At least I know she's safe living on her own. Not wanting to alert her I'm coming, I hug the bumper of the car in front of me to get through the front gate. Then I park in front of her apartment building. It's nice. I look around at the other cars. Most of them are far nicer than Betsy. I wonder if she's gotten a new one yet. If not, that can be my Christmas gift to her. I mean, I have a gift already—sort of—but a car would be the *real* one.

I squint at the numbers on the apartments, surmising hers is on the second floor. I get out, retrieving one of the gift bags from the back. No way can I carry in everything I brought with me. I'll just come back for the rest.

Taking a deep breath, because I truly have no idea if I'm an idiot or a saint for doing what I'm doing, I climb the stairs and knock on the door to apartment 502C.

There's no answer. I knock again. Then I step to the right and look through the front window.

It's dark inside. I came all this way and she's not even here.

Asher's. Of course she would be at Asher's place. She said they always spend holidays together. Maybe that means Christmas Eve as well as Christmas.

Even more nervous now that I have to do this in front of her older brother, I make my way back down to the car and do some stealth googling until I find the address. I actually find the addresses of a few Asher Andersons in the Orlando area, but I narrow it down to the closest one to my location, figuring she wouldn't live too far from her brother.

In ten minutes, I'm standing in front of another door, scared shitless at what might transpire over the next few minutes. *Grow some fucking balls, Montana*, I tell myself.

I ring the bell, and seconds later, a girl with blue hair opens the door. She looks down at my hands. "Delivery?" she asks, excited by the large decorative bag.

"You must be Bug."

She side-eyes me, closing the door just a little and wedging her foot behind it. "Do I know you, or are you some creepy lonely old guy who stalks girls on the internet and tracks them down on holidays?"

Yup. Definitely Bug. I'd recognize that snarky attitude anywhere. She must've gotten it from her aunt.

"I'm looking for your aunt. Is Marti here?"

"No. She flew up to New York City to go to some hick place. Conway Creek or something." She turns. "Dad! Where did Aunt Marti go?"

Asher comes up behind his daughter, stunned to see me. "Dallas. You're… here." He doubles over, laughing.

"Wait." I drop the bag on the threshold. "*She* went to see *me?* And… she got on a *plane?*"

When he's done being amused at my expense, he invites me inside. "You might as well have a drink and settle in. You'll never get a flight back on this short notice."

I come in, but before I talk to them or do anything else, I pull out my phone and place my second call today to Quinn Thompson. "Quinn, I'm gonna need another favor."

Chapter Forty-four

Martina

"Mommy, how much longer?" Charlie whines.

After two flights, including a three-hour layover, a thirty-minute train ride, and waiting another half hour for an Uber, my son is exhausted.

"We're almost there, buddy."

"I can ride the elvator?"

I snicker. "Yes, Charlie, you can ride the elevator."

I hope.

The streets are near empty. Donovan's Pub is dark despite the fact that it's only 7:00 pm. This is nothing like what we saw in New York City an hour ago, where no matter the day, people are out and about. But this town is different. Everyone is home spending time with family. I sigh and wonder—not for the first time today—if this is a good idea. It's been weeks and he hasn't reached out. If he wanted me—really wanted me—he'd have given me some kind of indication.

Am I the most pathetic woman on the face of the earth showing up unannounced on a man's doorstep on Christmas Eve of all days? I close my eyes and breathe, feeling anxiety take hold.

I could have called him. Or emailed. Or even sent a letter. Why did I have to take my son away from his family and drain my bank account on a whim?

Because you love him.

And you have to know.

Not for the first time today, or even over the past three weeks, I gaze down at the picture on my phone. The only photo I have of Dallas. The one with the snowman between us. The way he's looking over at me—I hold onto that. The eyes don't lie even when the lips do.

It crosses my mind that I've been reading far too much into this photo and I just happened to snap it at the precise moment that made it look like he was looking at… I don't know, an angel. Am I completely off base here?

"Ma'am?" I look up at the driver, who's staring at me in the rearview. "We're here."

My chest tightens. It's hard to take a deep breath. My hands shake. Is this what a panic attack feels like?

"Right. Thank you."

I quickly swipe away the photo and pull up the app to give the driver a larger-than-normal tip.

He gets our single suitcase from the trunk, and I slip Charlie's small backpack onto his shoulders.

"Merry Christmas," the driver says, resuming his place behind the wheel.

For a moment, I contemplate asking him to wait. Because the only thing more pathetic than me showing up here would be Dallas rejecting me and then having to wait on the curb with Charlie for another half-hour for another Uber—which might even be the same guy. I can't imagine there are many people who require an Uber on Christmas Eve. Not here.

Instead, I pull my big-girl panties on, and hope for the best. "Merry Christmas."

Charlie beats me to the front door by a mile. He's talked about this place for weeks. As I approach, I look up at the massive house with its extensive outdoor balconies lining the entire second floor, the gorgeous colonial architecture, the eight garages.

And the cars. My heart seizes for a second. There are plenty of extra cars in the driveway. An indication there are more people inside than just the few I was hoping for. I think about those people. How inviting they were. How down to earth and hospitable for a bunch of billionaires. *The people inside.* My heart stutters at the thought that Dallas might not even be one of them. He's almost twenty-nine years old. Would he even be living here? It's been weeks. Maybe he's gotten his own place.

I swallow. Or maybe… he's back at the cabin, having decided this wasn't what he wanted after all.

I scan all the cars in the driveway, noting his truck is not among them. Then again, there are eight garages. If he's living here, he could be parked in one.

My mouth goes dry.

Lord, I could be crashing this family's Christmas. And if I'm not wanted, there will literally be no place for me to go. I should have researched hotels before coming. Or better yet, I should never have come.

Charlie reaches up and presses the doorbell before I have a chance to back out.

A bark coming from the other side of the door gives me hope that he's here.

Charlie peeks through the sidelight. "Bex!"

The door opens and Sarah stands there, looking stunned, as Bex all but tackles my son to the ground and covers him with dog kisses.

"Marti."

She hesitates long enough after saying my name that a dozen bad scenarios run through my head. Bad scenarios like what if he is here, but he's not alone. What if he's here with a woman? A date. A new girlfriend even.

But before I pass out from crippling stress, she pulls me into her arms. "What a lovely surprise."

I relax into her and return the hug. Surely she wouldn't have said it if he were inside sharing eggnog with a slender beauty without any so-called baggage.

"I'm so sorry to show up like this. I know it's a terrible imposition but—"

"Nonsense. I said you were welcome here anytime and I meant it. And it's Christmas Eve. The more the merrier." She squats down and hugs Charlie now that he's done greeting Bex. "And you. I'm so happy to see you, Charlie."

"Mommy said I can ride the elvator."

She laughs. "As much as you want." She stands and moves aside. "Come in out of the cold. You can leave your suitcase here in the foyer. We'll get you situated later."

I do as she says, still terrified of what's inside. Am I about to walk in on a huge family dinner?

She escorts us to the living room where the massive Christmas tree is twinkling with gorgeous lights. Under it are more presents than I've ever seen in my entire life.

Charlie's eyes go wide and he races over, past the many people now looking at us. "Mommy! Look!"

Guilt crawls up my spine. I came empty handed. I'm imposing on this family, and I didn't so much as bring a bottle of wine or a bouquet of flowers. I packed a few of the smaller presents I picked up for Charlie, but as this was a spur-of-the moment decision, that was the best I could do.

I'm truly out of my league, element, and socio-economic class.

As Charlie scans the presents, I peruse the room. There are a lot of people here. Many I recognize from Lucas's birthday party. They aren't sitting down to a big family dinner, but they are all staring at me, many with slack jaws and surprised looks on their faces. Some are snickering.

Why are they laughing? Have I made a colossal mistake?

The one person I don't see, however, is the very person I flew up here for.

Allie steps forward wearing a gorgeous silver, red, and green mini dress that shows off her amazing figure. She's got the biggest smile of them all. "Marti!" She practically laughs out my name. "Oh my god. No freaking way."

She looks genuinely happy to see me, but something seems… off.

Whispers ensue behind her. Ones I'm sure I'm the topic of.

"And Charlie," she adds, plowing through the crowd. She looks at her mom. "Did you tell her?"

Sarah smiles and shakes her head like they all have this huge secret I'm not privy to.

"Come," Allie says, pulling me toward the bar that's manned by an actual bartender wearing a uniform. "She'll have the eggnog. Make it strong. She's going to need it."

Those words have dread tightening my stomach once again.

The man behind the bar quickly does her bidding and hands me the drink, topped off with a sprinkled holiday nutmeg pattern. I take it, but don't sip. I'm far too nervous and fear it may end up all over my shirt.

"Allie, what is it?"

The room is silent but for a few lingering whispers. It's like everyone is waiting to see what I'm going to do. I hate being the center of attention.

"Dallas isn't here."

I feel ill. All I can do is nod and hold back tears.

She tilts her head, looking amused. "Aren't you going to ask why?"

"I'm not sure I want to know the answer."

She giggles. "Oh, I think you do."

I blow out a breath. "Okay then. Why?"

She glances at a huge clock on the wall that must be eight feet wide and has roman numerals as numbers. "I'm guessing right about now he's knocking on *your* door."

"*My* door?" I almost hyperventilate. "What do you mean?"

"I mean, my idiotic brother finally came to his senses about seven hours ago and chartered a jet to fly him to Orlando. He's probably standing outside your place wondering where the hell you are, looking about as confused as you do right now." She laughs again. "I'd give anything to see the look on his face when he finds out you're here."

It takes a minute to digest this information. He flew to Orlando. *For me?* "Are you serious?"

Lucas and Blake come over, smiling. "It's true," Lucas confirms. "You can't even imagine the hell it's been to be around him lately. The pain in the ass did nothing but sulk and work. I told him what a fool he was and convinced him to do something about it."

Blake elbows him. "Hey now, *I'm* the one who convinced him."

"Boys," Sarah says, joining the conversation. "I'm not sure anyone needed to convince him of anything. He just needed time to realize it himself."

"Realize what exactly?" I ask.

Sarah grins. "I suppose that's something you should ask *him.*"

"Do you… think I should call him?"

"Won't do any good," Lucas says, holding up his phone. "He just texted that he's flying back. He may even make it by midnight."

My eyes bulge. "How is that even possible? It's Christmas Eve."

"My dear," Sarah says, "I get the feeling my son would move mountains for you. Now, come, we were just getting ready to sit down for dinner. Two more place settings have already been added."

Before I can even thank her, Charlie comes plowing over, pointing back at the tree. "Mommy, is there pwesents for me?"

I sigh, eyeing the massive pile that must have a hundred expertly wrapped gifts, because I only have two in my bag.

"Of course there are presents for you," Sarah says. "Lots and lots of them."

Charlie claps excitedly and Allie whisks him off to the dining room.

"Sarah, I—"

"You only have one suitcase, Marti. I know what you're going to say. I'll take care of it. We have an arsenal of toys we bought when Maisy came into our lives. She's already outgrown many of them. They'll be wrapped and under the tree by morning."

Tears come to my eyes. "I don't know how to thank you. I wish I could repay your kindness. I'm so sorry I came empty-handed."

"I'm confident you're about to make my son happier than he's been in many years. Believe me, that's all the thanks I need. And it's a million times better than anything you could put under that tree."

~ ~ ~

Hours later, after being fed, showered, and dressed up—thanks to Allie's extensive designer wardrobe—Allie and I are sipping eggnog by the tree while Charlie is fast asleep in a guest room.

"Does your family not stay up until midnight on Christmas Eve?" I ask.

"They wanted to give you some privacy. I'm not as discreet. I'm here for the show."

Butterflies flutter around my stomach knowing he's going to arrive any minute. Will he take me in his arms? Kiss me? Tell me he loves me?

I think back to when he told me about the butterfly effect, and I wonder just how it applies to us. Did a butterfly flap its wings in Connecticut, causing a shift in the wind that had me skidding off the road? Did a group of them migrating to Mexico create a disturbance in the atmosphere, instigating the blizzard that snowed us in? Did one of them—

My thoughts are cut short when the security system chimes, a sound I've learned means the front door has been opened. My whole body stiffens. This is it. Heat not coming from the fireplace burns throughout my body.

When Dallas steps into the living room and sees me, the rest of the world falls away. When he locks eyes with mine, and gooseflesh prickles my skin, I know with one-hundred-percent certainty that I love this man more deeply than I ever thought one could love. When his mouth turns up in a small smile, my heart thunders with hope. Hope that even though he's had a true, mad, deep love, there is still room for more.

"Hey," he says, dropping his bags as a sultry grin slowly overtakes his handsome face.

Without a second of hesitation, I run straight into his arms.

Chapter Forty-five

Dallas

She jumps into my arms, wrapping her legs around me. My eyes close at the feel of her. The weight of her. The mere presence of her.

When our lips meet, it's like they never parted. Our soft and welcoming kisses soon turn desperate. There's so much to say, but right now, I plan to do all the talking with my body.

I carry her back to my room, barely even registering the squeal behind me when my sister realizes what I've brought with me.

Setting Marti on my bed, I stand and stare at her for a moment. Is it possible she's gotten even more beautiful over the past few weeks? Her hair is soft, flowy, a bit shorter perhaps. Her eyes sparkle with a glittery shadow on the lids. Even her smile seems brighter, and easier somehow. One thing that hasn't changed is her scent. How I've missed that sweet vanilla aroma enveloping me. I'll never smell it again without thoughts of her invading my mind. Now, she's here. And I don't ever want to be without her again.

Our eyes connect, the heat passing between us more intense than ever before. She says three words that set my world on fire.

"I want you."

I get on the bed and climb on top of her. "You fucking have me."

She reaches up, weaves her hands through my hair, and pulls my face toward hers.

We kiss until we're breathless and desperate for more. Our hands tear at each other's clothing, both knowing the thirst we have for each other can only be quenched once I'm deep inside her.

I flip her over and unzip her dress, pulling it off her body in one fell swoop. Leaving her on her stomach, I work my lips over her shoulders, her back, the sexy dimples below her waist. I tug down her panties and work my mouth over the soft globes of her ass, continuing down to lick the backs of her thighs, her knees, her calves.

The sexy noises coming from her heighten my arousal and my cock throbs painfully. I want to take my time with her. Explore every goddamn inch of the body I've dreamed of every night for the last two-and-a-half weeks. But right now, more than anything, I need to be inside her.

I turn her onto her back, and I swear the way she looks at me makes me feel ten feet tall. I'm the king to her queen. The Clark to her Lois. The fucking yin to her yang. We belong together. I've never been more sure of anything.

"Dallas," she begs. "Make love to me."

The rest of my clothes are gone in seconds. I hover over her, my engorged dick pressing against her entrance. I run a finger down the slope of her nose, along her jaw, down a pulsating cord of her neck, amazed that she came all this way for me. That she took a leap of faith. That she's… mine.

Before I sink myself inside her, there's one thing I have to do. For weeks I tried to deny it. I ran from it like I've run from so many things. But the truth is clear. I can't hide from it any longer. Because I know beyond the shadow of a doubt that I can't fucking breathe without her.

I draw in a breath and say the words I never thought I'd say again. "I love you."

She nods over and over, tears streaming down her beautiful face. "I know."

It's a declaration I didn't expect. She, like everyone else, knew the truth even before I did.

I swipe a piece of hair behind her ear. "And you love me."

She cups the side of my face. "More than you can possibly imagine."

I swallow, a tear of my own dropping down onto her cheek. "I'm going to need you to say it."

"I love you, Dallas Montana. I love you so much."

I close my eyes and let the words sink in, my heart expanding with every passing second. She was right. Phoebe was right. My heart is so goddamn full. Fuller than I thought it could be. There *is* room for both. Hell, there's room for both *and* room to spare.

As I slide into her, I see my future in her eyes. A future I couldn't even dream of a few weeks ago. A future I was sure wasn't in the cards for me. A future that will exist only because she exists.

This woman was made for me. Placed on this earth for me. Designed by God for me.

We make love like we're the only two people who ever have. As if the act was created for us. Invented *by* us. And when we come together spectacularly, my entire life makes sense.

I slump down on top of her, both of us breathing heavily and holding on to each other in a way that lets us both know this is a feeling we intend on having over and over again for the rest of our lives.

I perch up on an elbow. "Let me get one thing straight. You got on a plane? I thought you said it would take an act of God."

She runs a hand through my hair that's hanging down and tickling her face. "Don't you know by now that I'd do anything for you? I mean, you got me to climb a tower, Dallas. Getting on a plane was just another leap of faith."

"You think all this is just some divine intervention?"

"I don't know. Could be." She shrugs. "Or maybe it's just the butterflies."

I smile then touch my forehead to hers. "Is it too early to ask you to marry me?"

She giggles. "Maybe just a bit. There are things we need to talk about."

I was kidding and she knows it. Or at least I *think* I was kidding.

She squeezes my arm then continues playing with my hair. It reminds me of the cabin.

"But just so you know"—she reaches between us and puts her hand on my heart—"when you do ask, the answer will be yes."

My heart pounds even harder than it did a few moments ago.

I roll off her and she rests her head on my chest. "How about for now, I just move to New York and we'll see how things go?"

"You'd… *move here?*"

"I love it here. And I love more than you, Dallas. I love your family."

"Yours is pretty great, too. They're here, you know."

She perches her head on a hand and looks up at me. "Asher and Bug are *here?*"

"They flew up with me." I shrug. "You said you always spend Christmas together. I didn't want you to miss out on that."

"How are you for real?" she asks.

"Sweetheart, I've been asking myself that same thing about you since the day we met."

Her smile is bright. "That's the first time you called me sweetheart when my life wasn't in danger."

I laugh. "Maybe it is in danger. I do plan on eating you alive every chance I get."

She lays her head back down on me, shaking my body with her silent laughter. Then she sighs deeply. "In all seriousness, there is something we need to talk about."

"Charlie," I say, running a hand down the smooth skin of her back.

"I'm a full-time mom now. We come as a package deal. I need to know you can handle that."

"I can handle it."

"How do you know?" She looks up. "What's changed?"

I snort and say the only word that can sum it up. "Everything."

"Aren't you scared?"

"Terrified. But the best things in life are worth fighting for, right?"

"Absolutely." She plants a kiss on my cheek then glances around the bedroom. "I slept in here the night of Lucas's party."

"I know."

"Your mom told you?"

"I smelled you." I lean close to her hair and inhale. "Vanilla. Always vanilla."

"I can't sleep in here tonight, Dallas. I want to, but Charlie might be afraid if he wakes up in a strange place and I'm not there."

"What room is he in?"

She nods to the bathroom. "He's next door."

"Well, then, you'll have to make sure you don't scream my name too loud when I make you come at least two more times before I let you leave."

She smiles. "Promise you'll never stop trying to make me scream."

I laugh. "Sweetheart, that'll be the easiest promise I've ever had to keep."

Chapter Forty-six

Martina

I awaken Christmas morning, happy to be sore in all the right places.

Rolling over, I watch Charlie sleep. He's too young to wake up early just because it's Christmas, but it won't be long, I'm sure.

I glance at the bathroom door that separates us from Dallas. Everything he said last night was everything I wanted to hear. But actions speak louder than words. He's never spent more than a few hours with Charlie. What if he was just caught up in the moment when he said what he said?

He said he loved me. I said I'd move here. Hell, I all but agreed to marry him.

I squeeze my eyes tightly shut, praying what he said will hold true.

When I hear distant voices, I put my mouth to Charlie's ear. "Wake up, buddy. It's Christmas."

It takes a moment for him to orient to where we are. When he fully wakes, he squeals, "Pwesents?"

"Yeah, buddy. Presents. But be patient, okay? We're guests here. We have to do things according to how they do them. They might want to eat breakfast first. I know you want to open your presents, and you will. You just might have to wait a little bit. Can you do that for me?"

He nods.

I kiss the top of his messy hair. "Okay. Bathroom first."

I glance down at my pajamas, unsure of what to do. Back home, we never bother getting ready. We'll wear whatever we slept in until every last present gets opened. What if they dress up? Or what if I do and they all come out in their robes?

There's a soft knock on the door. "Come in."

Dallas peeks inside. "Is the coast clear?"

"He's in the bathroom. We have a second."

He pulls me into his arms. "Merry Christmas."

I weave my arms around his back and hold him tight. "Merry Christmas."

"The first of many," he says, making me smile.

The toilet flushes. "Don't forget to wash up!" I shout.

Dallas reluctantly steps away. Maybe he doesn't want Charlie to see us embrace. I'm not sure how I feel about that either. We'll have to test those waters at some point. I'm just not sure when.

Belatedly, I notice he's wearing sleep pants and a plain blue T-shirt. "Is that what you're wearing this morning?"

"What kind of freak would I be if I actually got dressed for Christmas morning?"

"Thank God," I sigh. "I love you and all, but I might have to draw the line at dressing up for presents."

He doesn't laugh. He holds me prisoner with his stare. "Say it again."

I replay the words in my head, understanding what he's asking.

I step forward and whisper loudly, "I love you."

His eyes close briefly. "I thought it might have been a dream."

"Me too."

Charlie emerges from the bathroom. I hold my breath, because I honestly have no idea what's going to happen next.

"Dallith!"

"Hey, bud. Are you ready for presents?"

Charlie hops up and down. "Yes! Did you bring me one?"

"Charlie," I admonish. "That's not polite. Besides, he didn't have time—"

"I got you more than one, Charlie." He holds out his hand. "Come on, let's go see."

I swallow the ginormous lump in my throat when Charlie's small hand lands in Dallas's large one. I can only hope I'm seeing a sliver of what lies ahead.

Dallas looks at me and nods. It's hard for him, I can tell. His features draw tight with nervousness. But he's doing it. And right now, that's all anyone can ask.

The first person I see when I step into the living room is Asher. I walk over and hug him. "I'm so happy you're here. Why didn't you come in with Dallas last night?"

"And steal his thunder?" He laughs. "The man spent some serious cash getting to you. It was *his* moment. But no way was I going to turn down hitching a ride on a private jet. Bug was thoroughly impressed. We brought all the gifts, too."

I glance over at the even bigger pile under the tree, knowing Charlie is going to be spoiled beyond belief. Probably on this day and every other, if I've learned anything about the Montanas.

Blue hair pops up from the couch where Bug must have been lounging. "Bug!" I head over and squeeze her shoulders. "How was the plane ride?"

"Dope AF," she says.

I laugh, amused by the way kids these days can curse without actually cursing.

When Allie walks in the room, she and Asher share a look that clearly tells me they were doing the very same thing Dallas and I were last night.

"Morning, Bug," she says.

Bug shoots her a disapproving look. "It's *Darla.*"

Uh oh.

"Of course," Allie says with a smile, not even looking offended. "Good morning, Darla. And Merry Christmas."

"Yeah, whatever," my niece retorts.

I know my brother. I'm sure he and Allie didn't have the reunion at the door that I had with Dallas. He'd be more discreet than that after Bug has been so difficult the past few years with any woman he's shown interest in. It makes sense. Her own mother didn't want her, and then the woman who became her stepmother, and who she thought of as a mom, also left.

I sidle up to Asher. "Trouble in paradise?"

"How the hell does she know?" he whispers.

"Have you *seen* the way you and Allie look at each other?"

His smile collapses. "My kid is too damn observant."

More people pile into the room, filling every chair, some even sitting on the floor. Blake, Ellie, and Maisy are here. Lucas is too. And they're all wearing pajamas—even those who didn't sleep here.

I'm loving this family more and more.

Chris and Sarah come into the room carrying big trays of pastries and orange juice and place them on the massive coffee table.

"Everything is peanut-free," Sarah assures me. "In fact, we've gotten rid of all peanuts and peanut butter products. It's all in the garbage, never to return."

"Thank you so much."

She puts a hand on my shoulder. "You're family now. It's what we do." Sarah turns to the ridiculously large display of presents and says, "Who wants to open the first one?"

Charlie and Maisy both raise their hands, Blake having signed every word for his wife and daughter.

Sarah picks up two gifts, handing them each one.

For the next two hours, people open presents, the pile of wrapping paper in the corner growing so large the kids could get lost in it.

Charlie has never gotten so many toys. Sarah really came through. So did Dallas. I'm floored. He got him an inflatable backyard spaceship playhouse, an AI robot, and a state-of-the-art ride-on electric car. I can't believe he hauled all of it to Orlando—and back.

He hands a gift to me. My eyes drop to my lap, feeling guilty because I don't have anything for him. When I hesitate, he says, "Go on. Open it. Believe me, it's not what you think."

That piques my curiosity and I tear into the package, laughing when I see what's inside. It's a bouquet. But it's not flowers. This is a bouquet of EpiPens.

He explains, "One for your car. One for my car. One for my parents. The school he'll attend. There's enough here so that anywhere we go in this town, there'll always be one within reach."

I make sure Charlie's busy and then I kiss his cheek. "I'm not sure I've ever been given such a thoughtful gift. But how did you get a prescription? And how did you get so many?"

He shrugs. "I've got connections."

"That reminds me. I know you paid his hospital bill. I really appreciate it. With the added expense of everything that happened around Charles's death and my accident, your generosity came at a good time."

He brushes off the compliment. "It was the least I could do."

"You really have no idea how charming you are, do you?"

"I'll show you charming," he whispers, then bites my earlobe. "Later, when we're alone, I'll charm you with my snake."

I laugh and hold up one of the many EpiPens. "Thank you so much for these. I don't have the insurance money yet, so I haven't gotten a car to put one in."

He leans close. "I'm getting you one. That's going to be your real present."

"Dallas, no. You've already done so much."

He pushes my hair behind my shoulder and whispers, "I've got money, Marti. I'm going to spoil you and Charlie, so you'd better get used to it. We'll go car shopping as soon as we get you moved up here."

I shake my head. It's all so surreal. "I don't have anything for you. I had no idea what to give a man who has so much money he can buy anything."

"You," he says. "You can give me you. Move in with me."

My eyes go wide. I'm excited, yet terrified. "Hold on, space cowboy. I've got more than just me to think about. We'll move here. We'll move here tomorrow if that's what you want, but we'll rent a place of our own. Charlie just lost his dad. He needs time to process that before having another significant father-figure in his life." I try to gauge his reaction. "Does that scare you?"

"Not anymore."

He pulls out his phone.

"What are you doing?" I ask.

"Looking for rentals. *Short-term* ones. One for you and Charlie. And one for me." He glances up. "They'll be close. I never plan on being far away from you again."

Lucas sits down and looks over Dallas's shoulder. "Rental properties, eh?" He turns to me. "So about that offer…"

"I accept," I say without hesitation.

Dallas's smile grows even wider as he continues to scroll on his phone.

"Fantastic," Lucas says. "Welcome to the Montana Winery family."

"I'm happy to be a part of it." I look around the room at their large family. *"All* of it."

~ ~ ~

After a long day of playing, eating, and socializing, I tuck Charlie into bed.

He pulls Grumpy close. "I like it here, Mommy."

"I like it here too, Charlie. In fact, we're going to move here. Not to this house. I mean we will probably come over here quite a bit, but we won't live here. We'll get an apartment. What do you think?"

"In Calla Creek?"

"Yes, we're going to move to Calloway Creek."

"Are Unca Asher and Bug coming?"

"No, buddy. They aren't. But I have a feeling we might be seeing them often, especially Uncle Asher."

"You can fly down to Orlando to see them anytime you want," Dallas says from the doorway.

"I like planes," Charlie says through a yawn.

"Me too." Dallas stares at me. "What about you, Marti? Do you like planes?"

I roll my eyes. "Let's just say my aversion to them isn't as strong as it was before."

How could it be? One of those planes brought me back to him. And him to me.

"Goodnight, Charlie," Dallas says, and disappears.

Charlie's eyes grow heavy as I read him *The Night Before Christmas* one last time. Then Bex hops up on the bed and protectively settles in next to him.

It warms my heart that Charlie's world has expanded so much over the past twenty-four hours.

We're moving here. I have a… boyfriend. And a lucrative new employment contract. One that will allow me to scale back on all my other clients and focus mostly on the winery and my son. I glance at the empty doorway. Well, and other important people.

I give Bex a pat and kiss Charlie. "Sleep well."

Dallas is sitting alone by the fireplace when I enter the living room. Lucas has long gone, as have Blake and his family. Chris, Sarah, and Allie took Asher and Bug on a tour of the Calloway Creek holiday lights.

Dallas pats the couch cushion next to him and hands me a glass of red wine.

"Thanks," I say and take a sip. My eyes snap to his at the familiar robust flavor. "This is the wine from… oh, you shouldn't have."

"We never got to finish the bottle. And I told you, I only drink it on special occasions."

I scoot next to him and he pulls my legs up onto his lap, giving me a foot massage.

I take another drink and savor it, eyes closed. "Mmm. I'd say today is definitely one of those. And not just because it's Christmas."

"You can say that again."

"So you don't want to live here with your parents until we figure things out?"

He shakes his head. "I haven't lived with my parents since I went away to college when I was eighteen. I'm only here temporarily. I was serious about getting a place close to yours." He squeezes my foot. "Very close. I found some decent properties. Nothing special, but nice enough. When we decide to move in together, that's when we'll go all out."

"I don't need a big fancy house, Dallas. Everything I need is right here." I touch his chest then gesture to the back hallway. "And in there."

"I know you don't. But you're going to get it anyway."

"You don't need to spoil me."

"Need and want are two different things. I'm sorry, Marti, but you're going to have to humor me on this one."

"Fine." I roll my eyes dramatically. "If you insist, I'll live in a castle on a hill surrounded by a moat. But just so you know, Dallas, I'd love you if you had nothing and we lived in a one-room shack without power."

He doesn't laugh as I'd hoped. "So about that."

"Don't tell me you sold the cabin already. Because I really think you should keep it. We could go up there from time to time and try to recreate the magic, minus a few near-death experiences."

"It burned to the ground, Marti."

I cover my mouth, shocked. "Were you there? Were you hurt?" I quickly scan him from head to toe even though I'd have noticed any injuries last night. "What happened?"

"I wasn't there. It was a few days after you left. I stopped staying there and only went back to keep the fire going so the wine wouldn't freeze. I don't know how the fire started, and I'm not really sure it matters, because in some strange way, I feel like it had to happen. It allowed me to finally let go and realize there was nothing left to hold onto." He looks guilty. "I'm so sorry I couldn't recover your bracelet. I promise I'll get you another one." He tickles my left ring finger. "I'll get you all kinds of jewelry."

"I'm sorry about the cabin."

"I'm not. There's nothing I needed there. Everything I want is right here."

"You really lost everything?"

"There's a ceramic vase Phoebe made. It came out totally unscathed. That's it. It was the only thing."

"I'm glad you still have that small piece of her." When the words come out of my mouth, I'm surprised at just how much I mean them.

"You were right the whole time, Marti. I didn't need all that other stuff to remember them. I have pictures. The vase. And my memories."

"And birthdays," I say. "You'll have their birthdays."

"Thanks to you, yes I will. Now listen, I know you want to sleep in Charlie's room. But until then, I thought maybe…" He nods to a book on the table. A very thick book.

A tingle of anticipation runs down my back. "Yes." I move my legs off him, set my wine glass on the side table, and pick up the book.

I turn to page one, then pat my lap. He wastes no time lounging on the couch and putting his head on my thigh. And as I read to him, I weave my fingers through his hair. I clear my throat, having a hard time forming words, because this is something I didn't expect to ever do again. But now… now I think it's something we might do every day for the rest of our lives.

Chapter Forty-seven

Dallas

I shovel the last of the chicken casserole into my mouth. I think I've gained five pounds over the past three months, courtesy of Marti's mad cooking skills.

Even though my house is three doors down from hers, we eat together almost every night. Then I leave, she puts Charlie to bed, and I come back. Sometimes we accidentally fall asleep in Marti's bed. I've almost been caught by Charlie a time or two.

I have the perfect house in mind for when she's ready for the next step. But I haven't pushed her. She's been worried about Charlie and moving on too quickly after Charles's death. Me—I've been ready to live with her since Christmas. And not only her… Charlie too. He is amazing. He's wormed his way into my heart in a way I never thought possible.

I stand and pick up the plates, always doing the dishes with 'help' from Charlie.

"Bex needs to go out," Marti says. "Charlie, will you take him?"

Her rental has a fenced-in back yard. It has three bedrooms, two bathrooms, and a two-car garage. Same as mine. Neither are anything special, but honestly, after living in the cabin for years, both seem palatial. And it wasn't the houses that mattered. It was my proximity to *them* that did.

Marti stands by the French doors, supervising her son and Bex as Charlie lets him do his business then throws him a tennis ball.

I snake my arms around her, sneaking a hug. I kiss her neck. "Those two are best friends if I've ever seen any."

She nods. "I actually think Bex is the reason he wanted to move here. He gets so excited on the days Bex sleeps here."

Marti and I share 'custody' of Bex. He alternates sleeping here and at my place. From the beginning, it's felt like he's been more *our* dog than *my* dog, so it was the only thing that made sense.

When Charlie and Bex come back inside, Charlie gets out his AI robot, Robbie, and Bex barks at it. He's still uneasy around the thing and it's become quite entertaining to watch Robbie chase Bex around the room.

Bex is incredibly intelligent for a dog. Sometimes I think he acts this way around the robot simply because he knows Charlie loves it. Charlie giggles at the controls, which he's nearly mastered by now, as he guides Robbie through the living room.

Marti and I watch this routine for nearly an hour, her sitting on one end of the couch and me on the other. Her feet are in my lap. It's the closest we've come to showing affection around Charlie. After all, his father only died four months ago. And I, of all people, have to respect that. Even though Charlie hasn't gone through the grieving process an older child would have, there are still moments when you can tell he really misses Charles.

"Time for bed, buddy," Marti says. "Go get into your pajamas and use the toilet. I'll help you brush your teeth in a few minutes."

"Okay then." I stand, recognizing my cue to leave. "I'll see you two tomorrow."

As he always does, Charlie trots over and gives me a hug. Today, however, he does something different.

"Dallith read to me?" he asks, looking at his mom for permission.

Her eyebrows shoot up in delight. "You want Dallas to read your bedtime story?"

Charlie nods excitedly.

Marti looks at me, not wanting to answer on my behalf.

"I'd love to."

He skips back toward his room, Bex at his heels.

"That was unexpected," I say.

"You sure you're okay with it?"

I draw her into my arms. "Sweetheart, I'd have been okay with it months ago. But what do you think changed? Why would he ask now?"

"I don't know." Her eyes dart from one side of the room to the other, as if she's deep in thought. "But now that I think of it, a few days ago at preschool, they had a 'daddy day' where all the dads came in and did projects with their children. I went myself, as did one other single mom, along with a woman who's part of a lesbian couple. Charlie drew a picture of Charles and Alex. It was very sweet."

"And you think that has something to do with him wanting me to read a book?"

She shrugs. "Every parent took turns reading out loud to the class. It's been a long time since Charlie's been read to by a man. That has to be it."

"Ready!" Charlie shouts from down the hall.

"On my way, buddy."

I smile at Marti, feeling a sense of pride that he asked *me* to do the honors.

Marti helps him brush his teeth as I peruse his collection of books. Bex has already picked out his spot on the end of Charlie's bed, as I imagine he does every night he sleeps here. My heart swells a bit knowing that I'm now a part of the nighttime ritual. It's something I always looked forward to with DJ—the day we'd be able to snuggle in bed and I'd read to him until he fell asleep. It's not anything I ever dreamed I'd do after losing him.

When Charlie races out of the bathroom and jumps onto the bed, a huge smile crosses my face. The vision I had may have involved different people, a different house, and no dog, but it's happening all the same.

And, not for the first time, I reflect back on what Allie once told me about Marti and I being perfect for each other because we each had voids that needed filling.

Unsure of when my little sister became smarter than me, I'm more than happy to accept the fact that she is.

I sit on the edge of the bed with an armful of books. "Which one will it be?"

He pulls one from the middle. *Are You My Mother?*

An odd choice, considering I'm the one reading to him. But I never claimed to know the inner workings of a child's brain.

I sit next to him, shoes off, legs outstretched on his bed. He lays his head on my arm, and I take it as a cue that I should wrap it around him. He tucks in close. I shut my eyes for a moment and think of DJ. *This one's for you, bud.*

Marti stands in the doorway, watching as I read the book, her face illuminated with a glow of happiness.

When I'm done reading, I close the book and set it down, wondering if he's going to ask me to read another as I imagine kids do.

"Are you Bex's daddy?" Charlie asks, looking up at me.

Interesting question. "I suppose I am."

He looks over at Marti. "Are you Bex's mommy?"

"I guess I'm the closest thing to it," she says. "So, yes."

Charlie glances between the two of us and settles his gaze back on me. "If you're his daddy and Mommy is his mommy, does that make you *my* daddy?"

My heart lodges square in the middle of my throat. I scramble for something to say because Marti seems as stunned as I am.

"You still have a dad, Charlie. He may not be with us anymore, but he'll always be your dad."

His little hazel eyes study me. "Scarlett has two mommies. And if mommies and daddies can have more than one kid, why can't kids have more than one mommy or daddy?"

I poke the tip of his nose. "You're pretty smart for an almost four-year-old."

He beams with pride even though I never gave him an answer. And he doesn't ask again. He simply picks up the same book we just read and hands it to me. I happily oblige his request, the book now having so much more meaning to me than it did a minute ago.

~ ~ ~

Marti lays her head on my chest as soon as I crawl into bed next to her.

I never did have to leave tonight and do the same dance we've done for so many other nights. Because tonight, I was the one putting Charlie to bed.

I'm still reeling from the experience.

I squeeze her shoulder. "I don't ever intend to take Charles's place. That wouldn't be fair to him. But I'm telling you right now, Marti, I'm ready to step up and be the man Charlie needs."

A warm tear falls onto my chest. "I know you are. And I think he's ready too."

My entire body stiffens in anticipation. "Are you saying you'll move in with me?"

She looks up at me and nods, biting her lip in a way that has me instantly hard.

But my cock has to wait its turn. I have something else I need to do first. "I want to show you something." I pull her up next to me so we're both sitting against the headboard. I get my phone off the nightstand and open up my photo app.

"What am I looking at?" she asks when I tilt my phone toward her.

"House plans." I swipe through them. "In January, I bought two acres of land in that neighborhood you love. I've had an architect working on these for months. You can make any changes you see fit. I just wanted something ready to go when the time came."

She takes my phone and enlarges the floorplan. "This is huge."

I elbow her. "That's what *she* said."

She giggles. "Seriously, Dallas." She enlarges it even more to focus on the bottom corner where it lists the square footage. "Oh my god. Charlie will get lost. And is that an… elevator?"

"I know how much he loves the one in my parents' house." I swipe again, showing her the design of the pool. "And he's going to love this."

Her head shakes over and over. She's still not used to the money. The not worrying about bills and budgeting and car payments. But she stopped protesting a while ago, which is why I know she's going to be on board with this.

She studies all the pictures at least two more times, then she hands me the phone. "He's going to love it. I love it. But more importantly, I love *you.*"

"There's something else my architect is working on, but I want you to help design it."

"What's that?"

"I'm rebuilding the cabin."

Her eyes widen. "You are?"

"At Christmas, when you said you wanted to go up there with me again, I knew right then that I'd be rebuilding. Will you help me design it?"

"There's nothing to design. I think we should build it exactly like it was."

I cock my head. "No bedrooms? What about Charlie?"

She nods to my phone. "Everything you've done in the new house is for him. The cabin—that's just for us."

My heart expands. That's the thing about Martina Alexandra Carver. Just when I think I can't possibly love her more, she says something incredible. Does something amazing. Makes me feel like the luckiest man alive—a herculean task I thought was damn near impossible.

I put my phone away, slide her back down so she's lying on the bed, and climb over her. "Sweetheart, I'm about to show you everything I plan on doing to you when we go there."

"Speaking of which." She flashes me a sexy smile. "I'm really glad you put the master bedroom away from all the others in the new house. Because I can't wait to be able to scream your name again."

"I fucking love you, Marti."

"Show me how much."

"Gladly," I say, my lips lowering to meet hers.

And for the next two hours, I show her. I show her over and over again.

Chapter Forty-eight

Martina

I come out of the kitchen holding the birthday cake and bring it to the dining room table where Dallas and Charlie are waiting.

Dallas gives me a sad, yet heartwarming smile.

He moved into my rental a week after Charlie asked him to read him a book. And for the past month, Dallas has effectively stepped into the role of father. Though he works at the winery most days, he sometimes drops Charlie off at preschool. He takes him to the park. And he's teaching him how to play baseball, convinced we'll be raising the next breakout star of the New York Nighthawks.

I set the cake in front of Dallas and hand him a lighter.

Charlie knows the drill. He's sat through many birthdays like this in his four years. For the grandma and grandpa he never knew, the sister he can't really remember, and a father he only had for three short years.

This one is different however, and even if Asher and Bug lived closer, they still wouldn't be here. This one is just for us.

With misty eyes, Dallas lights the candle on the cake. "Happy birthday, Phoebe."

"Happy birthday," I repeat, as does Charlie.

There's a photo of Phoebe across the table. Next to it is the vase she made, filled with her favorite flowers. In the picture, she looks young and vibrant, and she's resting a hand on her pregnant belly. I know it's one of his favorites.

Out of respect to me, Dallas doesn't display photos of her on our walls. He keeps them in a special drawer in the room that has become his office. I don't begrudge him that. He had a whole other life before Charlie and me. One that deserves to be remembered, recognized, and revered.

Dallas has opened up about her to me more and more over the past four months. But today… today I get to hear about everything. How old she was when her family moved to Calloway Creek. How she finally gave in and agreed to date him when they were seventeen. How she loved being pregnant and swore they would have a dozen kids.

As the three of us eat cake and Charlie and I patiently listen to Dallas recall every happy memory, I realize there's no jealousy. No bitterness toward a past he still holds dear. No resentment over the woman who had his heart for more than half his life.

Later, after Charlie is in bed and I'm cleaning up, I pick up the photo of Phoebe. "You must have been one heck of a woman to deserve the love of a man like him."

Arms wrap around me from behind. "How in the hell did I get so lucky to have not one, but two amazing, selfless women in my life?"

In bed that night, we lay close and hold hands. But we don't make love. And that's okay. This is Phoebe's day, not mine. I get him the other three hundred and sixty-four days a year.

And that's enough.

Epilogue

Martina

Two years later

"Way to go, Charlie!" Dallas yells from the stands as Charlie crosses home plate. He turns to me, his smile huge and full of pride. "What have I been telling you? That kid is going to play in the MLB one day."

I roll my eyes at the way he thinks Charlie walks on water. It goes both ways, though. Charlie loves him like a father.

"Dad!" he calls from the dugout. "Did you get a picture?"

"Better," Dallas assures him. "Video."

Charlie gets high-fives from his teammates, loving every second.

I marvel over the fact that Dallas has never missed any of Charlie's sporting events. And it still warms my heart every time I hear Charlie call him Dad. I try to keep Charles's memory alive as often as possible. Charlie knows he was loved fiercely by him. My ex is who he resembles. But Dallas is the man who will raise him.

That was made official a year ago when I walked down the aisle on a beach in Antigua and Dallas became Charlie's stepfather.

Understandably, Dallas didn't want our wedding to be at the winery. He already had one wedding there. And I didn't want to take away from those memories. So we settled on a destination wedding and flew all of our friends and family down for a week's vacation before we said our vows. Chris and Sarah flew back with Charlie in tow while we spent the second week there on our honeymoon.

"Damn, I love that kid." Dallas turns, looks me straight in the eyes and says, "I'm ready."

I glance at the scoreboard. We're winning by a landslide, and although Charlie probably won't be up to bat again, there's still one inning left. "Ready for what? The game's not even over."

He nods to the dugout. "I'm ready for another one of those." He rests a hand on my tummy.

His unexpected declaration robs me of my breath. It's not something we've ever talked about. Not even when my doctor suggested I start using a diaphragm instead of the pill due to hormonal issues I was having.

I've always had the desire for more children. But even more importantly, I wanted Dallas Montana. I made the decision long ago that if he couldn't ever bring himself to have a child with me, so be it. I've never pressured him. Never even hinted at it. It had to be his choice. But he knows me better than anyone ever has. We didn't have to have a conversation for him to know my thoughts.

My heart pounds. "Are you serious?"

He leans close. "Martina Alexandra Montana, I'm not sure I've ever wanted anything more." Then he stands and offers me his hand.

My eyebrows jog up my forehead. "Wait… *now?*"

He pulls me up. "Right now." He turns to Asher, sitting on the other side of him. "You think you can take Charlie for some ice cream after? There's something we need to do."

Asher looks between us. I'm sure it wouldn't take a genius to figure out what's about to happen with the way Dallas is looking at me.

"You got it, brother," Asher says, chuckling.

Dallas takes my hand and leads me down the stands like a man on a mission. I get the feeling he'd sweep me up and carry me away if it weren't for the venue. He winks at me and then shouts over his shoulder. "Better make it a triple scoop."

I'm sure my face turns bright red, but at this moment I don't care. Because my husband has just given me the greatest gift I could have ever asked for. Sure, he's given me cars, houses, jewelry, and exotic vacations, but this… he's giving me a part of *him*. A brother or sister for Charlie. A son or daughter for him—one who will have the best father any child could have. One who will grow and thrive and become everything he'd ever hoped for DJ. And everything I'd ever wished for Alex.

I laugh at how quickly he's pulling me along. "Boy, when you get your mind set on something…"

Almost at the car, I see a butterfly dancing around some flowers. I thank him out loud.

"What's that?" Dallas asks.

"The butterfly." I nod to it. "I was thanking him. I know they only live for a few weeks, but who knows, one of his ancestors could be responsible for"—I look right into my husband's eyes, tears of pure joy flooding mine—"everything."

Bonus Epilogue

Dallas

Marti grips my hand so hard it goes white and loses all feeling. But it's nothing compared to what she's going through, so I let her do it. As hard and as long as she wants to.

"That's right," Dr. Hudson McQuaid says, glancing up with an encouraging nod. "It won't be long now, Marti. You're doing great. Relax for a second. When the next contraction comes, give it your all."

I wipe Marti's brow and kiss her forehead. "You've got this, sweetheart."

She closes her eyes and takes a few cleansing breaths knowing we're about to cross the finish line. She's been a trooper. Labor hasn't been easy. It started yesterday, a full fourteen hours ago. It's been slow and arduous. And my amazing wife hasn't complained about it for a second.

My heart thrums with anticipation. Boy. Girl. At this point I don't care. I just want a healthy brother or sister for Charlie. Another child I can hold, raise, and spoil.

We didn't find out the gender. It was a mutual decision. We never really talked about why, but we both knew the reason. I was worried having a boy would remind me of DJ. She was concerned a baby girl would stir up all the bad memories of Alex's death.

But in this moment, I'd welcome another son. And I'm willing to bet she'd be more than happy to give birth to a daughter.

I can see in her face that the next contraction is starting.

"Dallas," Hudson says. "You might want to step down here and see this."

Even as Marti's face scrunches up and turns red, she releases my hand, wanting me to witness our child coming into the world. The nurse steps in and takes over at Marti's side as I glide past her and take my place at the foot of the bed, more than ready to dive into this next chapter in our lives.

I wipe my eyes, ridding them of the tears fogging my vision, wanting to savor every second of the magnificent event that's about to happen.

"Push, Marti," Hudson says. "Your baby's almost here."

The head is halfway out. My entire heart resides in my throat and my breath is trapped. For the second time in my life, I'm witnessing my child being born. But instead of being gripped by fear, I'm flooded with hope. I spare a glance at the woman responsible for all of this. For changing the way I look at life. For always looking toward the future instead of living in the past.

Our eyes link. Somehow we both know this time is going to be different. We know our pasts have made us stronger. We know there are so many opportunities waiting for us. For him or her. For all of our children. There are endless possibilities to where life will take us. And we know that together, we can conquer all.

Marti's eyes scrunch tightly, and she screams one last time as I shift my gaze to the lower part of the bed and see our child slip out of her. Hudson swiftly places the baby on a large pad the nurse draped over Marti's chest. He rubs the baby's back for a moment, and then we hear the best sound a parent could ever hope for—the first explosive cry of our child.

Laughter and tears fill the room—both mine, I think—as a myriad of emotions overcome me.

Marti wraps her arms around our child, sobbing with joy. I perch on the bed next to her and kiss the sweaty crown of her hair. "You did it."

"Is it a boy or girl?" she asks through the rapid rise and fall of her chest.

My head cocks to the side and I chuckle. Because I have no idea. I lean down and look, my heart expanding tenfold when I discover the answer to her question. "Sweetheart, we have a daughter."

Marti cries out. Not in pain, but in pure, unadulterated joy. "We have a girl?"

I lean down and capture her mouth with mine. "We have a girl."

"Dad," Hudson says, the word bathing me like a warm blanket. "Want to do the honors?"

I nod eagerly and accept the blunt-ended scissors. He holds up the cord and shows me where to cut. And as I untether my daughter from her mom, I silently welcome her to the world. Silently, because I'm one hundred percent sure no words could get past the giant lump in my throat.

While the nurse takes the baby, and Hudson does whatever he needs to finish doing down there, I cradle my wife's shoulders and praise her for a job well done.

A few minutes later, our baby girl is swaddled and placed into Marti's arms.

"We'll give you a moment," the nurse says. "I'll be back to take her for the usual tests." She picks up a clipboard and a pen. "Do you have a name?"

Marti and I look at each other. Because we don't. We never even considered coming up with names. I'm sure we were both thinking about it. Would we try to honor those we lost? We'd already had children named after us, so I'm sure we'd agree that wasn't going to be an option. And as I gaze down into my daughter's eyes, I try to imagine who she is. Who she's going to be.

A flash of DJ's face comes before me. He can never be replaced. He'll always be my child. But this precious little girl—she's going to be my legacy. She and her big brother, who I love like my own.

"That's okay," the nurse says. "She can be Baby Girl Montana for now."

Dr. McQuaid offers his congratulations and exits the room behind the nurse.

We're finally alone, just the three of us. I smile at the thought of Charlie waiting outside with… well, with *everyone*. He's going to make the best big brother. He's going to protect her and love her and champion her every cause. He's going to do all that because he got the very best parts of Marti.

Marti reaches up and touches my cheek. "I don't think I've ever been so happy. Thank you, my love."

I grip her hand and hold it tightly against me. "I'm the one who should be thanking you. You were my exit."

"You've totally lost me," she says on an exhausted sigh, the tired grooves under her eyes doing nothing to keep me from thinking she's the most beautiful woman in the world.

"You once told me that if you're in hell, the only thing to do is keep going until you find the exit." I lean down and kiss her salty lips. "You were my exit, sweetheart."

"You saved me too, you know." She chuckles quietly so she doesn't wake our daughter. "Maybe with a little help from the butterflies."

I stiffen with an idea and get out my phone.

"Checking in at the office?" she teases.

I do a few internet searches and then show her my phone.

"What a beautiful butterfly," she says, eyeing the picture.

"Look at the name," I say.

She studies it, her face growing with a smile. Our eyes lock and she nods, both of us spilling tears. She breaks our stare and leans over to place a kiss on our daughter's ever-so-fine tuft of brunette hair. "Welcome to the world, Holly Blue."

Emotions swirl through me as I think of what this precious creature might become. I hope she's exactly like her mother. Kind, thoughtful, witty, and most importantly, capable of so much love.

"Holly Blue," I whisper, leaning over to kiss my daughter. "I think I love it." I scoot close to Marti on the bed and watch Holly's little chest rise and fall with each breath.

Marti cups my cheek. "She's you."

I swallow, shaking my head. "She's *you.*"

My wife smiles sweetly. "She's *us.*"

I clear the knot in my throat. "I'm glad she has your hair. I even hope she has your cowlick."

Marti giggles. "I hope she has your dark chocolate eyes."

"She's going to be a badass just like her mom."

She tears up once again, recalling this same conversation from long ago. "She's going to be strong like her dad."

"Maybe she'll cure cancer," I say, keeping in stride.

Marti's head cocks to the side. "How can she do *that* when she's running the winery?"

"This girl's going to be so smart she'll do both."

The past three years play in my head like a movie reel. It's almost surreal to think I'm sitting here with the woman I love, welcoming our daughter into the world, feeling as if somehow, my life is just beginning.

Most of all though, I know the precious little bundle lying on my wife is *exactly* like her mother. Because the hope she's just given me is the greatest gift any man could ask for.

Marti's head dips and a happy tear rolls down her cheek as she traces the outline of Holly's face. "She's going to change the world, this one."

I give my wife a squeeze. "She already has, sweetheart. She already has."

Acknowledgments

Eeek! My 30th book! I'm pinching myself.

This year (2024) marked my 10th anniversary as a published author, and now I've passed another milestone. This crazy, wonderful life I lead is only possible because you, my dear readers, have shown my books so much love.

I hope you found Dallas and Marti's story to be as emotional as I was while writing it. And, who knew this would spark ideas for a 4th Montana book about Allie and Asher? Yes!

There are many people to thank. At the top of the list is my amazing assistant, Julie Collier, who organizes me in a way I never could. Your eyes are always the first on my books. You tell it like it is and make me strive to be better.

To my editor, Michelle Fewer, and my beta readers, Shauna Garness, Joelle Yates, Laura Conley, and Kellie Shanks, I value your thoughtful remarks, suggestions, and criticisms.

It has been an honor to write these two books about truly stand-up men and their strong, supportive partners. The Montanas have proven to be in a class all by themselves. Will Lucas live up to the precedent his brothers have set?

I guess we'll see!

About the author

Samantha Christy's passion for writing started long before her first novel was published.

Graduating from the University of Nebraska with a degree in Criminal Justice, she held the title of Computer Systems Analyst for The Supreme Court of Wisconsin and several major universities around the United States.

Raised mainly in Indianapolis, she holds the Midwest and its homegrown values dear to her heart and upon the birth of her third child devoted herself to raising her family full time.

While it took time to get from there to here, writing has remained her utmost passion and being a stay-at-home mom facilitated her ability to follow that dream.

When she is not writing, she keeps busy cruising to every Caribbean island where ships sail.

Samantha Christy currently resides in St. Augustine, Florida with her husband and the two of her four children who haven't yet flown the coop.

You can reach Samantha Christy at any of these wonderful places:

Website: www.samanthachristy.com

Facebook: https://www.facebook.com/SamanthaChristyAuthor

Instagram: @authorsamanthachristy

E-mail: samanthachristy@comcast.net

Printed in Great Britain
by Amazon